W9-CHR-810

GLORIANA

Or, The Unfulfill'd Queen

ALSO BY MICHAEL MOORCOCK

ELRIC

Elric of Melniboné and Other Stories

Elric: *The Fortress of the Pearl*

Elric: *The Sailor on the Seas of Fate*

Elric: *The Sleeping Sorceress*

Elric: *The Revenge of the Rose*

Elric: *Stormbringer!*

Elric: The Moonbeam Roads
comprising—
Daughter of Dreams
Destiny's Brother
Son of the Wolf

CORUM

Corum: The Prince in the Scarlet Robe
comprising—
The Knight of the Swords
The Queen of the Swords
The King of the Swords

Corum: The Prince with the Silver Hand
comprising—
The Bull and the Spear
The Oak and the Ram
The Sword and the Stallion

HAWKMOON

Hawkmoon: The History of the Runestaff
comprising—
The Jewel in the Skull
The Mad God's Amulet
The Sword of the Dawn
The Runestaff

Hawkmoon: Count Brass
comprising—
Count Brass
The Champion of Garathorm
The Quest for Tanelorn

JERRY CORNELIUS

The Cornelius Quartet
comprising—
The Final Programme
A Cure for Cancer
The English Assassin
The Condition of Muzak

Jerry Cornelius: His Lives and His Times (short-fiction collection)

A Cornelius Calendar
comprising—
The Adventures of Una Persson and Catherine Cornelius in the Twentieth Century
The Entropy Tango
The Great Rock 'n' Roll Swindle
The Alchemist's Question
Firing the Cathedral/Modem Times 2.0

Von Bek
comprising—
The War Hound and the World's Pain
The City in the Autumn Stars

The Eternal Champion
comprising—
The Eternal Champion
Phoenix in Obsidian
The Dragon in the Sword

The Dancers at the
End of Time
comprising—
An Alien Heat
The Hollow Lands
The End of All Songs

Kane of Old Mars
comprising—
Warriors of Mars
Blades of Mars
Barbarians of Mars

Moorcock's Multiverse
comprising—
The Sundered Worlds
The Winds of Limbo
The Shores of Death

The Nomad of Time
comprising—
The Warlord of the Air
The Land Leviathan
The Steel Tsar

Travelling to Utopia
comprising—
The Wrecks of Time
The Ice Schooner
The Black Corridor

The War Amongst the Angels
comprising—
Blood: A Southern Fantasy
Fabulous Harbours
The War Amongst the Angels

Tales from the End of Time
comprising—
Legends from the End of Time
Constant Fire
Elric at the End of Time

Behold the Man

Sanctuary of the White Friars
The Whispering Swarm

SHORT FICTION

My Experiences in the Third World War and Other Stories: The Best Short Fiction of Michael Moorcock Volume 1

The Brothel in Rosenstrasse and Other Stories: The Best Short Fiction of Michael Moorcock Volume 2

Breakfast in the Ruins and Other Stories: The Best Short Fiction of Michael Moorcock Volume 3

GLORIANA

Or, The Unfulfill'd Queen

Being a Romance by

MICHAEL MOORCOCK

Edited by John Davey

SAGA PRESS
LONDON SYDNEY NEW YORK TORONTO NEW DELHI

Dedicated to the memory of Mervyn Peake

1230 AVENUE OF THE AMERICAS, NEW YORK, NEW YORK 10020

Interior design by Ellice Lee
The text for this book was set in Dante.
Manufactured in the United States of America
First Saga Press Edition November 2016
2 4 6 8 10 9 7 5 3 1
CIP data for this book is available from the Library of Congress.
ISBN 978-1-4814-8738-2
ISBN 978-1-4814-8739-9 (eBook)

Introduction to *Gloriana; Or, The Unfulfill'ed Queen*

John Clute

HE IS NOW over 70, enough time for most careers to start and end in, enough time to fit in an occasional half-decade or so of silence to mark off the big years. Silence happens. I don't think I know an author who doesn't fear silence like the plague; most of us, if we live long enough, can remember a bad blank year or so, or more. Not Michael Moorcock. Except for some worrying surgery on his toes in recent years, he seems not to have taken time off to breathe the air of peace and panic. There has been no time to spare. The nearly 60 years of his active career seems to have been too short to fit everything in: the teenage comics; the editing jobs; the pulp fiction; the reinvented heroic fantasies; the Eternal Champion; the deep Jerry Cornelius riffs; *New Worlds*; the 1970s/1980s flow of stories and novels, dozens upon dozens of them in every category of modern fantastika; the tales of the dying Earth and the possessing of Jesus; the exercises in post-modernism that turned the world inside out before most of us had begun to guess we were living on the wrong side of things; the invention (more or less) of steampunk; the alternate histories; the *Mitteleuropean* tales of sexual terror; the deep-city London riffs: the turns and changes and returns and reconfigurations to which he has subjected his oeuvre over the years (he expects this new Collected Edition will fix these transformations in place for good); the late tales where he has been remodelling the intersecting worlds he created in the 1960s in terms of twenty-first-century physics: for starters. If you can't take the heat, I guess, stay out of the multiverse.

His life has been full and complicated, a life he has exposed and hidden (like many other prolific authors) throughout his work. In *Mother London* (1988), though, a nonfantastic novel published at what is now something like the midpoint of his career, it may be possible to find the key to all the other selves who made the 100 books. There are three protagonists in the tale, which is set from about 1940 to about 1988 in the suburbs and inner runnels of the vast metropolis of Charles Dickens and Robert Louis Stevenson. The oldest of these protagonists is Joseph Kiss, a flamboyant self-advertising fin-de-siècle figure of substantial girth and a fantasticating relationship to the world: he is Michael Moorcock, seen with genial bite as a kind of G.K. Chesterton without the wearying punch-line paradoxes. The youngest of the three is David Mummery, a haunted introspective half-insane denizen of a secret London of trials and runes and codes and magic: he too is Michael Moorcock, seen through a glass, darkly. And there is Mary Gasalee, a kind of holy-innocent and survivor, blessed with a luminous clarity of insight, so that in all her apparent ignorance of the onrushing secular world she is more deeply wise than other folk: she is also Michael Moorcock, Moorcock when young as viewed from the wry middle years of 1988. When we read the book, we are reading a book of instructions for the assembly of a London writer. The Moorcock we put together from this choice of portraits is amused and bemused at the vision of himself; he is a phenomenon of flamboyance and introspection, a poseur and a solitary, a dreamer and a doer, a multitude and a singleton. But only the three Moorcocks in this book, working together, could have written all the other books.

It all began—as it does for David Mummery in *Mother London*—in South London, in a subtopian stretch of villas called Mitcham, in 1939. In early childhood, he experienced the Blitz, and never forgot the extraordinariness of being a participant—however minute—in the great drama; all around him, as though the world were being dismantled nightly, darkness and blackout would descend, bombs fall, buildings and streets disappear; and in the morning, as though a new universe had taken over from the old one and the world had become portals, the sun would rise on glinting rubble, abandoned tricycles, men and women going about their daily tasks as though nothing had happened, strange shards of ruin poking into altered air. From a very early age, Michael Moorcock's security reposed in a sense that everything might change, in the blinking of an eye, and be *rejourneyed* the next day (or the next book). Though as a writer he has certainly elucidated the fears and alarums of life in Aftermath Britain, it does seem that his very early years were marked by the epiphanies of war, rather than the inflictions of despair and beclouding amnesia most adults necessarily experienced. After the war ended, his parents separated, and the young Moorcock began to attend a pretty wide variety of schools, several of which he seems to have been expelled from, and as soon as he could legally do so he began to work full time, up north in London's heart, which he only left when he moved to Texas (with intervals in Paris) in the early 1990s, from where (to jump briefly up the decades) he continues to cast a Martian eye: as with most exiles, Moorcock's intensest anatomies of his homeland date from after his cunning departure.

But back again to the beginning (just as though we were rimming a multiverse). Starting in the 1950s there was the comics and pulp work for Fleetway Publications; there was the first book (*Caribbean Crisis*, 1962) as by Desmond Reid, co-written with his early friend the artist James Cawthorn (1929–2008); there was marriage, with the writer Hilary Bailey (they divorced in 1978), three children, a heated existence in the Ladbroke Grove / Notting Hill Gate region of London he was later to populate with Jerry Cornelius and his vast family; there was the editing of *New Worlds*, which began in 1964 and became the heartbeat of the British New Wave two years later as writers like Brian W. Aldiss and J.G. Ballard, reaching their early prime, made it into a tympanum, as young American writers like Thomas M. Disch, John T. Sladek, Norman Spinrad and Pamela Zoline found a home in London for material they could not publish in America, and new British writers like M. John Harrison and Charles Platt began their careers in its pages; but before that there was Elric. With *The Stealer of Souls* (1963) and *Stormbringer* (1965), the multiverse began to flicker into view, and the Eternal Champion (whom Elric parodied and embodied) began properly to ransack the worlds in his fight against a greater Chaos than the great dance could sustain. There was also the first SF novel, *The Sundered Worlds* (1965), but in the 1960s SF was a difficult nut to demolish for Moorcock: he would bide his time.

We come to the heart of the matter. Jerry Cornelius, who first appears in *The Final Programme* (1968)—which assembles and coordinates material first published a few years earlier in *New Worlds*—is a deliberate solarisation of the albino Elric, who was himself a mocking solarisation of Robert E. Howard's Conan, or rather of the mighty-thew-headed Conan created for profit by Howard epigones: Moorcock rarely mocks the true quill. Cornelius, who reaches his first and most telling apotheosis in the four novels comprising *The Cornelius Quartet*, remains his most distinctive and perhaps most original single creation: a wide boy, an agent, a *flaneur*, a bad musician, a shopper, a shapechanger, a trans, a spy in the house of London: a toxic palimpsest on whom and through whom the *zeitgeist* inscribes surreal conjugations of "message." Jerry Cornelius gives head to Elric.

The life continued apace. By 1970, with *New Worlds* on its last legs, multiverse fantasies and experimental novels poured forth; Moorcock and Hilary Bailey began to live separately, though he moved, in fact, only around the corner, where he set up house with Jill Riches, who would become his second wife; there was a second home in Yorkshire, but London remained his central base. *The Condition of Muzak* (1977), which is the fourth Cornelius novel, and *Gloriana; or, The Unfulfill'd Queen* (1978), which transfigures the first Elizabeth into a kinked Astraea, marked perhaps the high point of his career as a writer of fiction whose font lay in genre or its mutations—marked perhaps the furthest bournes he could transgress while remaining within the perimeters of fantasy (though *within* those bournes vast stretches of territory remained and would, continually, be explored). During these years he sometimes wore a leather jacket constructed out of numerous patches of varicoloured material, and it sometimes seemed perfectly fitting that he bore the semblance, as his jacket flickered and fuzzed from across a room or road, of an illustrated man, a map, a thing of shreds and patches, a student fleshed from dreams. Like the stories he told, he seemed to be more than one thing. To use a term frequently applied (by me at least) to twenty-first-century fiction, he seemed equipoisal: which is to say that, through all his genre-hopping and genre-mixing and genre-transcending and genre-loyal returnings to old pitches, *he was never still*, because "equipoise" is all about *making stories move*. As with his stories, he cannot be pinned down, because he is not in one place. In person and in his work, it has always been sink or swim: like a shark, or a dancer, or an equilibrist. . . .

The marriage with Jill Riches came to an end. He married Linda Steele in 1983; they remain married. The Colonel Pyat books, *Byzantium Endures* (1981), *The Laughter of Carthage* (1984), *Jerusalem Commands* (1992) and *The Vengeance of Rome* (2006), dominated these years, along with *Mother London*. As these books, which are non-fantastic, are not included in the current *Michael Moorcock Collection*, it might be worth noting here that, in their insistence on the irreducible difficulty of gaining anything like true sight, they represent Moorcock's mature modernist take on what one might call the rag-and-bone shop of the world itself; and that the huge ornate postmodern edifice of his multiverse *loosens* us from that world, gives us room to breathe, to juggle our strategies for living—allows us ultimately to escape from prison (to use a phrase from a writer he does not respect, J.R.R. Tolkien, for whom the twentieth century was a prison train bound for hell). What Moorcock may best be remembered for in the end is the (perhaps unique) interplay between modernism and postmodernism in his work. (But a plethora of discordant understandings makes these terms hard to use; so enough of them.) In the end, one might just say that Moorcock's work as a whole represents an extraordinarily multifarious execution of the fantasist's main task: which is to *get us out of here*.

Recent decades saw a continuation of the multifarious, but with a more intensely applied methodology. The late volumes of the long Elric saga, and the Second Ether sequence of meta-fantasies—*Blood:*

A Southern Fantasy (1995), *Fabulous Harbours* (1995) and *The War Amongst the Angels: An Autobiographical Story* (1996)—brood on the real world and the multiverse through the lens of Chaos Theory: the closer you get to the world, the less you describe it. *The Metatemporal Detective* (2007)—a narrative in the Steampunk mode Moorcock had previewed as long ago as *The Warlord of the Air* (1971) and *The Land Leviathan* (1974)—continues the process, sometimes dizzyingly: as though the reader inhabited the eye of a camera increasing its focus on a closely observed reality while its bogey simultaneously wheels it backwards from the desired rapport: an old Kurasawa trick here amplified into a tool of conspectus, fantasy eyed and (once again) rejourneyed, this time through the lens of SF.

We reach the second decade of the twenty-first century, time still to make things new, but also time to sort. There are dozens of titles that have not been listed in this short space, much less trawled for tidbits. The various avatars of the Eternal Champion—Elric, Kane of Old Mars, Hawkmoon, Count Brass, Corum, Von Bek—differ vastly from one another. Hawkmoon is a bit of a berk; Corum is a steely solitary at the End of Time: the joys and doleurs of the interplays amongst them can only be experienced through immersion. And the Dancers at the End of Time books, and the Nomad of the Time Stream books, and the Karl Glogauer books, and all the others. They are here now, a 100 books that make up one book. They have been fixed for reading. It is time to enter the multiverse and see the world.

September 2012

Introduction to *Gloriana; Or, The Unfulfill'd Queen*

Michael Moorcock

By 1964, after I had been editing *New Worlds* for some months and had published several science fiction and fantasy novels, including *Stormbringer*, I realised that my run as a writer was over. About the only new ideas I'd come up with were miniature computers, the multiverse and black holes, all very crudely realised, in *The Sundered Worlds*. No doubt I would have to return to journalism, writing features and editing. "My career," I told my friend J.G. Ballard, "is finished." He sympathised and told me he only had a few SF stories left in him, then he, too, wasn't sure what he'd do.

In January 1965, living in Colville Terrace, Notting Hill, then an infamous slum, best known for its race riots, I sat down at the typewriter in our kitchen-cum-bathroom and began a locally based book, designed to be accompanied by music and graphics. *The Final Programme* featured a character based on a young man I'd seen around the area and whom I named after a local greengrocer, Jerry Cornelius, "Messiah to the Age of Science." Jerry was as much a technique as a character. Not the "spy" some critics described him as but an urban adventurer as interested in his psychic environment as the contemporary physical world. My influences were English and French absurdists, American noir novels. My inspiration was William Burroughs with whom I'd recently begun a correspondence. I also borrowed a few SF ideas, though I was adamant that I was not writing in any established genre. I felt I had at last found my own authentic voice.

I had already written a short novel, *The Golden Barge*, set in a nowhere, no-time world very much influenced by Peake and the surrealists, which I had not attempted to publish. An earlier autobiographical novel, *The Hungry Dreamers*, set in Soho, was eaten by rats in a Ladbroke Grove basement. I remained unsatisfied with my style and my technique. *The Final Programme* took nine days to complete (by 20 January, 1965) with my baby daughters sometimes cradled with their bottles while I typed on. This, I should say, is my memory of events; my then wife scoffed at this story when I recounted it. Whatever the truth, the fact is I only believed I might be a serious writer after I had finished that novel, with all its flaws. But Jerry Cornelius, probably my most successful sustained attempt at unconventional fiction, was born then and ever since has remained a useful means of telling complex stories. Associated with the 60s and 70s, he has been equally at home in all the following decades. Through novels and novellas I developed a means of carrying several narratives and viewpoints on what appeared to be a very light (but tight) structure which dispensed with some of the earlier methods of fiction. In the sense that it took for granted the understanding that the novel is among other things an internal dialogue and I did not feel the need to repeat by now commonly understood modernist conventions, this fiction was post-modern.

Not all my fiction looked for new forms for the new century. Like many "revolutionaries" I looked back as well as forward. As George Meredith looked to the eighteenth century for inspiration for his experiments with narrative, I looked to Meredith, popular Edwardian realists like Pett Ridge and Zangwill and the writers of the *fin de siècle* for methods and inspiration. An almost obsessive interest in the Fabians, several of whom believed in the possibility of benign imperialism, ultimately led to my Bastable books which examined our enduring British notion that an empire could be essentially a force for good. The first was *The Warlord of the Air*.

I also wrote my *Dancers at the End of Time* stories and novels under the influence of Edwardian humourists and absurdists like Jerome or Firbank. Together with more conventional generic books like *The Ice Schooner* or *The Black Corridor*, most of that work was done in the 1960s and 70s when I wrote the Eternal Champion supernatural adventure novels which helped support my own and others' experiments via *New Worlds*, allowing me also to keep a family while writing books in which action and fantastic invention were paramount. Though I did them quickly, I didn't write them cynically. I have always believed, somewhat puritanically, in giving the audience good value for money. I enjoyed writing them, tried to avoid repetition, and through each new one was able to develop a few more ideas. They also continued to teach me how to express myself through image and metaphor. My Everyman became the Eternal Champion, his dreams and ambitions represented by the multiverse. He could be an ordinary person struggling with familiar problems in a contemporary setting or he could be a swordsman fighting monsters on a far-away world.

Long before I wrote *Gloriana* (in four parts reflecting the seasons) I had learned to think in images and symbols through reading John Bunyan's *Pilgrim's Progress*, Milton and others, understanding early on that the visual could be the most important part of a book and was often in itself a story as, for instance, a famous personality could also, through everything associated with their name, function as narrative. I wanted to find ways of carrying as many stories as possible in one. From the cinema I also learned how to use images as connecting themes. Images, colours, music, and even popular magazine headlines can all add coherence to an apparently random story, underpinning it and giving the reader a sense of internal logic and a satisfactory resolution, dispensing with certain familiar literary conventions.

When the story required it, I also began writing neo-realist fiction exploring the interface of character and environment, especially the city, especially London. In some books I condensed, manipulated and randomised time to achieve what I wanted, but in others the sense of "real time" as we all generally perceive it was more suitable and could best be achieved by traditional nineteenth-century means. For the Pyat books I first looked back to the great German classic, Grimmelshausen's *Simplicissimus* and other early picaresques. I then examined the roots of a certain kind of moral fiction from Defoe through Thackeray and Meredith then to modern times where the picaresque (or rogue tale) can take the form of a road movie, for instance. While it's probably fair to say that Pyat and *Byzantium Endures* precipitated the end of my second marriage (echoed to a degree in *The Brothel in Rosenstrasse*), the late 70s and the 80s were exhilarating times for me, with *Mother London* being perhaps my own favourite novel of that period. I wanted to write something celebratory.

By the 90s I was again attempting to unite several kinds of fiction in one novel with my Second Ether trilogy. With Mandelbrot, Chaos Theory and String Theory I felt, as I said at the time, as if I were being offered a chart of my own brain. That chart made it easier for me to develop the notion of the multiverse as representing both the internal and the external, as a metaphor and as a means of structuring and rationalising an outrageously inventive and quasi-realistic narrative. The worlds of the multiverse move up and down scales or "planes" explained in terms of mass, allowing entire universes to exist in the "same" space. The result of developing this idea was the *War Amongst the Angels* sequence which added absurdist elements also functioning as a kind of mythology and folklore for a world beginning to understand itself in terms of new metaphysics and theoretical physics. As the cosmos becomes denser and almost infinite before our eyes, with black holes and dark matter affecting our own reality, we can explore them and observe them as our ancestors explored our planet and observed the heavens.

At the end of the 90s I'd returned to realism, sometimes with a dash of fantasy, with *King of the City* and the stories collected in *London Bone*. I also wrote a new Elric / Eternal Champion sequence, beginning with *Daughter of Dreams*, which brought the fantasy worlds of Hawkmoon, Bastable and Co. in line with my realistic and autobiographical stories, another attempt to unify all my fiction, and also offer a way in which disparate genres could be reunited, through notions developed from the multiverse and the Eternal Champion, as one giant novel. At the time I was finishing the Pyat sequence which attempted to look at the roots of the Nazi Holocaust in our European, Middle Eastern and American cultures and to ground my strange survival guilt while at the same time examining my own cultural roots in the light of an enduring anti-Semitism.

By the 2000s I was exploring various conventional ways of story-telling in the last parts of *The Metatemporal Detective* and through other homages, comics, parodies and games. I also looked back at my earliest influences. I had reached retirement age and felt like a rest. I wrote a "prequel" to the Elric series as a graphic novel with Walter Simonson, *The Making of a Sorcerer*, and did a little online editing with *Fantastic Metropolis*.

By 2010 I had written a novel featuring Doctor Who, *The Coming of the Terraphiles*, with a nod to P.G. Wodehouse (a boyhood favourite), continued to write short stories and novellas and to work on the beginning of a new sequence combining pure fantasy and straight autobiography called *The Whispering Swarm* while still writing more Cornelius stories trying to unite all the various genres and sub-genres into which contemporary fiction has fallen.

Throughout my career critics have announced that I'm "abandoning" fantasy and concentrating on literary fiction. The truth is, however, that all my life, since I became a professional writer and editor at the age of 16, I've written in whatever mode suits a story best and where necessary created a new form if an old one didn't work for me. Certain ideas are best carried on a Jerry Cornelius story, others work better as realism and others as fantasy or science fiction. Some work best as a combination. I'm sure I'll write whatever I like and will continue to experiment with all the ways there are of telling stories and carrying as many themes as possible. Whether I write about a widow coping with loneliness in her cottage or a massive, universe-size sentient spaceship searching for her children, I'll no doubt die trying to tell them all. I hope you'll find at least some of them to your taste.

One thing a reader can be sure of about these new editions is that they would not have been possible without the tremendous and indispensable help of my old friend and bibliographer John Davey. John has ensured that these Gollancz editions are definitive. I am indebted to John for many things, including his work at Moorcock's Miscellany, my website, but his work on this edition has been outstanding. As well as being an accomplished novelist in his own right John is an astonishingly good editor who has worked with Gollancz and myself to point out every error and flaw in all previous editions, some of them not corrected since their first publication, and has enabled me to correct or revise them. I couldn't have completed this project without him. Together, I think, Gollancz, John Davey and myself have produced what will be the best edition possible and I am very grateful to him, to Malcolm Edwards, Darren Nash and Marcus Gipps for all the considerable hard work they have done to make this edition what it is.

Michael Moorcock

AUTHOR'S NOTE:

While it is neither an "Elizabethan Fantasia" nor an historical novel, this romance does have some relation to The Faerie Queene.

The First Chapter

In Which Is Presented the Palace of Queen Gloriana Together with a Description of Some of Its Denizens and a Brief Account of Certain Activities Taking Place in the City of London on New Year's Eve Ending the Twelfth Year of Gloriana's Reign

THE PALACE IS as large as a good-sized town, for through the centuries its outbuildings, its lodges, its guest houses, the mansions of its lords and ladies in waiting have been linked by covered ways, and those covered ways roofed, in turn, so that here and there we find corridors within corridors, like conduits in a tunnel, houses within rooms, those rooms within castles, those castles within artificial caverns, the whole roofed again with tiles of gold and platinum and silver, marble and mother-of-pearl, so that the palace glares with a thousand colours in the sunlight, shimmers constantly in the moonlight, its walls appearing to undulate, its roofs to rise and fall like a glamorous tide, its towers and minarets lifting like the masts and hulks of sinking ships.

Within, the palace is rarely still; there is a coming and going of great aristocrats in their brocades, silks and velvets, their chains of gold and silver, their filigree poignards, their ivory farthingales, cloaks and trains rippling behind them, sometimes carried by little boys and girls in such a weight of cloth it seems they can barely walk. There is precise and delicate music to be heard from more than one source, and nobles and retainers all pace to the music's time. In certain halls and rooms masques and plays are rehearsed, concerts performed, portraits painted, murals sketched, tapestries woven, stone carved, verses recited; and there are courtships, consummations, quarrels, of the intense sort always found in the confines of such a universe as this. And in those forgotten spaces between the walls live the human scavengers, the dwellers in the glooms—vagabonds, disgraced servants, forgotten mistresses, spies, ostracised squires, love children, the deformed, abandoned whores, idiot relatives, hermits, madmen, romantics who would accept any misery to be near the source of power; escaped prisoners, destitute nobles too ashamed to reveal themselves in the city below, rejected suitors, defaulting husbands, fear-driven lovers, bankrupts, the sick and the envious; all dwell and dream alone or in their own societies, with their own clearly marked territories and customs, living apart from those who exist in the brilliantly lighted halls and corridors of the palace proper, yet side by side with them, rarely suspected.

Below the palace lies the great city, capital of an Empire, rich in gold and fame, the home of adventurers, merchants, poets, playwrights, magicians, alchemists, engineers, scientists, philosophers, craftsmen of every sort, senators, scholars—there is a great University—theologians, painters, actors, buccaneers, moneylenders, highwaymen, dancers, musicians, astrologers, architects, iron-masters, masters of the great smoking manufactories on the outskirts of Albion's capital, prophets, exiles from foreign lands, animal trainers, peace-keepers, judges, physicians, gallants, flirts, great ladies and noble lords; all bustle together in the city's alehouses, ordinaries, theatres, opera houses, inns, concert halls; its forums, its wineshops and places of contemplation, parading fantastic costumes, resisting conformity at any cost, so that even the wit of the city's urchins is as sharp as the finest conversation of the rural lord; the vulgar speech of the street arabs is so full of metaphor and condensed reference that an ancient poet would have given his soul to possess the tongue of a London apprentice; yet it is a speech almost impossible to translate, more mysterious than Sanskrit, and its fashions change from day to day. Moralists decry these habits, this perpetual demand for mere empty novelty, and argue that decadence looms, the inevitable result of sensation-seeking, yet the demand on the artists for novelty, while it certainly means that bad artists produce only fresh and shallow sensation, causes the best of them to fire their plays with a language that is vital and complex (for they know it will be understood), with events that are melodramatic and fabulous (for they know they will be believed), with argument on almost any subject (for there are many who will follow them), and so it is, too, for the best musicians, poets, philosophers—not excluding those lowly writers of prose who would claim legitimacy for what everyone knows is a bastard art. In short, our London is alive at every level; even its vermin, one might suspect, is articulate and flea discourses with flea on the question whether the number of dogs in the universe is finite or infinite, while rats wrangle over such profundities as which came first, the baker or the bread. And where language catches fire, so are deeds performed to match, and the deeds, in turn, colour the language. Great deeds are done in this city, in the name of its Queen, whose palace looks down upon it. Expeditions set forth and discoveries are made. Inventors and explorers enrich the Realm—twin rivers flow into the city, one of Knowledge, one of Gold, and the lake they form is the stuff of London, equal parts intermingled. And there is conflict, of course, and crime here—the passions are high and heady, the crimes are fierce and horrible, for the stakes can be enormous; greed is a giant, ambition is Faith to more than a few—a drug, a disease, a cup that can never be drained. Yet there are many, too, who have learned the virtues of the rich; who are enlightened, humane, charitable, generous; who live according to the highest Stoic tradition; who display their nobility and offer themselves as examples to their fellows, both rich and poor; who are mocked for their gravity, hated for their humility, envied for their self-sufficiency. Pompous piety, some would call their state, and so it is, for some of them, those without humour, without irony. These proud princelings and captains of industry, merchant adventurers, priests and scholars follow a code, but they are individuals nonetheless—even eccentrics—though all would serve the Nation and Empire (in the person of their Queen) at any cost to themselves, even, should necessity demand, with their lives; for the State is All and the Queen is Just. Only secondly, to a man and woman, would they consult private conscience, on any matter whatsoever, for they would deem all personal decisions subservient to the needs of the State.

It has not always been so in Albion, was never as completely true as it is, now that Gloriana rules; for these people who, through their efforts, hold this vast Commonwealth in balance, who make it a coherent entity, who ensure its stability, believe that there is only one factor which maintains this equilibrium: the Queen Herself.

The circle of Time has turned, from golden age to silver, from brass to iron and now, with Gloriana, back to gold again.

Gloriana the First, Queen of Albion, Empress of Asia and Virginia, is a Sovereign loved and worshipped as a goddess by many millions of subjects, admired and respected by many more millions throughout the globe. To the theologian (save for the most radical) she is the only representative of the gods on Earth, to the politician she is the embodiment of the State, to the poet she is Juno, to the common folk she is Mother; saint and villain alike are united in their love for her. If she laughs, the Realm rejoices; if she weeps, the Nation mourns; if she has a need, a thousand would volunteer to satisfy it; if she is angry, there would be scores to take vengeance on the object of her anger. And thus is created for her an almost unbearable responsibility: Thus she must practise diplomacy at all levels of her life, betraying no emotion, expressing no demands, dealing fairly with all petitioners. In her Reign there has never been an execution or an arbitrary imprisonment, corrupt public servants have been sought for actively and dismissed, courts and tribunals deal justice to poor and powerful equally; many, who offend against the letter of the law, are released if the circumstances of their crimes are such that their innocence is evident—so thus, effectually, the injustice of the Law of Precedent is abolished. In town and meadow, in village and manufactory, in capital or colony, the equilibrium is maintained through the person of this noble and humane Queen.

Queen Gloriana, only child of King Hern VI (despot and degenerate, traitor to the State, betrayer of his trust, whose hand caused a hundred thousand heads to fall, unmanly self-murderer), of the old blood of Elficleos and of Brutus, who overthrew Gogmagog, is forever aware of this love her subjects have for her and she returns their love; yet that love, both given and received, is a burden upon her—a burden so great that she can scarcely admit its presence—a burden, it might be thought, that is the chief cause of her enormous private distress. Not that the Realm is unaware of her distress; it is whispered of in Great Houses and common ordinaries, in country seats and clerical colleges, while poets in verses refer obscurely to it (without malice) and foreign enemies consider how they might make use of it for their own ends. Old gossips call it Her Majesty's Curse, and certain metaphysicians claim that the Curse upon the Queen is representative of the Curse lying upon the whole of humankind (or perhaps, specifically, the people of Albion, if they wish to score a provincial point or two). Many have sought to lift this Curse from the Queen and the Queen has encouraged them; she never quite gives up hope. Dramatic and fantastical remedies have been tried, without success; the Queen, whisper the gossips, still burns; the Queen still groans; the Queen still weeps, for she cannot be fulfilled. Even common alehouse jesters make no jokes concerning this; even the most puritanical, the most radical of evangelists draw no morals from her predicament. Men and women have died grotesquely (though never with the Queen's knowledge) for making light of the Queen's Trouble.

Day upon day Queen Gloriana, in her beauty and her dignity, her wisdom and her power, conducts the business of the State according to the high ideals of Chivalry; night upon night upon night she seeks that satisfaction, that final abandonment, that release which sometimes she has almost reached, only to fall back from the brink of fulfilment, back into an agony of frustration, of misery, of self-hatred, of conscience, of confusion. Morning after morning she has risen, suppressing all personal grief, to continue with her duties, to read, to sign, to confer, to discourse, to receive emissaries, petitioners, to christen ships, to unveil monuments, to dedicate buildings, to attend entertainments and ceremonies, to show herself to her people as the living symbol of her Realm's security. And in the evening she will play hostess to her guests, converse with those courtiers and friends and relatives closest to her (including her nine children); and thence, again, to bed, to her search, to her experiments; and, when, as always, they end in failure then she will lie awake, sometimes voicing her agony, not knowing that the secret halls and passages of her vast palace catch and amplify her voice so that it may be heard in almost every corner. Thus the Queen's Court shares her grief and her sleeplessness.

"Ah, the yearning! I would cram whole planets into my womb, could they but fill the void in me! This torture is too great. I could bear any other. Is there nothing, no-one, to sate my need? If in dying I could experience release, just once, I should willingly submit to any horror . . . But this is treachery. We are the State. We serve, we serve . . . Ah, if there were but a single being in all our Realm who could serve us . . ."

In his great bed of sable and beaver, a naked wife on either silk-clad arm, Lord Montfallcon lies; listening to these words which come to him as whispers and occasional cries, knowing that they issue from the lips of his Queen a quarter of a mile distant in her own lodgings. She is the child, the hope he guarded with mad idealism through all the terrible, euphoric tyranny of her father's monstrous reign. He recalls his own loyal attempts to find a lover for her, his failure, his considerable despair. "Oh, madam," he breathes, so that his loved ones shall not hear, "if thou wast only Woman and not Albion. If thy blood were not the blood it is." And he draws his wives to him, so that their hair shall cover his ears and he need hear no more, for he would not weep tonight, this brave ancient, her Chancellor.

". . . Nothing can destroy me. Nothing can bring me to life. Has it been so for a thousand years? Three hundred and sixty-five thousand aching days and wasted nights . . ."

Skulking through one of his discovered tunnels on his way to snatch food from the palace larder, Jephraim Tallow, outcast and cynic, a little black-and-white cat, his only friend, upon his shoulder, pauses, for the words boom in his eardrums, boom through his bones, boom in his belly. "Bitch! Ever on heat, never brought to the boil. One night, I swear, I'll sneak into her rooms and service her, for my satisfaction if not for hers. I can sniff her sex from here. It will lead me to her." The cat makes a small sound, to remind him of his quest, and digs claws through thin, patched cotton. Tallow turns a mild, shifty eye on his companion and shrugs. "But so many have tried in so many ways. She's a much-explored maze, without a centre." He slides around a bend of metal, reaches an air-duct of stone which leads to a disused sewer, finds himself in a gallery of creaking beams and dripping pipes, scuttles through dust, his candle guttering, and into a rotted doorway like the entrance to a kennel. His nose twitches. He catches a whiff of lately roasted meat. He licks greedy lips. The cat begins to purr.

"We're none too close to the kitchens, Tom." He frowns, then lets the cat jump down and pass through the little door, wriggling after it until both are stopped by a lattice of carved wood behind which firelight bounces. Tallow puts an eye to an opening. Here is one of the palace's great public rooms. The fire is dying in the grate directly opposite. A long table is scattered with what is left of a feast—and some of the feasters who lie on and about the table. There is beef and mutton and poultry, wine and bread. Tallow tests the panel. It rattles. He seeks for catches and finds nails instead. He reaches for his little knife, on a cord at his throat, draws it up and prises at an edge, pushing it back from the nail until it threatens to splinter. He works his knife around the entire panel, loosening it. Then, grasping the lattice with his fingers, he pushes with his free hand so that the whole is detached. He pulls the panel in and places it carefully behind him, then looks down. It is a fair drop to the flagstones; there seems no easy way of returning, save by moving a piece of furniture, which would betray his means of entrance. The cat, disdaining his master's caution, and with a noise in his chest, half-purr, half-growl, springs from vent to table in one long leap. His mind made up for him, Tallow swings out, hangs by his fingers, then drops, grazing a small bench he has not seen from above, barking his shin. He curses and hops, re-sheathing his knife inside his shirt, turning and limping rapidly for the table where the cat already tugs at a turkey. It has been cold in the tunnels and Tallow realises the extent of his discomfort as the fire warms him. He carries a good part of a baron of beef to the fire, sits himself in the inglenook and begins to chew, cocking one eye at the snoring guests—entertainers, by their costume, who entertained themselves too well. Light suddenly falls on these figures and Jephraim is alerted until he looks up to see that there are windows set near the roof; he is unused to windows in his own dominion. Moonlight enters. White clowns and patch-coat harlekins lie upon cloth-of-silver, like dead geese on snow; their disguises are stained with wine which turns from black to red as the strength of the moonlight grows. Their powdered, masked heads are twisted, lying on outstretched arms; their crimson mouths gape, their painted eyebrows twitch, and Tallow fancies they are all murdered, looks about for weapons, sees only slapsticks, bladders and a wooden cucumber, subsides to give his full attention to his meat, feels his belly begin to swell, and sighs, turning a newly ruddy, grease-smeared face towards the dying fire, licking the savoury beef juice from his curved lips (a permanent smile which has saved him from as many disasters as it has threatened to create). It is the cat who looks up first, a whole roasted wing in its mouth, and Jephraim is not slow to hear the footfall. He rushes for the wine bottles, picks one which is too light, grabs another almost full, glances at his doorway, realises he cannot leap for it without abandoning meat and wine, ducks beneath the table, disturbing a grunting Zany whose sacklike smock is sour with vomit and whose left hand is buried in the clothing of some ambiguous Isabella who smells altogether too strongly of violets. Cross-legged behind his companions Jephraim watches the far door, through which, clumping gloomily, comes one he recognises, for no other would wear such ornate and useless armour so late at night without a ceremony of some sort to demand it. It is

Sir Tancred Belforest, the Queen's Champion, miserable as ever—as unfulfilled in his way as the Queen he serves, for Gloriana has demanded his word that he will not do violence in her name, nor in the name of Chivalry. Sir Tancred stops to gaze around the room. He crosses to the mirror which reflects the fire. His long moustaches are drooping and he tries to curl them, twisting them around his naked fingers (which jut oddly from the mass of metal encasing the rest of him). He has some success, but not enough. He sighs, clanks to the table and, so Jephraim guesses, pours himself a cup of wine. Studying the noble knight's gold-spiked knees, Jephraim lifts his own bottle and joins Sir Tancred in a gulp or two.

The door creaks and Tallow cranes his neck, observing first a trio of candles, burning cheerfully, then the outline of the young woman who holds the candelabrum. She wears a bulky robe pulled over her scarcely less bulky nightgown. Her face is in shadow, but seems soft and young. There is a further bulk above it, a bulk of dark red hair. From this young woman's mouth comes a strong impatient sigh. "You are too quick, Sir Tancred, to retreat into silly sulking."

Sir Tancred creaks a trifle as he turns. "You blame me—and yet it's you, Lady Mary, who spurns my embrace."

"I merely feared a spearing from your ornaments and suggested you remove your armour before you took me in your arms. I reject not you, Tancred, my dear, but your suit."

"This armour is the badge of my calling. It is as much a part of me as my soul, for it displays the nature of my soul."

Lady Mary (Tallow guesses her to be the youngest of the Perrott girls) moves across the floor and Tallow feels her warmth as she comes close to Sir Tancred. Tallow begins to lust for her, to scheme, a little hopelessly, for a means of making love to her. "Come back with me now, Tancred. The Old Year has passed, as I swore it would not, without a sharing of love between us. Let us, I beg you, begin the New Year in proper resolution."

The Zany groans and stirs. A little more vomit bubbles in his throat. He coughs, soiling his smock again. He takes a firmer hold on whatever it is that he grips in or upon his Isabella and begins to snore in a loud, somewhat self-satisfied tone, disturbing the lovers.

"My dear heart," murmurs young Mary Perrott.

"Oh, indeed, my dear heart!" replies Tallow very quietly.

Mary tugs at Tancred's hand.

Unable to resist an impulse, Tallow takes the arm of the Zany and stretches it out towards the Champion's foot, but delays Tancred's iron ankle with his own hand so that the Champion is checked, kicking loose all too soon, seeing the innocent fingers of the Zany there, and pausing to tuck them, with a fastidious metal toe, back beneath the table. Tallow has done all he feels he is able to do and watches sadly as the lovers depart, rustling and clattering, to Lady Mary's rooms.

Glad to be free of the Zany's company, Tallow emerges from beneath the table, finds a cork, seals his bottle, and puts it in his belt, whistles softly for Tom, flings the cat accurately through the panel, stands tiptoe upon the bench which grazed his shin, reaches long fingers to grasp the ledge and hauls himself upward until he is in his hole again, replacing the panel as best he can, feeling the cold of the tunnels ahead and already regretting his haste in leaving the fire. He sighs and begins to wriggle forward. "Well, Tom, so it is New Year's Eve we celebrate." But Tom is racing ahead in pursuit of a rat and does not hear his master. As Tallow crawls behind the eager beast, he hears from beyond the panel a high, fluting wail.

Master Ernest Wheldrake has been in a corner of the hall all this time. He has seen Tallow come and go, he has overheard the lovers, but he has been too drunk to move. Now the poet rises, finds his quill where he dropped it an hour since, finds the notebook in which he had begun to write his verse, treads upon the fingers of the Zany and, believing he has crushed some small rodent, tears at near-scarlet hair and wails again: "Oh, why is it that I must destroy so much?"

He leaves the hall, still seeking ink. It was for ink that he originally left his own apartments, a mile or more away, as he sat writing an accusatory sonnet to the wench who broke his heart that morning and whose name he cannot now recall. He stalks the lamplit corridors, a small flame-crested crane wading through shallow water, seeking fish, his arms stiffly at his sides, like starched wings, the quill behind his ear, the book in the large purse at his belt, his eyes on the floor, mumbling snatches of alliteration—"Sweet Sarah sate upon the starry step . . . Proud Pamela this poor ploughman's heart hath pierced . . . A doom did Daphne declare that day . . ."—in an effort to recall the offending maid's name. He takes a turn or two and discovers himself at an outer door. A tired man-at-arms greets him. He signs for the door to be opened.

"'Tis snowing, sir," the guard declares kindly, hunching himself in his own furs, by way of emphasis. "Perhaps the coldest night of the winter, with the river threatening to freeze."

Gravely Master Wheldrake signs again, piping: "Temperature is merely a state of mind. Anger and other passions shall warm me. I go down to the Town."

The guard takes his cloak from his shoulders. It engulfs the tiny poet. "Wear this, sir, I beg you, or you'll be a statue in the gardens by dawn."

Wheldrake becomes sentimental. "You are a noble knave, a brave, bold, bragging bear of Albion, the best of Boudicca's valiant breed, a warrior whose goodly deeds shall boast more fame than any limping line that Wheldrake pens. I thank thee, fellow, and bid thee fond farewell." With which he flings himself through the door, into the dark and shivering night, into the snow, and plunges along a path which winds towards the few lights still burning in a London that largely sleeps. The guard wraps his arms around himself for a moment, watching the poet depart, then draws the door shut with a bang, regretting generosity which, he knows, will not be remembered when the morning comes, yet superstitiously glad to have performed a good deed so early in the year and thus almost certainly assuring himself of a little reciprocal luck.

Master Wheldrake's own luck pulls him, oblivious, through two snowbanks, across a frozen pool, through a gate in the wall, into the outer lanes of the town, where the snow has not settled so thickly. He takes a familiar road, by instinct rather than judgement, which brings him at last to the shuttered walls of a large, ramshackle building which sports a bush on a pole above its main arch and a sign on the door proclaiming itself the Seahorse Tavern. Lights behind the shutters, noise behind the doors, tell Master Wheldrake that this, one of his favourite drinking places and a notoriously unwholesome den, will give him the welcome he most desires, provide the comforts his blood demands, and he knocks, is admitted, passes through the courtyard with its ranks of galleries in the darkness above, enters the public room and sinks into the stink and din of coarse laughter, vulgar jesting and bad wine, for it is amongst ruffians like these, amongst whores, amongst the resentful, cynical, ill-natured and desperate men and women who inhabit this riverside rats' nest, that the wounded poet can most easily find release from all that burdens him. He lets the guard's fur fall, cries for wine and, when he produces gold, is given it. The familiar whores come up to him, scratching at his neck, threatening him with all the delights he craves; he grins, he bows, he drinks; he greets those he recognises and those he does not recognise with equal good humour, encouraging their mockery, their contempt, giggling at every insult, screaming delightedly at every pinch and shove, watched by the quiet, cruel eye of a man who sits in a gallery above, sharing a bottle with a burnoosed, bearded and beringed Saracen who is a little disturbed by the crowd's treatment of Wheldrake.

The Saracen leans towards his companion. "They mean that gentleman harm, I think."

The other, whose face is largely hidden by heavy black locks and by the brim of an outlandish sombrero which sports the tattered feathers of a crow, whose body is wrapped in a black, stained seacloak, shakes his head. "They perform for him, sir, I assure you. It is how they earn his gold. He's Wheldrake, from the palace. A protégé of the Queen's, son of some noble Sunderland family, Lady Lyst's lover. He spends much of his time in taverns like this one and always has, since he was at Cambridge's University."

"You've known him so long?"

"Aye, but he has never known me."

"Oh, Captain Quire!" The Saracen laughs. He is drunk, for he is not used to wine. He is a handsome young merchant, a minor lord in Arabia, that most ambitious of all lands under the Queen's protection. Doubtless he is flattered by the fact that Captain Arturus Quire has befriended him; Quire knows the whole of London, knows how best to find the most enjoyment in the city. The Moor half-suspects Captain Quire to have an eye on his purse, but he carries only a moderate amount of money, to which the captain is welcome, for the pleasure he has so far provided. The Moor frowns. "*Would* you be bent on robbing me, Quire?"

"Of what, your honour?"

"My gold, of course."

"I'm no thief." Captain Quire's voice is cold, bored rather than offended.

The Saracen reaches for his wine-cup, watching curiously as two of the whores begin to lead Master Wheldrake up the stairs and around the gallery, into a passage. "Arabia gathers power daily," says the young man significantly. "You would be wise to cultivate her merchants; to consider advantageous trading alliances. Our fleets dominate Asia, second only to Albion's."

Quire darts him a glance, searching for irony. The Moor raises a glittering hand and smiles to reveal more gold. "I speak of mutual gain, nothing else. It is well known how much our young Caliph loves Queen Gloriana. Her father conquered us, but she redeemed us. She gave us back our pride. We remain grateful. It is in our political interest to retain her protection."

There comes a sudden yell from below and the flames of the fire roar up for a moment; a lamp has been flung into the grate. Two bravos battle, cutlass and dirk, amongst the benches. One is tall and thin, in worn velvets; the other is of medium height, altogether a better swordsman, and, in his leathers, almost certainly a professional soldier. The Moor leans forward towards the rail, but Quire leans back, fingering his lantern jaw, bringing thick, black brows together, considering his own thoughts. Meanwhile Master Uttley, the innkeeper, acts with habitual speed, rolling across the filthy floor to the door. He is round-faced, pasty-fleshed, this publican; there are black spots under his skin, like figs in duff, giving him a piebald look. The door is opened and the room begins to chill. Master Uttley clears the crowd, this way and that, a dog with its sheep, leaving an avenue for the duellists, who gradually back towards the door, then disappear, clashing, into the night. Master Uttley bars and locks the entrance. He glares towards the sputtering fire. He stoops to pick tankards and plates from amongst the rushes and sawdust. One of his whores attempts to help him, knocks his shoulder, and is cuffed with a jug before Uttley returns to his own den, immediately below the gallery where Captain Quire and the Saracen sit. The fire throws long shadows and the tavern becomes suddenly still. "Possibly we should seek a warmer place?" suggests the Moor.

Quire sinks further into his seat. "This is warm enough for me. You spoke of mutual advantage?"

"I assume that you have shares in ships, or at least command of a vessel, Captain Quire. There is information to be acquired in London which would be denied to me, but which could easily be available to you . . ."

"Aha. You want me to spy for you. To learn of ventures early so that you may send your own ships ahead, to catch the rival's trade?"

"I did not mean to suggest that you spy, Captain Quire."

"Spy's the word, though." A dangerous moment. Was Quire offended?

"Certainly not. What I suggest is common practice. Your own people do it in our ports." He is placatory.

"You think I'm the sort to spy upon my countrymen?"

The Arabian shrugs and refuses the challenge. "You are too intelligent for this, Captain. You deliberately bait me."

Quire's thin lips part in a smile. "Aye, sir, but you're not being frank."

"If you think so, we'd best terminate our conversation."

Captain Quire shakes his head. Thick, long ringlets swing from beneath his sombrero. "I must tell you that I own no interest in a ship. I command no ship. I am not even an officer aboard a ship. I am not a seaman. I serve with no company, either ashore or afloat. I'm Quire, nought else but Quire. Therefore I cannot help you at all."

"Perhaps you could help me more." Significantly, yet uncertainly.

Quire raises the shoulder nearest the Saracen and leans his chin on it. "Now you intend frankness, eh?"

"We would pay for any kind of information concerning the movement of Albion's ships, whether military or civil. We would pay for rumours from the Court concerning official adventures. We would pay considerably for specific news of Queen Gloriana's private converse. I'm told there are means of overhearing her."

"Indeed, my lord? Who told you so?"

"A courtier who visited Baghdad last year."

Quire draws in his lips as if considering all this. "I'm not rich, as you may observe."

The Moor pretends that he has noticed this for the first time. "You'd be improved by a new suit of clothes, that's true, sir."

"You are not a fool, my lord."

"I think that I am not."

"And you guessed from the first I was neither master nor merchant."

"There are men of a certain disposition in Albion who affect poverty. One cannot judge . . ."

Quire nods. He clears his throat. Along the gallery now comes a scrawny, snagtoothed villain wearing leggings of rabbit fur, a torn quilted doublet, a horsehide cap pulled down about his ears. He wears a sword from the guard of which some of the rust has been inexpertly scratched. His gait is unsteady not so much from drink as, it would seem, from some natural indisposition. His skin is blue, showing that he has just come in from the night, but his eyes burn. "Captain Quire?" It is as if he has been summoned, as if he anticipates some epicurean wickedness.

"Tinkler. You are just in time to be my witness. This is the Lord Ibram of Baghdad."

Tinkler bows, leaning one filthy hand upon the table. Lord Ibram looks uncertainly from Tinkler to Quire.

"The Lord Ibram, I'll have you know, Master Tinkler, has just insulted me."

The Moor is at last on his guard. "That is untrue, Captain Quire!" He cannot rise, for the table stops him. He cannot leave without pushing past either Quire or Tinkler, who is evidently a familiar accomplice of the captain's. "This is to be a quarrel, then," he says, drawing a sleeve back from his right arm. "Premeditated?"

Captain Quire's voice grows colder. "He has suggested I spy upon the Queen herself. He tells me that young Sir Launcelot Teale revealed to him a means of doing this."

"Ah!" says Lord Ibram loudly. "You know everything. I am trapped. Very well." He makes to push the table back but Quire holds it. "I admit I attempted to make a spy of you, Captain Quire, and that it was a foolish attempt—since you are plainly already a professional. But I trust you are also a good diplomat and will understand that if I am captured, or tortured, or slain, it will have repercussions. My uncle is brother-in-law to the Emir of Morocco. I am also related to Lord Shahryar, ambassador to Albion, who arrives shortly. I'll leave now, admitting my folly." He manages to stand at last. He lets his robe fall away to emphasise the fact that he is armed. He has made a further mistake, for Quire grins quickly and triumphantly at him.

"But you have, after all, insulted me, Lord Ibram."

Lord Ibram bows. "Then I apologise."

"It will not do. I am a loyal subject of the Queen. She probably has few better servants than Captain Quire. You are not a coward, sir, I hope."

"Coward? Oh! No, I am not."

"Then you'll allow me . . ."

"What? Satisfaction? Here? You want to brawl, do you, Captain Quire?" With a dark eye cocked, the Moor draws on a jewelled glove and lets the gloved hand fall upon the ornate hilt of his curved sword. "You and your accomplice hope to kill me?"

"I'll make Master Tinkler my second and give you the opportunity to seek a second for yourself. We'll find some private place to fight, if that suits you better."

"You intend to fight fairly, Captain Quire?"

"I have told you, Lord Ibram. You have insulted me. You have insulted my Queen."

"No, I have not."

"You have made insinuations."

"I spoke of common gossip." The Saracen realises he has betrayed his own pride and bites his lip as Captain Quire again grins up into his face.

"It is unseemly, in a great lord, surely, to give such gossip credence? And as for reporting the tittle-tattle of the gutter, that is certainly dishonourable."

"I admit it." The Moor shrugs. "Very well, I'll fight. Must I find a second from this rabble? Are there no gentlemen upon whom I can call?"

"Only Master Wheldrake. Shall we see how much liquor is left in him?" Quire makes no move around the table. Tinkler steps back to let Lord Ibram pass. Quire begins to walk along the gallery towards the passage where Wheldrake disappeared, but the Moor stays him. "The poor creature would not be capable."

"Then one of these." Quire indicates the population below. "Any will do it, if you pay."

The Moor leans over the rail. "I require a second in a duel. A crown to the man who comes with me." He displays the silver coin. The ruffler in leather, who lately went fighting through the door, has returned, presumably by means of another entrance. He is red-faced and there are two long scratches across his forehead, a bruise on his bald scalp, and his ear has been cut—he holds a sponge against it.

"I'll do it. I'd rather be a witness than a participant."

Quire smiles. "What became of your opponent?"

"He ran off, sir. But he left this behind." He reaches to the table nearest him and displays a severed nose. "I bit it off. He wanted it back so that he might find a barber to sew it on again. I won it fairly and refused to return it." Laughing, he flings it towards the fire, but it falls short and begins to roast on the tiles.

Lord Ibram turns to Captain Quire. "You know something of me? Sir Launcelot will have told you?"

"That you're a good swordsman?"

"Then you reckon yourself a better?"

Quire will not answer.

The party leaves the tavern by the back entrance, moving along the river path to where a carriage still waits. It is the one that brought Quire and Ibram to The Seahorse. They are all shivering as they clamber in and Quire gives the coachman directions for the White Hall fields. Quire looks out once at the broad, black river. Snow falls upon it. It seems to move more sluggishly than usual. Through the snow he sees the faint outline, the lights of a good-sized ship, hears the splashing oars of tugs towing it in to the dock at Charing Cross. He glances at the glowering Moor, whose anger seems primarily directed inwards, he winks at Tinkler, who grins a snagtoothed grin, but he does not look at the soldier with the red sponge who begins, perhaps by way of earning his silver, to try to engage Lord Ibram in friendly conversation.

The carriage bumps over frozen ruts and is swallowed.

On board the ship coming so late and with such difficulty up the Thames, Sir Thomasin Ffynne stamps one foot of flesh and one of carved bone upon the timbers of his bridge and thinks his breath must freeze before his eyes. He hopes the dawn will come before the ship reaches her dock, for he mistrusts the tugmen hauling her. There are not too many lights burning and those he can see are obscured by the weather.

Heavy snow coats the whole ship, yards, rigging, rails and decks. It settles upon Tom Ffynne's hat, his shoulders; it threatens to slip between boot and stocking and freeze his remaining foot so that it will also have to be removed (it was frostbite took the other, on his famous voyage into the Arctic Circle).

Tom Ffynne is back from his pirating—toll-gathering, he calls it—in the Mexican Sea. He had hoped to be back for the Yuletide Festival, then for the New Year's Masque, but has missed both and so is in poor temper. Yet he looks gladly at his London, at the distant great glistening palace, and he even thanks the lad who brings him a tin cup of hot rum from the galley. He sips, the metal burning his bearded lips, and grunts, and stomps, and sings out in his sharp falsetto at the tugboats whenever it seems to him that the ship moves too closely to the high embankments of the riverside. Diminutive, plump, ruddy-faced and twinkling, Sir Thomasin

Ffynne's appearance disguises one of the shrewdest brains in all Albion. An admiral at twenty-six, he sailed with the war-fleets of King Hern, in the old days of conquest and pillage, and it was under Hern that he became known as Bad Tom Ffynne, in an age that had many bad men in it. Yet his love for the Queen is as strong as Lord Montfallcon's, one of the few others who survived Hern's reign with some sort of honour, and one of the few still to hold office under Gloriana. It was Tom Ffynne's uncle who took the Moorish Caliphates for Hern, but it was Tom Ffynne who held them, made them almost totally dependent upon Albion for their defence, their survival. Two revolts in the great continent of Virginia were also put down by Ffynne, assuring his nation's power; and in Cathay, in India, in all the kingdoms of Asia and on the coasts of Africa, Tom Ffynne has fought, with absolute savagery, to maintain Albion's dominance over these lands which are now Gloriana's protectorates and which she does conscientiously protect, forbidding violence, demanding justice for all those for whom she accepts responsibility. Baffling days for Ffynne, who once possessed a reasonable trust in terror as the best instrument for maintaining Order in the universe; who saw all this new Law as an unnecessary expense, a wasteful business that was, moreover, abused by those it was intended to benefit; yet he has come to respect his Matriarch's wishes, maintains a grudging inactivity where the Queen specifically forbids his movements, and contents himself with exploratory journeys involving a little incidental piracy, so long as the ships involved are not under the protection of a far too generous monarch. The holds of his tall ship, the *Tristram and Isolde*, are currently full, half with the treasure of some West Indian emperor, whose cities Tom Ffynne visited on a voyage along a broad river which took him hundreds of miles into the interior, and half with cloth and ingots taken off two Iberian caravels after an engagement lasting five hours near the coast of California, that most westerly of Virginia's provinces. Tom Ffynne intends to deliver all to his Queen, but retains an educated hope that the Queen will let a large share be kept back for the *Tristram and Isolde*'s officers and men. He is anxious to be granted an audience for another reason:

he has news which he knows will interest Montfallcon and possibly alarm the Queen.

Ffynne realises that the dawn has come without his noticing it, the snow is so thick. Gradually the horizon grows pale, revealing a palace like some gigantic Alpine peak, a London half-buried in snow, a Thames on which ice is forming even as the ship moves through it.

All is white and silent. Tom Ffynne stops his stamping to stand in wonder at the sight of Albion's capital on this New Year's Day, beginning the thirteenth year of Gloriana's peaceful reign and, according to old Doctor Dee, the Queen's astrologer, the most significant both in her life and in the history of the Realm.

Tom Ffynne lets out a huge, billowing breath. He claps mittened hands together and shakes little icicles from his dark beard, grunting with pleasure at the sight of his home port, in all its proud, frozen glory; its temporary tranquillity.

The Second Chapter

In Which Queen Gloriana Begins the First Day of the New Year, Receives Courtiers and Learns of Certain Alarming Matters

FROM WHITE SHEETS, in a huge ivory gown trimmed with silver lace, her hair enclosed in a cap of plain linen, her pale hands decorated by nothing but two matching rings of pearls and platinum, Queen Gloriana pushed back bleached silk bed-curtains, rose and crossed to the window. On snowy lawns albino peacocks paced between carved yew hedges which this morning were like marble. A few flakes still fell to cover the darker tracks of the birds, but the milky sky grew lighter as she watched and there was even a trace of the faintest blue. She turned to where her little maid of honour, Mary Perrott, stood beside the breakfast tray with its heavy burden of silver. "You're very pretty this morning, Mary. Good colour. Womanly. But tired, I think."

In affirmation, Lady Mary yawned. "The festivities . . ."

"I fear I left the Masque a little early. Did your father like it? And your brothers and sisters? Was it enjoyable to them? The entertainers? Were they amusing?" She asked many questions so that none might be answered.

"It was a perfect night, Your Majesty."

Seating herself at the delicate table, Gloriana lifted covers to choose kidneys and sweetbreads. "Cold weather. Are you eating enough, Mary?"

As her mistress began to devour the food, Mary Perrott seemed to quiver slightly, and Gloriana, detecting this, waved a fork. "Return to your bed for an hour or two. I'll not need you. But first place another log on the fire and bring me the ermine robe. That dress is a new one, eh? Red velvet suits you. Though the bodice seems too tight."

Lady Mary blushed as she leaned over the fire. "I had intended to alter it, madam." For a moment she left the chamber, to return with the ermine, placing it across her mistress's broad shoulders. "Thank you, madam. Two hours?"

Gloriana smiled, finished the kidneys and started quickly on her herrings, before they should grow cold. "Visit no swain and let none visit you, Mary, but sleep. Thus you'll be able to fulfil all your duties."

"I will, madam." A curtsey and Lady Mary slipped from the Queen's austere room.

Gloriana found that the herrings were not to her liking and rose from them suddenly. She walked to the mirror on the wall beside the door, grateful for unanticipated privacy. She investigated her long, perfect face, her delicate bones. Her large green-blue eyes contained an expression of faint, objective curiosity. The cap gave a starkness to her features. She removed it, releasing her auburn hair, which curled immediately against her cheeks and on her shoulders; she unlaced her gown, threw off her ermine, so that she was naked, soft and glowing. She stood a full six inches over six feet, yet her figure was ideally proportioned, her flesh unblemished for all that, like some lovers' oak, she had been carved, in her time, with a dozen initials or more; struck, since girlhood, with almost every sort of whip and weapon, tortured with fire, scored, bruised, scratched—first by her father himself or by those who, serving her father, sought either to educate or to punish her; secondly by lovers whom she had hoped might rouse her to that single important experience still denied her. She stroked her flanks, not from any narcissism but abstractedly, wondering how such sensitive flesh as this could be so thoroughly stimulated and yet refuse to reward her with the release it had afforded the majority of those she lent it to. A little sigh and the robe was re-donned, the fur drawn around her, in time to call "Enter" when a knock came and in walked her closest friend, her Private Secretary, her confidante, Una, Countess of Scaith. The Countess wore a grey brocade marlotte, its high collar completely enclosing her neck and emphasising, with its short puffed sleeves, her heart-shaped face, flaring to reveal her gown's hooped skirt, dark red and gold. Una's grey eyes, intelligent and warm, looked into Gloriana's—a brief question already answered—before they embraced.

"By Hermes, let there be no further doctors like those that were sent to me!" The Queen laughed. "They pricked me all night with their little instruments and bored me so, Una, that I fell solidly to sleep. They were gone when I awoke. Will you send them some gift from me? For their trouble."

The Countess of Scaith nodded, being careful to share her friend's deliberate mood. She left the bedchamber and entered an adjoining room, unlocking a small writing desk and taking from it a notebook, calling back: "The Italians? How many?"

"Three boys and two girls."

"Gifts of equal value?"

"It seems fair."

Una returned. "Tom Ffynne is just come home. The *Tristram and Isolde* docked at Charing Cross not three hours since and he's eager to see you."

"Alone?"

"Or with the Lord Montfallcon. Perhaps at eleven, when your Privy Council meets . . . ?"

"Discover from him something of the nature of his anxiety. I should not like to offend the loyal admiral."

"He has no loyalties but to you," agreed Una. "These old men of your father's place a higher value on you than do the young ones, I think, for they remember . . ."

"Aye." Gloriana became distant. She disliked memories of her father or comparisons, for she had loved the monster increasingly as he grew older and sicklier and, at the end, had learned to sympathise with him, knowing that he had been too weakened by the burden she herself was barely strong enough to shoulder. "Appointments, today?"

"You wished an audience for Doctor Dee. That is arranged to follow the meeting of the Privy Council. Then there is nothing until after you have dined (at twelve until two) with the ambassador from Cathay and the ambassador from Bengahl."

"They dispute some border?"

"Lord Montfallcon has a paper and a solution. He'll tell you of that this morning."

"After we've dined?"

"Your children and their governesses. Until four. At five, a ceremony in the Audience Chamber."

"The foreign dignitaries, eh?"

"The usual presents and assurances, for New Year's Day. At six, the mayor and aldermen—presents and assurances. At seven, you agreed to consider the case of the new buildings by Greyfrairs. At eight, supper: the Lords Kansas and Washington."

"Ah, my romantic Virginians! I look forward to supper."

"After supper only one thing. Sir Tancred Belforest requests an audience."

"Some new scheme of chivalrous daring?"

"I think this is a private matter."

"Excellent." Gloriana laughed as she entered her dressing room, ringing the bell for her maids. "It will make me happy to grant at least one boon to the poor Champion; he yearns eternally to please me, but all he knows is battle and gymnastics. Have you any inkling of his desire?"

"I would say he asks your permission to marry Mary Perrott."

"Oh, gladly, gladly. I love them both. And I'd grant any boon to distract his noble concentration!" The maids of honour entered. Pretty girls, every one had been a lover of the Queen and had been employed as a result, for she could not dismiss any who had tried to please her and who did not wish to be free. "So the day is relatively light."

"Depending on Tom Ffynne's news. He could bring reports of wars—in the West Indies."

"We are not concerned with the West Indies. Save for Panama, they do not come under our protection, thank the gods. Unless they should attack Virginia—but which of their nations is powerful enough?"

"With Iberian help?"

"Oh, with Iberian help, aye. But I think the West Indians mistrust Iberia now, so many of their peoples have been sent to the slaughter. No, for danger, we must needs look closer to home, dearest Una." She leaned to kiss her secretary as maids tugged at her stays to produce the conventional peasecod-bellied figure demanded of her station. She grunted as the wind left her. "Ugh!"

"I'll go to tell Sir Tancred he is blessed."

Una departed while Gloriana continued to suffer the somewhat comforting constrictions of her costume as she was fitted, tight and tidy, like some man-o'-war, for her day's duties: stomacher and farthingale, a starched wired ruff, stockings of silk and tall-heeled shoes, embroidered petticoat, gown of golden velvet set with jewels of a dozen kinds and little stitched flowers, cloak of dark red velvet trimmed with ermine, hair bound with pearl strands and topped by a coronet, face powdered, gloves on hands, rings on gloves, mace and sceptre held to left and right, until she was ready to glide about her business, surrounded, a frigate by gulls, by her little pages and maids (some of whom took up her train), on her way to the Privy Chamber where her councillors awaited her. She sailed down corridors hung with silken flags, with tapestries and paintings; corridors decorated with glowing panels showing scenes of Albion's glories and vicissitudes, beasts, heroes, pastoral scenes, scenes of exotic Oriental, African or Virginian landscapes. And she passed courtiers, who bowed to her, or curtseyed to her, who complimented her, and with some she must share a "Good morning" or an enquiry as to health; she passed squires and ladies-in-waiting, equerries, stewards, butlers, footmen, servants of every description. Her feet trod on carpets, mosaics, tiles, polished wood, some silver, a little gold, marble and lead. She took a corner, gracefully, through the First, Second and Third Audience Chambers, her skirt's hoop swaying, where courtiers and petitioners awaited her favour and Gentlemen Pensioners, her personal guard, Lord Rhoone's men, in scarlet and dark green, saluted her with their pikes while footmen pushed open the doors of the Audience Room, which she crossed without pause to enter the Privy Chamber, where her councillors rose, bowed, waited until she seated herself in her chair at the head of the long table before resuming their own positions, those twelve gentlemen in gowns of rich materials, with golden chains upon their chests.

Through the splendid window at Gloriana's back came light filtered by the thousand colours in the huge stained scene of Emperor and Tribute: Gloriana's father pictured as King Arthur, with London as New Troy (legend's citadel of that Mystical Golden Age Britannia, founded by Gloriana's ancestor, Prince Brutus, seven thousand years before), with representatives of all the nations of the world bringing gifts to lay upon the ninety-nine steps of the Empire's throne where maidens, Wisdom, Truth, Beauty and Mercy, flanked a radiant crown. Privately Gloriana considered the window to be in poor taste, but respect for tradition and her father's memory demanded she retain it. Six to a side of the dark table, with silver-chased inkhorns, goose quills, sand-shakers and paper in order before them, her Privy Councillors sat, twelve familiar faces, according to their rank. On her immediate right, Lord Perion Montfallcon, in his blacks and greys, and his great grey leonine head half-bowed, as if he slumbered, her Lord Chancellor and Principal Secretary; on her immediate left, pensive, aquiline, with a long, square-cut white beard, in brown cap and cloak, a belted doublet and a golden chain made up of six-pointed stars, sat Doctor John Dee, her Councillor of Philosophy. Next to Lord Montfallcon, Sir Orlando Hawes, the blackamoor, thin and pinched, in plain dark blue, with a parsimonious collar of lighter blue lace, a chain of silver, small black eyes upon his papers, her Lord High Treasurer; opposite him, stiff as stone, controlling the pain of gout, a ruddy-faced and stern old man, Albion's most famous navigator, Lisuarte Armstrong, Fourth Baron of Ingleborough, Lord Admiral of Albion, in purple velvet and white lace, his chain heavy, like an anchor's, on his neck, his eyes blue as the palest northern oceans. Next on the right was Gorius, Lord Ransley, Lord High Steward of Albion, in ruff and cuffs of pale gold, quilted doublet of deepest russet, his chain of office embellished with rubies;

then Sir Amadis Cornfield, Keeper of the Royal Purse. In white-and-blue-striped silk, turned back at neck and wrist to display a crimson lining, over which was laid a large loose collar and broad cuffs, his linen; and in his silver chain, thin and delicate, made to match the silver buttons of his coat, he was a handsome, sardonic, wide-mouthed, dark-haired gallant, taking his duties seriously. He appeared to be studying some aspect of the window he had not noticed before. Facing Sir Amadis was Sir Vivien Rich, plump and hairy, in country-woven clothes making him resemble some yeoman farmer, this Vice-Chamberlain to the Queen. Seated almost primly beside Sir Amadis was Master Florestan Wallis, the famous scholar, all in black, sporting no chain, but a small badge on his breast, his thin, straight hair covering his shoulders, his strong lips pursed; he was Secretary for the High Tongue of Albion, the language of official proclamations and ceremony, and he was a writer of small plays performed at Court. The next pair: Perigot Fowler, Master of the Horse, in dark browns, and Isador Palfreyman, Secretary for War, in blood-red. Both bearded, almost twins. Lastly on the right Mr. Auberon Orme, Master of the Great Wardrobe, in somewhat unseasonal lilac and Lincoln green, with a huge ruff from both these colours, emphasising the length of his nose, the smallness of his mouth, the suggestion of crimson in the whites of the eyes; and, on the left, Mr. Marcilius Gallimari, a dark, amused Neapolitan, his doublet slashed, puffed and gallooned to reveal almost as many colours as those of the window; his hair was waved and there was a diamond in one ear, an emerald in the other; he had a thin, pointed beard and just the trace of a moustache, this talented Master of the Revels.

The Queen smiled. "There's a light, merry atmosphere in the chamber this morning. Am I to take it that the holiday continues?"

Montfallcon climbed to portentous feet. "In most matters, Your Majesty. The world is quiet. As the grave, today. But Sir Thomasin Ffynne brings news . . ."

"I know. I intend to see him when this conference is done."

"Then Your Majesty's aware of what he has to say?" A significant grunt.

"Not yet, Lord Montfallcon."

"Come, come, my Lord Chancellor!" Doctor Dee was his old rival. "You hint so ominously one might suspect the world ends, at last! Are you dissatisfied because there is no threat current upon Albion? Would you like an omen? Shall I consult the Talmud? Shall I conjure you a disaster? Release a few devils from bottles, find a dark future in the stars, frighten us all with talk of the possible plagues one might catch if this warning isn't heeded or that one ignored?" Being virtually without timbre, his voice always made some think he spoke, as now, sardonically; by others he was almost always taken literally. Thus he surrounded himself with more ambiguity than he could ever understand and was often, in turn, greatly baffled by his fellows, simply because, unknowingly, unreasonably (he could not help his voice), he had baffled them.

Perion Montfallcon was by no means baffled, for he was used to Dee's raillery. Neither loved the other even a little. Lord Montfallcon made a display of patience, giving his attention wholly to the Queen. "Your Majesty, it is a small matter, but it could be the nut from which would grow an exceedingly tangled root."

Anxious to avoid a full-fledged drama between these two seasoned players, Queen Gloriana raised both hands. "Then shall we have Tom Ffynne before us now, to explain?"

"Well . . ." Lord Montfallcon shrugged. "It can do no harm. He is without, in the First Presence Chamber."

"Then have him fetched, my lord."

Lord Montfallcon turned from his chair and moved slowly for the little door behind him which led to the anteroom between the Privy Chamber and his own offices. He opened the door, gave a word to a footman; a pause, then in stumped Ffynne. Sir Tom had trimmed his beard a little for the occasion and there were five purple ostrich feathers in his hat, a short, pleated bottle-green cape on his left shoulder, a white, starched ruff, emerald-green doublet, belted at his corseted middle, wide gallyslop hose tied below the knee with ribbons, white stockings and gold-buckled black shoes.

He had donned his best. His little twinkling eyes widened a trifle as he saw the Queen and he doffed his hat, bowing low, clip-clumping forward on his carved foot which had been so designed that the stump of his ankle could be pinned perfectly into it. "Your Majesty."

"Good day to you, Sir Thomasin. We expected you earlier. Were there storms?"

"Many, Your Majesty. Every league of the way. We were badly damaged. All rigging gone but a couple of stays, most yards down by the time we sighted the coast of Iberia. We limped through the Narrow Sea and put into The Havre to make minor repairs before coming on. That was four days ago."

"Your news is of France, then?"

"No, Your Majesty. It was got from France. While we were in the harbour, further delayed by the incompetents sent us as joiners and sailmakers, there came to port a large, old-fashioned galleon, of some forty oars. She flew the Polish flag and I became curious, for she was evidently a ceremonial craft, with a great deal of gilt and gold braid on ropes and rails. She wallowed in and dropped anchor quite close to us. Being interested, I sent my compliments to the master, who consequently invited me aboard. He was a civil old gentleman. A noble, too. And glad to meet me, for he was full of Queen Gloriana and Albion and eager for any happy intelligence concerning both. He praised our land and its Queen and flattered me, when he learned my name, with remembrances of my own adventurings."

"So that's your news, eh, Sir Thomasin," said Doctor Dee, entirely to spite Lord Montfallcon. "We are loved by Poland."

"Doctor Dee!" The Queen flashed an eye and the doctor subsided.

"Certainly," continued Ffynne, "for this ship is even now awaiting Poland's king, who comes overland, by coach, to board her—and from The Havre he intends to sail for London."

"For what purpose?" Sir Amadis Cornfield drew reluctant eyes from the windows. "The king himself? Without a fleet? With no retinue?"

"He comes as a suitor," said Tom Ffynne quietly. "Nay, almost a bridegroom. He seems, according to my noble Pole, convinced that Your Majesty will accept him in marriage."

"Ah." Gloriana's sideways look to Lord Montfallcon was embarrassed.

"Madam?" The Lord Chancellor lifted his head.

"An oversight, my lord. I had meant to inform you. I sent letters to the King of Poland."

"Consenting to marriage?"

"Of course not. It was while you were suffering the fever, in November last. There came a message from Poland. Formal enough. Suggesting a visit—a private visit from the king—perhaps a *secret* visit, now I think on it—but a visit incognito, at any rate. I agreed. Two swiftly penned letters, one assuring him of our affection for his nation, the other suggesting an early date in the New Year. No reply received. Perhaps it went astray. He is reckoned a kindly man and I was curious to meet him."

"And from this he deduces—doubtless because he interprets Your Majesty's gesture in terms of some custom in his own country—that you are ready to hear his proposals of marriage." Lord Montfallcon cleared his throat and pressed a palm flat against his chest. "And if you refuse him, madam?"

"He must be informed that he has misinterpreted our letters."

"And will suspect a plot. Poland is a good friend. Her Empire's a powerful one, stretching from the Baltic to the Middle Sea, with forty vassal states. Between us we hold off Tatary . . ."

"We are familiar with the political geography of Europe, Lord Montfallcon." Doctor Dee drew a long nail down the side of his jaw. "You suggest that if Poland believes himself a rejected suitor—a jilted lover, even—he will revenge himself with war upon us?"

"Not war," Lord Montfallcon spoke as if he answered his own voice, "probably not war, but strained relations we cannot afford. Tatary's ever ready. And Arabia's ambitious, too."

"Then perhaps I should marry Poland." Queen Gloriana was for a moment a wild young girl. "Eh? Would that save us, my lord?"

"The Grand Caliph of Arabia comes soon upon a State Visit," Lord Montfallcon mused. "There is every hint he, too, intends a proposal. Then, next month, there's the Theocrat of Iberia—but he knows his cause to be hopeless, since there could not possibly be issue. Yet Arabia, Arabia . . ." He became decisive: "There's nothing else for it! They must appear together!"

"But Poland's imminent," pointed out Tom Ffynne. "Any day he arrives in The Havre. One more day or so, and he's docking in London!"

"When was he due to arrive?" Montfallcon paced back and forth alongside the table while his fellow councillors tried to follow both his reasoning and his movement.

"Forty-eight hours, I think, behind me. And I left on the morning tide, yesterday."

"So we have perhaps three days."

"At most."

"I am deeply sorry, Lord Montfallcon, for forgetting to inform you . . ." Gloriana's voice was small.

Suddenly Lord Montfallcon straightened, ceased his musing, shrugged. "No matter, madam. It will be an embarrassment, nothing more. We must pray Poland's delayed a little longer and coincides with Arabia."

"But why should that improve the situation, my lord?"

"It is a question of pride, madam. If you should wound the pride of one or both, then our relations deteriorate, naturally. But if Poland wounds the pride of Arabia, or vice versa, we are strengthened. Neither thinks ill of the Queen, each thinks worse of the other. I consider not the immediate problems, madam, as you know, but those potential problems. Arabia and Poland would make an unlikely alliance, but not an impossible one. They share a seaboard—the Middle Sea—and yet the entrance to that sea is pretty well controlled by Iberia, who, in turn, would ally herself with Arabia against us . . ."

"Ah, the convolutions of your thinking, sir!" A black hand raised as if to ward off assault, Sir Orlando Hawes spoke for the first time. "Do they baffle only me?" He spoke with courtesy. He admired Montfallcon.

"They baffle all of us, save the Lord Chancellor, I think." Queen Gloriana rustled a cuff. "Yet I respect his concerns, for he has more than once anticipated an important threat to this Realm. We must leave it to your diplomacy, my lord. And I shall honour any decision you take."

A low bow. "Thank you, madam. I am almost certain the matter will resolve itself."

"I am entirely to blame, sir, for this trouble. The exchange of letters occurred when . . . I was obsessed with so many other problems . . . It seems . . ."

Lord Montfallcon was firm. "The Queen need not explain herself."

"He's considered something of a clown, I gather, this Poland." Lisuarte Ingleborough made an enquiring eye. "Or, at least, an eccentric. Strange that he sent no emissaries. If that had been done, we should not now be so surprised."

"Lord Ingleborough speaks the truth, as I understand it." Tom Ffynne fingered the plumes of his hat. "Count Korniovsky—if I remember his outlandish name accurately—said much the same, though not directly. His master has little grasp of statecraft, is primarily obsessed with music and such things. Platonically speaking, the nation's entirely decadent. There is a parliament in Poland, representing the interests of commons and nobles alike, and this makes all the king's decisions for him, Your Majesty, so it's said." The little admiral gave vent to a high-pitched giggle. "A strange land that has a king and doesn't use him, eh?"

Queen Gloriana smiled slowly, almost wistfully. "Well, we thank thee greatly for this service, Tom Ffynne. Have you more news? Of your own venturings in the West Indies?"

"Golden ballast saw us through the storms, Your Majesty, and it's still aboard, at Charing Cross, awaiting your pleasure, in the holds of the *Tristram and Isolde*."

"You have an inventory, Sir Thomasin?" Sir Orlando Hawes's manner was almost warm towards the mariner.

"Aye, sir." Tom Ffynne hobbled forward, drawing a roll of paper from his belt and, bowing with great ceremony, handed it up to Queen Gloriana. She unrolled the document, but it was obvious to most of those who watched her that she did not read it.

"Enough to build and fit a whole squadron of ships!" Gloriana rolled the document and passed it to Lord Montfallcon, who gave it to Sir Orlando. "Would you divide a tenth part between yourself and your crew, Sir Tom?"

"You are generous, madam."

"A tenth of this!" Like a startled stallion, the Lord High Treasurer's nostrils flared. "It's too much! A twelfth, Your Majesty . . ."

"For so many lives risked?"

Sir Orlando sniffed. "Very well, madam."

Queen Gloriana peered the length of the table. "Master Gallimari. Are entertainments prepared for all today's functions?"

"They are, Your Majesty. While you dine, the music of Master Pavealli . . ."

"Excellent. I am sure all other choices will be appropriate. And the gown for this evening is ready, eh, Master Orme?"

"To the last button, madam."

"And you, Master Wallis, have prepared the speech for this afternoon?"

"Two, Your Majesty—one for foreign ambassadors, one for London's mayor."

"And there are no decisions I need make concerning dinner or supper, I gather. And, Sir Vivien, I regret we shall not be able to go to the hunt until next week, but I beg you hunt without us."

Thus the Queen improved the atmosphere in the Council chamber, causing all to laugh, for Sir Vivien's passion was a standing joke.

Slowly Gloriana got to her feet, smiling back at her suddenly jovial councillors. They rose, in formal respect. "There are no urgent matters, then? That was the only pressing problem, Lord Montfallcon?"

"It was, madam." The old Chancellor bowed and handed her a scroll. "Here's my suggested solution for Cathay and Bengahl." She accepted it.

"I bid you all adieu, gentleman."

Thirteen legs bent. Gloriana departed this worshipping concourse and was at once surrounded, again, by pages and maids, on her voyage back to her own lodgings where she might gain, with luck, half an hour in which to indulge an inquest on the matter of Poland with her co-conspirator in innocence, the Countess of Scaith.

Perion Montfallcon, frowning, signed first to Lisuarte Ingleborough and then to Sir Tom; the three were cronies, survivors of a tyranny they had sworn must never return. Montfallcon bid a hasty farewell to his fellow councillors, and led the two through the small door, across the antechamber, into his own offices. These were huge rooms. They were filled with books of Law and History. Some of the volumes were as large as Montfallcon himself. The rooms were lit by high windows arranged so that none might ever spy upon the occupants. Diffused light entered, seeming to settle near the ceilings, and scarcely any of it reached the floor where the three men now stood, beside Lord Montfallcon's ordered desk.

The Lord Chancellor sighed and rubbed his heavy nose, shaking his head. "It is the first time she has acted so whimsically. Was it because I lay on my sickbed and she felt abandoned by me? 'Tis the action of a foolish child. From birth she was never that."

The Lord Admiral leaned his bones on the desk. "Perhaps she yearns to be unburdened?"

Tom Ffynne refused the notion. "She is too conscious of her responsibility. Perhaps she was ill."

"More likely." Montfallcon rubbed at an arm which seemed suddenly to ache as if he'd been in battle. "Yet—did you detect pain? Perhaps, for a few moments while she penned and sent those letters, she hoped to be free."

"It would be the only time she's displayed such an aberration." Lord Ingleborough sighed and laid a hand flat against his left thigh. His own agony threatened to wrench his body entirely out of shape.

Lord Montfallcon said: "We must make it our duty to ensure it does not occur again. And save her pain, if possible."

"You grow sentimental, Perion." Tom Ffynne uttered, quietly, a chuckle which had chilled the blood of thousands. "But how are we to solve the dilemma?"

"It must solve itself," said Ingleborough. "Surely?"

Montfallcon shook a determined head. "There's another way.

There's more than one, but I'll try the least dramatic first. I'm used to such manipulations. If the Queen but knew what I do to ensure her Faith and that of her subjects! In this case the art is to trick and delay all suitors, to keep all in hope, to give no true assurances, to offend none, to weary the persistent and to give a touch of encouragement to the crestfallen. Thus I play the flirt for the Queen." And he performed a small, uncharacteristic dance, which perhaps he thought flirtatious, before he sat himself down. "Decadent Poland comes from this direction, warlike Arabia from that. The secret is to let them arrive at about the same time in the hope they'll collide—look, as it were, into a mirror and mislike the reflection—and leave in dudgeon."

"But Poland comes too soon for that!" Tom Ffynne insisted.

"Then I'll stop him."

"How?"

"Sabotage. His ship can be delayed awhile at The Havre."

"He'll find another."

"True. Then closer to home . . ." A knock on the door and a frown from Lord Montfallcon. "Enter."

A young page came in. There was a sealed envelope in his extended right hand. He bowed to the company. "My lord, a message from Sir Christopher, to be delivered urgently."

Lord Montfallcon received the envelope and broke off the seals, reading swiftly, then glaring. "The very man I considered—the only man I considered—and he's pronounced a murderer and hunted. By Zeus, I'd be glad to see that toad hopping on a gibbet."

"A servant of yours?" Tom Ffynne grinned. "A bad servant, by the sound of him."

"No, no. The best I have. There's none so clever. There's none so wicked—but he has over-extended himself, it seems. And an Arabian princeling, at that. Of course! Sir Launcelot's Arab!"

"We'd be illuminated, Lisuarte and I," said Tom Ffynne, and twinkled very merrily, making it obvious to his two friends that he was more than a little curious as to the letter's contents. But Lord Montfallcon screwed the message up, then burned it, without thinking, in a grate already black with past papers.

"There's no more." Lord Montfallcon became cunning. "Now I must plot to save my toad, my unwelcome familiar, from his roasting. How may I defeat the Law we both support?"

"This seems secret and weighty." Sir Thomasin Ffynne limped for the door. "Will you dine with me, Lord High Admiral? Or better yet, make me your guest to dinner?"

"Gladly, Tom." Lord Ingleborough, noblest of these survivors, seemed troubled by the Chancellor's words, as well as by his actions. "By the gods, Perion, I hope you will not bring back the bad days with these schemes of yours."

"I scheme only to prevent that event, Lord Ingleborough." With gravity the Lord Chancellor bowed to his friends and wished them good appetite before pulling at a rope to sound the bell that would bring Tinkler from the shadows to bear a message to his master, Quire.

The Third Chapter

In Which Captain Quire Ensures Himself of Future Comfort and Good Will and Receives an Unwelcome Message

Captain Quire sat up on his grey and grease-veined bedsheet, flicking an ankle free of a blanket which clung to it like a dying rat, staring at a diffident young girl who, with a basket, had entered the seedy room. "The sewing?"

"Yes, sir. I was sent to fetch it." Bodice, petticoats and embroidered skirt too lavish for her station and evidently her own work. A good pair of hips; shy, sensual features. Quire grunted.

In his shirt Quire stretched a hand to the stool where all his torn and bloodstained clothing lay, black, damp, muddy. The shirt itself had blood on it. He peeled some patches off as his eye caught them; he brushed his thick hair back from his wide forehead and stared as she moved towards the stool. "My clothes are important to me. Those clothes. They are me. They are my victims. It's why they must be washed and mended well, my girl. Your name?"

"Alys Finch, sir."

"I'm Captain Quire, the murderer. Shakestaffs of the Watch seek me. I slew a Saracen last night. A young noble with a perfect body, unblemished. It's blemished now. Twenty times my sword slipped into him."

"A duel, sir, was it?" Her voice was trembling as she reached for the rags.

He drew out his blade from beneath the bedclothes; a finely made sword, a perfect weapon, the best of its kind. "Look! No, it was clever murder, disguised as a duel. We went out to the fields behind White Hall and there I killed him. You're a pretty little dell, ain't you. That's good hair, brown and curly. I like it. Big eyes, full lips. Are you broken yet, young Alys?"

She took his breeches up and put them in her basket while his calm, terrible eyes looked at her bodice. "No, sir. I hope to marry."

His smile was almost tender as he touched her shoulder with his unclean sword, as if he dubbed her a Lady. "Unlace, Alys, and let me see your buds. This sword"—he stroked her throat with it—"has killed so many. Some were fairly slain. But, at my suggestion, last night's Moor was tying back his robe's hems, bending, when I took him first, below the ribs and ripping up, swiftly, in and out. There were witnesses I could never have suspected on such a dark cold night." Quire's tone became momentarily bitter. "The trees were frozen. Our lanterns were shielded. But two soldiers, more's the pity, of the Watch, came by—and one of them recognised me." He directed her fingers to her laces and the blouse began to loosen, though she fumbled a great deal, out of fear. His voice was distant. "They attacked before my Saracen was properly dead—the slashes in my coat and doublet are theirs, and so's this cut on my thigh." He patted a place beneath his shirt. "The hole in the hose is where the Saracen struck at me with a knife from the ground, the traitor—I'd thought him dead—even as Tinkler took his boots from him, his lantern set aside. Fine, fancy boots, but Tinkler daren't wear 'em now. See his blood, there? And that, closer to the tip? A soldier I dispatched before his comrade ran away." He held the point under her eye so that she became very still; he touched it to her lips. "Taste."

The blouse entirely loosened, he pushed the linen back. She had small breasts, not full as yet. He prinked at the tip of one with the sword. "You're a good girl, Alys. You'll come back to me soon, eh? You'll bring my sewing?"

"Yes, sir." She breathed heavily but cautiously, having turned a strong colour.

"And you'll be an obedient girl, shall you, and let Captain Quire be first to your treasures?" His sword-point fell from cleft to cleft. "Shall you, Alys?"

Alys's eyes closed, rose lips parted. "Yes."

"Good. Kiss the sword, Alys, to seal our pact. Kiss the soldier's brittle blood." She kissed as the door thumped. He directed her hands to her laces and looked lazily towards the sound. "Aye?" As an afterthought he pricked her shoulder for a red pearl, which formed. "Good girl," he whispered. "You are Quire's now." He stretched up, grasped her, sucked the wound, then fell back upon the stained linen. "Who's there?"

"The innkeeper's wife. Marjorie, sir, with the food you ordered, and the suit."

Quire wondered for a moment, then shrugged, keeping a good grip on his Toledo sword. "Come in, then."

The woman floundered through, a coarse sea-cow, frowning at Alys Finch who, with a quick breath, bobbed and made for the door.

"Soon, Alys." Quire spoke affectionately.

"Yes, sir."

Taking the dark suit from under his fat landlady's arm, Quire began to dress, in evident dismay, while she placed the tray of mutton stew, bread and wine upon the chest at the foot of the bed. "These were the best you could find, Marjorie?"

"And I was lucky, Captain."

"Then here you are." He handed her an angel, a piece of gold.

"It's too much."

"I know."

"You're evil, through and through, Captain, but you're a generous devil."

"Many devils are." He drew the stool to the chest, grasped the big spoon and began on the mutton. "It's in their interest." He was wiry, muscular and dangerous as he ate.

Marjorie lingered. "There was a fight up at The Seahorse, then? A rough place."

"No rougher than this, and better booze. It was in White Hall fields, though. A duel, interrupted by the Watch, who now seek me."

"It's a foolish law that stops men duelling. Why shouldn't they kill one another, useless slopgollops? The Queen's too soft."

"Ah, well, better that than too hard." Quire, so used to being lured, adopted an instinctive neutrality. "And the law's to stop murder under the guise of the duel, and to stop the decline in gentlemen bridegrooms. They were slaying one another at far too fast a rate. The Queen feared for the continuation of the aristocracy. No nobles would mean a dissolute future, in Chaos!"

"Oh, Captain!"

"'Tis true as this stew is tasty." He did not flatter her.

"It's good, that, you monster." Mistress Marjorie folded her arms. "What were you doing with Crown's dell?"

A dark grin. Quire put bread to stew, knowing a would-be cohort in sin. "Quickening her interest, awakening her blood, warming her up for the time I'll need comfort, maybe."

"You'd terrified her. She has a lad. Starling's son."

"Of course I frightened her. 'Tis the best way to enrich her imagination and guarantee her curiosity, for she'll want to test herself against me—and all the time tremble for enslavement. Don't I frighten you, Marjorie?"

"I think I can control you." But she was doubtful, holding on to her gold in one fist. She picked at the corner of her mouth.

"I'm glad you think so." He was not ironic.

"But Alys Finch is no doxy for the likes of you." Weakly. "She's a good girl."

"She is indeed. The Watch?" He had his doublet belted. He wriggled uncomfortably; he tied faded cotton about his long throat. He sat to drag on his jackboots, lacing them above the knee.

"No closer. But they will be. Many know you stay here."

He downed a sparing glass—"Aye"—found his hat, smoothed the feathers. "Finch and Starling? She'd lay a strange egg if allowed to pair, what?"

"Leave her to him. He's a hot-tempered boy."

"Oh, Marjorie, my interest wanes already. Let them build their nest." He fingered the hat on his head and tilted it. He grinned at her, thin-lipped. "Maybe I'll play cuckoo, later, when it's Spring."

"You'll be hanged by then."

"Not Quire. Besides, Gloriana hangs no-one. And even if the Law were changed I'd survive. For I am Quire the Trickster, Quire the Thief—I've too many deeds undone, as yet—too great a fascinated audience for my art, awaiting my masterpiece." He sheathed the long sword, slipped knife in boot, poignard at his back. "And I'm Quire the Shadow. I'll need a cloak."

She shrugged, her smile doting, as upon a wicked, charming son. "Downstairs. Choose one on the run and it may be the owner won't notice."

"Thanks." He pinched her arm to show gratitude and she watched him go through the door, into the glooms, the light from the landing window catching his gleaming eye for a moment before he had flown down the stairs, taking her advice. She heard a scuffle, a bench go over, a yell, then prepared herself to soothe the fresh-robbed diner.

Quire plunged in stolen fur through the dirty snow of London's lanes, where men and women cursed and slipped and children slid and giggled in and out of the mist while breath and steam mingled at foodstalls set up to provide high-priced soups, pasties and nuts to the shivering, desperate crowd as it flowed. His pursuer was too cold to follow far, and Quire took Leering Street, piled at the sides with frozen snow mixed with urine and manure from the mews flanking it, turned into covered Rilke's Passage, into Craving Lane, beside the Gothic walls of the Platonic College, to a plaza in which a frozen fountain (Hercules and the Hydra) shone with pink and green lights, reflections of the lanterns on the walls of some fashionable ordinary. Another archway or two, through a crowd of snow-fighting boys, into a darker mist, half-fog, half-smoke, from a glueman's brazier, out of that and Quire was back at last in his alleys, slowing his pace as he reached the peeling door of an alehouse most men would have preferred to pass, Bale's. Quire sniffed the hop-sweet air before he tried the door and found it open. He left cold and damp behind him and entered stifling heat while unshaven features turned suspicious eyes over hunched shoulders, for there was not a client of Bale's who did not earn a living by thievery or begging; the place was shunned by the jack-thieves and other rogues of higher rank, and this suited Quire, for he found no enemies here, only admirers, or those who betrayed a thin, safe sort of envy, not worth his considering. At the far end of the long, narrow room, behind his counter, lounged the unwholesome Bale with his jugs of beer and cider and his pouch of farthings and ha'pence, and on the left of him, leaning where the bar met a black beam set into the lath-and-plaster wall, snagtoothed Tinkler, sword jutting under a dead watchman's leather coat.

Quire was surprised. He approached the counter, waving aside the mug Tinkler offered him. "Here already? Did you visit our friend as I told you?"

"Aye. I'm from there, just now."

Quire put out his hand. "You have the documents to save us further dodging?"

Tinkler scratched his exposed tooth and shook his head, his eyes confused.

"What? Are we without a patron, all at once?" Quire betrayed a hint of frustration, perhaps of consternation. He lifted his arm and placed it round Tinkler's bony shoulders.

"He refuses a blank this time. It's too serious, Captain." Tinkler whispered, even though Bale, tactful from experience, had moved to the far end of the counter and was counting copper.

"I thought he wanted his oriental extinguished."

"He calls our work clumsy. He disapproves very greatly."

Quire agreed. He sighed. "So it was. But it was an accident, the Watch. You paid the ruffler? King?"

"Half an angel, as agreed." Tinkler showed the split coin on his palm and grinned. "There it is."

"You killed him?"

"No. I took it back from him at dice before I left for our friend's. So much terror filled him, because of the Watch being on the hunt, that he could not think. I was good to him, Captain, as you suggested. He has all the Saracen's effects now and doubtless will have tried to pawn some ring, or that jewelled cutlass."

"He'll betray us, of course, when caught." Quire laid a palm upon his heavy jaw. "I expected no more. But without our papers we've no alibi."

"Bale here would speak for us. Or Uttley, at The Seahorse."

"No good. Who'd believe 'em? We need our patron's powerful signature. Won't he scrawl it at all, Tink?"

"He's angry. He says to give yourself to the Watch. Then to Sir Christopher Martin's inquisition. You must plead a plot against you, speak of King's rivalry—a common ruffler. Something of a stolen hat and cloak—yours. And so on."

"And I'm transported."

"No. If you're swift to do this our friend will send Sir Christopher evidence that you were elsewhere—on Queen's business—and you're free. But he says you must act immediately, for you're needed—an urgent task. You must be clean before you begin, or his plans are tangled. See?"

"Aye, but he could be tangling me."

"Why be so complicated?"

"Because he knows I'm hard to murder. He could use this to ensure my exile. But it doesn't smell of that sort of scheme. Every spider spins his own web and the work can always be recognised, after a while."

"Then you'll present yourself to Sir Christopher's men?"

"No choice, Tinkler. Still, I'm resentful of the time it'll take, particularly if there's urgent business to follow. When shall I sleep?"

Tinkler, putting a leather cup to his twisted lip, looked surprised, as if he had never imagined his master anything but forever awake.

The Fourth Chapter

In Which
Doctor John Dee the Magus Considers
the Nature of the Cosmos

COLD LIGHT, ENTERING from high windows in the domed roof, made the Audience Room brilliant. Each window contained a rainbow of coloured glass: abstract patterns as complicated and geometrical as snowflakes. There were no areas of shadow anywhere in the great circular chamber, save behind the throne, where curtains hid the door by which, on ceremonial occasions, Gloriana entered. The door led also to her Withdrawing Room. Panelled and bearing chiefly pastoral scenes in light colours (greens, blues and browns), the walls were white and silver, curving up to join the roof. Six doors gave the Throne Room a deceptively hexagonal appearance, and across these, too, were curtains, some in plain colours, some of tapestry. Footmen stood at the main doors, which were tall and double and painted like the panels, and through them now came venerable Dee, white-bearded, in scholar's cap and gown, charts under arm, spectacles like a badge of office on nose, bowed at the shoulders as if by knowledge, yet almost the height of the Queen herself, entering the Audience Room in the wake of his sovereign to see that she held private court, for there was no-one present but Una, Countess of Scaith, smiling in blue, and Lord Montfallcon, massive and stony, who seemed unusually agitated and unwilling to be present.

Queen Gloriana was settling herself in her padded throne of gold and marble, her outline clarified by the pure light from above, her face framed by her high collar of wired gauze, her golden velvet kirtle winking with all the tiny jewels set into it. "You've brought your diagrams, Doctor Dee?"

He waved them. Lord Montfallcon rubbed rapidly at his nose and looked from Queen to magus. In common with most of his contemporaries he regarded Dee as a charlatan—his appointment as Councillor of Philosophy a woman's folly. Montfallcon was aggressively sceptical of Dee, and Dee in turn was almost entirely amused by the Chancellor's scepticism.

"You promised to describe your cosmological theories in detail," the Queen reminded Dee, "and the Countess of Scaith would hear them. Lord Montfallcon is invited in an effort of ours to broaden his mind."

The Lord Chancellor grunted and sighed. "I would remind Your Majesty that I have urgent duties. Poland . . ."

"Of course. We'll detain you a few moments." She looked towards the great filigree silver clock on the distant wall facing the throne, and seemed to sway in time with the pendulum, as if mesmerised. With neat fingers, she pulled a petticoat in place, gestured for Una to seat herself in the chair at the side of the dais, enquired with an eyebrow of Lord Montfallcon if he'd take the chair on the other side, shrugged when he shook his head and smiled upon her magus.

"Do you require assistance with the charts?"

Dee wiped moisture from his brow. The room was heated from pipes below the flagstones, in the Roman manner. "A boy?"

"Lord Ingleborough's page is here, awaiting his master's return." She pointed towards a scarlet curtain half-hiding a polished door. "There."

The Countess of Scaith rose. "I'll fetch him." She crossed to the curtain, pulled open the door. "Ah, it's Patch."

A sweet voice from the page. "Good morning, your ladyship."

"Join us please, Patch." Una spoke warmly. There were few at Court who were not charmed by Lord Ingleborough's boy.

In came Patch, elegant and tiny, in a suit of dark green, with ruff and cape, all green; green cap in hand. His curls were cut short and were almost white. He bowed prettily and looked at Doctor Dee with large brown eyes that were courteous and intelligent.

"Master Patch, please aid the doctor."

"Sir?" Patch presented himself to Dee and seemed unembarrassed when the magus reached out exceptionally long fingers to pat his head.

"Good boy, Patch."

Doctor Dee looked about him, sighted a sideboard, and went to place the majority of his charts upon it; he selected one and returned to the foot of the dais. "Take an end, lad. There." Cheerfully Patch obeyed. "Move away a little. Excellent." They unrolled the chart and stood with it between them, displaying it to the Queen, who, in concert with the Countess, bent forward, while Lord Montfallcon looked steadily and somewhat longingly at the door to the Privy Chamber.

The Queen's scent reached Doctor Dee's nostrils and he felt his old knees tremble. For twelve years he had loved her, lusted after her. There had been hardly a moment, even during his most profound contemplations, when he had not desired her; but he lacked the means to tell her. For so long had he been regarded as a sage, a mentor, a metaphysician, that he had been trapped entirely in his rôle, did not dare leave it for fear of disappointing her. He loved her too much to risk such disappointment. *O, Madam*, he thought, *if only I could disguise myself one night, as a devil, as a rogue, to creep into your bedchamber and bring you what you yearn for. What we both yearn for, by the gods . . .* He realised that she was asking a question. "Madam?"

"These spheres?" she said. "All these circles intersecting. There are other worlds, eh?"

He peered upon his own charts. "Yes, madam (*why must she rustle so seductively?*), the broad diagram—not specific, but to show the theory. The central sphere is ours, though no more central than our own in the universe we know—these others are (*those brows!*) representative of worlds which exist in parallel to our own (*ah, and in one Dee must be the master, you the slave*) and mirror our own, perhaps exactly, perhaps only in approximate detail, some with continents where our seas are, or with dominant beings descended, perhaps, from apes—anything imaginable . . ."

"How are these worlds reached, Doctor Dee?" Lord Montfallcon challenged. "Where have you seen them?"

"I have not seen them, my lord."

"You know travellers who have? Mariners?"

"Not mariners, but perhaps—yes, travellers . . ."

"They came by ship?"

"Most did not, my lord."

"By land?" Lord Montfallcon threw back his shoulders, prepared for further conflict.

Queen Gloriana laughed. "Hush, Lord Montfallcon." She was delighting in this unusual pettiness on the part of her greatest minister. "You are a bad scholar, sir!"

"I wish to know, madam"—heavily, turning to her—"for it is my business to protect your Realm. Therefore I must be wary of all possibilities of attack."

John Dee smiled. "I think there's little chance these worlds threaten our security, my lord."

"In no way at all, Doctor Dee?" Lord Montfallcon glanced significantly at the magus.

"I can think of none." Innocently.

"You waste your own time and ours, my lord." Gloriana became gently impatient. "These are but the doctor's theories . . ."

"Based on certain evidence, however, Your Majesty," muttered Dee.

"Of course . . ." She picked up her sceptre.

"How do these travellers reach our shores?" Lord Montfallcon became more stubborn as the smiles around him broadened.

"The spheres, I believe, occasionally intersect. When that occurs, they come willy-nilly, through no intention of their own. At least, most of them do. Others, by the practice of certain arts unknown to us, come deliberately, perhaps. But, sir, we move too far from what I present as a pure idea, nought else. Plato himself suggests . . ."

Lord Montfallcon let a breath loose from between his teeth. He put a hand to his belt. "I am not obtuse, I think. I have studied the classics. I have a reputation, moreover, for subtlety, yet I still do not understand!"

"You do not will it so, that's all. (*Oh, this dolt knows what I am feeling! He is aware that the only knowledge I truly desire is the knowledge of her high-strung flesh . . .*) I suggest, Your Majesty, that we pursue this discussion at another time."

"No, no, no. On with it, Doctor Dee." Gloriana tapped with the royal baton.

"Yes, Your Majesty. (*On with it, aye. On to your warm bones with mine . . .*) I have another plan, more detailed, of a section of our cosmos." He moved towards Patch, rolling the chart as he approached, plucked the end from the boy's soft hand, strode to the sideboard and, selecting another chart, returned. Again the boy and the man moved, as if in a dance, to display the next chart. "Here are familiar constellations, marked in red. Behind these are the same constellations, but at a different angle, in blue—then the constellations again, in black—and again, and again, in these yellows and greens. The constellation in red is the one we observed with the naked eye. The constellations in other colours are those which might exist, but which are separated from our ordinary perception by some means—layers of ether, perhaps, hiding one from the next. (*Oh, those fingers! Her hands! Would that they tickled my manhood now . . .*) I have not, Lord Montfallcon, observed such constellations through telescopes. They are theoretical constellations. There have been reports, of course. I am even now, alchemically, devising a means of crossing from one world to another, but so far I have had poor success."

"You have no need to defend yourself from Lord Montfallcon's ignorance, Doctor Dee." Queen Gloriana reached out towards her Chancellor, placating him with a gesture as she placated her Philosopher with a word. "You seem distracted, Doctor Dee."

He looked up, controlling the fires which sprang behind his eyes. He ignored the enquiry. "Certain persons have been brought to me in the course of the years, gracious Majesty, who have seemed mad. These men and women have all claimed to originate upon other worlds. I have found them logical and consistent—sane, save for their single, central delusion, that this world is not their own. I have had them draw their spheres for me. They are all, in basic, the same as our own. The names for nations and continents are sometimes different. The societies described are often alien and barbaric." He rolled the second chart, moved to the sideboard, came back with a third. "This is one, for instance. Similar to ours, yet not entirely the same." Patch took the left, Dee the right, to display a detailed map of the globe. "See. The names are not at all like ours, though a few correspondences exist. I had this from a poor lunatic who claimed to have been a king over all the German states, some Emperor Charlemagne, though with considerable magical powers . . ."

"With designs on Albion?" The grey voice.

Pedantic Lord Montfallcon was ignored. Una, Countess of Scaith, looked with great interest at the map. It was almost as if it was familiar to her. "It is very good."

"Fanciful, you mean, my lady?" asked Dee.

"If you like."

"I believe it to be a true representation. This is the only full one I have made. My informant, as it happened, was obsessed with maps. I have yet, gracious Majesty, to map the geography of any other spheres." He let Patch roll up this last map and take it to place it with the others. "However, from reports brought to me I can produce a scheme—a broad plan of the positions of these spheres and how they might relate to our own. We are at the centre (again for argument's purpose) of a pool. Our activities produce ripples and eddies throughout this pool. We are for the most part unaware of these movements, save when, by fluke, a backwash, a momentary current, brings us evidence. This evidence was feared by our ancestors. Devils, angels, poltergeists, pixies, elves, gods and their works were held to be the cause of these disruptions to our ordered world. Why, there are those who still call that noble musician Lord Caudolon a demon, because he came so suddenly to our sphere, speaking of strange lands and works and wondering of everything he found (*Lady, I would your lips would touch this pounding prick*), yet soon he calmed and judged himself recovered from our enchantments—or a dream. As I said, some spheres are not dissimilar. Their histories, even, have resemblances—there are other Glorianas, other Dees, other Lords Chancellors, no doubt—shadows, sometimes faint, sometimes distorted, of our own selves."

Gloriana eyed the distance. "Doctor Dee, think you we shall one day travel between these spheres?"

"I work, intermittently, upon that very problem, madam (*your lips and then your legs shall part for me*), and hope one day to effect the means of moving freely from sphere to sphere, as a pike crosses beneath the surface of his pond."

"Sorcery!" grunted Lord Montfallcon. "Is this not always where your mathematick leads? Now you see, great Majesty, why I'd abolish such studies—though I blame not the misguided scholar." A sidelong glance of malice. Doctor Dee shrugged it back.

"It is our wish," murmured the Queen, "that all arts shall be studied at our Court."

"Then let the Queen look to the security of her Realm, lest she find it torn asunder by warring demons admitted to our sphere by Doctor Dee's experiments." Lord Montfallcon spoke without a great deal of conviction.

"My sovereign," a wincing bow from Dee, "the Science of Cabalism . . ."

Her foot moved. "You think this diversion likely, Doctor Dee?"

He bowed again, sucked in a breath or two. (*Blood of Zeus! These pantaloons will make a eunuch of me yet!*) "I fear not, my sovereign. Devils are the name we give to beings whose origins are obscure to us. Those few travellers who have passed between the spheres are men and women like ourselves. Sometimes they think they are reincarnated, in past or future; sometimes they find our sphere Heaven, sometimes Hell. Doubtless, if we visited them unwillingly, we should think of their worlds in a similar way (*I swear it—your breasts shall bloom to the heat of my tongue*)."

"Look to your soul, madam!" The Chancellor's words were actually addressed to his rival. A warning. "The Pit lies, inevitably, at the end of Doctor Dee's dark road."

Dee was evidently astonished by this expression of a previous century's superstition—words which might have come from Montfallcon's famous witch-seeking grandfather. He decided diplomacy: "The Universe, madam, is not our concern, perhaps. (*To have her arse in love and pain!*) This planet and its facets, its shadows, is complex enough, without our needing to discourse on the question of rival spheres. (*Oh, she is the universe, mother of galaxies—I would grasp her tits until she gave voice to the Last Trump!*) If my lord the Chancellor cautions discretion . . ."

"It is my duty to protect the whole Realm—including you, Doctor Dee—as best I can." Frowning, Montfallcon drew a fold or two of heavy cloth about him.

"I respect your sincerity, my lord." Dee's tone showed puzzlement. "However, you seem unusually disturbed by what is, after all, no more than a discussion of possibilities."

Montfallcon snorted. "My business is with possibilities. I have many to consider at this moment."

"You are agitated, my lord, because we keep you from your Duty." Gloriana became placatory, impressed by Montfallcon's manner, at last. "You may go to it."

"I am grateful, madam." A bow, a swift, disapproving glance at Dee, and Montfallcon fled for his mysterious rooms.

"I had no intention . . ." began Dee, biting his lip a little, his white beard flat against his chest.

"Lord Montfallcon is distracted. Matters of State, as you know. I am to blame. It was capricious of me. You'll need finance for further experiments, I take it, Doctor Dee?"

"Madam, I did not come . . ."

"Neither did I. But you'll need gold. It will have to be extracted from the Privy Purse, I think, for the Council will never agree—why should it?—to patronise your Science. I shall speak to Sir Amadis and you shall tell him of your needs."

"I thank thee, madam. (*Needs, needs! Ah, if she knew!*) If I could find two people, for instance, from the madhouses, who independently raved the same logic, then I could test them. The Thane of Hermiston has offered his help."

"But all believe him a clownish boaster!" The Countess of Scaith stroked the velvet of her chair's arm. "These claims of adventurings in fairy realms! Isn't he, at best, a mediocre poet and a poor liar?"

"I think not, your ladyship. There are his prisoners. His trophies."

"We have had them at Court. Mindless savages. Lunatics. Nothing more." She smiled. "They make bad sport. He is vulgar, the Thane, in guessing his victims will amuse the Queen."

Doctor Dee thought he detected more than mere scepticism in the Countess of Scaith's voice. It was almost as if she tested him.

"There was the magus who came and went," said Dee carefully, his voice soft, "called Cagliostro. He appeared suddenly, vanished as quickly. He was one who controlled his own journeys through the spheres. I conversed with him. I learned from him. There was the woman, Montez . . ."

"She was not at all coherent, Doctor Dee," said Queen Gloriana. "We interviewed her. The poor creature was completely deranged. And those clothes! The work of some addle-pated designer of masques who had escaped the same hospital!"

"I did not disbelieve her, Your Majesty, though I would agree she seemed very ordinarily crazed. Her claims and notions were familiar delusions."

"Where is she now?" asked the Countess of Scaith.

"She joined a travelling mummers' show, I think, but died near Lincoln."

Una leaned her face in her palm.

"And this German Emperor of yours?" Queen Gloriana signed for Patch to seat himself on the steps of the dais. "Is he still with us?"

"Adolphus Hiddler, Your Majesty? A suicide. I liked him the best. A splendid barbarian, much interested in alchemy, as well as geography. Apparently his alchemical experiments brought him here. A scholar, in his own way, he claimed to have conquered the world."

Queen Gloriana put a finger to smiling lips. "Hush, Doctor Dee, lest Lord Montfallcon hear. You'll keep us informed of your experiments?"

"I shall, madam (*Ah, the pressure! There is only one experiment I must perform before I die! One instrument to play. I'll make you sing like Orpheus's harp. . . .*), and I thank you for your interest."

"We are always interested in investigations which can increase our knowledge of the natural world, but you must be careful, Doctor Dee. There could be truth in Lord Montfallcon's warnings.

A demon could be summoned from one of these other worlds whom we could not control."

"Do not venture too far into fairyland without letting us know where you go, sir," added the Countess of Scaith with a friendly smile, "and do not trust yourself too readily to the Thane of Hermiston's ramshackle contraptions."

"Or the mechanical dragons of his friend Master Tolcharde!" Gloriana was laughing. "Poor Tolcharde! He works so hard on his toys. I have had to devote several rooms to their storage. And he makes more and more! You saw the telescope, did you not, Doctor Dee, that Tolcharde made for studying the inhabitants of the Moon? Their behaviour was extraordinary and, I'll admit, entertaining for a while, but such things pall all too quickly. Since then, I've heard he plans to make a ship which will carry him there."

"To be fair to Master Tolcharde," said Dee, "he has been of help to me in certain matters. He has considerable skill as a craftsman and can make almost anything I need."

"He lives only to make more and more fantastical devices." Una laughed in concert. "He cares not if they are used. The Queen accepts the gifts, admires them, sends them off to be incarcerated. He is content to make her others. There must be a score of mechanical birds and beasts, at least—each increasingly elaborate!"

Doctor Dee had begun to pick up his charts. His face was red and sweat darkened his beard.

"I did not intend to make too much fun of Master Tolcharde," said Una. "In reality, I respect his gifts. . . ."

"Are you well, Doctor Dee?" The Queen was solicitous.

"Well? Aye, madam. (*O, gods, would that I had the courage to pull you from that throne and bear you down upon this floor and plunge flesh into flesh. . . .*)"

"You have a fever?"

"No, madam. Perhaps the heat. My own rooms are cooler. (*They must be, or I should burst into flame!*)"

"You'll be with us, later, at dinner?"

"With your permission, madam (*though I'd rather chew at your sweet shoulder*)." He bowed, and gasped. "Ah!"

"Doctor Dee?"

"Until dinner, madam!" His voice was high as, in blustering cloak, he fled the Throne Room, out into the passage which branched to the left, head down, as if he pressed urgently through a powerful wind, so that when Lady Lyst, the beautiful young drunkard, most brilliant of scholars, turned a corner and fell, with a hiccup, against him, he did not recognise her and made to push her from his path.

"Good morrow, Doctor Dee!"

"Aside, fair maid, aside!"

But she clung to his jerkin and at last he saw her face. "Advice, good sage, I pray."

"Advice?"

"On a matter of philosophy." Glazed, cheerful eyes looked up into his. A warm hand encircled his waist as she steadied herself.

"Aha!" He could think of no lovelier substitute. He became avuncular. He, in turn, squeezed her shoulders. "To my apartments! Come quickly, Lady Lyst, and I swear I'll fill thee *full* of my philosophy."

Amiably, he helped her mount the steps to take them to the East Wing and his tower, where, a traditionalist in all things, he maintained his studios, his laboratories.

The Fifth Chapter

In Which Captain Quire Is Brought Secretly to the Palace, and Lord Montfallcon, to Be Apprised of a Desperate Mission

Lord Bramandil Rhoone, huge and jovial, Captain of the Gentlemen Pensioners, the Queen's Guard, received charge of Quire (hooded like a querulous hawk) from Sir Christopher's men and immediately began to brush and primp at the shrinking spy, whose clothes (borrowed) bore more than a fair share of the contents of Marshalsea Jail; dung, straw and mould gave Quire something of the odour of a long-deserted farmyard.

"This won't do, villain, if ye're to have audience with the great Lord Montfallcon. Though why the identity of such as you should be protected I don't know." The round, red face beamed above the scarlet ruff, the ruddy hands straightened Quire's collar while Quire promised himself that if ever Lord Rhoone should fall foul of Lord Montfallcon, or if he should ever stray into the thieves' twittens in the city, he would take precisely forty-eight hours to kill him, giving him mercy on the sixtieth second of the forty-eighth, while he smiled beneath his hood and came close to curtseying, bobbing in the big man's grasp. "Thank you, my lord. Much obliged to you, my lord." And suffered Rhoone to slide his good sword from its sheath.

"This must be kept. No swords at Court, save for the Queen's Gentlemen and her Champion." He tapped his own. "Come." Striding rapidly along the corridor, a hand on Quire's arm, so that the half-blinded captain was forced to run, aching as he was already from the buffets of his jailers and from the bench and stones of the prison in which he had spent an entire night.

"A little slower, my lord. I have not been well."

"Lord Montfallcon is anxious to see you. Perhaps he'd question you further concerning the Saracen. You're lucky Lord Montfallcon spoke for you, saying you were on his business in Notting village that night and that the man mistaken for you was a scoundrel similarly dressed." Casting his eye over patched motley, Lord Rhoone relished the telling of what he strongly suspected was a compendium of lies. "Still, I've no fondness for Saracens. Or murderers," he added piously, "whatever their reasons. The Queen has made her views plain."

"I agree entirely, my lord." Quire panted and clutched at his side. "A stitch, I fear."

Lord Rhoone's thick lips flapped like the lips of an overheated stallion. "We'll soon be there, man." They reached a large hall, the Third Presence Chamber, wide enough to be a good-sized market square, in which courtiers conversed in clusters, taking a passing interest in the hurrying pair. Lord Rhoone greeted some, here and there. "Sir Amadis. Good morrow, Master Wheldrake. Lady Lyst."

Captain Quire, on the other hand, was careful not to recognise his few acquaintances, though with his hooded head he drew more attention than Lord Rhoone. They took the central passage, turning aside before they reached the doors of the Throne Room, stepping before a door whose handle only could be seen, for the rest was hidden by a tapestry. Lord Rhoone rapped. They were admitted.

Lord Montfallcon stood beside his fire, his back to them, his warrior's shoulders hunched. "Rhoone?"

"My Lord Chancellor. He's here."

"I thank you."

Lord Rhoone flicked at Quire's shoulders once more, then, smiling to himself, he departed, bearing the Toledo sword away. Quire looked after it once, furiously, then composed himself. He did not want to waste time, however, on feigning humility. He scanned the room. It held nothing unfamiliar. He scratched his ear. He removed his sombrero from beneath his borrowed cloak. He tugged his hood free to disclose his dark little self.

"Captain Quire, sir. I did your bidding and here I am."

Lord Montfallcon nodded, pulling a coat of silk and beaver about his chest as he began to turn. "You are lucky, Quire, aren't you?"

"As ever, my lord."

"Not even on the night of New Year's Eve. You were clumsy, overreaching, and you were seen."

"I was not clumsy, my lord." Quire threatened to flare.

Lord Montfallcon sighed and revealed a frozen, angry eye. "Tinkler brought me your note. The intelligence concerning Arabia was useful. But Lord Ibram was well-connected. Indeed, we had assured his uncle he would be safe in London. If it were not for a reputation for wildness in him, which went a way to explaining what happened, we should be mightily embarrassed, Quire. Perhaps I should have let you suffer the full consequences. An unlucky Quire is no use to me."

Quire warmed his hands. He did not posture, but spoke with reasonable pride. "Slay me? Aye, in the cause of Knowledge, perhaps—for an I die, then the foot I keep on Pandora's lid shall lift and out shall pour all those secrets best left bottled. Or perhaps you'd disagree, sir, with such cautious philosophy, and play Doctor Fauste with the Queen's darker mysteries?"

Montfallcon listened, not from interest in the subject, but because he believed he gained insight to Quire's soul.

Quire continued. "However, sir, I know this cannot be your thinking. You've already seen the point of preserving Captain Quire's life. At all costs, sir, eh? At any cost, what? For I am guardian Cerberus turned to keep the devils and the damned from 'scaping Hades. I am the protector of your security, Lord Montfallcon. You do not honour me sufficiently."

Thinking Quire had gone too far, and thus betrayed himself, Lord Montfallcon became more relaxed. "Ah, it's a misunderstood dog, is it?"

"A badly treated dog, my lord. Sir Christopher's constables handled me ill and I was given the worst cell in the Marshalsea. I expected better, for agreeing to your schemes. Also, my identity was not completely concealed. . . ."

"My reward to you, Quire, is your freedom. I saved it."

"I risked it, sir—and did not flee. I'm the best man you have in London—in all Albion—in the Empire. For I am an artist, as you know. And I am not vulnerable."

"That makes you a doubtful servant in some ways, Captain Quire. You are too intelligent for this work. You spring from excellent yeoman stock, you were educated at John's in Cambridge, where you might have become a much admired theologian, but you refused all respectable opportunities."

"Creative inclinations of a stronger sort sent me to exploring my senses, my lord, and the geography of the world. I have no talent, save for what's called evil, and in your service, sir, I am enabled to pursue my studies further. I've considered many callings, but all seem worthless. I like not the examples of the various professions I have encountered and I believe my own occupation, at your service, my lord, and therefore the Queen's, to be as good as, if not better than, any. At least, you'll agree, I'm able to judge the exact degree of evil I perform—if evil it be. These others, these scholars, lawyers, courtiers, merchants, soldiers, statesmen, who are pillars of our Realm, they throw stones over their shoulders, anxious in case they should see what or whom they strike. But I look in the eyes of those I strike, my lord. I tell them what I am doing, as I tell myself."

Lord Montfallcon had become calmer. He was not offended by Quire's speech, as Quire had known he would not be. Quire was given to such speeches, defining his work as a poet might define his calling. If Quire had sought to apologise, had been placatory, Montfallcon would have become suspicious of him. He employed Quire for his impertinent creativity, his courage as well as his cunning. The old Chancellor seated himself behind his desk. Quire remained by the fire. "Well, you have inconvenienced me badly, Quire. At a time when I needed no more complications. Still, it's done."

"Aye, my lord. King's to emigrate for a murder he did, after all, help at, even if he didn't initiate the deed."

"Few believe that. Sir Christopher does not. I doubt if the Saracens will for long, when they receive their own reports of the affair. You'd best be wary, Quire. They can be a vengeful race."

"I'm always wary, my lord. What's my new commission?"

"You must go to the coast. You're to play wrecker to a galleon due on tomorrow's early tide. If possible I want no-one killed, but she must come onto the sands at the mouth of the river at Rye. Already I've sent a skiff to intercept the pilot and place one of our own people on board. He'll redirect the ship to Rye—claiming the frozen Thames as excuse."

"A fair one. No ship could move into or out of London at present, without threat to her timbers. But what's my function? This pilot can perform the task unaided."

"Not easily. You'll give the plan a twist and make sure it all goes smoothly. Then the sequel's entirely yours. I leave its details to your imagination."

"I'm glad you continue to trust me, my lord."

"In such matters, Quire, you're always the most inventive. The King of Poland's ship, the *Mikolaj Kopernik*, must run aground, the king must be captured as if by common wreckers, as a noble held to ransom. Here's a rough likeness I had drawn for you. If he speaks our tongue, he must be led to believe that he's been mistaken for nothing more than a foreign dignitary. Use your knowledge of the High Tongue only if you must. He must then be held for a time—I'll tell you when and by what method he'll be released."

Quire was amused. "A king? Well, my lord, you set me after splendid quarry. But I'll need a full pack for this hunt."

"Pick 'em."

"Tinkler. Hogge. O'Bryan . . ."

"You'll employ that braggart, still?"

"He'll do well at this. Moreover he's spent two years in Polish employ, as a soldier, and we might need him for his language. I'd consider Webster. . . ."

"No! The rogue's been associated with certain young men at Court. He could be recognised later."

"Kinsayder?"

"None of that gang of ink-stained would-be gentlemen will do. Some fools already think they represent the Queen. Fools who do not know the Court but merely its detritus." Montfallcon frowned. "Besides, they're gossips. You'd be carrying a hen-house with you."

"Good fighting cocks, my lord, and braver than your common ruffler."

"Aye, and more ambitious. And more inventive. I employed their kind under old King Hern, but you're the only half-gentleman I'd care to use now, for you are not, like them, addicted to grog, airy language and promiscuous comradeship—for which they must always pay with the only currency they have in quantity: small-talk, scandal, embellished anecdote."

Quire's thin lips moved. "Your point's made, my lord. I'll draw my list later, following your advice."

"Send me word when all's accomplished."

"I will, my lord."

"Protect this secret from your hirelings, if you can."

"I will. But it's an unsubtle scheme."

"The best there's time for. We must retain Poland's friendship. If we used diplomatic means, they'd guess at once. This plan's so desperate none will suspect devious Montfallcon's hand."

"But the consequences . . . ?"

"There'll be none that are unwelcome, if you play your part correctly and with your usual skill."

Quire sniffed. "My sword—that stickler Rhoone took it. I'll leave through the Spiders' Door." He tugged the hood back on.

Montfallcon rang a brass bell for a lackey. "Clampe: Ask Lord Rhoone to give you this man's blade." He came to stand by the fire.

"The plot belongs to King Hern's time," continued Quire. "Let us hope none recollects how you served him. I remember. . . ."

"You were a boy when Hern took his life."

"I feel no nostalgia. Did I say so?"

Montfallcon passed fingers over his lids. "You and I, for all that forty years separate us, are both of another age. It's ironic we should work together to resist a return to that darker past."

Quire humoured him. "Or that I, most villainous of villains, with my love of such an antique art, should benefit for living in a world where justice is so much stronger. Where Virtue rules."

Montfallcon raised his right arm and stretched it, saying acidly: "I am needed while such as you remain on Earth."

Quire considered this, then shook his head. "On the contrary. It could be argued that I am needed while noble souls of your sort continue to exert themselves. After all, Plato tells us how vulnerable is the age of the perfect monarch. . . ."

Montfallcon was baffled. Angrily, he changed the subject. "Some roads are impassable with the snow. You've good horses, I hope."

"They'll have to be rented."

"Gold?"

"Aye."

The lackey returned with the sword as Montfallcon took out his key. Quire stepped forward to draw the blade from the man's hand. "Thanks." He sheathed.

Montfallcon waited until the servant's back was to them before he unlocked the box. When the servant had gone he opened it. He counted coins. "Five nobles?"

"Aye—that'll pay for horses and men."

Montfallcon put the gold into Quire's careless palm. "You'll leave before dark, this afternoon?"

"As soon as all are hired and I've dined and cleaned myself."

The two men entered a smaller room and then another still smaller. A third door, hidden in a panel behind a chair, led into the walls: a way from the palace which Quire, Tinkler and their patron believed only they knew. Quire gently pulled back fresh webs, as if he handled ancient lace, and let himself through. A muffled farewell to Montfallcon before the panel closed on him and he dragged off the hood and dropped it, reversed his cloak so that, with his sombrero on his head again, he was all in black. The place he entered was full of grey light, the source obscure, in which thousands of spiders crawled, upon floors, walls and pearly silk. He stood upright and moved carefully, to crush as few of the spiders as possible. The tunnel was of glass and had perhaps once been an orangery, for there were remains of tubs and pots, rotted branches. Now dust covered the glass and a roof had been erected some distance above that. It was through windows at the far end of what appeared to be a gigantic shed that the light came. The tunnel curved gradually, horseshoe fashion, and the air grew colder, the spiders fewer, until Quire came at length to a repaired door which he used, crossed a hard, littered floor until he reached a wall which must once have been an outer wall, to a garden. Through a gap in this he went, into semi-darkness; down steps, over a patch of naked earth. Now he shivered and dragged his cloak to his body, approaching a high, vast wall. A shoulder against one part and it swung so that he half-tumbled into daylight, into deep snow. He pushed back the brick door. He stood beneath a tall cliff of weather-yellowed brick and before him was a long, narrow ornamental garden, abandoned, overgrown, forgotten, whose outlines were made more precise by the snow and the ice. Black branches spread against the sky, broken statues stared from beneath a clothing of snow—the demigods of some sunnier realm, in ermine, frozen. Quire's breath seemed grey against all this. Stepping high, he plunged booted feet along a familiar, but unseen, path, between the squares, circles and oblongs of barren flower beds and clogged fountains, turning left towards another wall overhung with evergreens, jumped a small, iron gate, entered a grotto and trod a few cobbles that were free of snow, coming at length to a larger gate which he opened with his picklock, to stand upon a hillside where there was no longer a road. He was hungry. He began to run down the hill towards a thick grove of poplars lining a pathway, black with cart-ruts, glimpsed beyond. Wind blew the light top-snow so that it resembled the rippling waters of a wide, shallow river. Quire fell, rolled, cursed, then chuckled, stumbling to his feet, reaching the trees and their shelter, pausing to catch deep breaths which cut his lungs, leaning his stiff back against a bole while he looked down at the smoke of the city, not too distant now. A fence was his final obstacle and he clambered carefully over, not anxious to be seen, dropping into the spoiled track and slithering on the ice of a puddle before he was on the run again.

Through the ruts and the snow flew Quire, the crow's feathers in his hat flapping in the wind, his cloak crackling like black fire, dropping faster and faster along the twists of the track until suddenly he had come to London's walls and the unguarded archway which took him into salubrious northern streets and a respectable inn where he maintained the persona and name of a visiting gentleman scholar whose studies brought him frequently to the nearby Library of Classical Antiquity. The original scholar Quire had slain, during an argument over the likely identity of the poet Justus Lipsius, and taken his character complete. Here Quire bathed, dined on a better meal than any he would be likely to find in his usual ordinaries, and hired a good black stallion for himself. The cold had increased, driving many inside; the streets were almost deserted as Quire galloped east, for the river and the Seahorse Tavern, to tell Tinkler which men to rouse and where to go for the best steeds. Tinkler, infected by Quire's briskness, hurried in his creaking new coat to the door and was gone, and Quire, finishing off a small measure of hot rum, was about to follow when Master Uttley's unhealthy features confronted him. In all his spots and pocks, his little eyes were almost lost as he laid a propitiatory hand on the captain's arm. "You've an enemy, sir, outside. Where your horse is."

Quire looked to the clock overhead (Uttley's pride) and saw that he had two hours before he was due to meet his men on the Rye road. "Some relative of the Saracen?"

"A lad you've done harm to, he says."

"Name?"

"He gave none. If you wish, Captain, I'll have the ostler lead your horse round to the back and you can join him there."

Quire shook his head. "Let's have a resolution, if it's possible. I remember no lad, however." With curiosity he approached the door and stepped outside, to lean against the jamb and study the slender boy who stood, with hot, uncertain eyes, near the horse and its wool-swathed ostler who held the bridle. The boy wore a hooded jerkin, rabbitskin leggings and patched shoes, and there was a quarterstaff in his mittened fists. Black, shining hair escaped the hood. He had dark, gypsy features, but it was his mouth which gave Quire a clue to his true character—it was wide, with a prominent, sulking lower lip. Quire grinned at him. "Me?" he said.

"You're the Captain—Quire?" The boy flushed, confused between his imagination's proposals concerning this encounter and the reality of it.

"I am, my beauty. What harm d'you claim I've done you?"

"I am Phil Starling."

"Aha. The chandler's child. Your father's a retired sailorman. A good fellow. Is it money you claim? I assure you I'm not one to be in debt, particularly to an honest seadog. Yet, if it will help to see him, I'll return with you, gladly. . . ."

"You know more of me than I know of you, Captain Quire. I come on behalf of a young lady who has but lately passed her fourteenth birthday and upon whom you have laid lewd hands, threatening her virginity."

Quire allowed himself a mild lift of an eyebrow. "Eh?"

"Alys Finch, servant to Mistress Crown the seamstress. An orphan. An angel. A sweet-natured paragon of goodness whom I shall marry and whom I now protect." Starling gestured somewhat aimlessly with his stick.

Quire feigned controlled rage. "And how have I offended this virgin? Lewd hands? Upon the girl who collects my sewing, whom I'd not recognise a third or fourth time she came? Who told you this?"

"She told me herself. She was distressed." The boy faltered. "She does not lie."

"Young girls, however, fancy many things to be true—often most positively when their imaginings are the strangest." Quire put fingers to jaw. "Visions, and such, you know. Visitations. They know so little of the world, they interpret the innocent remark as a vicious one, while the vicious suggestion is taken for virtue." Quire became friendly. "What has she told you, lad?"

"Just that. She was distressed. Lewd hands."

Quire held his gloved palms before him as if to inspect them. "I doubt they touched her. She took my clothes for mending. Was there another guest, in the same lodgings, whose clothes she collected?"

"It was you. You are known to be a very Prince of Vice."

"Am I?" Quire laughed easily. "Am I, indeed? By whom?"

"It is the talk of all at the King's Beard."

"And you're one to believe 'em—these scandalmongers? Because I do not mix with the crowd, I am envied, I am a mystery, I become an object of scandal. Have you heard of those who accuse honest men of vice they dare not or cannot perform themselves?"

"What?"

"Even you, lad, must indulge fancies of that sort. You hear that a man is wicked—and you guess what you would do in his shoes. Eh?"

A carriage, all creaking metal and leather, bounced past, drawn by two pairs of grey horses, its windows covered, a mingled scent of roasted duck and heavy musk drifting from it, as if a rich whore dined on the jog. The black stallion shifted his rump and the boy was gently pushed closer to Quire.

"That's a good strong staff," said Quire. "Is it for me?"

"You swear you did not touch Alys?" Starling was entirely confused.

"What does she say I did?"

"That you made her—that you forced her to show herself . . ."

Quire seemed stern. "I cannot remember ever laying a hand upon her." Quire's fingers encircled the boy's stick. "But I'll get to the bottom of this one, if I can. Let's analyse the tale together, eh? Over a noggin? It could be, you see, that inadvertently, I made some gesture she misconstrued."

Starling nodded, impressed by Quire's gravity. "It is possible. I would not blame a gentleman unjustly."

"I can read as much in those large eyes of yours. You're a fine, upstanding lad. Sensitive, too, to the misfortunes of others. But a little quick to spring to the defence of those who do not always deserve it, eh? I can tell that, too, from your face. No wonder you are loved, for you have a beauty rarely granted a young man." Quire removed the staff and placed it against the wall. He slipped a comradely arm about the boy's waist. "I would be happy if I fathered a son as manly as yourself, sweet Phil."

Warmed suddenly and euphorically by Quire's flattery, Starling relaxed, and was lost.

The Sixth Chapter

In Which Queen Gloriana
Continues to Pursue Her Familiar and
Hopeless Nightly Quest

THE SCARLET LIGHT which filled the small chamber came from a score of hanging candles in parchment shades, after the fashion of the Cathay court, and through shadows of darker scarlet moved the Queen, back and forth, on the pace, hands on waist, on thighs, on breasts, folding, unfolding, against the face, upon the shoulders, as if she feared her trembling body might at any moment fly apart. She took wine from a ruby beaker, poured from a ruby flask, she pushed back her robe of silk-lined wolfskin; save for a pair of linen under-hose, from waist to knee, she wore nothing else. She combed at her auburn hair with long fingers on which red gold glinted; she strode to the fire and stood before it, straddled, as if she prayed the heat would burn her tension from her. "Lucinda!" It was almost a scream.

From heaped scarlet cushions in a corner a sleepy, dark-skinned child peered.

"No!" Gloriana's hand waved Lucinda back to sleep. Her conscience could not let her further tire the girl. Besides, her tender mood had passed, much earlier in the night, and now she craved sensation as her only substitute for satisfaction. Her fist ground at her groin. She removed a key from the mantel above the fire; she pulled aside heavy drapery, unlocking a door to apartments still more secret than those she presently occupied.

A short flight of stairs took her up into barbaric, blazing torchlight, into a hall of asymmetric splendour, whose ceilings rose and fell and whose walls were studded with huge gems, like the walls of some faerie cavern, whose carpets sank deep beneath her naked feet, whose tapestries and murals showed crowded, obscure scenes of antique revels. At the far end of the hall two giants drew themselves to attention. One was an albino, red-eyed, white-haired, muscular and naked—the other was a blackamoor with jet eyes, jet hair, and yet the absolute identical twin of the albino. The merchant adventurer who had found these two and matched them had discovered the albino in Muscovy and the blackamoor in Nubia and, seeking trading rights in Albion, had brought them as a clever gift to the Queen. Now they bowed, awaiting her pleasure, adoring her as they had always done; but with a word of affection she passed them by, pushing open the doors into another, darker cavern, filled with the odour of heated flesh, of blood, of salty juices, for this was where her flagellants convened, men and women, passive and dominant, who lived only to enjoy or wield the lash. And, as she passed, some raised gasping heads and recalled the ecstasy they had enjoyed, could only enjoy, at her kindly, knowing fingers, and some paused to stare and remember her wounded flanks and how their piss fell from her inviolable body, and these called out after her, but she was not, tonight, obedient. A short, connecting passage, another key, and she was amongst her boys and girls, smiling but impatient, as she continued on, through a series of chambers where her geishas, male and female, whispered greetings. And in her wake, half-dirge, half-celebration, her name: *Gloriana, Gloriana, Gloriana*—rising, louder and louder in her ears—*Gloriana, Gloriana.*

"Ah!"

Past the beasts and their lovers, past frigid beauty and sensual ugliness; past old men and youths, past the naked and the fancifully costumed, past baths of milk or wine or blood, past blocks and beds and gallows—these were the ones who chose to live here, who had begged to remain, for Gloriana would keep none against their will; past her young girls, her matrons, the crèches and the nurseries, schools and gymnasiums, libraries and theatres; past the blind, the mad and the overly sane, the crippled, the dumb and the deaf; past faces innocent and lustful, generous and greedy, past bodies gross and beautiful, thin, fat, exquisite and ordinary; past nobles and commoners —

Gloriana, Gloriana, Gloriana . . .

—Past orgies, banquets, games and dances, past consorts of music, of players, gladiators and athletes; through chambers pale and featureless, through peculiarly shaped rooms which were dark and populated, furnished with the treasures of the world; through halls, along galleries, cloisters, dormitories, past alien statuary and paintings —

Gloriana, Gloriana!

"Oh!" She sobbed, half-running now. "Ah!"

To a quiet hall. Hairy men, lazy and huge, looked up from where they lounged, in a pack, beside a heated pool of blue and gold tiles. She scented them, half-apes, and went to sit amongst them. They were scarcely aware of her at first, but slowly their curiosity was aroused. They began to inspect her, pulling at her wolfskin coat, stroking her hair, her body, sniffing at her breasts and hands.

"I am Albion," she told them, smiling. "I am Gloriana."

The hairy men grunted and puzzled at the sounds but, as she knew, they could not understand her—neither could they repeat the names.

"I am the Mother, the Protector, the Goddess, the Perfect Monarch." She lay back and their fur was coarse against her flesh. She laughed as they stroked her. "I am History's Noblest Queen! The most powerful Empress the world has ever seen!" She sighed as their hot tongues licked her, as their fingers touched her sensitive places. She embraced them. She wept. In turn she reached below their hairy stomachs and tickled them, so that they grunted, frowned and grinned. She stretched. She writhed. "Ah!" And she smiled. She groaned.

They began to shove each other gently, in order to be closest to her. She embraced one, taking him down onto her. While he snuffled and moaned she stroked his muzzle, his head and his hairy back. She scarcely felt him enter. She pushed; she seized his buttocks; she pulled him; she heaved. He shuddered and she opened her miserable eyes to see his grinning, sated jaws, his benign beastly countenance staring mildly down at her.

A few moments later he and his fellows lost interest in Gloriana and wandered over to the side of the hall to seek food, leaving the Queen of Albion sitting cross-legged beside the pool, looking into the foul tranquillity of the water.

The Seventh Chapter

In Which Captain Quire Attempts the Wreck of the Mikolaj Kopernik *and the Capture of Her Chief Passenger*

WITH CONSIDERABLE SATISFACTION Captain Quire watched the bank of cloud gradually move across the moon. Ahead, the horizon vanished, the sea no longer gleamed. The lights of the Polish galleon, the *Mikolaj Kopernik*, had already been pointed out by O'Bryan, the Erin renegade, who sat comfortably upon the dying bulk of the light-keeper, puffing his pipe and sniffing the wind. "She should be aground within half an hour, Captain."

The light-keeper moaned. There was a round-pommelled dirk in his back, O'Bryan's.

"By Jupiter, O'Bryan," said Tinkler, blowing on his gloved hands, "won't you finish off that poor devil?"

"Why should I?" O'Bryan spoke reasonably. "The longer he lives, the warmer he stays. In this weather a man must make use of everything possible to keep him from freezing. That's the trick of survival, Tink, look you."

Quire put his spyglass to his eye. As he lifted his arms, the wind caught his cloak and blew it back from his shoulders. He tucked the glass in his belt and recovered the cloak, fixing it at the throat by the silver clasp he sometimes wore. He repositioned the spyglass and thought he sighted the galleon. The brim of his hat was bent back against the crown, his hair was blown like weed in a whirlpool, and the spray from the sea below, a curling streamer of foam, pricked that part of his face not protected by the cloak's collar.

"A perfect night for a wreck." O'Bryan re-lit his long clay pipe and shifted his rump a moment, to give the keeper a few extra breaths. O'Bryan wore a huge fur hat, after the Ukrainian fashion, and had on a bearskin coat made from the whole pelt, so that the claws hung about his hands and the beast's head acted as a high collar. His square, ruddy features bore the drinker's mark and his eyes revealed his character even if his smile and easy manner did not. He looked up at the tower, a scaffold set above the watchman's two-roomed cottage, where a red light gleamed to warn ships to hold off approaching the channel until morning. At the sides of this were two unlit lanterns, one yellow and one blue, to indicate, in good weather, which side of the light the ship should go, for the warning beacon was positioned on this small island at the centre of the sandbar; the waters here ran very erratically, sometimes deep, sometimes shallow, depending on the position of the shifting, unstable sands.

Tinkler stared down to the beach where the rest of their men stood, close to the horses they had ridden here while the tide was out. "If it's more than half an hour those ruffians'll be too stiff to act and the plan's wasted, and all this work."

"The plan can't be wasted," Quire told him. "It's the only one."

"And a mad scheme." O'Bryan was approving. "A Polish noble will fetch a good price. They're rich, the Poles. Probably richer, head for head, than Albion. I was in Goddansjik for a few months and saw more gold than I'll ever see in London. But they have strange laws, made by commoners, and it's hard for a free spirit to earn a living there, save as a soldier in the East, where it's poorer."

Quire had decided not to give O'Bryan the full story and intended to betray him as soon as he had served his turn: he knew O'Bryan for a fool with more greed than intelligence who could not be controlled as the others were controlled. "We'll all be rich within the month, O'Bryan. It'll be your task to carry our message to Poland."

O'Bryan had agreed to this and, since Quire had already been generous, had seen no snags to the scheme. The Irishman warmed his hands over the bowl of his pipe and kicked with his heel at the ribs of his victim, as another man might stir the embers of a fire.

Quire now had the ship in focus. He thought he heard a trumpet sound, as the ship signalled. It was rolling in rapidly, borne by the notorious quicksilver tide. Quire could make out figures—the pilot in conference with one who was doubtless the captain, pointing in their direction. And on the high deck, astern, the untidy figure he had had pictured for him, the Polish king.

Quire began to climb the ladder of the tower, while Tinkler took up the trumpet and blew a deep blast to answer the ship's.

Thus, as the shaggy king of Poland looked shoreward from his stern castle, did Captain Quire put lips to lamp and extinguish the red signal, lighting instead, with casual fingers, the green. Next, he leaned to light the blue lantern on the left, to guide the ship directly onto the sands where his men waited. He could see the *Mikolaj Kopernik* with his naked eye. She had most of her sails reefed and her oarsmen were backing water. A few moments, while the signal was interpreted, and then the galleon advanced more swiftly, heading, to Quire's relief, in exactly the direction he had anticipated. Hastily he swung down from the tower, tapped O'Bryan on the shoulder, winked at Tinkler, and began to run, his spurs silvery and jingling, down to the beach to await his lumbering prey.

"She's on her way, lads." Quire stooped to pull up the folded-down flaps of his jackboots, lacing them tight at the thigh. The wind made so many scarecrows of his men, all wild rags and hunched figures, and gave the horses haloes of their own manes. Some distance away the sea slithered over the sands or struck flat and wet against the smooth stones; Quire could smell it. He could taste its salt on his lips. He had no liking for the sea. It was too large.

"Guns, Captain?" One of the hirelings spoke, half-muffled, from his cloak.

"That's what we brought 'em for, Hogge. More for the noise than anything. The trouble with a task of this kind is that unless you advertise your presence like mummers at the fair you'll not be noticed. And unless you're noticed, nobody's afraid. And if nobody's afraid they can all get away from us without ever knowing we were here!" Quire enjoyed this speech, but he left his men bewildered. "Guns, yes. Fire 'em willy-nilly—into the air until we've got our man at least. We don't want to put a ball through his head and have no ransom. I've told you who to look for."

O'Bryan came stiff-legged down the sands. He rubbed at his bottom and farted. He drew two great horse-pistols from the pockets of his bearskin coat and held them close to his face in the gloom, inspecting the locks.

"And careful with those pistols, O'Bryan." Quire patted the Erin man on the arm. "If you let 'em off too soon the ship'll think she's attacked by a man-o'-war and fire a broadside to destroy the whole island."

O'Bryan appreciated this compliment to his weapons and laughed loudly.

Quire detected a different note to the tide and turned, taken unawares, to see the jigging lights of the *Mikolaj Kopernik* as her keel shuddered into sand and her oars began to smash, cracking one by one; so many whiplashes. The wind droned like an organ around the huge ship and the cries and shrieks from the decks were like the sound of gulls. Quire and Tinkler began to run towards her.

As Quire made out the ship's bulk he saw that she yawed markedly to starboard, seeming to lean on her broken oars like a monstrous wounded crayfish. The wind found her staysails and moved her intermittently, adding to the impression of a helplessly landed sea-beast. From above came the sound of every sort of human distress. The oarsmen had doubtless been the worst hurt and from the rowing ports issued wailing screams that had an extra eeriness in conjunction with the notes of the wind.

Tinkler shuddered as they got closer. "Ugh! It's like banshees. Are you sure we haven't taken some ghost ship, Captain? There's so many have gone down in these waters. . . ."

Quire ignored him, pointing to the ornamental stair built into the ship's side. "We can climb that easily enough. Quickly now, Tink—while they're confused."

They were knee-deep in the surf, creeping under the splintered shafts of the huge sweeps, when they reached their goal, to see that it was further from the ship's bottom than Quire had originally judged. Weed tangled itself about his boots and caught in his spurs.

The ship creaked and groaned and sank a little deeper on its side so that for an instant Quire thought they would be crushed, but it brought the gilded stair a little closer.

"On my shoulders, Tink." Quire bent and lifted his swaying accomplice. Tinkler grabbed for the stair's rail, missed, shifted himself and grabbed once more, catching it, swinging himself onto the lowest step, then leaning down so that Quire could jump, clasp his hand and be hauled up. The great ship settled again. Overhead, orders were being given in a language entirely unfamiliar to Quire and it seemed that some sort of discipline was in danger of being restored. Then, thankfully, Hogge and O'Bryan began their barrage and sent almost everyone crowding forward. Up the angled stairway they went, bodies against the ship's side, until they had reached the main deck and could raise their noses high enough to inspect the scene. There were corpses on the deck, where men had been flung from the yards, and there were crippled sailors, with broken limbs and ribs, being tended by their fellows. Lanterns moved here and there and Quire glimpsed the captain in conference with the pilot, who was shaking his head and either pretending ignorance or professing it in good faith (Quire did not know how much Montfallcon had involved the man). He tried to see if Poland's king was still in the stern castle, but it was too dark. Boldly, with Tinkler in his wake, he climbed rapidly for the stern, like two black shadows cast by the flapping sails above as the moon appeared mistily behind thinner cloud. Though many mariners passed them and some glanced curiously at them, Quire and Tinkler were only challenged when they reached the companionway to the castle itself. Quire held up his lantern to reveal the face of an armoured musketeer. "We're from the shore. To help. We saw the wreck."

The musketeer shook his head. Quire laughed confidently and held up the lantern again, clapping the guard on the shoulder as he and Tinkler squeezed past and continued on their way, to find Poland sitting up against the rail, blinking and perplexed, with some noble greybeard bending over him in concern.

"I was sent here," said Quire in a harried tone, "to attend a gentleman. Does anyone speak our tongue?"

The old noble, swathed in sable, looked up, his speech halting and guttural. "I speak it, sir. You're from the shore? What happened? The shots." He blinked. He was short-sighted.

"You're wrecked, sir. Smashed up, sir. And you'll be breaking before long if you don't get off." (This last, a lie.)

"What shall we do?" Peering. "Who are you?"

"Captain Fletcher. Coastguard, sir. The shots you heard were ours, driving off brigands who attend wrecks like crows attend a corpse. You were lucky we were close. Come now, where's your women and children?"

"There are none."

"This passenger looks like someone of quality."

"In truth, sir, he is."

"Then let's get him over the side, and you too. Who else?"

"This one first. I'm not important. And there are valuables. In the cabin. They must be saved. They are gifts. . . ."

"Valuables may be salvaged later, sir, but not lives," said Quire chidingly.

"These valuables are of great importance. Help His—this gentleman—to the shore. I'll fetch the treasure." He spoke to the king in Polish. The king smiled, vaguely.

Quire appeared to debate with himself. Then he nodded. "Very well, if you think that's for the best. My lieutenant here will go with you." He offered his gloved hand to the king, who looked at it without understanding at first, then accepted it. "Up you get, Your Worship."

The king climbed unsteadily to his feet and Quire supported him, helping him to the companionway and down it.

"Carefully, now, sir."

"I am much obliged to you, sir," said Poland in the High Speech used for diplomacy throughout the globe, but Quire had to pretend hearty ignorance.

"Sorry, sir, but I don't know a word of whatever it is you talk."

They got to the deck and began to move back towards the point where Quire and Tinkler had boarded. The ship shuddered again, quite dramatically, and Quire was flung hard against the rail. The wind's note changed, became shrill. The moon vanished. Water dashed itself aimlessly around the ruined ship. Quire staggered back, still half-carrying Poland, who murmured with hazy cordiality, permitting himself to be guided to the leaning steps and down them, while Tinkler cried "Here!" from behind and waved a bundle, the old nobleman at his rear calling out to the crew to follow, which was what Quire had feared would happen. "Easy, sir. Easy, sir." He helped an irresolute Poland into the shallow water. "This way." He took Poland's arm and tugged. Tinkler was next, but the old man remained on the steps, still calling back for his men.

Quire and his charge left the water and began to trudge up the beach as O'Bryan and the others came in sight. "Off we go, O'Bryan!" he called. "Hold them, Tink, and we'll meet you at the mill."

O'Bryan put out a hand to take the king's, leading him to their spare horse. "Up you go, my lord."

The king chuckled and shook his head. O'Bryan said something in Polish and the king laughed again, readily straddling the sorrel. Quire found his black and was up, too, taking the sorrel's bridle while O'Bryan mounted. He heard Tinkler yell an order as sailors began to wade ashore, seeking their liege, and musket and pistol fire roared in the hands of the half-score knaves Tinkler commanded, cutting down the first rank of sailors.

The king shouted a question to O'Bryan, who replied again, as he and Quire had arranged, that there were brigands along this coast who always came out in the hope of attacking a wreck but that their coastguards were holding the villains off.

They were galloping rapidly through the shallows separating the island from the mainland before Poland cried out and tried to draw rein.

"What's he want, O'Bryan?" shouted Quire above the wind.

"Says he's concerned for his people, that he should stay."

"Very worthy. Tell him the tide's due in and all must get to high ground, that our men are looking after the rest."

O'Bryan spoke slowly in Polish. The king replied, still reluctant.

"What's up now, O'Bryan?"

"He says the tide appears to be going out."

"So it does!" Quire grinned. If the tide were not retreating, they would not have been able to cross this wide strip of sand at all. "He's observant in some ways, eh? Tell him it's deceptive. Put a bit of urgency in your tone, O'Bryan!"

The bitter wind grabbed at them, struck them with such force that the horses staggered. "Ride, by Mithras!" yelled Quire.

More gunfire sounded from behind. The king tried to turn the sorrel. "Oh, sweet Ariadne!" Quire rode in close, removed the king's cap, drew a pistol from the holster on his saddle even as Poland began to crane to see what happened, and struck him hard at the base of his unkempt skull, grasping him before he fell too far, leaning him across the pommel, wrapping reins to hold him in position, taking the bridle and leading the sorrel on. O'Bryan fired off one of his pistols, apparently for the fun of it, and waved the other. They were almost at the grassy dunes where glinting snow displayed the evidence that they left the tidal flats behind and would soon be on true land.

They rode at a gallop, inland and eastwards, away from the harbour city of Rye, for Quire had determined that they should put at least fifty miles between them and the wreck if they were not to be accidentally detected.

Quire looked back and saw a few flashes, heard a few shots and yells. If he guessed right, Tinkler and the men had had less trouble than any of them had anticipated and were even now horsed, leaving the *Mikolaj Kopernik* and her crew to fare as best they could until news reached Rye and help was sent. By then it would be morning and the rufflers well on the way to London, while Tinkler joined him at the spot they had agreed, bringing with him, by happy chance, the King of Poland's treasure.

As they galloped, Quire began to utter a series of sharp, barking notes, between the sound of a wolf and a raven, which made O'Bryan somewhat nervous even after it had dawned on him that Quire was laughing.

Some hours later a bedraggled, shivering Tinkler, his snag fang dancing in unison with his other, less visible teeth, a bundle clutched between legs and saddle horn, his face blue and his eyes glazed, as if ice covered them, sighted the windmill where they had agreed to meet. It stood out as a black silhouette against the early light, its old sails squeaking as they tried to turn in the wind. The horse splashed through the shallow water of the fen; its hoofs broke thin ice with every step; the frozen grass cracked as it bent. There was scarcely any colour to the scene and it seemed to Tinkler that everything which was not white was black. Even Quire's hunched form, sitting outside the mill beside a small fire, was completely black to Tinkler's eye. He called out and then became nervous as his voice bawled with startling loudness from his lips and sent some white geese flapping into the pale sky. "Quire!"

Quire looked up and waved cheerfully. There was a dead, plucked fowl on his knee.

Tinkler walked the horse over the small, decaying bridge crossing the clogged stream. "Where's our charge?"

"Inside, tied and sleeping."

"O'Bryan?"

Quire gestured with the knife he had been using to gut the goose. The mound on which he sat stirred and groaned. Tormented, bloodshot eyes peered from out of bear-fur. "He's served his first purpose, to communicate to our charge. Now he's serving a second. One he suggested himself. He's kept me pleasantly warm for the last two hours, while the fire drew."

O'Bryan's mouth opened and groaned again. Blood ran from between his clenched teeth and over his lips. Thoughtfully, Quire took some of the goose's feathers and stuffed them tight against the teeth, so that the blood would not run onto the bearskin coat and spoil it. O'Bryan whimpered, imploring Tinkler for help, but Tinkler glanced away and entered the mill, noticing, as he did so, the three carefully placed daggers which stuck from O'Bryan's twitching back.

"What's next?" he called, looking down at the King of Poland, who snored on ancient straw. He seated himself on part of a broken millstone and began to unwrap the bundle.

"Montfallcon will pretend to send out men. Hogge will take

the ransom note to one of the Polish merchants in London—making it clear that we have no idea whom we have captured—and eventually, after much fuss, our victim will be found, none the worse for wear—and with only a few of his valuables gone." Quire spoke over his shoulder at Tinkler, who was holding up a golden figurine to the shaft of light which fell through the gap in the mill's roof. "Just a few, Tink. If we were caught with too much, we'd hang this time, for certain, even though it entailed a change in the Law. Montfallcon couldn't afford to save us. Poland would demand our lives. The treasure—or most of it—will be rescued with its owner."

Tinkler put the things back. He picked up the bundle and placed it casually in a corner. "And when will that be, Captain?" He scratched, characteristically, at his exposed tooth.

"Shortly before Twelfth Night, Tink. In time for the Court Masque, when so many dignitaries and sovereigns shall be present that our poor king will be lost amongst them and his gestures, speeches, protestations—all will fall flat. He'll be able to blame himself—as well as brigands—for his failure—but he'll not blame Albion or Gloriana. And that's the issue."

Tinkler had not been listening to most of this. He stepped over O'Bryan's head again, studying Quire's efficient hands. "How long will he take to cook, eh, Captain?"

And he reached to pinch the goose.

The Eighth Chapter

In Which the Mad Woman in the Walls Observes Some of the Many Comings and Goings in the Outer Palace

LYING FLAT, WITH her eyes close against the grille which was immediately and coincidentally opposite to that which Jephraim Tallow had used on New Year's Eve, the mad woman stared into the hall, her ears filled with the beauty of the choir's single voice as it entertained the dining nobles below. She was starved, as she usually was, but she was not hungry. Thin fingers held the grille, occasionally combing the tangled, red-brown hair or scratching at the grey flesh of her long body while parasites ran in and out of her rags, unheeded. There was a seraphic smile upon her filthy face—the music and the beauty of the diners filled her with so much pleasure that she was almost crying. Already sweetmeats and savouries had been served and wine waved away, heralding the end of the meal. As another might watch a favourite play, she tried to will the guests to stay, but gradually they rose, taking their leave of the grey lord in his chair at the head of the table, going about their business.

The mad woman focused all her attention on the two who remained. The Arabian ambassador and the lord, who was her greatest hero and whose name she knew, as she knew most of those at Court.

"Montfallcon," she whispered, "the Queen's trusted adviser. Her Right Hand. Incorruptible, clever Montfallcon!"

The choir's chant ended and the choristers began to file from the hall, so that now she could overhear some of what was being said between Montfallcon and the proud, brown man, in braided white silk and gold-twined plaited ropes at head, wrists, neck and waist.

"... my master married to the Queen? Security for all time, for us both. Such an alliance!" she heard the Moor remark.

"We are already allies, however." Montfallcon smiled delicately. "Arabia and Albion."

"Save that Arabia's hampered against expansion because Albion protects her. We are frustrated in our ambitions—as are all children who have grown and whose parents do not recognise the fact."

Montfallcon laughed aloud. "Come now, Lord Shahryar, you cannot misjudge my intelligence or expect me to misjudge yours. Arabia is protected by Albion because she has not the resources to defend herself against the Tatar Empire. She has no alliance with Poland because Poland shares her fear of the Tatars but hopes the Tatars will leave Poland alone and concentrate on Arabia, if Arabia is weak. On the other hand ..."

"My point, my lord, is that Arabia is no longer weak."

"Of course she isn't, for she has Albion's aid."

"And the Tatar Empire could be conquered."

"Gloriana will not make war unless the security of the Realm is threatened—and is seen to be threatened. We fight only if invaded. Tatary knows this and therefore does not invade. The Queen hopes by this policy eventually to create habits in nations, so that they will not automatically go to war to gain their ends. She visualises a great Council, a League. ..."

"Lord Montfallcon's tone betrays him." Lord Shahryar smiled. "He believes no more than I in this easy feminine pacifism. Oh, such yearnings are to be admired in any woman. Yet a balance must be established between the Male and the Female instincts. But here there is no balance. There should be a man, as strong in his way as the Queen. My master, the Grand Caliph, is strong. ..."

"But the Queen does not wish to marry. She regards marriage as a further burden—and she already has many responsibilities."

"She favours others?"

"She favours none. She is flattered, of course, by the Grand Caliph's attentions. ..."

Lord Shahryar stroked his head. "It is for me now to remind you of my intelligence, Lord Montfallcon. What I have said, regarding the Queen and her needs, is well-meant. We are concerned for her."

"Then we share that," said Lord Montfallcon. "And if you respect her, as I do, you will respect her wishes, her decisions, as I do."

"You do nothing without her approval?"

"She is my Queen. She is Albion. She is the Realm." Lord Montfallcon lifted his chin. "She is the Law."

"Not always effective."

"What?"

"Your Law. It seems it does not bring criminals to justice on every occasion."

"I cannot understand you."

"My nephew, Ibram, was killed in London, even as I took ship from Ben Gahshi. I arrived to learn of his death—murdered—and that his murderer has gone free."

"King? He's to be transported next week."

"There was another involved, however—the one who actually performed the deed—whom you spoke for, as I hear it, my lord."

"There was another accused, aye. I spoke for him because in truth he was on my business and could not have become involved in the brawl, even if he was the kind of knave who would."

"So you are completely certain of your servant's innocence?" Lord Shahryar looked hard at Lord Montfallcon. "This black-clad swordsman, this spy of yours . . ."

"Quire? A spy? A courier for the Queen, no more."

"Quire's the name." Lord Shahryar nodded. "I'd forgotten it. This Quire is known for his duelling skills. He lured my nephew into a fight in order to rob him, do you think?"

"I know Quire well. He would never waste his time in such a scheme. He is too proud."

"You give your word then, my lord, that your Captain Quire could not possibly have killed my nephew."

"I give my word, Lord Shahryar." Lord Montfallcon stared unblinkingly into the Arabian's eyes.

"Can I, perhaps, interview him—just to satisfy myself that he has not deceived you?" continued Lord Shahryar softly.

"He is on another mission for me. He is not in London."

"Where?"

"He helps in this business concerning the King of Poland. If you listen to rumours, my lord, you'll have heard that one, eh?"

"That Casimir was taken by brigands, for ransom? Yes. Do you think he's still alive?"

"A ransom note was received by the Polish merchants. The villains think they have nothing more than an ordinary aristocrat in their hands."

"Well, I trust he fares better with your justice and its keeping than did my nephew." The Saracen rose in his chair. "Albion fast becomes a lawless land, it seems, with brigands and murderers allowed to range wherever they will, slaying nobles, capturing kings. . . ."

"There are no murderers in your own land, my lord?"

"Some, of course . . ."

"There were many more before Albion protected you and brought her Law to you."

"When King Hern sat on this nation's throne, that's true," said Lord Shahryar pointedly. "If the land is to be properly ruled, then there must be a man . . ."

"The Queen is the greatest sovereign Albion has ever known. The world envies us our monarch."

"As a mother she is sometimes just a little too fond of her children. Thus she cannot see either their faults or the faults of those who, pretending friendship, threaten them. With a good, stern husband at her side . . ."

"She has the help of men such as myself." Lord Montfallcon inspected a dish of dried figs, selected one and placed it on the plate before him. "Are we not experienced—and stern?"

"But you are not her equal, my lord."

"Her equal, my lord, does not exist."

"I'd hoped to convince you of our sincerity, of my master's admiration for your mistress, of the need to unify our two lands completely, in the traditional manner of kings. The Grand Caliph is young, virile and handsome. If you have heard any rumours concerning him, I assure you that they are without foundation."

"The Queen allows no suitors, my lord. That way she favours no-one. Your master could be old, diseased, a follower of the habits of Sodom, he would stand as excellent a chance as any other . . ."

"So you will not speak for us? I'd hoped you would. Yet I thought the King of Poland came incognito for one reason only . . ."

"If so, he was misled. He was not encouraged."

"No love letters from the Queen?"

"None, sir."

"So that is why he's captured?" Lord Shahryar grinned to himself.

"You are too devious, my lord. I have ceased to follow you."

"I suspect that my nephew was slain because he tried to spy on Her Majesty. I suspect that King Casimir was taken because he hoped to woo the Queen in secret."

Lord Montfallcon began to laugh. "We are not savages, Lord Shahryar, in Albion! Our diplomacy is entirely of a subtler sort!"

The Moorish lord pushed back his chair. He was glowering, but attempted to disguise or dismiss the expression. "I must apologise, my lord."

"My good lord, I accept your apology. There is much more amusement in your suggestion than there could possibly be insult!"

Lord Montfallcon stood up and embraced the Saracen, who made an effort to smile. "I must assure you of our greatest friendship. We admire Arabia over all other nations of the world. . . ."

"As we admire Albion. When the Grand Caliph arrives tomorrow . . ."

"Our partnership requires no traditional union to ensure it shall survive a thousand years."

"Our concern is for the Queen, as well as Albion."

"They are the same."

The mad woman above crept away, crawling on hands and knees through the dust, to her next vantage point, where, through a small window which could scarcely be detected from the floor, she observed Master Ernest Wheldrake, naked and draped in gold chains, kneeling before his mistress, the amiable Lady Lyst, as she sipped from the goblet in her hand, the mock crown askew over one eye, swiping a leisurely whip as he grovelled ecstatically and moaned some name which the mad woman could not catch. The scene was altogether too familiar and she crawled on, seeking something fresher for her entertainment. Another ten minutes and she was able to take up her usual place at the mousehole looking into Lord Ingleborough's bedroom, but the old lord was not in evidence. She caught sight, briefly, of his catamite, Patch, playing with some wooden soldiers, but he did not return. She wriggled on, to see how Sir Tancred and Lady Mary Perrott fared in their relationship. She was greatly jealous of this relationship, largely because it seemed so perfect. She envied it the more because she herself required a diet of Romance and Intrigue rather than mere Sensation, which as often as not saddened her. She had never known the love Sir Tancred gave to Lady Mary, though she dreamed of possessing it one day.

But it was to be a dull tour for the mad woman. Neither Sir Tancred nor Lady Mary was present. Lord Rhoone snored in his formal uniform, at his desk, black beard pushed against his lips by his green ruff, speckled with cream. Sir Amadis Cornfield was also behind his desk, bent over his accounts and receipts, his fingers dark with ink. Una, Countess of Scaith, was disrobing, removing the complicated dress she had had to wear while entertaining the Saracen ambassador on the Queen's behalf. There would be nobody in Lord Montfallcon's study, so the mad woman decided not to descend the chute which would take her there. She considered a visit to the seraglio, but this, too, depressed her. She spent a little while watching the mummers rehearsing the mime they were to perform for the Twelfth Night festivities tomorrow, but she did not have much interest in symbolic drama. She was returning to her crypt, passing on the other side of the dusty and web-festooned glass of the forgotten orangery, when she observed a shadow, making its way towards Lord Montfallcon's secret entrance, and she paused, hidden in gloom, to see who visited the Chancellor.

It was Tinkler. He was jaunty.

The mad woman drew her tall body back in case Tinkler should glimpse it. Doubtless this varlet was in Montfallcon's employ and had come to receive his instructions. The King of Poland would be rescued by morning. She had overheard the scheme discussed. She chuckled to herself, shaking her head in admiration of her two heroes—Montfallcon, whom she dreamed of as a father, and Quire, whom she yearned for as a lover. The scheme appeared to be working exactly as they had planned.

The Ninth Chapter

In Which the Queen and Her Courtiers Celebrate the Twelfth and Final Night of the Yuletide Festival

Una of Scaith drew deeply on the stem of the tobacco pipe and stretched herself at ease over her tapestry couch. She lay upon woodland scenes (the Hunt, Nymphs and Fauns, Diana and her Maidens) before a magnificent fire, her farthingale askew, like a badly hung bell, her bodice loosened, gauze-wired collar on one side of her pearl-stranded head, as she enjoyed the few minutes before the festivities and ceremonies which, as the Queen's friend, she must attend. She stroked the orange back of a large cat which lay asleep against the couch, and she gave herself up to the tobacco while in the next room her maids prepared the rest of her ensemble.

The Countess hated almost all public events, particularly those where she was expected to perform some function—tonight the Queen had asked her to announce the programme at the beginning of every section, which meant she would have to be present through the entire celebration of the Twelfth, from Bounty Giving to the Final Feast, which was certain to last into the early hours. Worse, the whole of the first half of the evening was to be spent on the ice at West Minster, where the river had frozen so thickly it had been possible to light bonfires and roast a pig (last night an enterprising Venetian innkeeper had done this to his considerable profit), and she would be chilled to her bones as, of course, would everyone else; and, like everyone else, would resort too much to the mulled claret which would be the main beverage and chief source of heat. And later, in elaborate costumes, would come the Masque in the Great Hall, and, with it, further discomfort, for she was bound to roast as Urd the Norn. Others would be equally suffering here, as well—there would be a Thor, an Odin, a Hela and the rest, and Gloriana would be Freyja, Queen of the Gods, in Master Wheldrake's subject entitled *The Eve of Ragnarok* from the Northern mythologies, in honour of Greater Poland, which ruled both sides of the Baltic Sea. Una, whose own estates and homeland lay on the large island of Ynys Scaith, far to Albion's north, and who was over-familiar with these gods, found them a thoroughly boring pantheon and hated the current fashion at Court for novelty, which put her own favourite Classical subjects out of vogue.

Una's pipe burned down and with a sigh she rose to adjust her clothes, to have her maids draw her together, covering her with a cloak of red velvet trimmed with green lake moiré fur, the large hood shading her face. The maids escorted her to the outer door of her apartments (really an entire house built, like many others, into the main structure of the palace and facing out upon a broad yard in whose centre was an ornamental lake containing a good-sized artificial island). The Queen's coach-cabined sleigh waited for her and footmen, in exaggerated coquard bonnets, short brocaded tabards and slashed canions of yellow and blue, attended her as she climbed aboard and plunged into darkness and soft cushions. A shout, a crack, and the vehicle lurched on its springs, to make the little journey around the path to the rather more elaborate façade of the private gateway of the Queen's gardens and a gathering of guards forming ranks at the command of Lord Rhoone, whose breath billowed with every staccato utterance, reminding Una how cold it was. She kept her hands in the muff beneath her cape and stared miserably through the far window at the darkening ornamental garden on which more snow was beginning to fall. It seemed that winter drew deeper and might never end, unless it was with the ending of the world—and she was reminded, with a shiver, of the Fimbul Winter, and wondered, with morbid relish, if perhaps it really was the Eve of Ragnarok and that they brought in Chaos and Old Night to engulf them, once and for all. She yawned. If the Lords of Entropy were to manifest themselves on Earth again as they had in the legendary past she felt she might welcome them as a relief, at least, to her boredom. Not, of course, that she believed in those terrible prehistoric fables, though sometimes she could not help wishing that they had really existed and that she had lived in them, for they must surely have been more colourful and stimulating than this present age, where dull Reason drove bright Romance away: granite scattering mercury.

It was with these thoughts in mind that she welcomed the platinum-crowned Queen as she stepped up into the carriage. "By Arioch! You're marvellous gaudy, tonight!" She smiled.

Gloriana returned the smile, relieved by Una's deliberate vulgarity (it was considered poor taste to exhort the names of the Old Gods). She was dressed in ermine, white silk, pearls and silver, for she must represent the Polar Monarch tonight, the Snow Queen; and all were expected to reflect this motif if they attended her Court. Una's own dress beneath the cape was pale blue, her collarette a slightly deeper blue, her petticoat white and decorated with small blue bows, a modification of the previous spring's Shepherdess.

Meanwhile, around them, the guard mounted white horses, drew silvery capes over their traditional uniforms, placed white beaver caps with white owl feathers on their heads and readied themselves. Lord Rhoone rode up, his black beard almost astonishing in all this paleness, and bent to show an enquiring eye.

Gloriana's lace glove waved, Lord Rhoone cried out his loud "At the trot, gentlemen!" and sleigh and escort were moving, with a screech of runners and a muffled drumming of hoofs, off to West Minster and the river.

"Good news," Gloriana told her companion. "You heard it? Poland's rescued."

"He's well?"

"A trifle frostbitten, I gather, but not harmed. Montfallcon told me this afternoon. He was found this morning at a mill. The villains who'd taken him had quarrelled and run off, leaving him in his bonds, killing one of their number in their argument. Perhaps they'd intended to return—but Montfallcon's men found Poland first and brought him to London. So all's well and we'll be plagued no longer by Count Korzeniowski's anxieties for his master."

"When shall you receive this unlucky monarch?"

"Tonight. In an hour or so. When I receive all the guests."

"But the Grand Caliph—this proposes a difficult diplomacy."

Gloriana pulled back the curtains for a view of the city's lights. "Montfallcon has solved it. Both shall be presented together, with Poland announced first, since he's Emperor."

Una bit an amused lip. "I thought they both hoped to pay more than formal respects to Your Majesty. Do they not come to Court to"—she was almost ashamed—"to court?"

"Poland, apparently, swears he'll marry none but me. And Arabia's protests are only a degree less fulsome which, considering his notoriety, must reveal as great a passion, eh?" Gloriana was sardonic. "Which would you prefer, Una?"

"Poland for companionship, Arabia for pleasure," said Una at once.

"Arabia would admire your figure more, I think. It's boyish enough for his taste."

"Then pray he'll accept me as a substitute and make me Queen of All Arabia." Una cocked her head. "The notion's excellent. But I suspect his ardour's politically kindled and Ynys Scaith's not a large enough dowry."

Gloriana enjoyed this. "True! He wants Albion and all her Empire, nothing less. Perhaps he can have them, if he'll give me what I cannot have." The sleigh lurched a fraction as it rounded a corner, and Gloriana sang the chorus of a favourite song:

Oh, could I be what I am not,
Then I could have what I have not,
If I had, I would not . . .

And Una, hearing that merry lament, became silent for a moment, causing Gloriana to regret her lapse and lean to kiss her friend. "Master Gallimari promises us many splendid diversions this evening."

The Countess of Scaith recovered herself. "Aye—diversions! They're what's needed, eh? Are all the foreign embassies invited?"

"Of course. And London's officers. And every noble from the

country who will come. And every courtier. Mithras!" She put a satirical hand to her mouth. "Will the ice hold 'em, d'you think, Una? Shall we all dance to watery doom, tonight? And half the globe's security float out, so many icebergs, on the dawn tide?"

Una shook her head. "If I know my lord Montfallcon he's seen that girders support the ice from bank to bank. Why, I suspect he's had the ice replaced with obsidian and painted, he fears so for any possible harm which might befall you."

"He's a tigress and I the cub, in that respect," agreed Gloriana. "But look!" She pointed through the gauze. "The ice is real!"

They were on a hill from which could be observed the curve of the great Thames, glinting with frost and snow, broad, shining black between the deeper black of the buildings which lay on both sides, like a massive forest hung with so many yellow lanterns. As they watched, more and more lights appeared and slowly the scene was transformed from black to glowing grey, and white, and hazy amber, and the river became pale glass in which moved small figures, seemingly reflections from an invisible source, and then the road had dropped so steeply it was no longer possible to see anything but the snowy hills and, ahead, the two battlemented towers of London's North Gate, the Bull's Gate, where the Queen's carriage must be greeted and she must be welcomed and formalities exchanged between Lord Rhoone (on behalf of the Queen) and the glowing, half-tipsy Lord Mayor.

All this over, the sleigh continued, bumping mightily now, for the snow was not so thick on the cobbles, between lines of waving, torch-bearing, cap-flourishing, cheering citizens to whom the Queen smiled, bowed, blessed with nodding hands, until the gates of the Little City of West Minster were approached and these passed and shut, so that for a few moments the sleigh slithered in comparative silence, along the broad avenue, past the great Colleges and Temples of Contemplation, the Ministries, the Barracks, to the wide embankment upon the quays where, in better weather, the ships of visiting monarchs would dock. On this embankment awnings were already arranged and Una could see carriages disappearing, having delivered their illustrious cargoes. Footboys and footmen sped from position to position, ostlers stood ready, a choir of trumpets was prepared, at the tall Graecian columns flanking the steps down to the quay. These steps were covered by awnings, also, and carpeted. Braziers burned, like warning fires, along the length of the embankment walls, to provide both light and heat, and above them waved ranks of banners in a glory of multicoloured silk reflecting flames and surrounding snow. And over these flags stood a rich ebony sky, in which no stars glowed. It was like a larger canopy, covering the whole of the city: a canopy through which a few flakes of snow dropped, to heap themselves where they could, or die spluttering in the fires.

Gloriana clapped her hands and nudged Una's ribs before she recalled her own majesty, and became the grave, beautiful symbol demanded by the occasion. Una assumed a similar gravity.

The door of the sleigh was opened by Lord Rhoone. The Queen descended. Una followed.

Between the columns they paced, whilst a brassy fanfare announced the Queen; down the steps to where two great torches burned, held in the hands of pages clothed from head to toe by the skins of the polar bear. Behind the pages lords and ladies bent their heads. Also in whites and blues and silver, with powdered faces, the courtiers in the shadows made by the torches reminded Una of a ghostly assemblage, as if the dead rose to pay homage to Albion's Empress on this misty Twelfth.

From quay to wooden steps the awning stretched, and down they went with measured dignity, to a side carpet laid across the ice where, covered still, a path led to their pavilion, three-sided, tall, of billowing silver silk, with a throne for Gloriana of delicate silver filigree, and a white-cushioned chair for Una, as the Snow Queen's chief attendant.

Above, on the embankment, Una saw, as she waited for Gloriana to seat herself, a lowing processing of reluctant oxen; she heard the honking of geese, who would share the oxen's fate, saw the stacked tinder and logs of the fires on which these creatures would be cooked, their juices soon to splutter, their skins to crackle, their savoury meat to swell, proud and tasty in the heat. Una licked her lip and, seeing that the Queen was down, went down herself with a shiver as her farthingale tilted and let a sharp breeze to her knees.

Over the centre of the ice was a platform, like a scaffold, on which the musicians sat, tuning their instruments as best they could. The awnings and carpets beyond the Queen's pavilion were, for contrast, green and gold, and the musicians wore dark green wool; in several layers, judging by their bulk. More trumpets blew a fanfare from the embankment, to hamper their tuning further, and the Queen looked questioningly at Una, who paused. Then she rose, as slowly the courtiers, having filed down from above, assembled.

A figure in rippling ivory appeared upon the carpet leading to the throne. He doffed an ermine cap, falling to one knee. It was Marcilius Gallimari, Master of the Queen's Revels.

"Your Majesty."

"Is all prepared, Master Gallimari?"

"It is, Your Majesty! They are ready!" He spoke with intense, earnest enthusiasm.

"Then we'll begin. Countess."

Una coughed quietly into her hand. Master Gallimari stepped into the shadows of the awning, to pass through the guards and vanish. Then Una cried:

"The Queen bestows her bounty on the Yuletide widows and the Season's orphans. Let them come forward now and receive their right."

The courtiers stepped to either side and a footboy handed Una a cushion on which rested a score of kidskin purses. Una took one of the purses and placed it in the Queen's palm as the first nervous commoner, a plump matron, came humbly up the carpet, her eyes lowered, a shy smile on her lips, in linen shawl and apron, to curtsey. "Your Majesty. The folk of the Southcheap send their loyal respects to Your Majesty and pray the plague will never come upon them."

"We thank you and the people of Southcheap. Your name?"

"Mistress Starling, Your Majesty, widow of Starling the chandler."

"Be wise, Mistress Starling, with this, and we pray you to do your duty. We are sorry for your grief."

"I thank Her Majesty." A shaking hand accepted the purse.

Then came two swarthy children, fingers linked, a boy and a girl, bobbing all the way.

"Your father and your mother are dead? How so?" Gloriana took a second purse from Una.

"Lost upon the river, Your Majesty," said the boy, "where they worked at their ferry, up above the Wapping Stairs."

"We are sorry for your grief." The words were ritual but the sentiment was not. Gloriana took a further purse, so that the children might have one each.

As the ceremony continued, Una stared beyond the crowds, at the far embankment, the twin of the northern one, with its columns and torches and fanciful stonework, its painted ceramics. Where the embankment turned, to her right, she could see a line of gargoyles on the piles, with mooring rings in their grinning mouths; above the gargoyles were the trees which grew over the high walls, their dark branches turned to stiff grey strands of velvet by the lantern's light, and then, a little further on, was the Water Gate of West Minster and its grille decorated with iron devils.

The bounty given, Lord Montfallcon came to stand beside the throne and whisper to the Queen while trumpets announced the two Guests of Honour, and the Queen's Tribune called out their names. Then, side by side they came, in ceremonial stockings and gowns, magnificent with jade, with diamonds, aquamarines, turquoises, sapphires and all manner of other pale gems.

"His Royal Highness King Casimir the Fourteenth, Emperor Elect of Greater Poland. His Royal Highness the Grand Caliph Hassan al-Giafar, Lord of All Arabia."

Two crowned heads bowed before the third. The crown of Poland's Casimir was white gold, with Gothic spikes and very light emeralds, while Hassan al-Giafar wore a turban about which was set a Moorish coronet, all floral abstracts, in silver and mother-of-pearl, and though their gowns were simple, according to tradition, they were trimmed with the richest threads permitted.

They used the High Speech for this ceremony. Fork-bearded Arabia spoke first.

"Gloriana, who is Ishtar upon Earth, Goddess of Us All, Whose Name is Honoured in the World's Four Corners and Whose Fame is Feared, Who is the Sun to Light our Days and the Moon to Illuminate our Nights, whose Splendour Dulls the Stars, We, Caliph Hassan al-Giafar, Descendant of the First Calligraphers of Sheena, Protector of the Raschid, Father of the Nomad, Chief of the Deserts, the Rivers and the Seas, Shield against the Tatar, Overlord of Baghdad and the Fifty Cities, bring Thee the greetings and the felicitations of All our Folk."

The Queen rose, taking the sceptre handed her by Una and lifting it as if, obscurely, she blessed the Caliph.

"Albion welcomes thee, great king. We are honoured by thine attendance at our ceremonies." She seated herself as Poland, fumbling with his cloak, his crown askew over one shaggy eyebrow, his hair falling across his face, his beard coming loose from its careful knots, blinked vaguely, his lips moving soundlessly.

"Um . . ." began Poland. "Your Majesty."

Hassan al-Giafar's handsome hooded eyes showed a hint of amused contempt as they looked upon his confused rival.

"Firstly—thank you—or thank your men—for my rescue. I am much obliged to you. It was foolish of me to trust those villains. I regret the trouble I have caused. . . ."

"No trouble," murmured the Queen. "But is there not some formal greeting, Your Majesty . . . ?"

He was grateful for the reminder. "Your Majesty, Queen Gloriana. Greetings from Poland." He frowned. "I am—we are Casimir—Emperor Elect of Greater Poland—you know that, eh? Just announced. There's a formal phrase, but I fear I've forgotten it—King of Scandinavia, what? And all the lands from the Baltic to the Black Sea. Great Jove! So I am. Well, it's a republic, of course. And a union of republics, essentially. Autonomous. But I serve my turn, I suppose, as a symbol. Oh, dear—I had a ring to give you. There are other presents. . . ." He looked behind him. "The presents? It was a lovely ring. . . . Didn't expect to have to appear in public like this. Rather shy of ceremonies. The presents . . . ?"

The Caliph was snapping his fingers for his own gifts, carried by turbaned boys. Gloriana inspected the usual treasures (including a necklace of carnelians and gold) and accepted them with ritual thanks, while Poland spoke anxiously to his aide, old Count Korzeniowski, and sent him on an errand.

"There were also several elephants, Your Majesty," the Caliph told her gravely, "but it was thought inadvisable to bring them onto the ice."

Una smiled behind her hand, imagining the effect of so many elephants losing their footing and crashing into the waters of the Thames.

There was a pause, after the Caliph's procession had come and gone. Casimir of Poland looked up. "Aha!" He waved. Another procession, of fur-clad footmen, with precious ikons and beautifully worked jewellery, lacking the magnificence of the Caliph's gifts but carrying the stamp of artists' perfection.

"There are some things missing, you see. Not much. We were lucky. But . . ." Casimir searched beneath his robes. "There was a ring. With a ruby. You might think it vulgar, of course. I had hoped . . . However, there is a time and a place, I know—don't have much in the way of formal ceremonies in Poland, these days—you must forgive me if I give offence. . . ."

"The gifts are exquisitely beautiful, King Casimir."

"They are, aren't they! But the ring . . . There was some fine Vienna stuff. Did that come? The ring. Gods! It's lost!"

"The brigands . . . ?" murmured Gloriana.

"The villains! The most beautiful of all my gifts."

"We shall catch the leader, never fear," she promised.

Lord Montfallcon cleared his throat to speak. "Her Majesty is grateful to both Your Majesties . . ."

Gloriana, recovering, nodded. "Albion welcomes thee, great kings. We are honoured by thine attendance at our ceremonies."

And chairs were fetched, almost thrones, for the two guests, both placed on the right of the Queen, and at angles so that one should not seem to take precedence, and the Countess of Scaith must smile and whisper and play host to the monarchs while the Queen received the rest of her guests:

Rudolf of Bohemia, the scientist-king, Casimir's vassal; Prince Alençon de Medici of Florenza, a youth whose chivalrous love for the Queen was famous; the Aztec ambassador, Prince Comius Sha-T'Lee of Chlaksahloo (who believed himself a demigod and Gloriana a goddess) in golden feathers and feathered cloak; the Chevalier Persivalle-Gallois of Britannia; Oubacha Khan, in painted armour, iron and fur, envoy from the Tatar Empire; Prinz Lobkowitz, in black and silver, from independent Prague; Prince Hira of Hindoostan, a protectorate of Albion's; Lord Li Pao, ambassador from the Court of Cathay, another vassal state; Lord Tatanka Iyotakay, ambassador from the great Sioux Nation, in eagle feathers and white beaded buckskins; the Lady Yashi Akuya, ambassadress from the Isles of Nipponia; Prince Karloman, the old king's son, to represent the Low Country Alliance; Count Rotomondo, Overlord of Paris; Master Ernst Schelyeanek, astronomer and physician, of Vienna; envoys from Virginia, amongst them hawk-nosed Lord Kansas and the tiny, contentious Baron of Ohio; Master Ishan the Mathematician from the Tatar protectorate of Anatolia; Caspar, the great engineer of Jawa; the Palestinian scholar Micah of Jerusalem; the explorer Murdoch, Thane of Hermiston, a white cape thrown carelessly over his plaids and bronze, a bonnet with white hawk's feathers jaunty on his red curls; and many more dignitaries, scholars, scientists, magicians, alchemists, engineers, adventurers and soldiers, taking more than an hour and a half to pass before the throne.

Then came the first entertainment, in torchlight, as the Ice Knight (Lord Gorius Ransley) and the Fire Knight (Sir Tancred Belforest) tilted in full armour, on horseback, on the frozen surface at the river's centre. Chips of ice flew, the breath of the horses was like dragons' vapour, metal rang as lance met shield and both were unhorsed at once.

Above them, on the embankment, leaning with elbows against stone to look down at this scene, stood a figure made shapeless by the huge bearskin coat clothing him from head to foot, the bear's skinned head forming a cap which hid the greater part of his face. Sometimes, when the light from the bouncing flames (on which geese and oxen now roasted) leapt high, his black, sardonic eyes would gleam.

Fire defeated Ice, according to arrangement.

Now he watched as the skating tumblers in the costumes of the Comedy—Harlekin and Pantalon, Cornetto and Isabella and the rest—began to leap and spin in time to the brisk and somewhat discordant music of the shivering consort on the platform, while beneath the awning the Queen bent her head to converse with her fellow sovereigns. Pages, their feet steadied by spiked irons, moved slowly through the gathering, bearing trays of boiling wine; cooks and their boys basted spitted meat; and on the far bank a huge scaffolding was being erected.

The figure in the bear coat left the wall and moved gradually down first one flight of steps and then another, until it stood with the crowd upon the ice, sipping a silver cup of claret, admiring the children of the nobles, Frost Fairies all, who carried the monstrous Twelfth Night Cake on a litter to the Queen, taking the meat and bread that he was offered and cramming it with some relish into his mouth as he continued to move here and there, keeping more by instinct than by judgement to the shadows, to the fringes of the crowd. There came a cracking from the far bank, a rush like mysterious wind as the observers gasped, and the first fireworks began to fizz and spin, forming a great "G" in an ornamental panel; then rockets shrieked and scattered diamond sparks and the whole of the ice was stark with sudden brilliance, causing the bearskinned figure to retreat a little to a corner where wharfsteps met wall. Flaring cartridges fell upon the ice, which hissed, causing alarm or feigned consternation amongst those who took heed of it.

Red and green fire bellowed and the scaffolding shifted a little once again, so that the ice appeared to creak.

Lord Montfallcon heard the sound and was instantly active, calling for Lord Rhoone, who stood with Lady Rhoone and their two children, talking to tiny Master Wheldrake and insouciant, swaying Lady Lyst. "Rhoone! D'ye hear?"

"What?" Lord Rhoone handed his cup to his elder boy who, glad of opportunity up to now denied him, began to sip.

"The ice, Rhoone. The ice is breaking. Out there."

"It's solid enough here, Montfallcon. It was tested. We still test it."

"Nevertheless . . ."

Rhoone rubbed at his beard, looking about him with some dismay. "Well . . ."

"We must transfer to the embankment." Lord Montfallcon looked to see the figure in the bear's coat moving casually up the steps, strolling into the darkness. More fireworks howled and burst. Lord Montfallcon glared at the figure, half-lifted his hand, then lowered it. "Your Majesties, my lords and ladies," he cried. "We must return to shore. The ice threatens to crack." But his voice could neither be heard above the roar and snap of the fireworks which still blazed, nor above the laughter and shouts of a drunken crowd.

Montfallcon pushed urgently through until he reached Gloriana's side. She was laughing at something the King of Poland had just said, to Hassan al-Giafar's annoyance, her face shining as she watched the explosions which grew louder and brighter in increasingly rapid sequence.

"The ice, madam. There's a danger it might collapse!"

A blinding burst of light and heat. Her lips parted. "Ah!"

"The ice is breaking!" screamed Montfallcon. "Your Majesty! The ice is breaking!"

The figure in the bearskin moved beside the embankment wall again, through the trees, looking back at the throng, hearing Montfallcon's voice as it called now into silence. He paused to watch as slowly the gathering began to move, following the Queen. She left the ice and returned to her carriage. Then, with an amused lift of his shoulder, he ducked down behind a shrub, through a gap in the West Minster wall, and out into a narrow alley which would take him eastward to a house where further entertainment awaited him.

In the Queen's sleigh, side by side, sat Poland and Arabia, while opposite them was the Queen herself, with her companion, the Countess of Scaith.

Shaggy Casimir the Fourteenth was in high spirits. "It's been fine adventure, since I came to Albion! By the gods, Your Majesty, I am glad I made my decision! If I'd come in state, with all my fleet and gentlemen, I'd have had a duller time, and no mistake."

Hassan al-Giafar put the nail of the little finger of his right hand to a gap between his front teeth and picked at a piece of meat, staring moodily out of the window at the retreating river. "There was really no danger," he said. "The ice is still firm."

"My Lord Montfallcon exists night and day only for the Queen's safety," said Una with a smile of irony.

The young Caliph scowled. "Do you permit this man to monitor your every decision, madam?"

Gloriana was dismissive. "He has protected me since I was born. I fear that I am so used to it, Your Majesty, that I should feel strange without Montfallcon clucking somewhere in the background."

King Casimir was shocked. "Hermes, madam! Are you never free?" He laid an innocent and sympathetic hand upon the Queen's knee.

Gloriana found herself with a further problem in diplomacy, but she was rescued from it as the sleigh struck an obstacle and Casimir was flung, chuckling, back on his cushions, sliding against Hassan, who sniffed: "If this Montfallcon were my vizier, I should have him whipped for spoiling my entertainment."

Gloriana smiled.

"But then, of course, I am a man," said the Grand Caliph of Arabia.

"It's true that women do tend to be more merciful," observed King Casimir. "To abolish death by hanging from your land and replace it with exile seems to me an ideal solution, if one suffers at all from conflict of conscience. I, of course, am not bothered with such conflicts, since my power comes to me from the Parliament."

"That is no power at all, in my opinion." Hassan was determined to be contentious.

"Actually it is the same, if one accepts that power is given to one as a responsibility by the people one serves, eh?"

"I think we are all agreed on that." Gloriana strove, as usual, for equilibrium.

The palace was reached and with bows and curtseys they went

to their separate lodgings to enrobe themselves in their costumes and study their parts for the Masque.

Gloriana was met by Lord Montfallcon as she returned. "I must apologise, Your Majesty, for cutting short the entertainment. It seemed to me . . ."

Gloriana nodded dumbly. The strain of maintaining a balance of attention between the haughty Hassan and the confused Casimir had been greater than she had expected, and she would be glad of the hour she had to herself. "You do your duty, my Lord Chancellor, as I do mine," she murmured. Her smile was thin. "Now you must don your disguise and join in the pleasure of the Masque. Do you know your lines?"

"I intend to read them, madam. There has not been time. . . ."

"Of course. In an hour, then, my lord." With a guilty movement of her hand she passed into her apartments and allowed the doors to be closed, for once, against her watchdog.

Lady Mary Perrott came forward, looking a little weary, as usual. Gloriana raised her arms. "Strip me off, Mary." She removed her crown with a sigh. "And then, I pray you, stroke me for a while, to rid me of my aches and pains."

Lady Mary took the crown and gestured for the maids to disrobe the Queen. Her own costume was ready, near Gloriana's.

She was to go as a Valkyrie while her demanding lover Sir Tancred went as Baldur.

In her own rooms, the Countess of Scaith inspected the jewelled casket which had been sent to her. She read the note, in Hassan's own hand. It thanked her for her courtesies and kindnesses (she recalled none) and begged her to remember him to the Queen with great affection. Una shook her head as her maids unlaced her, wondering if she should tell the Queen of this development or leave the story for an airing when they both relaxed. She decided on the latter.

In nothing but her shift she resumed her position on the couch, took another pipe of tobacco and cast her eyes over Master Wheldrake's opening lines for the Masque.

In Winter, when the Year burns low
As Fire wherein no firebrands glow,
And Winds dishevel as they blow
The lovely stormy wings of snow,
The hearts of Northern men burn bright
With Joy that mocks the Joy of Spring
To hear all Heaven's keen clarions ring
Music that bids the Spirit sing
And Day gives thanks for Night.

They lacked his usual intensity, she thought, but then he was usually reluctant to write for the Court Entertainments, and it seemed that of late he had been particularly distracted, spending most of his time with that ruined intelligence, that fragile beauty, the haunted Lady Lyst.

The pipe smoked, Una considered her costume; then, with an effort, got to her feet and moved to the cupboard where it was kept. Her fellow Norns, the Lady Rhoone and Lady Cornfield, would expect her to be on time.

Una paused, looking about her, certain that she was watched, but the room was empty save for herself and the maid's cat. She looked up into the shadows of the ceiling where a small grille admitted air, then shrugged and reached for her corselet.

In the Great Hall of the palace, decorated now in symbolic representation of icy mountains and doomy skies, the masquers took their sieges, wearing furs and brass and silver and all the barbaric magnificence of some Arctic castle's denizens, while the audience, comprising most of those who had been presented earlier to the Queen, sat, rank upon rank, in chairs, and the musicians in the gallery began to play the music composed by Master Harvey for the occasion, full of sonorous horns and bass viols.

The Countess of Scaith, in hood and black fur, had already spoken her gloomy introduction and stood back so that Odin and

Freyja might come forward. Odin, in eye-patch and flop-brimmed hat, a stuffed raven swaying on his shoulder, a plaster head in one hand, was played by reluctant Lord Montfallcon. Queen Gloriana played Freyja.

Lady Rhoone, as Skaal, the Norn of the Future, gave her lines in a voice to rival her huge husband's (Lord Rhoone played Thor):

Now Fimbul Winter falls upon the fields,
The Age of Knife and Axe and Cloven Shields,
And violent deeds are wreak'd on men of peace
While Odin, holding Mimer's sever'd head,
Plans the Last Fight 'gainst those living and those dead,
And in Black Grief's Gulf the Fenris wolf's releas'd!

Awkwardly Lord Montfallcon held the plaster head aloft and read from the page he tried to hide, while in the farthest rank poor Wheldrake winced and clutched at his body, feeling an agony he could never experience at Lady Lyst's hand.

Hearken! Heimdal's horn is blown
And nine worlds wake!
Across our ancient bridge the Giants do come
And Bifrost breaks!
Soon Skoll shall swallow up the sun
The world-ash quakes!

It was now Gloriana's turn. She had seen Master Wheldrake and wondered if his grief were not, in some degree, inspired by guilt. She drew breath and, as Freyja, intoned:

On Ironwood's hill Storm Eagle's wings
Flap wild wind across the world
While in Midgard commoners and kings
To Hela all are hurl'd
And Fjular-Suttung in disguise goes he
To steal the Sword of Victory.

Next, burly Lord Rhoone, as Thor, sporting a good-sized hammer:

The Gods of Asgard do not fear their Dusk
But to the Battle gladly go.
I'll dare the Midgard serpent's tearing tusk,
Destroy mankind's most deadly foe,
Then die midst fire and snow!

And on in this vein for a while before Una must step forward again to conclude the Masque with:

Thus Ragnarok is come and gods lie dead!
In noble conflict were they slain —
Bluff Thor, sly Loke, fair Frey—none fled
The final battle or the fiercest pain.
And so the World's New Age they ascertain'd
That Glorious Albion might their burden bear
While in Albion's Glory shall the whole globe share!

Una noticed that Master Wheldrake had not waited for the applause but was already, with desperate glance to Lady Lyst, sliding from the hall. It seemed to Una that if the quality of Master Wheldrake's masques continued in this course then the Queen must soon admit that a new poet should be found for the Court, but the hands of the audience were clapped with gusto and Casimir and Hassan leapt forward, almost colliding, to congratulate Gloriana on the beauty of her performance, the nobility of the lines, the wisdom of the sentiments, the appropriate sonorousness of the music, and Una was able to slip behind one of the screens on which the scenes had been painted and tear off her uncomfortable hood, finding that Lady Lyst was already there, giggling uncontrollably to herself. Fearing that if she caught Lady Lyst's eye she would also be infected, Una returned to the front and was immediately taken up by Lord Montfallcon, who was almost gay. He was most definitely warmer than usual towards her, for he disliked her, regarding her as a rival to the Queen's ear, a disruptive voice that lured the

Queen away from duty. "Fine words, eh?" said Montfallcon. "Wheldrake excelled himself this Twelfth. We must give him a knighthood in the spring. I'll speak to the Queen. 'That Glorious Albion might their burden bear, While in Albion's Glory shall the whole globe share!' Very true, eh?"

Delighting to find their normal rôles so thoroughly reversed, Una grinned, "Oh, yes, my lord! Very true, my lord!"—and heard a further burst from behind the screen. She moved, with Montfallcon on her arm, towards the centre of the Great Hall, where the Queen enjoyed the flattery of kings and princes and, in her present mood, might set an earldom on the shoulders of the poet whom, a few minutes before, she had been ready to thrash as thoroughly as, in his secret thoughts, he desired. Thus with inadequate verse did Master Wheldrake find honour and lose the only reward he would ever value.

Doctor Dee passed by, giving his close attention to the words of his old friend King Rudolf of Bohemia, who was explaining the results of his latest experiments.

"And was the transmutation then attained?" asked Dee. Una saw him lift his eye in one swift, stealthy glance at the Queen's neck.

"Unfortunately the success was only partial. The theme of the Masque reminds me of something I was reading concerning the true nature of the dwarves who featured in the old sagas. They were, in fact, powerful sorcerers, not originally of this planet, who journeyed from another world, bearing with them all the alchemical secrets they had learned there. This is the basis of our own fragmentary scientific knowledge, you see. If their writings could be found—perhaps somewhere in the North Pole—we should truly be embarking on a new age in mankind's history. I have sent out three or four expeditions, but unfortunately none has, as yet, returned. . . ."

The music, lively and delicate now, had begun again and, still in costume, masquers joined with audience in the Trippe, a complicated form of gallimard, which was currently in fashion, but not at all suited to someone dressed in the costume of the Norn of the Present. Una of Scaith began to look forward to the Feast.

* * *

In the wide yard of the Gryffyn Inn there blazed a magnificent Twelfth Night bonfire hot enough to warm everyone who stood around it. Hot enough to warm even those who lounged in the open galleries above, pouring beer upon the heads of friends and enemies, guffawing at the antics of the troupe of dwarf fiddlers who pranced in a circle around the fire and squeaked and scraped in a boisterous parody of music. Feeling for the parts of their companions denied them, for one reason or another, through the earlier days of the festival, tearing at pieces of meat and bread and cheese, capering, dancing or merely swaying from side to side, pissing, farting and vomiting in less than private corners of the innyard, claiming everlasting affection for acquaintances of that night or eternal hatred for their oldest comrades, they filled every space. The cold air seemed to burn and was rich enough to nourish anyone who breathed it, carrying as it did the fumes of boiled beef and roasted fowls, of wine and rum, of sweat and spunk, of blistering wood and melted snow. There came yells of laughter from all corners of the inn, and sometimes, as when Tinkler was pushed backwards into the fire by a doxy who did not favour him, the laughter was so loud that the timbers trembled. Here, too, were professional clowns—some of those who had earlier entertained the Queen herself—the zanies, the harlekin, the bragging, strutting gallant, the old dotard, the beautiful ladies—in clothes of an Italian cut, though most of them were native to London—in their cups thanks to the Queen's gold and giving to this audience free what the Queen had paid for.

Into the noisy mob, with his arm about the waist of his paramour, stalked cocky Captain Quire, his sword jutting behind him like the wagging tail of a triumphant mongrel who has found the way into the butcher's store. The elaborate white and silver costume of his companion, the little tinsel crown upon the coiffured head, face powdered white, eyes hugely exaggerated, lips a startling crimson, were in evident parody of the Queen as she had appeared during the festivities on the ice.

Tinkler, patting at the back of his singed coat, staggered up to greet his master and was shocked. "Hermes, Captain, what's this?"

"Our very own queen, Tink, come to see her people. Pay your respects, Sir Tinkler. Let's see you make a good leg."

And Tinkler, infected as always by Quire's confidence, fell in with the charade at once and bowed deep, whipping off his tattered cap, his gag tooth twisting upwards in a grin. "Welcome, Your Majesty—to the—the Court of King Booze!" He giggled and staggered, grabbing hold of dark-chinned Hogge who passed with two tankards in either hand. "May I present to Your Majesty Lord Grunt of Hogge and"— he pulled on the wrist of the wench who had pushed him into the fire—"Lady Sow, his beautiful wife." She pushed him again and he sat down in the slushy mud of the yard, still grinning. "But which queen is it we honour? What's her name?"

"Why, it's Philomena," said Quire, struggling from the bear-skin coat to reveal his own black cloak beneath. From his belt he took his folded sombrero and smoothed it out, brushing at the crow's feathers. "Queen Philomena—the Queen of Love!" Quire pinched his queen upon the painted cheek, upon the silken bottom, and caused a simper, though the huge, hot eyes were also a little startled, a little wary. The pair moved closer to the bonfire and Quire took one of Hogge's tankards for himself, another for the Queen. "Ladies and Gentlemen of the Gryffyn. A cheer, if you please, for your sovereign, Queen Philomena, who dubs this night a Night of Love and bids you celebrate in her name."

As the crowd began to cheer, and some of them cried out bawdy promises to Quire's queen, the captain looked about him in mock astonishment.

"I see no throne. What's become of it? Where's the Queen's great Chair of State? What shall she sit upon?"

The answer was loud and conventional. Quire continued to play to the crowd. He held up his hands. "You are bad hosts. Sir Harlekin here will tell you that the Queen's guests were better treated." He put his arm around the patch-coated shoulder of the comedian, who hiccupped theatrically in his face and scratched his eye under his mask. "All had chairs, did they not?"

"They did, sir."

"Good, solid chairs?"

"Excellent chairs, sir. Your queen's a beauty and I'd swear she's —"

But already a large, high-backed chair was being passed over the heads of the mob and placed so that it was framed by the firelight behind. Again Quire bowed. "Be seated, madam, if you please." With an awkward curtsey the mock queen sat and stared around at the new-found Court who, slack-mouthed, stared back. It seemed that she was drunk, or drugged, for her eyes were glazed and her own mouth moved oddly, though she showed lechery enough for Quire whenever he tickled her and licked her ear and whispered into it.

"Oh, Phil, how you'd satisfy the Caliph now—so much better than the real Queen." Quire grinned, and hugged his concubine tighter.

And Phil Starling, gone quite Eros-mad, simpered at his lover, his master, and looked at the wonderful ruby ring upon his finger and could not believe that such riches could be his.

The Tenth Chapter

In Which Some of the Queen's Subjects
Consider a Variety of Alchemical, Philosophical
and Political Problems

"It seemed so permanent," said Lady Lyst, kneeling on her window seat and looking down into the February morning. "I thought the snow had come to stay for ever. Look, Wheldrake, it's melting. See, crocuses and snowdrops!" She stared over her shoulder at her untidy room, scattered with books, papers, ink, instruments, dresses, bottles, stuffed animals and living birds, where her tiny crimson-combed lover strutted, in a black dressing gown, a sheet of paper in one hand and a pen in the other.

"Um," he said. "Well, spring won't be long now. Listen —" and he quoted the sheet:

"And Ada's Ardour's slowly growing cold
'Neath leaden hammer blows
Of Slavic Prose,
As picking at his Academic nose
He'll pass in Public as a Wit
And Labouring Iron transmute to Gold.

"Well, what d'you think? Got 'im, eh?"

"But I don't know who you're talking about," she said. "A rival poet? Really, Wheldrake, you become increasingly obscure and decreasingly inventive as time goes on."

"No! It's him! *He* grows obscure!" Master Wheldrake's arms flapped as if some primitive pterosaur tried desperately to take to the air for the first time. "Not *me*!"

"You, too. And I don't know *him*." Her lovely blue eyes were wider than ever as they regarded him with a certain distant sadness; her lovely golden hair fell in unruly strands across her golden face. "And I doubt, Wheldrake, dear, from your tone, if he knows *you*."

"Damn him!" Wheldrake stalked, as best he could, through the rubble of her room. Parrots and macaws cackled and fled for the thicker growths of ivy near the ceiling. "He's rich—because he panders to the public. Makes 'em think they're intelligent! Bah! While I'm here for ever, dependent on the Queen's patronage, when all I want is her respect."

"She said how much she liked the last Masque, and Montfallcon murmured of an imminent knighthood."

"I'm wasting my time, Lucinda, writing indifferent attacks on rival poets, self-pitying verse against women who've rejected me, and earning my keep by writing elephantine, grandiloquent farts to be performed by the Court's Philistines. My poetry, my old poetry, is slipping away from me. I lack stimulus. . . ."

"Arioch, Wheldrake! I'd have thought you'd have had enough of that to last you through a hundred sonnets at least!"

He frowned and began his return flight, ink from his pen splashing upon her upturned chests and draperies, her half-read metaphysical tomes, crumpling the paper as he came. "I told you. No more scourges."

She turned again to the window. She was neutral. "Perhaps you should return to your North Country, to your borders?"

"Where I'm even more misunderstood. I'd considered a journey to Arabia. I have an affinity, I believe, with Arabia. What did you think of the Grand Caliph?"

"Well, he was very Arabian. He had a good opinion of himself, I think." Lady Lyst vaguely scratched her ribs.

"He was confident."

"Aye, he was that." She yawned.

"He impressed the Queen, you could tell, with his exotic sensuality. So much more than poor, bumbling Poland."

"She was kind to Poland," said Lady Lyst.

"Yet both departed, frustrated in their ambitions, with Albion unconquered. They made the mistake of laying siege when they should have delivered themselves as captives at her feet."

Lucinda Lyst was dry. "You invent a Gloriana for yourself, I think. There's no evidence. . . ."

He blushed so that skin and hair were, for one radiant moment, of the same colour. He began to uncrumple his satire. A maid came in. "A visitor, your ladyship. The Thane."

"Good. It's the Thane, Wheldrake. A fellow countryman."

"Scarcely." Wheldrake sniffed and came to join her on the window seat, lounging a little theatrically, unaware that he had exposed a scrawny knee.

Gaunt but hearty, in strode the Thane of Hermiston, in flapping filibeg and monstrous bonnet, his sporran slapping and his hands already on his hips as he jutted out his red beard and grinned down at the couple. "Ye're a pretty pair, just fresh from yer beds, eh, like lazy kittens. Well, well, well!"

Wheldrake brandished his accomplishment. "I have been writing, sir, a poem!" His voice squeaked with passionate indignation. "It has taken me all morning!"

"Oh, has it indeed? It has taken *me* all morning, Master Wheldrake, to cross five worlds, just to come here to pay a call upon old friends."

Lady Lyst clapped her hands once, then paused, startled by the sound. "And what have you brought back from those metaphysical regions?"

"Your usual rude romances?" Wheldrake was sceptical. "Tales of gods and demons, of swords and sorcery?"

The Thane of Hermiston ignored the jibes. "I thought I'd captured a beast, but when I arrived here, it was gone. I intend, later, to confer with Master Tolcharde, who invented the carriage in which I travelled to those spheres."

"A carriage pulled by spirits, eh?" said Wheldrake. "The spirits which drugged you and made you dream."

The Thane laughed heartily. "I like ye, Master Wheldrake, for ye're a fine sceptic, like meself. I'd brought this beast, I told you. A great reptile. A veritable dragon. 'Tis called an aligarta."

"Virginia has them in her southern counties," said Master

Wheldrake. "They swarm in the swamps and rivers. Huge beasts. I have seen one stuffed. Like the Tigris crockodyl."

"But this is bigger," said the Thane, and sulked. "Or was," he added. "Master Tolcharde's carriage rocked and roared so, and I'd swear its invisible attendants played tricks upon the poor mortal they escorted. I caught my head a terrible blow, having already battled two demigods and survived unscathed."

"By Hermes, sir, I'll never know if you believe it all, inspired by that foul distilled grain you drink, or if you lie because you think it entertains."

The Thane took this well. "Neither, Master Poet—it's simpler. I tell the truth. I had a unicorn, too, but it was eaten by the aligarta."

"You journey through lands that are nought but mere metaphors! The sort we poets can invent daily!"

"But I'm no poet to invent such places. I visit 'em, instead. Lady Lyst, d'ye come with me to Master Tolcharde's manufactory?"

"I'll dress."

"I'll come too." Wheldrake was jealous, though he knew the friendship was innocent. "Unless there are secrets the chosen alone may share."

"There are no secrets, Master Wheldrake—only knowledge. It is the open knowledge men always reject, though they look everywhere for secrets."

As they dressed, the Thane poked about the room, picking up half-written theses, abandoned by Lady Lyst, opening books of philosophy and mathematicks and history, on alchemy and astronomy, being interested by none of them. He was a man of action. He preferred to test a metaphysical guess with the point of his sword if possible. Out they came again, Lady Lyst in rumpled blue silk, Master Wheldrake in black velvet, the pleats of his ruff unstarched and hanging loose around his throat, and they followed the gaudy Thane as he marched from the apartments, through the royal corridors, up the royal staircases, along the royal galleries, until they reached an older part of the palace, the East Wing, and could detect acrid smells, as of smelting iron and cooking chemicals, took one wide, near-derelict marble staircase, two flights of granite steps, and came to a gallery hung with faded lace, with a great dusty fanlight above it, to let in the morning's watery rays, to a tall door which, in contrast to the roof and columns of the gallery, was cast in an ancient near-barbaric mould, the pointed style, with pitted timber, brass and black iron.

Upon this the Thane of Hermiston flung a fist, so that it shook and rattled and was opened almost immediately by a bespectacled, blinking youth, one of Master Tolcharde's many apprentices, in leather apron and shirtsleeves, whose scowl cleared as he recognised the Thane. "Good morning, sir."

"Good morning to ye, Colvin. Is your master at his business or can we enter?"

"He's expecting you, I think, sir." Young Colvin stepped aside and they all filed in, to dusty gloom, while he closed the door carefully behind them and locked it. A little smoke drifted into the antechamber, almost as if brought by curiosity to spy upon the visitors. Yellowed astrological tables peeled on the walls, while below them were stacked dusty, unused boxes and books. The smell was more intense, and Wheldrake began to cough, putting a kerchief to his mouth, afraid he might choke to death, coming last as they continued through several such chambers which opened out eventually into a vault so filled with curling copper tubing that it seemed they inhabited the guts of some extinct leviathan. Through this rococo maze they could see a bench on which retorts belched and, on the far side of the bench, a small, sharp-featured man with a fixed, unnatural grin, who sat watching the retorts and saying not a word.

Master Tolcharde appeared from behind a great copper sphere on which he had been hammering. "With this machine, Hermiston, I intend to send you off through Time!"

"Not today, I hope, Master Tolcharde."

"Not for months. There is still a great deal to do, both theoretically and mechanically. Doctor Dee is aiding me. He's not with you?" Master Tolcharde's fanatical and friendly eyes rolled this way and that. He exposed his broken teeth in an enquiring grin. He wiped his bald head on which sweat gathered.

The Thane shook bonneted locks. "But who's this?" A thumb for the little man on the other side of the bench.

"A traveller. He came here not long since, by means of a glowing pyramid which dissolved and stranded him."

Master Wheldrake turned away, studying his own features in the gleaming copper of the globe. "So there's an exchange between the worlds?"

"Aye," Master Tolcharde innocently responded. "The Thane brings many back—but many are taken, too. And some come and go without help of either the Thane or myself. If you would see some of the creatures . . ."

Master Wheldrake raised a wing. "On another day, sir. I would not waste your time."

"But I am always willing to instruct those whose search for Truth is genuine."

"Instruct me later, Master Tolcharde. You were telling us about your visitor."

"His name is Calhoun and he claims to be from the White Hall—to be a Baron, indeed. He understands much of my scientific philosophy, but little of aught else. He's sympathetic enough, however, of the same kidney as myself. But mad, d'you see? Aha! Here comes Doctor Dee."

In brown, with white points jutting from chin and neck, the great sage strode, greeting all with some gusto until his eye fell upon Lady Lyst and he became embarrassed. "Very pleasant . . . I regret I did not . . . ?"

Lady Lyst drew her brows together. She could think of no explanation for this display. "You promised me something, Doctor Dee?"

"Oh, madam, I beg thee. . . ." He cringed. "I beg thee!"

Lady Lyst's great eyes grew rounder still. "I'm at a loss, sir, but if my presence is unwelcome to you, I'd be pleased to leave."

"No, no. It is an honour to have so famous an intellect among us. Indeed, there is someone"—he looked behind him, through the curling tubes—"there he is—you must meet, if you have not already." Doctor Dee appeared to turn purple for a few seconds.

He pushed an index finger between ruff and throat. "Harrumph! Your Majesty!" In the darkness a voice cried:

"Here, Dee!" In a strong accent.

"King Rudolf. We are gathered near the sphere."

It was the young scientist-king of Bohemia, strolling enthusiastically towards the bench to peer upon the retorts, his hands behind his back, clad in hunting green; doublet and breeches and peaked cap. "What's this?"

"I would introduce you to Lady Lyst."

King Rudolf looked up with a smile. "We are old friends. We corresponded some years ago, when Lady Lyst's first treatise was published in Prague. And we have spoken once or twice since I've been visiting the Court. I am most flattered to be in such company. And we have met, also, I believe, Master Wheldrake. I admired your poems. Though lately, I've seen little. . . ."

"I am dead!" pronounced the miniature poet. "That is why. I have been dead for a long while."

"Then you have come to Doctor Dee for resurrection?"

Doctor Dee smiled. "My reputation is a burden, Your Majesty. Many come with just that request—on behalf of relatives and loved ones, of course. But if you are right, then Master Wheldrake's the first who's asked in person."

Wheldrake leaned his stiffening body against the curve of the globe.

"Perhaps you should ask Master Wheldrake to attend the Court of Bohemia," suggested Lady Lyst. "He claims we're Philistines here. And it's well known that the Elfbergs are great artists in their own right—and scientists."

Doctor Dee clapped the king on the back. "And this is the finest Elfberg of them all. Soldier, poet, scientist!"

"And I fear, a dreadful dilettante." The Bohemian king was charming. (He had published three excellent books of verse, two scientific treatises and a work on natural history, and had led the successful Macedonian campaign against the Tatar Empire some five years before.) Wheldrake loathed him mightily and consoled himself with a brooding line or two (*How condescending is this King /*

Who turns his hand to everything / Let's lesser folk his praises sing).

"Not as a scientist," said Wheldrake aloud.

Lady Lyst looked about the laboratory. "Perhaps we should offer the king hospitality, Master Tolcharde?"

"Eh?"

"A drink of wine, perhaps?" said Lady Lyst. "Have you some?" She added: "Or anything?" She picked up a large phial. "This?"

"That's the urine of a pregnant toad," Master Tolcharde said. "I don't think it's alcoholic."

Doctor Dee was helpfully knowledgeable. "Not urine, no. There are few kinds of urine which are . . ."

Lady Lyst had moved away from the bench, into the shadows, peering into alcoves. "What are these?"

"They are some of my mechanical comedians. I'm intending to make a whole set, then present them to the Queen."

The metal figures, life-size, swung like corpses on a gibbet, and clanked a little: Columbina, Pierro, Captain Fracasse, Scaramouche—the latest costumes, the figures of the fashionable Comédie Parisienne, in bright brass, silver and glowing enamels.

"Excellent," murmured Lady Lyst. She bent and picked up a dusty flask from the floor. "How do you give them life?"

"Cogs and springs, Lady Lyst, according to my own design." He patted a dangling leg, which seemed to twitch. He reached up to turn the elaborate puppet; it stared, with an impression of dignity, into the space above his head. "There are rods, yet, to be positioned—and a mainspring—otherwise I would demonstrate . . ."

The Thane of Hermiston had flung an arm around King Rudolf's shoulders and was pointing out some of the features of a baroque iron carriage on the far side of the vault, while Colvin kindly helped the senile Baron Calhoun from his chair and away into an antechamber. Doctor Dee joined Lady Lyst and Master Tolcharde to stare up at a silver-skirted Columbina as yet lacking hair, pirouetting, as if on an invisible surface.

"And who can say, Master Tolcharde, when your work is finished, whether these creatures are any less alive than we, of fresh and blood?" Doctor Dee became momentarily introspective. "Flesh and blood."

"Ah," said Master Tolcharde. "Indeed." He rubbed, in a perplexed way, at his glinting head.

Doctor Dee cocked a significant eye. "And how goes your other work, Master Tolcharde . . . ?"

"The sphere?"

"No, no. The work you do for me."

"Of course!" Master Tolcharde exposed his potion-stained teeth. "Almost ready, Doctor Dee. The final stages, however, must be left to you."

"I understand that." Doctor Dee brightened. "So it goes well?"

"Modestly, I must say that it is probably my finest creation. My skills, my ideas, seem at their peak. Inspiration comes, as ever, fast and furious, but increasingly I have the means of translating that inspiration into disciplined, practical invention. The Queen's praise, as always, spurs me. She was very pleased with the little falcon, so I heard, Lady Lyst."

"I heard the same. A pity you gave it no homing instinct. It flew off, over Norbury Woods, in pursuit of a plover, and never returned."

"They are easily made. I'll produce another soon." Contentedly Master Tolcharde turned back towards his benches.

Master Wheldrake handled a silver-framed mirror, of polished quartz, in which he saw his own birdlike features reflected and distorted. "A magic mirror, Master Tolcharde?"

"From the West Indies." Doctor Dee took it. "Brought by Sir Thomasin Ffynne. Part of some Iberian booty, I gather, and originally used for summoning the images of gods (or demons) by the priests of the Ashtek Empire. Up until now we have had no success with it. It is always difficult, and sometimes dangerous, in these cases, to try incantations and potions at random. But we persevere, Master Wheldrake, in the Cause of Science." He placed the mirror into a box of plain, polished wood and put the box under his arm. "The king seems ready to stay a while. I'll let the Thane escort him and get on with my appointments. I thank you, Master Tolcharde, for your good news. Lady Lyst." He bowed. "Master Wheldrake."

His brown gown lifting, as if he were about to ascend into the air, he hurried through the tangle of tubes towards the door.

Making the long, complicated journey back to the modern court, Doctor Dee left the old part of the palace behind and had reached the brighter, airier atmosphere of the Long Gallery when he came upon two of his fellow ministers in conversation with Sir Thomasin Ffynne himself. The admiral wore plain black and white and was dressed for the open sea rather than the Court, in contrast to the lavish brocades, starched ruffs, puffed velvets, stomachers and chains of his companions, Lord Ingleborough and Lord Montfallcon.

Montfallcon's bow to Dee was small and stiff, but Ffynne greeted him with the somewhat patronising good humour he usually reserved for Dee, whom Sir Thomasin regarded as a harmless and pleasant old eccentric serving the Queen rather as a jester might. "Good morrow, Doctor Dee! How go the spells and charts?" He had made use of Doctor Dee's excellent geography more than once and, in return, had added information to the sage's store.

"You are returned from another voyage, Sir Thomasin?"

"Your sense of dates is not your strongest point, Dee." Tom Ffynne's shrewd eyes shrank as he laughed and stamped his ivory foot upon the marble tiles. "I've been back from the Indies scarcely more than a month. No, I'm off this morning to trade with Tatary and take tolls from any Iberian ships I find in the waters we protect. I've come from the Queen a few moments since." He held up a packet. "And have my documents. Now I bid farewell to my old friends. The *Tristram and Isolde* awaits me at Charing Cross, and the river's free enough of ice to make the journey to the sea. So I go while I can. A month on land's too much for me. I'll keep an eye out for trinkets, Doctor Dee, of the sort you seek."

"I'm always obliged to you, Sir Thomasin." With a nod to Ingleborough and Montfallcon he was bustling on. "A safe journey, sir. Farewell! Oh! My apologies, boy!" He had bumped into Patch the page. "It's you. Good lad. Charming. Farewell!"

Patch moved to be closer to his master. Ingleborough smiled fondly. "Are you harmed, Patch? What a blunderer is Dee!"

"In all things," agreed Lord Montfallcon, scowling at the brown robe as it turned a corner, "save cunning. It pains me that he should so influence the Queen."

"But in no important way," said Tom Ffynne. "And, besides, my navigation's considerably improved by his knowledge. He is not altogether a fool. He has done much for the mariner, Perion."

Lord Montfallcon ignored this unwelcome praise. He folded his arms upon his broad old chest and looked down at his friend. "You must be careful, Tom, to abjure piracy. Particularly in the Middle Sea where witnesses abound. And no Moorish ships. No ships of Poland—and none, of course, of Tatary, at this time."

"That leaves Iberia, the Low Countries, a few independents . . ."

"Fair game, surely," said the Lord High Admiral, in thoughtless support of a disappointed Ffynne. Absently, with a gnarled hand, he stroked the head of Patch. "Eh?"

"You know the rule, Tom. Do nothing to embarrass the Queen. Do nothing to bring shame to Albion. Do nothing to complicate my diplomacy."

Tom Ffynne let loose a high-pitched chuckle. "Oh, aye—do nothing, in short. Methinks I'll stay in the Narrow Sea and try a little fishing. If the herring nation is still uninvolved in your plots, Perion!"

Montfallcon was adamant. "I know you will respect the Queen's honour, Tom."

Ingleborough nodded, becoming grave. "Albion is an example to the world."

"I'll remember. Well . . ." He put out two scarred, strong little hands and gripped the arms of his friends. "Let not the air of this peaceful Court lull you too softly or you'll sleep so well you'll never wake. And look to your health, Lisuarte."

Ingleborough touched his pale cheek. "I merely suffer the common ailments of the winter. When you return, Tom, I'll be ruddy and as active as ever."

Then Sir Thomasin Ffynne turned on his ivory heel and rolled, *clack-slap, clack-slap*, away.

Montfallcon and Ingleborough, with the beautiful lad following a yard or two behind, continued their journey, upon a constitutional they often made when exercise outside was impossible, and their steps took them gradually from the populated, busy corridors of the palace towards the East Wing, into the parts John Dee had recently left behind, though they went deeper, through wider, vaster halls, full of decaying pageantry—banners, armour, weapons—dull and dusty, into the echoing gloom of that cathedral of tyranny, the Throne Room of Gloriana's father, King Hern, where rats ruled now, and spiders danced their precise, oft-repeated steps; where shadows moved, scuffled, and were gone. Here only one beam of light entered directly: it fell upon a mosaic floor silvered by the trails of slugs and snails. In that pool of light Hern's captives—any prisoner or perhaps a courtier who had fallen from favour—were once displayed to those who, with Hern, hid themselves in the shadows. The throne remained; its shape asymmetrical, its back like a warped half-globe, on a dais reached by thirteen black steps. Here Ingleborough and Montfallcon came to remind themselves of the iron past they had plotted to destroy and against the return of which they still worked. It was cold; but the two old men remembered when braziers had burned in the glooms, their bloody coals stinking and hissing. They remembered the whisperings, the vengeances planned and taken, the poison, the corruption of any innocent spirit who ventured into this arena.

Their human figures were dwarfed by obsidian statues of grotesque and anthropoidal aspect—brooding statues, perhaps still dreaming of the heated, morbid and fantastical past, when Hern's Throne Room rang with the wailing of wretched victims and the coarse laughter of the drunken, the degenerate and the despairing, too fascinated or too frightened to depart from the addictive atmosphere accompanying the indulgence of self-hating Hern's horrible appetites.

The place disturbed Patch, who moved closer to his master and took his hand, for comfort. "Was King Hern mad?" he whispered. "Was he, sir?"

"His madness brought wealth to Albion," Montfallcon answered. "Possessions of all kinds. For though he had no political ambition, in the ordinary sense, he encouraged such rivalries amongst his courtiers that they were forever adding to their own wealth and Albion's. However, towards the end, it was almost certain that everything would be lost. Our enemies were ready to snatch them from us, for they thought we should have civil war on Hern's death. Instead, young Queen Gloriana ascended the throne—thanks to the efforts of men like your master and myself—and in the thirteen years of her rule our world has changed from a Realm of dreadful darkness into one of golden light."

"The only pity of it all," said Ingleborough sadly, "is that we should have been touched by Hern's madness. There isn't one of us from that time who was not in some way corrupted, distorted or harmed."

"Not the Queen!" insisted Montfallcon.

Lord Ingleborough shrugged.

"And not you, sir!" said Patch to his master in loyal astonishment.

"Lord Montfallcon and myself served King Hern and served him well, make no mistake. But we dreamed of nobler future, Albion's Periclean Age, if you like. We guarded Gloriana as the symbol of our hope, turning the king against those who supported him most strongly, filling his poor mad brain with evidence of plots against him so that gradually he destroyed the worst of his supporters and employed the best—men like ourselves who had no stomach for the things that went on daily in this room. . . ." Ingleborough sighed and hugged the boy to him. "And the Queen has nine children, none of whom are legitimate. It terrifies me. She will not deny that they are hers. She cannot name the sires. If she should die . . . oh, it would be Chaos. Yet, if she should marry . . ."

"Strife," said Montfallcon. "Sooner or later. Certainly, if it were a man of Albion, such as we should wish, it would silence certain tongues. But she'll only marry the one who will bring her to—who will give her peace. . . . And none has ever succeeded." He looked up at the grinning statues. "Gloriana falls—and Albion falls back to this—or worse—inturned, cynical, greedy, unjust and weak—we should become small again and we should rot. Arabia wishes to preserve what we have gained, there's no question of it—but Arabia would rule Albion, and thus disaster would come, inevitably. Arabia is too intractable, too proud, too masculine . . .

We survive through the Queen, her character, her very sex. She fills our people with her own idealism, with a sense of all that is best in Albion. Indeed, she infects the world. But as some men would drag the sun from the heavens so that it might be theirs alone, so do some who love Gloriana most see her as the fulfilment of their private desires: unable to see that Albion created her as much as she has created this Albion, and that if they destroy the root they destroy the blossom, too."

"Is there no prince, I wonder," said Ingleborough, "in all the world, who would give himself to Albion so that he might then win Gloriana?"

"None we have met." Montfallcon turned suddenly, thinking he had seen a tall figure moving behind the statues. He smiled at himself. "And no-one who matches nobility of spirit with the means of comforting the Queen. By Xiombarg! Enough have tried, Lisuarte. Soon, I think, she must reconcile herself. . . ."

"I fear a reconciled Queen might also become a moody Queen—a careless Queen—for I have it in my mind that Albion and Gloriana's circumstance are interdependent—that should she ever lose hope, then Albion's hope, too, vanishes." Ingleborough led Patch by the hand from the old Throne Room. Montfallcon hesitated for a moment before following them.

As they left there came a rustling behind the throne itself and, cautiously, the ragged, unkempt frame of the mad woman rose to stand with one hand upon the chair's black arm, poised on tiptoe, alert in case they should return. Then she danced gracefully down the steps, curtseyed once to the empty throne, and drifted away into the shadows as mist might join smoke.

Jephraim Tallow, who had been following her, emerged, standing with hands on hips, cat on shoulder, to look about him. He had lost the mad woman.

"Well, Tom, she's led us nowhere. I'd hoped for a pantry, at least. I think we've exhausted her possibilities as a guide and must find some other old inhabitants to show us more secrets."

He stalked to where a narrow stair ran up the wall to a gallery. He climbed. He found a bell-shaped arch and went through, crossing a narrow bridge with a parapet higher than his head. Above was darkness. Below were echoes, perhaps the sound of water. He walked quickly, found more steps and then was opening a door which took him onto a little balcony, set into a tower, and he was in daylight. He shivered, glancing down once at the two figures far below in the garden, before he went inside again.

Oubacha Khan, son of the Lord of the Western Horde and ambassador from Tatary to the Court of Gloriana the First, clad in a long ponyskin coat that reached to his ankles, ponyskin boots that reached to his knees, and a cap of chainmail lined with wool, was walking the grey garden with the Lady Yashi Akuya who, kimono-clad, was forced to take several little steps for every stride of his but, since she was secretly in love with the thin Tatar, she bore all discomfort (including the cold) with an eager smile. Tatary and Nipponia had long been traditional enemies, which was why the two found one another's company so comforting at this alien Court.

Certain that they were not observed in their distant and forgotten garden, they spoke casually of the matters most frequently upon their minds.

"Last night it was the little ones again, and the swimming pool," the Lady Yashi Akuya informed Oubacha Khan, "or so I had it from my girl." (She had introduced a geisha to Gloriana's seraglio and now the geisha sent regular reports.)

"Followed by some obscure activity involving toy sheep, as I understand it," said the young Khan, fingering long moustaches and causing Lady Yashi Akuya to blush. He maintained his own spy, Mauretanian, to keep him informed not of Gloriana's specific amusements (if amusements they were) but of her condition, of her state of mind and her state of health. Several nations pursued a theory of diplomacy based very closely on their own interpretations of Gloriana's private misery.

"But without result, as usual," added the Lady Yashi sympathetically. She suffered much as Gloriana suffered, but rather less intensely. Also, she was convinced that she would soon know the pleasures of orgasm, when Oubacha Khan at last decided to have his will with her.

"She remains frustrated."

The Nipponian ambassadress made a small noise through her rounded lips.

"And no suggestion that either Poland or Arabia visited her secret apartments?"

"None. Though both were eager. Attempts were made. Notes were sent, and the like. But in the end Poland left, assured of a sister in the Queen, while Arabia consoled himself with a page or two and—this is a mere rumour—the Countess of Scaith."

"He hoped the Countess would provide a way to Gloriana. We can reasonably guess that it was with this in mind that he broke a lifetime's habit." The Tatar ambassador uttered a frosty chuckle to disguise the jealousy he felt. Although he had absolutely no ambitions concerning the Queen, he had for two years entertained a passion for her closest friend and would have courted her long since, had he not, when leaving home, taken the vow of celibacy demanded of all Tatar nobles who went as emissaries to foreign lands.

"And yet," said Lady Yashi Akuya enthusiastically, "both Arabia and Poland appear to have committed themselves even more closely to their alliance with Albion."

The Tatar nodded. "It is a tribute to Gloriana's innocence and Montfallcon's guile. I had thought, by ensuring Lord Shahryar's discovery of the truth concerning Montfallcon's part in his nephew's murder, that I had provided a substantial subject for contention, but evidently Arabian ambition is so great they would relinquish all honour if it meant one slender chance of winning the Queen." He was disapproving now. "If such a thing had happened to a Tatar, vengeance would have been taken immediately, no matter what the political gains at stake."

Extended lashes fluttered. "Honour is not dead," she said, "in Nipponia, either."

He put habitual prejudice behind him. "The Nippon Isles are a synonym for selflessness," he told her generously. "Our two nations stand alone as upholders of the old values in a world where pacifism has become a creed in itself. I am all for peace, of course—but a proper peace, won by victorious arms, a well-deserved rest after manly conflict. Battle clears the air, decides the issues. All this diplomacy merely complicates, confuses and suppresses problems a decent war would bring immediately into the open. The victors would know what they had won and the vanquished would know what they had lost—and everyone would have a perfectly good idea of their position, until things became cloudy again. As it is we know that Arabia wants nothing more than to go to war with Tatary, but Albion frustrates her, and that is why Arabia grows degenerate, because her energies are not naturally employed."

They had reached the door which led into Lady Yashi Akuya's quarters. "How refreshing it is," she said, "to listen to such direct and healthy talk. Would you consider it self-indulgent if I invited you to talk with me so that I might listen a little longer to your thoughts?"

"Not at all," replied the Khan. "I am flattered by your interest."

She stepped aside to admit him to a room which was, like all her rooms, excessively black and white. "And you must tell me more about the Arabian murder." She clapped her hands for her servants to come to take Oubacha Khan's tawny coat. "Montfallcon did it, you say?"

"His creature."

The Eleventh Chapter

In Which Captain Quire
Brings a New Client to Josias Priest,
the Dancing Master

WITHIN THE NARROW confines of a sedan chair carried by four none-too-healthy lackeys cursing and stumbling on rain-slippery cobbles, Captain Quire sat staring almost tenderly at Alys Finch who sat with back straight, hands folded and knees together, in respectable stomacher, gown and petticoats, with a starched ruff like an aurora about her throat, emphasising her high, unnatural colour; she was as carefully costumed as her ex-swain, and as carefully trained by the demon who had mastered them both. His tone was approving:

"How swiftly you rise in society, Alys. I shall soon be proud of you."

"Thank you, sir." The voice was small and automatic.

"You had natural manners and I have needed to do little in that area. I improved your taste in clothing, taught you to eat properly and to speak and so on, but I have not the time to teach you the most important accomplishment, which is to be able to laugh, smile, make witty observations at will, yet never once relax into genuine and dangerous happiness. I feel a responsibility to you, Alys, as any father might (for I am creating you more consciously, more carefully, than a natural father would), and I cannot allow you to be vulnerable. I promised to make you strong, to make you reliant only upon yourself and your master. And to that continuing end we visit Josias Priest."

"Yes, sir."

"You thought yourself weak and Phil so strong. I proved you wrong. It is you who are strong, Alys, and who will be stronger still anon. An able lieutenant for Captain Quire in his constant war against the world's weaklings. For Quire is Mother Nature's thresher." His black eyes smouldered with self-mockery which she, mesmerised for almost two months, could neither understand nor recognise. "And that is why I have never insulted your strength and your intelligence by demanding love from you. Instead I have demanded disciplined obedience and given you power and security in return. For few men understand what Quire understands—the extent of a woman's physical fear. It is what I exploited in you at first. And now I offer you release from that fear. I have trained you as a sergeant trains his troops. I have said, 'Trust me with your life, your soul, your freedom—and I will protect you and teach you how to protect yourself.'" He stretched his cruel, muscular hand towards her and lifted her chin. "Do you feel safe, Alys, and strong?"

Her grey eyes were steady, though without much vitality. "I do, sir."

The chair swayed from side to side and came to the cobbles with a bump. Quire opened the door and sprang out. They stood before the gates of a high-walled courtyard. Beyond the courtyard, surrounded by tall shrubs and ornamental trees, was the white wall of a two-storeyed house of the sort that might belong to a well-to-do merchant.

Leaving Alys Finch within the sedan, Quire rattled the gate and called a halloo. "Priest! Are you there, man?" Dogs barked. Two lanterns appeared from the left side of the house. They were carried in the hands of middle-aged footmen in short smocks and hose. "Priest! It's Quire!"

Before the footmen could reach the gate a door in the house had opened and more light filled the courtyard. A skinny silhouette. A hand lifted. "Admit the gentleman, Franklin."

Quire went back to the sedan and helped Alys Finch, whose natural grace had, in his eyes, been improved and who was now demure by intention rather than instinct, to the stones of the street. He gave the rogues twice the fee they asked for, ignored their honestly expressed gratitude, and led his girl through the gate, calling out, as it was shut and locked behind him: "Master Priest, I have brought a young lady to you, for training in deportment and the dance, and to learn the ways of the Court."

Josias Priest, the Dancing Master, continued to wait at his threshold. He had a velvet evening cap upon his lank, mousy hair. His eyes were shifty and his mouth hung open, like the soft mouth of a petulant and pampered pony. On his scrawny body, a head taller than Quire's, was a long gown of the same dark velvet as the cap. He held a dinner knife in his right hand, though his stance was entirely without aggression.

"It's late, Captain Quire," he said, as his visitors came in.

"You needn't begin your work tonight." Quire was bluff. Josias Priest's watery eyes became even more alarmed. "She's to stay here, so that she can be trained thoroughly and swiftly."

"I don't accommodate my pupils, Captain. . . ."

Quire led the way into Priest's dining room. Here a large table had been laid with a supper so mean that it would have shamed a river scavenger. Quire looked sadly at the cheese rind and the ham fat, the crust. "She'll expect better food than this. She is my particular charge, my ward, and I'll want her fed heartily, with all kinds of nourishment." He drew back a chair for her and, eyes upon the surface of the table, she sat down. "Succeed with this one and I've another for your troupe."

"It is not good policy, Captain, to have young lady pupils staying on the premises. For one thing, there is the gossip. It also produces undue excitement in the other pupils. Moreover, there is always the danger that the young person will conceive a—an infatuation. . . ."

"Do you think you're in danger of falling in love with Master Priest, Alys?"

"No, sir."

"There! You're safe, Priest. With such guarantees, how can you refuse? I want her to have everything—and you must do your best. You are good at your profession. You must teach her to walk, to dance, to make entertaining conversation. Most of all, you must teach her how to flatter. You know how to flatter, do you, Priest? Of course you do, it's your greatest skill—indeed, it's your philosophy! Good, then—deportment, dancing and flattery. I shall drop in from time to time to see what progress you are making. I shall expect considerable progress, Priest."

"Captain Quire! I have no room!"

"You have a large house and several servants. Dismiss one of the servants, if you must. It would be a charitable act, come to think of it." Quire adjusted the sombrero on his thick, black hair, admiring himself in one of Master Priest's many mirrors. "Be a good girl, Alys. I shall be watching out for you."

"Yes, sir."

"I'll have clothes sent round," Quire told Master Priest.

Priest laid down his knife with a clatter, making some attempt to resist. "Lessons? Accommodation? How will she pay?"

"I'll pay, Master Priest."

"How much?"

"In my usual currency, where you and I are concerned. I'll pay you with six months' silence."

Master Priest sat behind his supper, pushing the plate aside. "Very well. But to what purpose do you want her trained?"

Quire paused at the door and scratched his chin. He shook his head and grinned. "None, as yet. There may never be one. My actions, Master Priest, as you must know by now, are often performed for their own sake."

"I can't understand you, Quire."

"I am an artist, and you, Master Priest, are a tradesman. For you, every action must result in an evident cash profit, however small, however indirect. You keep accounts. I create events. There's room for us both in the world. Do as I tell you. Do not try to understand me. Remember both those things and you'll be a happier Priest, Josias."

A hard, important look into Alys's eyes, and Quire was gone.

The Twelfth Chapter

In Which Queen Gloriana Entertains Guests to Supper and Considers Her Condition Together with That of Albion

THE LONG TABLE resembled to Gloriana a white path along which she must run, as in a nightmare, with traps at regular intervals on both sides and a tangle of obstacles (a silver net for spices, elaborate salts shaped as fabulous beasts) to block her progress down the centre; each place-setting representing a malevolent spirit. She took more wine—for once abandoning her normal caution—and pretended to listen to her nearest guests, on left and right, while making abstracted expressions of interest, astonishment or sympathy. Refusing both apathy and cynicism, she must suffer her pain, her yearning, unadulterated (for the wine did nothing but remove a little of the accompanying tension).

Indeed, my lord. How true, my lord. What a pity, my lady. How clever . . . How sensible . . .

Lord Montfallcon, as grey as granite, in black plush, with a grey, starched ruff, and a chain of ebony and gold upon his chest, spoke portentously across the table to Sir Amadis Cornfield, who tried to ignore the murmurings of his small wife and hear his lordship.

"There are those, Sir Amadis, who would take Poland's example and make a democracy of Albion. I have heard such views expressed here, in the palace itself. Some would do away with our monarchy complete! The penultimate step to total decadence, as Plato says, is the establishment of Democracy in a land."

Oh, to have the burden lifted! But no, there is Duty . . . Duty . . .

Sir Amadis, in his conservative elegance, in contrast to his wife's rather lively gown of purple and green, put a morsel of partridge between moustache and beard and chewed slowly, to show that he listened with appropriate gravity. "And Arabia? Are there not others who look to tyrannical Arabia—and would make Albion a warlike nation, an all-devouring dragon?"

"To weaken herself for ever in one great, bloodthirsty rampage." Sir Orlando Hawes waved a black, short-fingered hand in which he gripped a pickle-fork. "Wars waste money as well as lives. They take a country's youth. All investments are squandered to gain glory, which we do not need, and land, which requires tending." Sir Orlando's economic theories were still sufficiently radical for the majority not to understand him.

"War!" called the Tatar ambassador from some distance down the table, as if he thought mention of the word might be sufficient to create the situation he most desired. "War strengthens the strong nation. Albion should not be afraid of war!"

But I fear war and all that attends it. . . . Violence simplifies and distorts the Truth and brings the Brute to Eminence. . . .

Gloriana had a clear image of the Brute in her brain. He was not unlike the father she had known as a little child. The threatening, weeping, malevolent creature of unchecked power, who could resolve too-complicated issues quickly, by means of the axe and the rack, and justify any decision by a mixture of self-pity and suspicion that his, and therefore his country's, security was threatened. . . . She recalled the madness and the sorrow. . . .

"Certain nobles of Virginia are declared republicans." My Lord of Kansas, splendid in sombre reds and dark yellows, with the wide, high collar that was fashionable in his own land. He smiled at his listeners, glad of the effect he had made, and took some wine.

"And yet I thought Virginia the loyalest nation in Albion!" Sir Amadis's wife (the eldest of the Perrott sisters) turned rounded, pretty eyes on Lord Kansas.

"So we are, ma'am. The Queen is worshipped there almost as a goddess. No question."

"And yet . . . ?"

"They're republicans, not anti-monarchists. Poland's their example. A hundred years ago the twelfth Casimir (known as the

Level-Headed) gave parliament all power and became the representative rather than the ruler of the State."

"And should war threaten Poland—serious war—" cried Oubacha Khan, "she'll be finished—a thousand decisions will be made where only one should exist!" He turned enthusiastic eyes to the Lady Yashi Akuya, whose approval he could always depend upon. "While commoners babble—a king acts. Ancient Athens is your example there!"

There were not a few who agreed with him. Even Count Korzeniowski, a trifle deaf as well as a trifle short-sighted, nodded in assent.

"A republican is a traitor to the State," said Lord Ingleborough, who was propped in his chair and wearing a fur robe over his ceremonial clothes. He had come late, a mild heart attack delaying him. He coughed. "That must be logical. Traitors should be—well . . ." He became confused, glanced at his Queen, looked away. "Exiled," he said.

He means killed. Executed, chopped, strangled, sliced, torn apart . . . There must be no more blood. . . . Too many died . . . too many . . . I will not kill in Albion's name. . . .

"A traitor, Lord Ingleborough," rumbled the fair-minded Rhoone from where he sat picking methodically at the bones of his bird, his black beard stained with its juices, "is one who would actively plot against the Queen's person or the security of the State. If the holding of republican views, or Stoical views, or theological views, or, truly, any views at all, does not directly threaten us, then those who hold them cannot be called 'traitor.' A well-run Court contains a composition of opinion and belief, for it must be representative of the Nation and, if possible, the world. A monarch is required to sit at the head of this Court, to be advised by sage, knowledgeable fellows, like yourselves, my lords councillors, and by any others whose wisdom is of usefulness, as to facts and understandings—then the monarch can reach a thoughtful decision."

Oh, trusting, faithful Rhoone. How ordered and unmalleable is your perfect universe! How strongly your faith enchains me. That sense of Liberty we share—it makes slaves of us. . . .

Lord Shahryar, the Caliph's envoy, set aside a plate almost untouched, saying: "Agreed, Lord Rhoone. Would you also agree with me that a nation's stability is maintained by means of a royal line, trained from birth in the responsibilities of government?" With bland calculation he raised a ghost, then hastened on: "I speak in abstract, Your Majesty."

Gloriana nodded, only half-hearing him, understanding from his tone what the familiar sentiments must be. She took more wine.

Lord Gorius Ransley, the Queen's High Steward, seated next to the Saracen, turned a head full of artificial curls so that he could look upon the speaker. He pushed lace back from both wrists and picked up a piece of fowl upon his knife. "In Poland, you'll recall, the king's elected."

"From those directly in line to the throne," Lord Shahryar pointed out. He refused to notice the glaring looks he received from more than the Queen's councillors. "But old King Hern," he continued, "so successfully destroyed his rivals that there are none in Albion who could ascend. . . ."

"Sir!" Mild Sir Vivien Rich sucked at his plump cheeks. "This is not mannerly intercourse!"

"I am sure I say nothing that has not already been a sober subject of discussion amongst those holding Albion dear," said Lord Shahryar in apparent humility. "I apologise if I have been naïve."

Doctor John Dee was not the only gentleman who felt acutely for the Queen, though the Queen herself appeared to overlook what had been said, with splendid insouciance. "You have been that, at least, sir." He attempted to dispel the growing atmosphere. "Besides, all this is speculative. It suggests our Queen is mortal! And all know she is immortal!" He raised his glass. The Queen smiled kindly and Dee interpreted this as approval for his words. "The whole of Albion is certain that the plague will never descend upon them!"

"The plague?" Oubacha Khan became nervous. "There is plague in Albion?"

"There is no plague in Albion," Sir Vivien explained, "because the Queen lives. Have you not heard the common folk's greeting—'Pray the plague will never come upon us'? You've heard 'em, eh? There's the legend that when Pericles died plague came to Athens."

"But all fear plague. What, Sir Vivien, is the significance?"

Sir Amadis Cornfield grinned, lending his own energies to changing the dangerous mood of the table. "They do *not* fear the plague—that's the point." His wife reached under his leaning body to take a piece of cheese. "The greeting indirectly refers to the Queen's health."

"My health?" Gloriana spoke as one waking from sleep. "My health?"

"The plague, Your Majesty," said Lord Montfallcon. "You know—the belief of the common people that if you should die a great plague would immediately fall upon Albion."

Gloriana drew up her shoulders and was valiant. "Aha! Then let 'em all believe so and I'll have no enemies in Albion. It could preserve my life for ever." She drained her glass. Some laughed with her.

But such false words from that sad mouth served to make the guests nearest her aware of her mood.

"Aye, ma'am," bravely answered old Lord Ingleborough. "Pray that those republicans who would destroy Tradition and therefore the cornerstone of our State take heed of the prophecy ever so profoundly!" And thus he added his own limp to that lame gait, that heartless measure.

Again Sir Amadis rallied himself and stood upon his feet, raising his golden goblet. "I would give all a toast. To the next half-century of our Gloriana's reign!"

Then all must stand and drink, save Gloriana.

Gods, would that I were old now, and my body suffering the simpler sensations of senility . . . Why cannot I be reconciled? Because to be reconciled is to let the Spirit die. Yet this is flesh that speaks to me, drives me, torments me. . . . Flesh, not Spirit. Oh, they are one, as Gloriana and Albion are one. . . . Am I doomed to my Quest, as Chivalry's knights were doomed to seek Bran's Cup and never find it, because they were not pure enough? Have I ruined myself through dissipation, have I lost the secret which I might have found in virgin innocence? Oh, Father, that knowledge you demanded and which I did not deny, because I feared you so, honoured you so, and, Father, loved you so . . . If you had only granted me and yourself a little more ignorance. . . .

"Gloriana! Gloriana!"

They were drinking.

Then, conscientiously, up she stood, and she raised her own glass. "To all my honourable gentlemen and their ladies, to all the envoys of the foreign courts, I wish you health!"

And this, because of the previous reference to the plague, seemed like a good joke of the Queen's at her own expense. Their enthusiastic merriment rang in her ears and she listened to their compliments and smiled, as if the joke had been deliberate, noticing that Oubacha Khan and Lord Shahryar in particular were looking at her shrewdly, misjudging vagueness for irony and believing themselves to have received a fuller impression of her character, since neither had recognised the deliberate ironies she had offered during their formal encounters. This amused her and she was forced to disguise it, to give undue attention to the servant who poured her fresh wine.

How I wish my Una were here, returned from Scaith. There's a consort for a Queen! Should I change the Law and marry the Countess? Una and I could rule better together. I wish she would take more power. I miss you, Una. . . .

She looked up. Near the end of the table was the battle-suited Sir Tancred Belforest, creaking to his feet, aided by Lady Mary Perrott, whose loss from her bed Gloriana now began to regret. Not long since Lady Mary had played boy for the Queen with enthusiasm. Now she played demoiselle to Tancred's sober chevalier, apparently delighting in his clumsy innocence; in love with him. Gloriana felt a threat or two of jealousy winding through her half-drugged heart and, disgusted by her ignoble thoughts, dismissed the sensation, though it was not Sir Tancred she envied, but Mary, who had found a focus for her faith in a single individual.

"Your Majesty," began Sir Tancred, his red face glowing from within its case of steel, his unruly moustache bristling, his huge plumes dancing, "as Your Majesty's Champion, as Albion's Champion, as Defender of the Queen's Honour, I offer my sword to you." He, the only one present allowed to carry a large weapon, dragged the heavy ornamental broadsword from its scabbard of Iberian enamel-work, and held it upright by the blade. "And I beg leave to challenge any one of these present who would insult Your Majesty or Albion's name." He paused, for he was considerably drunk. Gloriana loved him, then. "To a tourney at arms—sword, mace, lance or any other honourable weapon—to the point of grave wounding or death."

Gloriana became a Queen, clear-voiced and kindly. "We are grateful for this display of loyalty, Sir Tancred, which is inspiring and worthy of the Court of the Bear and the Great Age of New Troy, when Chivalry was at its height. And should there come a time when we are insulted here, we shall command you to avenge that insult by force of arms. In the meanwhile we pray you to conserve your energies for the May Day Tilt."

Sir Tancred blinked. "But, Your Majesty, there's more than one here, tonight, who has so insulted you!"

"We heard no insults, Sir Tancred—only innocent jests. We all make merry and forget formality, for we are good friends at this table."

Oubacha Khan turned eagerly to look up into Sir Tancred's frowning face, murmuring: "Honour. Aye, honour." He fingered the pommel of his little dress dagger.

Sir Tancred opened his mouth again, but was tugged by his paramour from behind, by a strap, and sat down with a sudden crash.

Oubacha Khan murmured very softly to the Lady Yashi Akuya, who nodded rapidly, even though she made out only half his words. "Thus are even the brave and the honourable turned to milksops by this over-loving mother." He looked across the table at Lord Shahryar and they exchanged mutually knowing glances.

Gloriana, recalled to diplomatic duty by the incident, singled out Lord Kansas. "You have been adventuring, far from Virginia, so I hear, my lord?"

"To the East Indies, madam, and to the interior of Africa, wherein I discovered several new nations ruled over by mighty kings, who treated me with great hospitality and sent their greetings to Your

Majesty." He spoke with modest, civilised good humour, conscious of his expected rôle.

"You must give them our greeting in return, my lord, if you should ever venture that way again. And there were savages, too, were there not?"

"Many tribes of them, madam. But again we were well and courteously received. I found the chiefs of these tribes as good company as any civilised man!"

"They are less restricted by formality and ritual, perhaps?" said she.

"On the contrary, madam, they seem to have more ceremonies and rituals than we do—though such things are not always recognised for what they are by those who practise them."

"True, Lord Kansas. You learned their tongues?"

"One or two, madam. I discoursed with their priests and their wise men. It is fairly said, madam, that while Man's store of knowledge increaseth, his wit doth not. So is the savage equal to the civilised sage."

"Well put, Lord Kansas!" She liked the long-faced, wry man with his dark-tanned, leathery skin, his simple Virginian Stoic costume (it had been Stoics who had settled Virginia originally) and his air of tolerance. She considered him for a lover. She went further, and considered him for a husband. For she must take a husband, soon. Though Lord Shahryar's remarks were resented, they voiced the thoughts of everyone there who valued Albion's continuing security. But to take a husband who could not please her, for whom she must also give up her Quest, would be madness. If she gave up her Quest, she felt, she gave up Belief—and Albion would have a hollow symbol that would crumble, causing the very structure of the State to crumble. She had a vision of Albion in flames, with thick black smoke drifting from coast to coast, from ocean to ocean of the Empire—of cruel war, carnage and waste. It was a vision instilled in her since she had been a child, by her mentor, Lord Montfallcon. It was a vision that would come true if once she forgot her Duty. And now all were agreed where her Duty lay—in marriage. . . .

But they do not realise how weak I am. I cannot maintain this responsibility for ever. If I marry I shall share my burden but cease to be Gloriana. And unless I remain Gloriana, Albion's endangered. Or does it matter? Perhaps I should proclaim Albion a republic? But no, this would make both commoners and nobles despondent and weaken us, making us vulnerable to our enemies. . . . Republics are born of necessity, not morality. . . . I must remain true to my instincts and my Duty. Or should I, like the princess in the fairy tale, make it known that I shall marry the first prince to bring me to fulfilment, or marry Arabia, utilising my energies to make war on Tatary, on Poland, on the rest of the world? To turn those energies, as Father did, into a kind of awesome, horrifying Art, bringing the turmoil of the liver and the heart, the kidneys and the brain, to the whole Realm, forcing it to reflect and feel the anguish he felt and which I inherit. No! For I swore this would never be—this need of mine must always be private and privately must it be satisfied. . . . Only twice did Father succeed in finding private release and, by his first action, created me, while by his second he placed his burden upon my womb as firmly as Montfallcon placed the public burden upon my head when, four years later, he supervised my coronation. . . .

The table had become a road again, the heads on either side so many carrion birds waiting to pick at her corpse. Firmly she drove the images away. Such images had belonged to her father as he grew increasingly insane, seeing every eye accusing him, every voice imploring him for a portion of his fragile substance, until, to close the eyes and still the voices, he had turned more and more to desperate murder in the guise of Justice. Thus had Lord Montfallcon's family perished, thus Lord Ingleborough's brothers and his father, thus Sir Thomasin Ffynne's mistress and son—whole households, whole villages had been slain. If he had lived, King Hern might have executed the population of Albion to the last baby, in an effort to deny the guilt he suffered for his rejection of Duty. And then Montfallcon, who had consoled himself with this ambition through all the terror and the danger, who had maintained his own sanity by making her his Faith, had crowned her Queen, announced a new Golden Age, named her a modern, female, pacific Pericles, named her Justice, Mercy, Love, Pity and

Hope, and banished Chaos, overnight, from Albion—brought Light to Albion, Trust to Albion, Truth and Dignity to Albion, across all the lands of her Empire—and Queen Gloriana the First, within five years of her rule, received all the credit for this transformation, while Montfallcon, made shy and reserved by habit and from character, still posed, when necessity demanded, as the Devil of the Past.

With an effort she made her mind turn outwards again, shaking her huge and lovely frame as a setter might rid itself of water and hearing Lord Kansas recall, with all the skill of one who relished the rôle of raconteur, his East Indian adventures.

"And so, gentlemen, sundry clattering knights met all in a hall of tall bamboo, which was cool and gloomy, for light did come only through tight-woven lattice. This great place was the Aviary of the King of Bengahl. Axe and shield, sword and spear, clanged and cracked, like white fire in that gloom, while all about us parrots and macaws and parakeets, jackdaws and birds of paradise, canaries and cockatoos, screeched and fluttered. Why, in the end *of it, there was more birds' blood spilled than men's. The thing was* settled amicably in the end, when all were exhausted, when Sir Colum Feveril undertook to pay the proper price for the girl he'd married out of love. It was the issue. They had not made it clear!"

Gloriana drew a deep breath and then her voice joined in the common laughter.

The Thirteenth Chapter

In Which Lord Montfallcon Fails to Give Due Appreciation to the Work of an Artist and in Which the Artist Meets Death and Begs a Commission from Him

March winds lifted the thick ivy about Lord Montfallcon's high windows; it billowed like the heavy skirts of peasant matrons, reminding Captain Quire of a sensation he could not identify; something from his childhood when, occasionally, the elements would inspire him, bringing him a luscious tranquillity he had never since known. With his hand upon his hilt and his sombrero under his arm he watched the clever old lord read from the printed pamphlet Quire himself had just delivered into his hands.

"No other copies escaped the fire?" Montfallcon asked heavily.

"None. And the manuscript, too, I burned."

"These Stoics. I respect them, Quire. I follow their faith myself, to a large degree. But when belief's turned to zealotry . . . Ah, the damage they can do. This makes out the Queen's a harlot, though a blameless one. Bad blood, it says! The blood's the best there is—'twas her sire soured it. Taking sensual pleasure while the enemy gathers, it says . . . Gods! If they knew how hard she works for Albion. I've read all this more than once. The author?"

"On his way to begin a new life, my lord, where he'll find plenty of discomfort to please him. In Africa. In irons, to the Shaleef of Bantustan."

Lord Montfallcon gave vent to a small chuckle. "You sold him, Quire? As a slave?"

"As a scribe. He'll be well-treated, by Bantustan standards. He claimed, in one paragraph, that he was no better than a slave. It seemed fitting to give him a taste of the reality."

"The printer of this?" He waved it as he walked towards the fire.

"An ignorant man. Fear was all I needed to use. He's back to making snatchsheets and placards."

"You're certain?"

"He claimed he read poorly, that he had not understood the import of the pamphlet. So I offered to insure him against further error by making certain he would be able to read nothing at all."

"Ah, Quire," said Lord Montfallcon with sudden gravity, "I wonder if you'll ever come to frighten me."

"It's not my business, my lord."

Montfallcon was in a restless mood. He studied Quire. He failed to find an answer to the question his eyes asked. "I wish I knew your purpose, Quire. You do not work for gold, I know, though you're paid well. How's so much spent, and you with the same suit of clothes, the same patched cloak? You're not a drunkard or much of a gambler." He frowned against the glare of the fire. "You do not pay for women. Do you save it, Quire?" The pamphlet was placed upon the fire and stirred with a long rod.

"I spend it freely, sir, on good deeds as often as not." Quire was puzzled, even discomforted, by this lack of understanding. "A widow here, a cripple there."

"You, Quire!" A grunt. "Charitable?"

"I am a sympathetic friend—but only to the weak. I will not tolerate the mad or the strong—those I'll fight or avoid. My good deeds, Lord Montfallcon, are, like all my deeds, self-interested. Your work and mine is greatly aided by my reputation for generosity. We employ a great army of loyal innocents, of faithful feeble-minded men and women, of dull, good-hearted, honest folk—for they are the people never reckoned with by one's enemies. They are always ignored, always condescended to. Therefore they are the most grateful for my good deeds and will bring me all kinds of information, not from greed but from simple loyalty. I am their hero. They worship Captain Quire. They'll forgive him any crime ('he has his reasons') and protect him, as best they can, from any consequences. They are the backbone of every scheme."

"I am almost flattered, Quire, by these confidences. Do you not fear to reveal the secrets of your trade to me?"

"Trade?" Surprised, Quire hesitated at the word, then shook his head to answer: "No, sir, for there are few men of my kidney in the world. Most thieves are fools, most murderers romantics, most spies self-important. I am proud to expound the theories of this profession, as any artist enjoys explaining his method, because he knows that only a rare few can follow him—and he's happy to encourage those few."

"What? You see me as a pupil?"

"Of course not, my lord. A peer."

Lord Montfallcon wagged a finger. "Hubris, Quire! I suspect that the abduction of kings gives your imagination a richer diet than you can afford. You've tasted strong wine and now you'd have no other kind. You'll fall—you become too cocky."

Quire was sullen. "It pleases me to be so. If I enjoy the emotion, I'll take it while I may, and not stifle it. I've little belief in any definite future."

"You expect to die?"

He was further surprised. "No, my lord. It is just that there are so many possible futures. I plan, to some degree, for all of them. And, in another way, I plan for none of them."

"You are not easy-going, Quire. Do not pretend that to me."

"My life is as disciplined as"—Quire pointed into the fire where the pamphlet had turned black and was disintegrating—"as was his—as his will be, indeed. But I play my emotions with the skill and care of a musician, as I play the emotions of those I'm inclined to use."

"But you must have an ambition."

"I've told you, my lord. To amplify and define my senses."

Lord Montfallcon became disturbed. "You use a scholar's words to justify base deeds, that's all." He seemed about to dismiss Quire. He returned to his desk, frowning more darkly than ever.

"My lord?" Quire took his sombrero in his hand, made a step towards the door, then turned. "You recognise me as an artist, surely? I spoke candidly. The best I can do. Such words should not affect you, my lord. They are objective."

Lord Montfallcon pouted his lips. "You relish your work!" It was an accusation and unexpected.

Quire's dark eyes were half-amused. "Aye."

"Zeus! I wish it were not necessary. . . . But it is necessary, and we must do it." He gave out a bitter noise. "That I should play Socrates to some modern-day Callicles!"

Quire combed his left hand through his thick locks, studying his patron. His cold voice sang out. "You are suffering, my lord?"

Montfallcon fumbled with a drawer. "I must pay you."

"You're ill, my lord?"

"Damn you, Quire, you know it's not a physical condition. Sometimes I wonder what I do and why I should bother to employ such as you."

"Because I am the best. At this work of ours, sir. But I'll not justify my rôle. I merely explained myself. Justification is for you to do."

"Eh?" Montfallcon brought out the box of gold. His hands shook.

"One acquires a necessary relish for the pain and humiliation of one's fellow creatures, my lord. It is in the nature of the work. Yet, as a soldier (when the battle's won) will wax sentimental over the shame and the waste and the pity of it, so could I weep, and cry *'Horror! But it must be thus!'*—and console myself (and you, my lord, for that is what you seem to expect of me today). I refuse such sophistry. Instead I cry *'Horror! But how sweet it is!'* Should I be the victim, I think I should still learn to relish my own misery, for that, also, is a means of amplifying and defining the senses. But I seek the freedom of power. It gives me a wider field. So do I grasp at privilege—which your patronage affords me—the privilege of power. I would rather relish another's pain than my own."

"Pain's for bearing, that's all. You are a creature, Quire, perverse and stunted in your soul." He put coins in a bag, counting them carefully.

"No, sir, my soul's as noble as thine own, sir. I merely interpret its demands in a manner different from yours, sir." Quire was offended not so much by Lord Montfallcon's insults as by his misreading of the truth.

Lord Montfallcon's hand shook as he held out the bag. "Admit it—you work for money!"

"I am not a liar, sir, as you know. Why do you wish me to reassure you in this way? We have worked together harmoniously up to now."

"I am sick of secrets!"

"You do not employ me, my lord, to console you."

"Go! Your vulgar ironies ring dull to me!"

A ragged bow from Captain Quire, but he would not leave. There was an unstated demand. He stood his ground. It seemed that he was furious. "For that, my lord, I'll readily apologise. I lack the practice. I can't aspire to sing as bright and clear as you lords of the Court, for my calling demands blunter tones."

"You bait me, Quire! I'm no bear for your amusement. Go."

Captain Quire took the money and tucked it in his belt, holding his stance. "I'm used to speaking to those who are near deaf with terror, or half dead with pain. Thus it is, also, with those who teach the young, or tend the mad and sick, sir. Their vocabularies wither, their style simplifies, their art becomes the art of the country mummer, their humour the bumpkin humour of the Fair."

"And your apologies bore me, Master Quire. You are dismissed." Montfallcon seated himself.

Quire took a step forward. "I offer you plain truth and you reject it. You questioned me, my lord, and I replied. I thought we both spoke truth. I thought there was no ambiguity between us. Must I lie to maintain your patronage?"

"Perhaps." Lord Montfallcon locked his drawer. He drew a breath and said: "Do you say I am an imperfect employer?"

"Perfect up to now, sir. Do we not possess an understanding, as between men of equal sensibility?"

"Indeed! We do have an understanding! I pay. You kill, kidnap and conspire."

"An understanding of the skill, my lord, involved."

"You're clever, aye." Montfallcon became baffled. "What more must I say to make you leave? Is there a charm? Do you seek public honours? Would you have me make you a Prince of the Realm?"

"No, my lord. I was speaking of the art of it, that is all. My belief that you appreciated that art for its own sake."

"If you like." Montfallcon waved him away.

Quire was shocked. "What?"

"Go, Quire. I'll send for you."

"You offend me deeply, my lord."

Montfallcon's voice rose, shaking. "I protect you, Quire. Remember that. Your wicked life is permitted to continue unchecked—your seductions, your blackmailings, your killings on your own account. . . ." Montfallcon placed thin fingers upon his grey brow. "I'll not respond to your ambiguous demands! This is no time. . . . I have important matters to consider. . . . matters more important, Quire, than the balming of a villain's pride. Go, go, go, Captain Quire!"

The flop of tawdry black, and Quire was vanished.

As Captain Quire left the shadows of the palace and entered the ornamental garden, now a tangle of budding brambles and unchecked creepers, he paused to look back at the high wall behind him, to frown, to shake his head. His pride was, indeed, most mightily injured. He began to investigate the sensation as he walked on, through the gates and down the hill to the line of trees where Tinkler leaned whistling against the fence, staring at the ragged, racing sky.

"Tink." Quire climbed the fence and stood with his back to Tinkler, looking along the road towards London's smoke.

"What's afoot, Captain?" Tinkler was sensitive to his master's moods as only one who fears for his life can be. He paced forward in his stiff, cracked coat, thumbs in his doublet belt.

"I'm shocked."

Captain Quire was murmuring, rolling a stone with the pointed toe of his jackboot.

"I thought I was respected. Aye, that's what's attacked, my self-respect. I am not understood as an artist. Hasn't anyone an idea of the skill, the genius involved in my work? Have I not proved it constantly? How else could I prove it? Who else could do what I do?"

"I admire you, Captain. Greatly." Tinkler was placatory without being truly sympathetic, for he had not the sense to interpret stance or gesture. "We all do—at The Seahorse, The Gryffyn and elsewhere . . ."

"I meant my peers. I thought Montfallcon sensible to a fellow artist, a realist. I'm stunned, Tink. He's nought but a pump-room cynic!"

Tinkler thought he guessed the cause of this. "He didn't pay, is that it, Captain? He always . . ." He was forestalled as Quire pushed the purse into his hand. "Ah, thanks."

"All this while I believed he understood the nature of my game. He doesn't appreciate the finesse, the comedy, the irony of it, but most of all he doesn't understand the structure, the vision, the talent, the hard, unblinking eye that looks upon reality and transmutes it into drama. Oh, Tink!"

Unused to this display of emotional confidence, this revelation of his master's inner life, Tinkler was at once fascinated and at a loss for words. "Well," he said, falling in beside Quire as he set off, flustered and flapping, down the track. "Well, Captain . . ."

"Every artist requires a patron." Quire looked about him at the black poplars waving in the wind. He yanked at his wandering cloak; he pulled his hat more firmly upon his head. The crow's feathers fluttered like little drumming fingers against his crown. "And unless he has an appreciative patron he can soon wither, turning his talent to mercenary gain, to please the majority. I have never pleased the majority, Tink."

"Indeed you haven't, Captain."

"My wealth has gone, every copper, on materials. Invested for the art's sake."

"You were always generous, Captain."

"That is what he failed to understand—that and my pride. I took his insults, his apparent contempt, for I understood it to be the part he chose to play."

"We must all play parts sometimes, Captain."

"And all the while he displayed his true character, his true opinion of me! Oh, the old fool!" Quire stopped in the middle of the track.

London was in sight—red, grey and white below. On the city's walls swayed the ramshackle shanties and tents of those who lived and worked there; beyond were roofs of green or silver slate, roofs of thatch, of copper and, in one or two places, of gold leaf. Spires, delicate and thin; heavy domes; battlemented towers; tall temples of knowledge—colleges, libraries in the latest Graecian mould, or in older pointed, Gothic shapes, of brick, granite and marble; theatres made of wood and brightly painted, pasted over with a thousand posters; street upon street of dwelling houses, inns, taverns, ordinaries, drapery shops, butchers' shops; the shops of fishmongers, greengrocers, signpainters, goldsmiths, jewellers, scriveners, makers of musical instruments, clothiers, saddlers, tobacco merchants, vintners, glaziers, barbers, apothecaries, carriage builders, blacksmiths, metalworkers, printers, toymakers, bootmakers, tinsmiths, chandlers; the high corn exchanges, the shambles, the merchants' meeting halls, the exhibiting galleries where painters and sculptors displayed their creations . . .

Quire was reluctant to continue. He stopped and sat down suddenly on a large, smooth rock. "And where may I show the world my works?"

"A drink?" suggested Tinkler. "At The Seahorse?"

Quire could see a squadron of cavalry, with banners and gilded cuirasses and helmets, plumes and embroidered cloaks, trotting down the broad Clerkenwell Road between the fine buildings of the great guilds. He looked towards the river, far across on the other side of the city, to Bran's Tower, a building of immense age, and beyond it at the barges, the wherries, and the galleons under sail upon the river. "I could have been a general or a famed navigator, employing my gifts to my own great public credit, a favourite of the people, and honoured by the Queen. With my talent I could have become the mightiest merchant in Albion, enriching myself and my nation, made Lord Mayor at least. But I shunned such unworthy pursuits. I lived only for my art and its improvement. . . ."

Tinkler became nervous. "Captain?"

"You go on down, Tink, and spend that gold. It could be the last you'll see."

"You are dismissed?" Tinkler was horrified.

"No."

"You have quit our friend's employ?" Tinkler's gag tooth twitched on his lip.

"I have not said so."

Tinkler, in relief, clapped his wincing master on the back. Since Quire's tone had changed, he instantly forgot his distress. "Then let's both to The Seahorse, Captain. This gloomy, windy weather spreads melancholy everywhere."

Quire lifted himself from the rock, his lantern jaw upon his chest, his face hidden by the unsteady brim of his sombrero. He was unusually and terrifying malleable. "Aye."

Tinkler was again disturbed. "A wench or two is what we need, Captain. To warm us up. To suck the poor humours from us."

"A wench?" The eyes moved in the wicked head, questioning Tinkler as if Quire no longer understood the term.

Tinkler trembled. "Every doxy at The Seahorse would be yours, if you desired. And every dell. It's love you need, master."

Quire turned bleak eyes away from his lieutenant and straightened a sturdy back. "I love my art."

"You're the best." Tinkler's voice thickened as his mouth dried. "Ask anyone."

They continued towards the wall, now not half a mile from them at the foot of the steep path.

"It's true," agreed his master.

"And you're strong, Captain. You love your work—your art, that is to say—and nothing else. But let them love you. Take your rewards."

Quire smiled at the ground. "I thought Montfallcon understood. I've no expectation where the rest are concerned. You and the others, Tink, will never be more than apprentices, to put a little colour to the outlines, paint in a background or two. Good, solid craftsmen, and none the worse for that. It's men like O'Bryan I despise—jacks of his order, who pretend to be great, who have ambitions towards greatness, and have no true talent, merely an instinct towards murder and treachery. I had to cultivate those instincts, discipline 'em, hone 'em, tune 'em. . . . Ah, and then to find I am considered to be no better than O'Bryan, that insensate, greedy, grandiose, bragging butcher. The kind I most despise."

"Well, you handled him as he deserved." Tink's cheer wore thinner still.

"And they think I cannot love, Tink. You think so. . . ."

"No, no, Captain. I meant only that you were dedicated, that you do not waste yourself . . . don't indulge in the softer sort of sentiments . . ." Tinkler drew his gag tooth into his mouth as if he wished he could follow it.

"But I have loved much and loved many, for I have defeated many. And I am a conventional conqueror. I fall in love with all I vanquish. Who could not? Some can feel affection only for children, if children seem not to threaten them. I feel affection for those who have threatened but are threats no longer. Is not my love the most rational, Tink?"

"Unquestionably, sir." Tinkler curbed an impulse to increase his pace and move ahead of his master. "And many love you, Captain, as I said."

Quire showed distaste. "I hope not. I do not wish that. I do not demand it."

"I meant," panted the bewildered lackey, "that you're admired, Captain, and so forth."

"Admired? By the mob? That's easily won, such admiration. A few dramatic actions, a cheap jest or two, a daring gesture—aye, and the rabble will continue to cheer you all the way to Tilbury and the hulks. I despise those who pander to the crowd for its own sake. My art must be appreciated by other artists, people who are great in their own spheres, as Lord Montfallcon is great. All those years he spent beside Hern's throne, calculating, plotting, scheming for Gloriana's succession. He was my hero, Tink, when I was younger. I recognised him for what he was. I still admire him. He has surely sensed my subtle appreciation of his achievements. But mine, in their own way, have been as great."

"Greater, Captain, considering all."

"I accepted his patronage in order to extend my experience, improve my skills—amplification, definition. . . . He was my only master. And he despises me."

"Despise him, Captain. He's the loser."

Quire brightened. "So he is. You're right, Tinkler." With some effort he lengthened his stride. They were almost at the walls. "You go to The Seahorse and I'll join you there. I'll to my respectable quarters and see how Mistress Philomena, the scholar's wife, fares without her loving mate." He cocked his hat and creased it. "I'll see you at The Seahorse, Tink."

Relieved to be dismissed, Master Tinkler ran ahead through the gate, waving once. "You'll soon be your old self, again, Captain!"

Quire's spirits were improving by the second. "Aye. Despise him. I've learned all I can. I'm better than our friend, Montfallcon. I'll leave him behind me!"

It was in this unreal and jaunty mood that he entered through the gate and was immediately attacked by half a dozen rogues, with nets and blankets, ropes and knives.

"Here he is!"

Quire's quick hand went to his sword hilt, but a noose had already settled over his shoulders. He wriggled. The noose tightened.

The six rufflers, half-masked by cloaks and hoods, were on him.

"Fools! I'm Quire. I've friends. All the jacks in town!"

They ignored him and had him trussed and aboard a stinking cart before he could think. He began to doubt his entire comprehension of himself and his world. He was blindfolded and his body was numb with the pressure of the ropes. He had received his second amazement of the day. If he had not been gagged and hooded, he would have sworn aloud.

Arioch! I'm captured. This is injustice to excess! In one day! I allowed myself to lose confidence and thus lost hope—and now I lose my life. Unless I can speak myself free. But what is it? What enemies would dare . . . ?

And then it occurred to Captain Quire that his interview with Montfallcon and the turn it had taken had something in common with this abduction.

He's delivered me up. He's betrayed me. He hopes to murder me before I can reveal his secrets. He must not believe the truth. Well, he shall know if I die. Every deed will be published in Captain Quire's Confession. Gods, it will bring Albion down! Oh, my friend Montfallcon, if I survive, you'll know still greater vengeance. Then you'll acknowledge the truth—that pupil has become master. I'll force you to appreciate that fact, if no other. . . .

His little finger sought his hidden dagger but could not reach. He bit carefully at the gag, to chew it loose. He tested the ropes and the nets that held him. He listened hard to the voices of his captors, but there were only three now—two on the seat in front and one in the wagon beside him—and they were all three taciturn.

Because he was not dead (it would have been as easy for them to murder him there, and then cart his body to the river) he guessed that a delayed death was to be part of his fate. Perhaps Montfallcon hoped to torture the hiding place of his Confession from him before he died. He determined to enjoy the agony as best he could—and to enjoy their frustration when he died. It meant, too, that he had a chance to live, to escape, for these fellows were not quick-witted. Mere Kent Street cutpurses of the lowest caste, they might be bribed, threatened or deceived, once his mouth was free. He wondered which lieutenant Montfallcon had commissioned to question him. There was none he had trusted to this sort of work for a long while, save Quire himself. Quire further determined that Montfallcon must personally supervise his torture and death, and this gave him so much satisfaction that he settled in the cart as comfortably as possible and, to the consternation of his captors, began to hum a tune through his gag.

At length the cart stopped; he was dragged from it and humped up a number of groaning wooden steps until a room was reached. It smelled very strongly of coffee and he guessed that he was therefore in one of the many Flax Hill coffee-merchants' warehouses. Two of his captors departed, leaving one to guard him. Quire began to wriggle across the boards to see what happened. He received a kick in the back. He subsided. The door was opened again and he heard a soldier tread, the chink of spurs, as of a man in authority. The hood and then the blindfold were removed and Quire grinned around his gag, believing he would see Montfallcon, then grinned wider (and more painfully) when he recognised, instead, the Caliph's envoy, Lord Shahryar of Baghdad, who smiled benignly back at him through a dark, carefully groomed beard and fingered the large curved dagger which hung by golden cords at his gown's belt. He looked towards the ruffian who stood unseen behind Quire's prone body. "This is Quire?"

"It's Quire, sir."

Coins changed hands and the ruffian was through the door and down the steps as if he feared to witness what followed.

The Arabian drew the dagger from its sheath and, with a menacing movement Quire found rather too obvious, set it against Quire's throat before swiftly cutting the gag loose and allowing Quire's grin to come to magnificent bloom. "I'm exchanged, am I?" He was abnormally incautious. "For some favour you've granted Montfallcon?"

Lord Shahryar was mildly surprised.

"I mean," continued Quire, "that he's delivered me up to you. If so, he grows senile, as I half-suspect, for I could tell you many secrets, as you doubtless know."

Lord Shahryar sheathed the dagger and straightened up, folding his gown fastidiously around him, touching his burnoose lightly with a finger almost solidly covered by gold.

"I'm not your man," Quire said, deciding that he had admitted too much. "Why have you had this done to me?"

Lord Shahryar rubbed at the point where his jaw met his skull, just behind his left ear.

"You are evidently," Quire continued with clever indignation, "a gentleman. You are not a vagabond out for ransom. Why am I captured, sir?"

"For several reasons, Captain Quire. You think Montfallcon betrayed you? Well, perhaps he did. And you know who I am—that I am the uncle of Lord Ibram, whom you lured into thinking he was fighting a duel, then slew in a most cowardly fashion."

"You suspect me of murder! My lord!" Quire steadied his eyes. "Then I beg you, sir, place me in the hands of Sir Christopher Martin's constables, that I may be given an honourable trial. I am a scholar, sir. I was on my way to the inn where I stay, when in London. Where my wife is, sir. Send a messenger. They'll vouch I speak truth. The name is Partridge."

Lord Shahryar smiled again. "Are you afraid, Captain Quire? Do you understand that you shall die, painfully and lingeringly. . . ."

"You've the common touch in your wit, sir. I'm the victim of a jape, eh?"

Lord Shahryar displayed some impatience. "I thought you were, at least, a professional rogue and that you would not try to deceive me in such a naïve fashion as this, Captain Quire. I know you killed my nephew."

"Lord Montfallcon hates me. He is jealous of me. He told you, eh?"

"You seem eager to believe Montfallcon your betrayer. Why?"

Quire blinked, then shut his thin mouth tight.

"Montfallcon will not protect you," continued Lord Shahryar thoughtfully, "if that is what you mean. And he will not much regret my killing of you, Captain Quire. Now what motive has Montfallcon in betraying you, d'you think?" The Saracen was shrewd, but Quire saw no harm in answering the truth:

"Because he sees me as a threat, perhaps."

"Why's that?"

"Because I'm the better artist."

"Spying, murder and betrayal as Art." Lord Shahryar found this idea attractive. "I suppose it is—as much as War is regarded as an art. I understand you, Captain Quire. You appear to be without rival in your chosen vocation."

He had made, because of recent circumstances, something of a friend. Quire determined to die as quickly as possible, without torture, and tell the Moor every secret he had. He could be generous—as any artist is when praise comes from an unexpected quarter.

"You have a reputation, Captain Quire, for honesty in your own field."

"I have. You'll not find me lying, save for specific reasons."

"Your word is said to be your bond."

"I give it rarely and never without full consideration of what's involved. I believe in the truth, you see." Quire shifted across the floor and inched up so that he could lean against the crumbling plaster of the wall. "An artist's life is full, by necessity, of ambiguity. It does not do to let ambiguity exist where it need not. Therefore truth and plain-speaking must be cultivated."

"You're a strange creature, Master Murderer. I believe you. Are you mad?"

"Most artists are thought so, sir, by those who do not understand them."

"You're a dreamer, then?"

"Perhaps. It depends how you use the word. I'd be free of these ropes, sir, if you please. Would you be kind enough to cut them off? The strands of the net in particular are prone to bite quite deep."

"You'll give me your word you won't make an attempt to escape?"

"No, sir. But your rogues must still be below. I'll promise to offer no harm to your person, which is, in reality, a better oath."

"I think it is." His eyes narrowing, the Saracen sliced at the bonds with short, cautious movements.

Quire took a deep breath and remained seated, rubbing at arms and legs. "I thank you, sir. Well, Lord Shahryar, I might or might not have been delivered up by Lord Montfallcon, but I know you've no immediate plans to kill me, so therefore you intend to bargain with me, eh?"

"I should kill you. To avenge my nephew."

"Who was robbing you, as you were aware."

"Blood is blood. How do you know I shan't kill you yet?"

"There are rituals attendant to these things, sometimes unconscious, as there are to all things—preliminaries, the working of oneself into a particular humour, the tone of the voice. I've heard many a death-song in my time, my lord, and sung many. I think I know all the tunes men sing before they kill. Similarly there are songs—words, phrases, rhythms, melodies, even—sung by those who would be killed. Have you ever detected such a song, my lord?"

"I do not hear you singing one, Captain Quire."

"I would not, my lord." Quire stood up and walked towards a bench, half-covered with old coffee beans. He swept the beans away. They rattled on the bare boards and echoed in that empty room. Quire watched them bounce. He stooped, seeing his hat nearby. He picked it up and dusted at it. "I relish life."

"And death?"

"Not mine." Now that he knew he was safe, for a while at least, Quire had regained all the pride his encounter with Montfallcon had temporarily taken from him.

"How many have you killed, Captain, in Montfallcon's service?"

Quire became vague. "You ask me a political, not a personal question."

"How many have you killed? How many lives have you taken, in your career?"

"An hundred, at least. Probably more. That is, myself. Scores have died in fights and such. But I remember only a few."

"My nephew's?"

Quire cupped his hand to his hidden ear. "Aha. I think I detect you tuning for that song I mentioned."

Lord Shahryar shook his head. "I'll assume you recall his death, since it was so recent."

"I remember only my best work, not the run-of-the-mill stuff. There was a little girl—part of a family—whom I skewered whilst coaxing information from her dam. But it sounds nothing retold thus, and I haven't the poetry to make it live for you."

"By what morality do you justify these killings?" Lord Shahryar asked an honest question, though his tone was neutral. "I should like to know."

"Morality? None. Morality plays no part in it. That would be offensive, my lord. I have killed for every possible reason—pleasure and gold and subtle sensation; curiosity, revenge, to preserve my skin, and so on—save one: I've never killed for a moral reason."

"Montfallcon must pay you very well. Where does your gold go?"

Quire laughed reminiscently. "I've been asked the same question twice. It is a day for inquisitions. My poverty's not spartan. If I possess nothing, I can lose nothing. I rent and I borrow my necessities of the moment. I disperse my money generously but rather whimsically—I cover possible retreats—paving a silver road back to safety, if you understand me. The money's turned into the best possible asset I could have—power. And therefore I lend my money not so that I may be paid back, but so that I have someone in my debt."

"I can see that." Lord Shahryar was amused. "I wondered what weaknesses you had, Captain Quire, and now I know one of them. You tend to long-windedness, eh?"

Quire opened his mouth to reply, but Lord Shahryar returned to the original subject. "Your sword is good, I hear."

"The best steel in all the world. Blood-forged steel from Iberia. My sword and my daggers are my only valuables. They are my tools—those and my quick brain."

"So you have no other weaknesses, Captain Quire." Lord Shahryar was frowning as he turned away, his finger still to his jaw.

"I am, as you say, prone to discourse on the nature and practice of my art. I am rather proud," Quire added, by way of helping the Moor. "I am inclined to finish work even though it is evidently spoiled when half-completed. I require resolutions. I resent criticism, when sometimes I deserve it. Oh, I am sure I have more weaknesses."

"But none of the conventional sort. Women?"

"I am satisfied in my sexual needs."

"Position?"

Quire laughed.

Lord Shahryar gave up this line of argument. "What would you do to save your life?"

"Most things, sir, I think."

"Relinquish honour?"

"Your interpretation of honour might not be the same as mine, my lord. I am true to myself, true to my art."

Lord Shahryar began to brighten, as if inspired. "I do begin to understand. Montfallcon employs you for your special gifts, I see. You are not an ordinary assassin."

Quire shifted his position on the table. "Lord Montfallcon employs me no longer."

"What? I understand your initial words at last. He has put you out!"

"No, my lord. I have given up his patronage."

Lord Shahryar nodded. "And that is why you thought he'd betrayed you to me."

"Now I know he did not directly betray me—perhaps only carelessly. I expected greater loyalty."

"From him?" The Moor flapped an airy hand. "Not Montfallcon. He respects no-one. He has long since rejected humanity in favour of idealism."

"I learned as much today."

"So you require a fresh patron, eh?"

"I did not say so, sir. But I tell you this: if you agree to spare my life and let me go away from here unharmed, then I will perform any service you require, save regicide."

"Any service, Quire?"

"One, sir. No more. A favour for my life. It's fair."

"You owe me at least that already. In return for my nephew's life."

"I did not say I slew him."

"But you did slay him. I spent a good deal of money investigating the crime, once given the initial clue."

"King's in Newgate for it—or already transported."

"And you and your varlet are free."

Quire shrugged. "Let's say I agree to that bargain. A favour for his life, a favour for my own. You already make a profit of one hundred per cent. Which two favours can I accomplish, Lord Shahryar?"

"None. I have agreed to nothing you propose. Yet I might be prepared to write off all debits and credits up to this moment. And offer you, instead, my patronage." Lord Shahryar was laughing delightedly as he turned with arms outstretched, almost as if he displayed his breast to Quire's knife. "A patron to honour you, Captain Quire! To offer you the greatest possible opportunities for the practice and enlargements of your Art. Montfallcon would not honour you. I shall."

"But what's the commission, Lord Shahryar?"

The Moor became ecstatic. Tears of joy were in his eyes as he looked upon his potential protégé. "Albion," he said.

Captain Quire set his hat back on his head and scratched his scalp. His luck and his mood had changed drastically in the last few hours. It was as if he had prayed for this opportunity and it had been delivered to him. He understood, in broad terms, what the Moor asked, but the commission very nearly daunted him.

"Gloriana?"

"She would be happier if wed to our Grand Caliph. The burden of State is too much for a woman."

"Montfallcon?"

"Disgraced." A shrug. "Whatever you wish."

"Specifically, what shall I do?"

"It would be your business to corrupt the Court. The details, of course, would be in your hands—blackmail, charm, deception, murder, what you will—so long as you encouraged cynicism and despair, suspicion and vice, in Gloriana's followers." Lord Shahryar's voice rose, a hymn, as he delivered a prospectus into which he, untrammelled by a Montfallcon's conscience and doubts, could pour fire—and transmit that fire to Quire—offering him the one thing he desired: respectful sympathy for his greatness in his chosen trade. "We grant you this opportunity, Captain Quire, as well as your life. Also, our gold."

Quire was excited and amused, wavering. "You win me by flattery, do you, my lord?"

Lord Shahryar said: "I have already praised your talents. The gold would be useful, even to you." He had missed Quire's meaning.

Quire stripped a black gauntlet from his hand and waved the conversation into a different course. "I asked for a specific commission."

"If I tell you, you could tell Montfallcon. . . ."

"Montfallcon's no longer my master."

"And I?"

"I still await the exact plot."

"You swear silence?"

"I'll say nothing to Montfallcon, if that's what you mean."

"The Grand Caliph desires to marry Gloriana so that Arabia and Albion are equal in all things. With this power, he would make war on Tatary and crush our traditional foe for ever. But before he can do this, Gloriana's own courtiers must see her as a weakling; her nobles must lose their faith in her omnipotence, as must the commons. The Court must be shown to be weak and corrupt. Montfallcon must be disgraced or made a fool in the eyes of the Queen—she listens only to him and the Council. The Countess of Scaith must be removed from Court. All the Council, if possible, must be seduced in some way. Murders must occur which will be blamed upon the blameless. Contention, suspicion, counter-measures. You follow me?"

"Naturally, but I am not sure it could be done."

"You could do it. No-one else, Quire."

Quire nodded. "It is true that if I refused you would be hard put to find one with my skills and my opportunities. There is Master Van Haag in the Low Countries, and one or two Florentines—a Venetian I can think of—but they do not know our Court as I know it. Well, the work would be hard and it would take a great deal of preparation."

"We are fairly patient. Our Grand Caliph wishes it to seem that he comes to Albion as a saviour, accepted both by the Queen and by the people." The Moor had Quire half-mesmerised. "Could you do it?"

"I think so."

Lord Shahryar said: "What we Arabians offer Albion is security, purity, morality. We are traditionally praised for these virtues. You must create the climate in which the folk of Albion would cry out for our virtues. We should come to save you—Queen and Realm."

"And I should have revenge," said Quire to himself. "I should be vindicated."

Lord Shahryar continued: "You would be rewarded, of course. Made great. Would Montfallcon elevate you?"

"No, my lord. I trusted him for that."

"Do not, Captain Quire, suggest you dislike power." Lord Shahryar linked an arm with that of his nephew's murderer.

"I have plenty."

"But no position."

"And therefore no responsibility. If I were Baron Quire I should have to set an example. Why, I'd be scarcely more free than the Queen herself!"

"A principality? A nation? To indulge your tastes with even greater imagination?"

Quire shook his head. "Like Lord Montfallcon you misunderstand me, sir. And besides, I know you would try to kill me when my work was done. This offer of a nation is nonsense. You would not tolerate a small world of my creation. No, I'll choose my reward when my task is done. I'll do it, as you've guessed, for the art of it. If I decide to help you, you will have won me from Montfallcon for a single reason—you appreciate that I am an aesthete. You have flattered me and tried to stimulate me in other ways. Well, I am flattered. I am stimulated. But it is only the commission itself that attracts. If I brought Albion down, Queen and all, and if you succeeded in killing me for my pains, I'd die in the knowledge that I had produced my greatest, most lasting work."

Lord Shahryar withdrew his arm from Quire's and looked into the Captain's glittering eyes. "Does Montfallcon fear you, Quire?"

Quire stretched himself and drew deeply of the coffee-flavoured air. "I think he will."

He contemplated a rich and bloody future, yawning like a waking leopard who opens sleepy eyes to see that, in the night, he has suddenly become surrounded by a herd of plump gazelles. He smiled.

The Fourteenth Chapter

In Which Gloriana, Queen of Albion, and Una, Countess of Scaith, Venture Upon an Exploration into the Hidden World

THE COUNTESS OF Scaith drew both her shutters back and felt the warmth of the sun on her face. She sniffed at her violets. From this bedroom window she looked across lawns and sprouting gardens to the ornamental lake which, this morning, had begun to lose the untidy sheen of winter. There were gardeners and the like about, trimming and twitching. The spring, when it came, thought Una with sudden melancholy, would be unwelcome. Behind her, in the curtained bed, Gloriana still slept. She had come here, weeping, at night, for comfort. In black damasked silk Una headed for the bell rope, understanding that the Queen must soon awake. But she hesitated, arms folded, to stare down at her friend, who seemed at peace. Gloriana's huge beauty filled the bed; her marvellous auburn hair lay all around her head and shoulders in great skeins and her fair, high-boned, innocent face, half-turned from the light admitted through the curtain's gap, showed a degree of childish wistfulness which brought tears to Una's eyes and made her pull the curtains tight, considering a means of distracting the Queen, for a few hours at least, and making her a girl again.

For some while Una had wanted (selfishly, she thought) to show Gloriana what she had discovered about the nature of the palace. She had hesitated for several reasons: Gloriana's time was rarely her own; Gloriana preferred to spend as long as possible in private company with Una; Gloriana carried so many concerns with her, regarding the palace, the city and the Realm, that further knowledge might increase her anxieties. And yet, thought

Una, she could offer Gloriana compensation for all this, for what she would offer would be a shared secret, clear of State and Politics—some private knowledge—potential, if temporary, escape. Though she could think of no appointments for today, Una continued to hesitate, impatient of Responsibility which hovered all around; yet trapped, unable to dismiss it, and in this she was almost as burdened as the Queen. She knew, too, that the bright, sharp thoughts of morning, when one was still allowed to dream unchallenged, might soon be muddied by the myriad considerations of commitment to lazily made promises and thoughtless assurances, not to mention established ritual and routine, of previous, more hectic moments. To wake Gloriana now, with breathless predictions of adventure and freedom, might serve to create a greater melancholy when the realisation of the day's prepared events occurred. Una decided that she would wait—test her friend's heart and discover both her public and her temperamental desires.

And so she moved from the room and its velvet-shielded bed, into the next. She moved in glinting black silk, like a supernatural being—half shadow, half silver fire—to the little bedchamber of her maidservant, and entered without warning, as was her habit, to find Elizabeth Moffett already dressed, in good plain linen, and brushing out her hair.

"Morning, your ladyship." Elizabeth Moffett was uninhibited by the presence of her mistress. Her face grew a little red, from the effort of the brushing. Her square, wholesome features were typical of her northern home. All Una's servants were from the North, for she was inclined to mistrust Southerners as muddle-headed and careless in their duties; an inherited prejudice which she knew to be unfair but which she preferred to follow in the hiring of personal staff. Una loved Elizabeth for her unimaginative relish of commonplace life.

"Good morning, Elizabeth. I have a visitor. Would you please have breakfast for two prepared and ensure we are not disturbed."

"Ho, ho, ho." Elizabeth Moffett winked at the Countess. Her interpretations of Una's life were always direct and never subtle.

Una smiled and returned, rustling, to her own room, where Gloriana could be heard awakening.

The bed-curtains parted and through them appeared the tangled head of the World's Ideal, shamefaced. "Oh, Una!"

The Countess of Scaith was at the window again, watching a carthorse, which drew a cargo of seedlings, cropping, unknown to the gardener, at some recently planted privet.

"Your Majesty?" Una's expression was gently sardonic and it made Gloriana laugh, as Una had known it must.

"Una! What's the hour?"

"Early enough. There's time to break your fast. What must you do today?"

"Today? But you know better than I. Tell me."

"There are no commitments until noon, when we dine with the ambassador from Lyonne and that wife."

"Ah, me!" Gloriana's head disappeared. Her muffled voice continued. "But we're free till then, eh?"

"Free," said Una, and dared herself to add: "For exploration. Just we two. If Your Majesty is of a mind . . ."

"What?" The head reappeared, eyes wide. "What?"

"I have a discovery I would share. The palace is ancient, as you know."

"As ancient as Albion, some think. Founded when New Troy was founded."

"Aye. Old roofs are said to lie below the ground now."

"So scholars speculate. What's this, Una? You have discovered an antique vault?"

"More. The secret passages . . ."

"No secrets, those. I dared them all, as a girl. They lead nowhere, most of them, save to blank walls."

"What's beyond those blank walls?"

"Eh? Montfallcon would know, if that were true. It's his business."

"If Montfallcon knows, he refuses to speak of them. I've sounded him. He's vague. Perhaps by decision. He allows the surface, accepts the possibility of certain depths, but no more."

"That is his temperament, I think."

"Aye. Well, then, we have a secret which Montfallcon will not share—whatever his reasoning."

"Oh, I should love such a secret!" Gloriana flung away the curtains and was on bare feet, in crumpled, musty white, to lift her friend almost bodily from the ground in her strong, enthusiastic arms. "Una! Escape!"

"Of sorts. Without anyone knowing where we go. I found the entrance shortly upon my return from Scaith. It leads to subterranean parts, full of old relics, rich with hints of a past our histories scarcely mention."

"We can visit those tunnels? You'll lead me?"

"If you're for it. We should dress in some rough disguise, I think. It would add to the excitement."

"Indeed. We'll go as young men. In those costumes of ours."

"I thought the same. With swords and poignards and feathered bonnets."

"Boots and leathern doublets. Aye. Now?"

"We have the moment."

"We'll seize it, then!" Gloriana kissed her friend upon the lips. "And then, when we've explored, we can tell a few companions. John Dee? What do you say? Wheldrake?"

"It might be best to make all this our own. No sharing. I'll show you why."

"You have our clothes, Una?"

"Where they always are. In the trunk."

"And lanterns? Shall we need lanterns?"

"We shall."

Gloriana frowned. "What if there's danger? Broken steps, hidden pits, quaking roofs?"

"We'll avoid them. I've already travelled the paths. I'll lead you." Una knew the Queen did not refer to her own danger but to her responsibilities as the Realm's cornerstone.

"Shall we find demons, Una?"

Glad of Gloriana's elation, anxious to maintain it by any means, Una cried: "Only those we can vanquish with glaive and valour, because our hearts are virtuous!"

"Where's the entrance?" Gloriana was opening the trunk and dragging out the disguises they had used some while before, when they had conceived the notion of courting maids together.

"Here." Una pointed at the far wall. "In the next room. A deep closet I'd scarcely used. It leads into a passage I knew was there. A few steps, then down to a blocked door which once led outside. There are many like it."

"Aye. Hern's Court created the fashion. But that's not all, of course. Go on."

"I found the wall behind the steps hollow. The bricks moved. I made a hole. And there it was!" Una tugged on loose breeches and buckled them up. She pulled a linen shirt over her naked chest and pointed it, fluffing at the lace on collar and cuffs before drawing the peasecod doublet round her body and buttoning it from navel to throat. Stockings and shoes, a scarlet slouch hat with a blue ostrich plume, and she was ready to sling the belt, with sword and dirk, about her waist. Gloriana rolled up her hair, which was much longer than Una's, and fitted it under a tighter cap, also feathered. She wore a short cape on one shoulder and her doublet was of brown padded velvet, but she resembled Una in essence. They stood, right hands on hips, left on hilts, and laughed at one another—two gallants of the town, poor younger sons, ready for any escapade.

"Breakfast first," said Una, always the leader when they were dressed thus. "And we must take one of those portable clocks of Master Tolcharde's, so that we know when to return. The pocket watch?" She found it, wound it and placed it in her purse. Its loud tick sounded against her thigh. She swaggered to the door, opened it a fraction. Elizabeth Moffett had done as asked and porridge, herrings and bread were ready on a crystal table which had been brought back as booty from some forgotten West Indian campaign.

The eating done, Una took them to the closet, sliding back a squeaking panel, lifting her lantern to show the steps and, in the wall immediately to her left, a newly made hole. "Here," she said. "I thought of it when I noticed that cold air came from a vent in one of my rooms downstairs—in what I had always considered solid stone. I discovered that there is an entire passage—too small for upright movement—which passes that room, which can be seen into in turn. If I wished, I could spy upon myself! But that's not of much interest. Here." She helped tall Gloriana through the gap. There were more steps, twin to the others, leading down.

The lantern light was almost too bright in the narrow chilly corridor. They whispered, yet their voices were amplified, as the light seemed to be amplified, at paradox with their confines, and oddly comforting. Dust in their nostrils brought unspecific nostalgia. They were both children now, holding hands and pressing on. A rat went by. They tipped their hats to him as he fled. Spiders were studied, patches of moss found to resemble the faces of certain courtiers. Their spirits rose so as to border on ecstasy while the tunnel turned, dropped, climbed, leading them away from Dignity and Charity and Grace and the other sober demands of office, until they entered a high gallery, all intricate, barbaric carving, with ancient beams supporting a ceiling of panelled wood, and the lanterns cast shadows, displayed inhuman faces and peculiar representations of animal forms, yet still they giggled, but more quietly, as if they feared to offend these ancestral monuments. Even when something moved, a larger shadow, not their own, they felt no anxiety, though they could not identify the source. They found grimy paintings and rubbed them clean to exclaim upon the unsuspected skills of ancient craftsmen. They seated themselves in dusty chairs and wondered how many hundreds of years they had waited here to be used again. They pretended to find human remains—sticks; fallen, rotted woodwork; rusting weapons; the bones of cats or rats—which hinted at epic murder from Albion's legends. They investigated little rooms which still contained narrow beds and benches, lengths of chain and manacles, as if prisoners had slept and worked here—perhaps those who had carved the gallery which lay behind them. They descended pitted stone and heard water but never saw it. They found wax, so fresh-seeming it might have fallen from a candle an hour or so since. They found scraps of food, doubtless borne here by the ubiquitous rats. They heard movements everywhere and guessed these came from the inhabited palace, unseen on the other side of several walls. It was strange to be so close to activity without being able to see or even to identify the source of movements. They heard voices, laughter, cries, the rattle of implements, footfalls—fragments of sound, sometimes quite loud, sometimes very faint, as if space itself possessed different qualities within the walls. They were haunted by the living.

Una led Queen Gloriana up a further, twisting flight and crawled along a little tunnel, cautioning her to silence, until suddenly there was dappled light ahead of them, with its source on their right, from the wall. Una turned with difficulty and crawled backwards so that, head to head, they could both look through the lattice at the room below.

Gloriana's astonishment gave Una considerable satisfaction. They could see Doctor Dee himself, pacing the length of a room half-full of curling parchments, of simple furniture, scientific glasses, instruments of brass and polished hardwood, untidy shelves and cupboards, crystals, mirrors, geographical globes, orreries, phials containing richly coloured liquids and powders, all the paraphernalia and stimuli for his myriad intellectual investigations.

He wore a loose robe, nothing else, and as he paced it opened to reveal his firm flesh, grizzled hair and, to their shared astonishment, his disproportionately large private parts, which he fingered absently all the while, as if to aid his concentration. Queen Gloriana bit her lip and shook with amusement, then became ashamed, tugging at Una to come away.

Una, however, crawled further back, to another square of light, and Gloriana was tempted to follow. Here they could see into John Dee's bedchamber. It was as littered with charts and books and pieces of alchemical apparatus as the other room. Only the bed, draped with black curtains bearing a variety of mystical and astrological symbols as befitted the couch of a follower of Prometheus, was free of paper. Gloriana frowned a question, but Una's hand begged her to be patient and to continue looking. Very soon Doctor Dee paced in, his robe sailing back from his bare body, his manhood now much huger in his sensitive hand. Gloriana gasped.

"Oh," they heard him groan, "if only there were an antidote for love. This exquisite poison! It fills my being. Some philtre which robbed the body of lust but left the mind clear. There is none. To dampen such desires is to extinguish the higher investigations of the brain. I must have both! I must have both! Ah, madam! Madam!"

Gloriana creased an unbelieving brow.

He drew the curtains of the bed gently and it seemed that there lay in shadow a figure, tall and giving off a very faint lustre, as a putrefying corpse might shine. They saw John Dee begin to stroke the object. He murmured to it. He lay down beside it and he flung his arms around it, flung a leg across it—twitch. "Oh, my beauty! Oh, my love. Soon your loins shall live—and throb to my pounding dork! Ah! Ah!"

Gloriana pulled at Una, retreating.

Eventually they stood upright upon the stair, their lanterns held loosely in their hands. Gloriana was leaning heavily against the wall, her mouth hanging open. "Una!"

"It shows us a mortal sage, eh?"

"We should not have watched! That thing he has—what is it? Is he in love with a dead creature? Is it human or animal? Or a demon, even? Perhaps it is a demon, Una. Or a corpse, waiting for the demon to inhabit it." The rustle and murmur from the walls had begun to disturb her now. "Does my Dee dabble in necromancy?"

"Not at all." Una began to lead the way down the stair. "That thing's probably no more than a wax effigy of someone. No-one. He loves you, Your Majesty, don't you see?"

"I thought so. But then I denied it."

"I've spied on him before. He speaks of you constantly. He is in a fever of wanting you."

"But he has never hinted. . . ."

"He cannot. He loves you. He fears—well, many things. He fears you will laugh at him. That you will be shocked by him. That you will become afraid of him. He is constantly in a quandary. And, it appears, he is incapable of satisfying himself with any other woman."

"He seemed confident with—that. . . ."

"He pretended it was you."

Gloriana began to smile broadly. "Oh, poor Dee. Should I —?"

"It would be poor politics, Your Majesty."

"But excellent sport. And it would make him happy. After all, he has given so much to me and done so much for the Realm. He should be rewarded. There are few who could understand his pain as I understand it."

"He does not suffer as you suffer."

"To a degree, Una."

"But not to the same degree. Be cautious, Your Majesty. Montfallcon . . ."

"You think it would be destructive. And so it would. It's four years since I entertained a courtier. They grow ambitious, or melancholy, or wild, then strange humours fill the palace. There are jealousies."

"And expenses," said the Countess of Scaith. "You have had to marry so many of them off, bestow estates. Your kindness to those who have loved you . . ."

"My guilt." Gloriana nodded to agree with Una. "But you're right, dear heart. Dee must burn on and I must do my best to continue to treat him as I have always treated him."

"You still maintain respect, surely."

"Of course. But it will be harder to milk humour from him, knowing his pain, by setting Montfallcon off against him, as I love to do. It's poor sport for me and none at all for Dee."

They crossed a low-ceilinged room and found a broken door through which to enter the tunnel they had left, but, as they stooped, torchlight flared from another door, to their right, and they turned, straightening, afraid.

A small man peered from beneath his upraised hand. He seemed to have a humpback or some other growth upon his shoulder. He wore a leather jerkin and breeches and a dark shirt, its collar folded at the neck. He had large eyes and a wide mouth, giving him something of the appearance of an intelligent frog. They raised their own lanterns, assuming the poses suitable to their disguise.

"What's this?" Una, lounging on the wall, was arrogant. "The dungeon keeper, left behind?"

She saw now that the man's shoulder carried a small black-and-white cat which sat very straight and still and looked at her with yellow, candid eyes.

"What's this?" echoed Jephraim Tallow, mocking her. "Two play-actors who've lost their way?"

"We're gentlemen, sir," said Gloriana boldly. "And might resent your insult."

Tallow opened his huge mouth and laughed. Una believed in her heart that she and the Queen had been recognised, but such thoughts were scarcely logical here. She stepped forward. "We're exploring these tunnels on Lord Montfallcon's business. Looking for traitors, renegades, vagabonds."

"Aha. Well, you've caught one, gentlemen." Tallow's smile was insinuating. "Or two, if you like. Me and Tom. Vagabonds the pair of us. Confirmed rogues. Scavengers. But not traitors, nor are we renegades, for we serve no-one and therefore can turn against no-one. We live on our own account, Tom and myself." He bowed. The cat clung on. "You'll see I'm swordless, sir, so cannot offer you the duel you desire."

"I spoke hastily." In return Una made a short bow. "We were startled by your sudden appearance here."

"And I by yours." Tallow found a stone bench in the darkness and seated himself, crossing arms and legs and staring up at them. "Well?"

"You know these passages, then?"

"They're my home for the moment. Until I grow tired of them and move on. But I've a poor understanding of the real world, which is why I prefer to be separated from it, as one is, of necessity, here. Though I'm fascinated by it, also. This is the ideal habitat for a fellow of my persuasion. And you are Lord Montfallcon's men, eh? On the Queen's business, then?"

"Indeed," said Gloriana with an irony Una felt was dangerously obvious.

"I guessed you to be some of the larger palace beasts at first," said Tallow. Una suspected this remark to be pointed failure to sense Gloriana's meaning.

"Beasts?" said the Queen.

"They hibernate in the winter. A few of them are beginning to rouse. Creatures of all sorts. They make life dangerous for the rest of us. Now, tell me the truth, gentlemen, Montfallcon will have no-one in the walls. It does not suit him. You are escaped from some imprisonment, or threat of it, and seeking a hiding place, I'd guess."

"Montfallcon knows . . . ?" Gloriana hesitated.

"Of the darker places of the palace? Oh, aye. Some of 'em, at least. But Tallow knows 'em all. Shall we be friends? You'll have me for your guide."

"Aye," said Gloriana, rather too readily in Una's opinion. "Friends it is—and a guide, Master Tallow."

"These rooms go down deeper and deeper," Tallow told them. "To natural caverns where blind, white beasts blunder and devour one another. To halls so ancient they were hewn from living rock before the first Golden Age. To strange cloisters inhabited by dwarfish men who were here before true men walked the Earth. All this lies below the palace which lies below the palace. These haunts are modern in comparison, a few hundred years old. The true antiquity is so alien to us that it plays tricks upon our minds should we merely be witness to it. And yet, I know, there are those who dwell there, no longer sane, in our eyes, though eminently sane in their own—men and women, once . . . They breed, some of them, I think."

Una lifted her shoulders back. "You seek to frighten us, Master Tallow?"

"No, gentlemen. I receive no relish from alarming others. I speak of it as a curiosity, that's all." He reached up and stroked his cat. "It's cold here."

"Aye," came Gloriana's small voice.

"I'll take you to the warmer parts," Tallow said. "Come. You can meet a few of your fellow exiles—those who have no objection to being met, that is. Most of the folk who dwell here are inclined to be reclusive. It is why they choose to live between the walls."

"How many?" Gloriana whispered.

"I've never counted 'em, sir. A hundred or two, maybe. We live, most of us, by scavenging. And there's superstitious servants to rely upon, too. Those who think us devils or fairies and put out titbits for us. But they misjudge our size. A strapping fellow like you, sir, needs meat every day to maintain such a huge frame. You have an unusual figure, sir." Tallow spoke casually as he led them on. "There's only one other I know who possesses such size. . . ."

"We'd best return," said Una urgently. She stopped in her tracks, taking Gloriana by the arm. "No time for further exploration now."

But Gloriana had shaken her off and advanced. Una was forced to follow.

The passage widened, opening upon a very large hall, like a covered market. Flickering torches illuminated the place and an unruly fire burned in a grate at one end, while around the walls, in changing flame-cast shadows, as nomads might camp, small tents or groups of tents: tiny territories marked out by means of ropes, or rubble, or pieces of half-rotten furniture, or blocks of stone torn from the very foundations of the hall. And white faces stared from shawls and hoods and hollows: thin faces, for the most part, with large eyes, as if already these people adapted to the glooms: another race.

Gloriana stopped dead when she saw the scene and was bumped against by Una who, lost in her own rapid thoughts, noticed it a few seconds later.

"Who are these?" the Queen whispered.

A great figure had risen from beside the fire and stood in silhouette, pausing as if to confront the newcomers. Then it had dashed into deeper darkness and was gone.

Una, full of dread, gripped the Queen's arm. "No," she implored. "We must return."

Tallow was amused. "She is shy, the mad woman. Of all of us. But you shouldn't fear her."

There was no curiosity in the faces of this lost gathering, and Tallow greeted none of them. It seemed that he did not regard himself as part of the tribe. He displayed it with a distant, proprietorial air, in his self-chosen rôle as their guide. "There are gentlemen here, like yourselves. And well-born ladies. Most, of course, claim to be a little nobler than they actually were. But why should they not? Here they create themselves and their surroundings afresh. It is all they have."

But Gloriana had at last broken free from the fascination and, in obedience to Una's terror, was in retreat.

Tallow called out from behind them. They ignored him. They ran through the passages, back to where they had first encountered the little man. They climbed and scrambled up passages and flights of steps, half afraid that they were lost, though the way was familiar: through the carven gallery, which now seemed to threaten, and along the narrow corridors to Una's rooms, to squeeze through the panel, and slam it shut.

Gloriana was paler than the nomads of the walls. She leaned, in dusty gallant's guise, panting against the wall. She attempted to speak, but failed. Una said to her: "It must be forgotten. Oh, Your Majesty, I have been so foolish! It must be forgotten."

Queen Gloriana stood upright. She recalled the great silhouette in the hall and her head filled with terror again. Her face was without expression. Tears ran from her eyes. "Yes," she said. "It must be forgotten."

The Fifteenth Chapter

In Which Lord Montfallcon Is Dismayed by His News and Begins to Regret His Poor Diplomacy

LORD MONTFALLCON LAY alone in his substantial bed while his wives in the next chamber rubbed ointments into one another's wounds, whispering and gasping. He was miserable, unreconciled, self-loathing that morning, for Gloriana's voice had sounded through the night, pathetic and full of grief, and he had awakened his wives so that their cries would drown the Queen's. Montfallcon moved his strong old body in the bed and rebuked himself for his lack of vigour, and wondered if, at this time of delicate crisis, his brain, which had held so much, controlled so much, was at last about to fail. The Queen was recently more melancholy than ever, and he could not name the cause. She had cleverly avoided the question of marriage when he had raised it. Lord Montfallcon had also received news of Tom Ffynne's capture in the Middle Sea. The old pirate, growing short-sighted, had mistaken an Arabian barquentine for an Iberian barque, and now Arabia complained loudly and at length, ritualistically, though the mistake was obvious. Then in the middle of all this, Sir Christopher Martin had died, poisoned, apparently by his own hand, as if he felt dishonoured. This was a bad omen to nobles and to commons. There were rumours of a quarrel between King Casimir and the Grand Caliph; other rumours of a pact between them. There were rumours out of Tatary, rumours from the German and Flemish States, from Iberia and the High Countries, from Africa and from Asia; and Quire, his eye, his hand, his weapon in the world, was missing.

Whether Quire, offended by Montfallcon's undiplomatic

response during their last encounter, played doxy-on-a-high-horse to further his own ends, whether his pride was genuinely wounded, whether he had taken a notion to visit foreign lands or even seek foreign employ, or whether he had paid a price, at last, for his crimes, Montfallcon did not know. And of all things, Lord Montfallcon hated ignorance. It was his impulse, his necessity, to be omniscient. Now not only was his main well of knowledge run dry, but the very location of that well was lost. Frustrated, having no news on which he could base further actions, Montfallcon knew a kind of terror, as a warrior in the heat of battle might feel to receive a hint of imminent paralysis and blindness. It seemed to Montfallcon that unseen enemies were creeping closer and that all he could sense of them was their unspecific malice.

He had failed to understand his tool, Quire, with sufficient complexity; he had imposed a view of the man's strange character upon the truth; he had broken a rule of his own, which was never to assume, always to interpret. And, because of one lazy failure to interpret Quire, he might have lost his control over the man. Quire worked for the love of his art, as Montfallcon worked for the love of his Ideal, represented in Gloriana. Their partnership, Montfallcon realised, had depended upon that understanding. But he had resented Quire's suggestion that they were equal, that they collaborated as poets collaborate upon a play. In the past Montfallcon had trained himself to deny any expression of pride which might be false or which might threaten his goal, but, in his last interview with Quire, he had let his anger, his arrogance, dominate him and so clash with Quire's own pride. He understood now that if Quire had attacked him on like grounds—accusing him, say, of base motives in his work for Albion—he might have felt the same fury. And yet Montfallcon respected Quire's intelligence. It did not seem typical of the man that he should sulk this long. A day or so, certainly. Even a week. It had been a month. It occurred to Montfallcon that Quire might be planning some form of vengeance against him, but Quire's particular nature was not of the sort to turn to petty revenge. More likely Quire proved himself by performing some complicated espionage, the results of which he would present to Montfallcon by way of a challenge.

Montfallcon, however, could be sure of none of this. Because he had misjudged once, he had lost some of his faith in his own judgement: he could misjudge again.

With a groan he floundered from sheets which stank of lavender and sweat. He must prepare himself for the day.

The gagtoothed knave, Quire's lieutenant, in his coney cap and his overlarge leather greatcoat, his gallooned doublet, his puffed hose and turned-down jackboots, who waited for Lord Montfallcon in the small chamber, striking a pose with longsword and cocked leg, was a sight to encourage Montfallcon that morning, so that he greeted Tinkler almost merrily, enquiring after his health and his fortunes. He bustled, in his usual grey and black, to his desk where, it seemed, more paper than usual had gathered. He frowned.

"Well, Master Tinkler?"

"My lord?"

"You've news of Captain Quire?"

"No, my lord. Nothing certain. I came because I thought that you might reassure me. Also, the debts mount, you know, and the Captain has not paid me in a month. I still work on his behalf. . . ."

Montfallcon studied a letter from Bantustan. "Eh? What is it, then, Master Tinkler? You've come for gold?"

"Or silver, sir. Something to keep me going until Captain Quire returns, or . . ."

"Have you heard aught of Quire?"

"There was some gossip, my lord, that's all. When we left you here last, we went together to the Ares Gate and then parted, agreeing to meet a few hours later. He never found me at the inn and, to my knowledge, has never been there since. The gossip concerned a scuffle by the Ares Gate. The Captain, or someone like him, was attacked and carried off, either dead or wounded."

"By whom?"

"No witnesses, sir. This news is all indirect, you see. A child saw it, maybe. Or a housewife behind a curtain. There's other rumours followed, but Captain Quire has taught me well—I go to the core and at the core remain, until there's more discovered."

"You pursued the tale?"

"Of course, sir, for Captain Quire's my friend. And my benefactor. And more. I asked at every house. I enquired the direction of every cart coming from the Ares Gate. I made enquiries of every ruffler and cutpurse I could find. It seems that a gang was recruited and that Captain Quire might have been their prey. But I know not who they are, nor who employed them, nor why they were employed."

"There's an angel for you, Tinkler." Montfallcon stretched his hand towards the scrawny rogue. "And I'll have more if you can prove Captain Quire's whereabouts or his fate. You think he's dead?"

"The Saracens are said to have been seeking him."

"It is not their custom to hide the body of a man on whom they've taken vengeance. They would display Quire."

"True. I've seen more than one corpse of theirs, when I was with the Captain on that errand in the Middle Sea, my lord."

Lord Montfallcon wondered if Tinkler spoke significantly, to remind him of service given to Albion. He looked at the thin-faced, gagtoothed scarecrow, fearing that he misjudged him, too, and that he might dismiss another Quire.

But Tinkler, glad of the gold, anxious to placate him, miserable as a dog deserted by its master, was not a substitute for the clever little Quire.

Lord Montfallcon became bitter. There had never been a servant as quick and brilliant. He had lost the best.

"If you see him, Master Tinkler—should he live—you'll give him my most anxious felicitations?"

"I shall, sir, of course. We're both loyal men, sir."

"Aye." Montfallcon picked up a letter, in code, from Bohemia. "You'll point out to him how much I miss him, how much the Empire needs him, how greatly his skills and his arts are appreciated here."

"It's what he was wondering about, my lord. That."

"What?"

"Whether you appreciated how finely he performed the deeds you set him. With what perfection he planned and composed his plots, to make all neat, to divert suspicion, to bring further information which might be of use. To put a stop to evil gossip and libels. He regarded himself as a poet might, my lord."

"And I?"

"His most understanding audience."

Lord Montfallcon sighed and let the coded note from Bohemia flutter down.

Tinkler, in a fit of honesty evidently against his own interests, burst out: "He's murdered, my lord. I know. He's dead. All those wits and all that courage, gone!"

"Bring me the proof of that, Tinkler, and I'll pay you very well. Or bring me disproof, and I'll pay you as much or more. Bring me Captain Quire, alive to this room, Master Tinkler, and I will guarantee a rich pension for the rest of your life."

Tinkler lowered his head, then looked up quickly, as if another thought had formed.

Lord Montfallcon's smile was grim. "And in the meanwhile, Tinkler, bring me what news you can from foreign sources. Your employment is secured."

Tinkler bowed and retreated for the Spiders' Door, to make his way along the very periphery of those forgotten vaults and catacombs, hidden in the palace as Hades itself might be hidden in Heaven's very heart.

While Tinkler broke, with some relief, into the damp, bright April air, Lord Montfallcon forced his hectic brain to dwell upon the matter of the forthcoming Celebration of Spring, at which the Queen must honour various worthies and placate a myriad of minor dignitaries. He was thankful that the main business would be left to Gallimari, Master of the Revels, and that only the diplomatic problems would be his. Such problems would be time-wasting, but at least they were not of any particular consequence. These public occasions were important in that they displayed the Queen's presence to the people, reassured them of her greatness and Albion's security, wealth and power.

He found Master Wheldrake's verses, submitted to him yesterday, as he had requested, and carefully read them through. He had always been a trifle suspicious of Wheldrake, especially when the poet had first arrived at the palace with a reputation of sensuousness and impiety, but there was no doubt Wheldrake's work had improved considerably under the influence and disciplines of the Court. Montfallcon regretted he had already drawn up the Spring Honours, but he determined to ask the Queen next season to bestow at least a baronetcy upon one who seemed to understand so well the Mysteries and Accountabilities of the Matter of Albion.

The Sixteenth Chapter

In Which Queen Gloriana Celebrates the Advent of Spring and Experiences the First Forewarning of Future Tragedy

IN A GOWN of white and green, stitched with tiny buttercups, daisies and daffodils, upon an open litter whose surrounding frame was woven with garlands of ivy, wallflowers, bluebells and marigolds, Queen Gloriana was borne by her bright gentlemen into the wide, walled park behind the palace. Here, fallow deer looked out from the dappled shade of oaks and poplars which thickly hid the high wall itself from view, while overhead, in the swaying Tree Walk, trumpeters placed brazen instruments to lips and blew G L O R I A N A, a greeting and a triumph.

For today she came as May Queen, into the grounds where the Maypole stood, and where courtiers already were arranged, as shepherds, shepherdesses, milkmaids and their swains; a scattering of Cupids and a Pan, some fauns, five dryads, and one gigantic Lamb. From the Tree Walk and from galleries in the palace, many other noble visitors watched the ceremony.

The litter was lowered, the gentlemen (among them the Countess of Scaith in huntsman's garb, with bow and quiver) took their positions on either side while the company made its obeisance and the trumpets sounded again.

G L O R I A N A.

High above on a balcony overlooking the park, Lord Montfallcon stood, giving his eye first to the pretty scene below and then to the grey cloud which gathered as it sped from the west, to obscure the sun. It had always been his regret that he had no control over the weather and that Doctor Dee, who might have been excellently employed in this manner, had discovered no magical method to exert Man's power upon the elements. Doctor Dee would suffer with the rest, should it rain, for he was amongst them, in woolly satyr's disguise, together with Lady Lyst (a water nymph in blue silk), Sir Amadis Cornfield (an elegant cowboy), Lady Pamela Cornfield (a shepherdess with crook and taxidermist's ewe), Sir Vivien and Lady Cynthia Rich (huntsman and huntress) and Master Ernest Wheldrake, in some sort of elaborate avian disguise (perhaps a nightingale) with nodding plumage and gilded beak, to read his greeting to the May Queen. As the first large spots of rain began to fall, Lord Montfallcon craned to hear the distant piping. . . .

Green grows the earth and blue the skies.
Love calleth both the foolish and the wise.
Omnipotent Nature ruleth over all
Ridding us at last of Winter's frigid pall,
Inspiring swains their troth to plight
And maiden's thoughts take crazy flight.
No face may frown beneath this shining sun.
All praises sing. The Earth is fresh begun!

Master Wheldrake pulled a sodden feather or two away from his eyes and read a little more rapidly as the ink began to spread across the parchment and blot lines he had made no effort to memorise. . . .

Racing blood and beating heart confirm
Every hint that MITHRAS *has returned.*
Garlands decorate the shrines and secret bowers:
In comes Great PAN *to banish darkling hours.*
Now across the land each jolly bell its peal doth ring:
As ALBION'S *Empress summons golden Spring!*

"Well put as ever, Master Wheldrake!" The May Queen waved her silver sceptre, twined with myrtle, while lackeys rushed to throw green canvas over the litter's frame and protect Gloriana from the drenching the others must expect before the awnings were around them.

Rain thudded like running feet above her head as she took up the sword which hobbling Lord Ingleborough brought her on a cushion, and dubbed brave sailors "Sir" before, as she put it, they drowned whilst awaiting their reward. A Lord or two was made and estates granted in Virginia, in Cathay, in Hibernia, to sober men whom Lord Montfallcon judged trustworthy to enjoy the responsibilities of wealth and, by sharing to a greater degree in the bounty of the State, support the Realm's interest with that much more resolution. Envoys were sent abroad, taking certificates and letters; foreign envoys were, in turn, received, and their letters read, greetings given. Nine little girls (each one a stage younger than the last, Gloriana's natural daughters) led lambs across the flooded lawns and, sneezing, lisped their pastoral rhymes until the Queen begged their nurses to hurry them within and dry them before they perished of a chill.

The Quintain was abandoned until the next day (or until the sun should shine). The Sun Chariot, in which posed an embarrassed, sorry Lord Ransley, as Mithras, God of Light, half-naked and damp in collapsed yellow ruff and breeches, drawn by youths and maidens, also in yellow, to represent the sun's beams, came and went, making dark marks across the squelching grass. The musicians, as satyrs and nymphs, were ordered to withdraw to the Great Hall, where the dance would now be held, and the Procession through the Tree Walk was abandoned. It was decided to continue with the ceremony whereby Gloriana would be bound to the Maypole by her courtiers and released by Sir Tancred who would represent the Chivalry of Albion, unless the rain grew heavier, for the pole itself was now protected by a large square of canvas, rigged like a sail above it. Master Wheldrake was asked to come forward and read another poem.

His feathers shimmering with water, which he scattered everywhere as he gesticulated, Ernest Wheldrake announced his intention to read some recent stanzas from his long epic romance, which he had been writing for the past six years, called *Atargatis; or, The Celestial Virgin*. "You'll recall, Your Majesty, that Sir Felicites, the Shepherd

Knight, has but lately left the company of Sir Hemetes, the Hermit Knight, who has set him again upon his true path in his quest for the Court of Queen Atargatis. But before he can reach the Court he must encounter many more adventures, each one of which teaches him a further lesson and so prepares him for his position as the Queen's Protector, who must encompass Wisdom, Temperance and Justice within him, as well as Courage, Virtue and Charity." A bead of water rolled along his beak and splashed upon his costumed foot.

"We recall your story, Master Wheldrake, and listen with considerable and pleasurable anticipation to its continuation," graciously replied the May Queen as Master Wheldrake drew a damp-stained volume from his plumage and cleared his throat:

"Now through a forest drear our goodly knight
Did slowly ride in doubtful fear,
Anon, he came upon a sight:
A woodsman tall with axe did shear
Through sturdy oak and noble ash
And elm and rowan tree
With flying blade did trunk and branches gash
So that FELICITES cried out to him to cease
While, lowering lance, he signall'd peace.

"'Woodsman, what art thou named?' Quoth he,
'You, who art so strong of loin and thew,
Pray tell me what your fearsome purpose be
To hew so heavily the pine and yew
And threaten this whole wood to slay
And cause the healthy roots to die
So turning all this green to black and grey
When not a trunk's left standing high.
How art thou named? Say I.'

"The woodsman's hair with radiant silver shone
So that his face could not be seen,
His beard, like burnish'd gold, it fell upon

A mighty chest of iron, both jet and green,
And eyes like two fierce stars stared out of him
While arms and hands were shimmering rose.
And now the knight in awefull woe fell back.
'My name be CHRONOS, Lord of Time!' the giant did cry,
'And LEVELLER, my axe, makes all comply!"

"'For, in truth,' this giant continued in sober voice,
'With Life and Death there must be always Harmony,
And, since Man's own mind cannot make the choice,
To regulate the spinning globe the gods entrusted me:
Thus hour shall follow hour and day pass day
And year pursue each rounded year.'
'But this be unjust tyranny,' FELICITES did say,
'Which causeth foolish folk to grieve and mourn,
To question: And they die then whyfore are they born?'

"'Time's circle turneth,' said the giant, 'as do the spheres,
And four ages quarter up the mortal span
As Seasons subdivide the steady years.
Thus do the gods describe a Sign for Man,
That when in his last age he'll wither
His birth shall surely come again.
And though DEATH's hand shall call him thither,
LIFE's gentle lips shall stir new breath in him;
And thus Man's Winter giveth way to Spring.'

"'Certes,' said FELICITES as he took rein,
''Tis true that all must die so all can live anon,
And if thine action, CHRONOS, bringeth Man to pain,
So also doth it bring great joy to every one.
And shall I ride this forest path another hour
I'll find that all yon ruin is no more,
That trees do bloom and beauteous plants do flower
While bounding HOPE doth take momentous wing
And GLORY rule throughout thy golden Spring!'"

In spite of the rain, it was Wheldrake's moment. Not a soul in that gathering failed to be fired by the ideals and wisdom of his epic lines, save perhaps Una, Countess of Scaith, who, joining in the general applause, somehow managed to clap just a fraction out of time with the rest. Even Wheldrake took congratulation with better grace than was usual, leading Una to believe that he had at last accepted the demands of the audience and determined to please their taste rather than his own.

The rain had stopped. A little sun shone through the cloud. The awnings were pulled free and rolled aside. Curious deer continued to chew and stare from the glinting cover of the sweet-smelling oaks.

"See, Master Wheldrake, your words banish the grey skies and lure the sun from hiding!" flattered the May Queen as she advanced towards the laurel-bound pole, to fling herself upon it and laugh as the musicians reappeared with tabor, horn and flute, to mingle with the courtiers as each took a strand of bunting and began to dance, twisting this way and that, to secure a girlish, joyous Gloriana to the mighty staff of Spring, to bind this innocent, flame-haired giantess as tightly as Lord Montfallcon had tied her to his Duty.

Montfallcon was on the balcony again. He had emerged to listen to Ernest Wheldrake's verses, but now he felt alarm as he watched the merry Court surround and fetter his Ideal (for all that the chains were made of daisies and silk), and he shuddered deeply as he restrained his impulse to rush down into the park and shout for them to release her. He controlled himself, took a deep breath and smiled at his stupidity. Sir Tancred would emerge from the palace at any moment, after the Queen had spoken her lines, and free her. This time their lines would be by Master Wallis, Secretary for the High Tongue. (Montfallcon found them dry and sterile in comparison with Master Wheldrake's.)

"Is there no noble knight of Chivalry
Who'll come to set the May Queen free?"

cried Gloriana, and looked expectantly towards the door into the park through which her Champion must emerge.

Sir Tancred did not appear.

The Countess of Scaith found that she had grown alert, suddenly, and wondered why. Perhaps it was that Sir Tancred, always eager to represent the Queen in these familiar rôles, was inclined to enter the scene too early rather than too late.

Gloriana shook her head and sang out her couplet for a second time.

There was a silence now. Water could be heard dropping from the surrounding trees, from the boards of the high Tree Walk. The rustling movement of the fallow deer gave emphasis to the general stillness. The sun disappeared.

And into that hushed, bewildered throng, Sir Tancred staggered. He wore no golden helmet and his golden, fanciful armour was only half buckled. Loose plates flapped about him and clattered as he walked.

Lady Lyst's high, gasping scream was echoed by more than one other in the company.

"Sir Tancred!" The Queen tried to struggle out of the bonds, but she was completely trapped.

There were bloody smears on Tancred's golden armour. There was blood on his face, on his moustaches, and on his hands. Tears sprang from his staring eyes and his red mouth gaped as if pain turned him dumb.

The Countess of Scaith was first to reach him, to take his arm. "Sir Tancred. What has happened?"

The Queen's Champion groaned and heaved words out of him. "She is dead," he said. "The Lady Mary. I have . . . I have come. . . . Oh, she is murdered!"

"Free me!" cried Gloriana, struggling from behind them, the great pole swaying. "Free me, someone!"

The Seventeenth Chapter

In Which Lord Montfallcon Begins to Fear a Return of Terror and the Queen Begins to Question the Value of the Virtuous Myth

"It has been thirteen years," said Lord Montfallcon distantly, "since I have seen so much blood."

He looked down at Lady Mary Perrott's head, half-severed at the neck, at Sir Tancred's sword, which had created the wound, and he was sad, not for the girl who had died so terribly, nor for Sir Tancred for his sin, but for the security of his great dream. Vice had been discovered to be disguised as Chivalry. He was resentful of both the killer and the killed, who so ominously disturbed a harmony he had maintained with such fortitude since Gloriana's accession.

Lord Ingleborough, gasping in his formal wear—with casque and breastplate squeezing throat and chest and threatening to bring another heart attack upon him—still uncertain as to what had taken place, said: "Why should Tancred destroy her? It is frequently jealousy, of course, which makes a man go mad. . . ."

Montfallcon was impatient of his old friend's platitudes. "I must report to the Queen. Is Sir Tancred restrained?"

"Lord Rhoone took him."

"He must be questioned."

"He is mad." Ingleborough sat himself weightily upon one of the few chairs which were still standing upright, for Lady Mary's room was all wreckage. "Oh, the poor child. And gay. A favourite of the Queen's. The Queen . . . ?"

"She is in her apartments," said Lord Montfallcon with a sigh. "The Countess comforts her, most likely. The Perrotts are one of the most powerful families in the land. They will need more than a conventional explanation for what has happened here."

"We'll try him, eh? In the old secret court." Ingleborough mopped his head. He was sweating, perhaps with fever.

"If the Queen allows it. But I see no good can be served by undue punishment. He can be confined to apartments in Bran's Tower. Where Prince Lamartis is—and those two nobles brought us by the Thane of Hermiston."

"But Tancred's no outland lunatic."

"Bran's Tower. 'Tis best," said Montfallcon firmly.

"If he's guilty." Ingleborough stooped, grunting and feeble, and attempted to pick up the sword, but he could not lift it. It fell back upon the blood-soaked damask of Mary's dress.

"Who else?" Montfallcon said. "In Hern's time there might have been an hundred to suspect. Now there are none. I am fearful, Lisuarte." With a final, disapproving glance at the young girl's corpse, Lord Montfallcon began to move through the apartment, a surviving ship sailing through carnage after a sea-fight. Ingleborough hauled himself out of it, like a weary, beaten beast.

"You are unwell." Lord Montfallcon gave his friend an arm. They stood in the corridor where green-clad Patch, a little faun, awaited them. "Patch, take your master home. Sleep, Lisuarte. Be firm with him, Patch." He smiled at the handsome boy.

"Aye, sir."

"You'll accompany me?" enquired Lisuarte Ingleborough, gripping Patch's slender shoulders and looking back at his friend. "Eh?"

"I must to the Queen to make my report."

"The Quintain is cancelled, then?"

Montfallcon was dry. "Aye, since the chief participant, the Champion, is indisposed."

Lord Ingleborough shrugged. "The Quintain is all I care for in these entertainments. And even those are tame compared to the tilts of my youth."

"By the Queen's command we mourn, all of us, for Lady Mary."

"Aha!" Ingleborough retreated.

Lord Montfallcon wondered if he, too, had become a dotard. He looked sadly after his hobbling friend.

"My lord?" It was Wheldrake, half-stripped of his feathers, his bird mask under his arm. "Is Lady Mary truly murdered?"

"Aye."

"By whom?" The poet's voice was so high as to be almost inaudible. "By Tancred?"

"It would seem so. His sword. Her throat."

"Hermes!"

Lord Montfallcon put a steady hand on the tiny poet's twitching shoulder. "A funeral ode, perhaps, eh, Wheldrake? The Court's in mourning from this hour, by order of the Queen."

"She was a child. Sixteen summers." Wheldrake trembled. "A merry child. And she loved Sir Tancred so, with such innocence. They were model lovers, we thought, and happy friends. She gave him all. . . ."

"But not enough for the romantic soul, perhaps. Such as Sir Tancred demand a response as intense as their own. Recall how he burns to serve the Queen. His belief in Chivalry is absolute. It is why such as he are so often rejected, so often thwarted or wounded in love. Too passionate, too furious in their loyalty . . ."

"No," said Wheldrake, "she was killed by another, I'd swear."

"Who else?" They walked slowly, side by side through the silent, golden halls.

"A servant? Who tried to seduce her and failed, taking vengeance?"

"Unlikely, Master Poet."

"Another lover?"

"She had none." Lord Montfallcon licked his lips. "Her father must be told. I'll send a messenger to Hever. I am full of doubt, Master Wheldrake. I suspect a portent. Once this palace ran with innocent blood. It stank of blood, you know. Blood bloomed on tapestries, stained walls, crusted guilty blades. Girls like Lady Mary died almost daily—stabbed, poisoned, strangled. It was a time of dark madness, and Fear drove Virtue into hiding. It was Albion's Age of Iron. I would not have even a hint of its return."

"One murder is not enough to call back tyranny." Master Wheldrake was comforting, though he also felt the chill, as of an ominous wind. "If Sir Tancred committed the crime then he'll be tried, found guilty, and we'll all be sad for a month or two, no more."

"If?"

"Aye. If." Wheldrake was confident. "The true murderer shall be found, however, if it be not Tancred. Lord Rhoone and Sir Christopher's successor, working together, will question any suspect person. There are so many who cannot be suspect, for so many attended the May Day ceremony."

"So you think a servant?"

"A mad servant, aye—for it's a madman's work, sure enough. If calculated, the crime could have been hidden. Poison, stifling, imitation suicide. A madman, without a doubt."

"But Sir Tancred seems mad." Montfallcon shrugged.

"With grief."

"Just that?"

They stood now outside the Queen's apartments.

"It's my instinct," said Wheldrake, "and I cannot give you rational explanation." He bowed, his feathers dripping, and made his adieux.

Lord Montfallcon knocked upon Her Majesty's door. He was brooding, for he could only agree with Wheldrake and he did not wish to do so. Sir Tancred was, at least, a convenient and uncomplicated culprit, with no surviving family. His own suspicions lay towards certain foreign envoys domiciled at Court. Oubacha Khan, for instance, was cold-blooded but determined and hated to be thwarted. Also his vow of celibacy would make him all the more tense. And the blow had been struck once, skilfully, by someone used to handling a large blade. Or there was the warlike ambassador from Bengahl, who, Montfallcon knew, had once killed two girls of Lady Mary's age when he had caught them together in his palace bedchamber. Or secretive Li Pao, who had courted more than one mistress here and who had revenged himself on Maeve ap Rhys by branding his family mark upon her buttocks. Or the Icelandic envoy, who had been Lady Mary's sister's lover until she had been married to Sir Amadis Cornfield. Or the envoy from Peru, a land notorious for its casual letting of blood, its human sacrifice. Montfallcon would investigate them all, and again he regretted Quire's absence, as he regretted Sir Christopher's death. But more he regretted the darkness, the confusion in his brain, a familiar Chaos he had fought daily in the reign of Hern.

Wearily, he knocked again upon the Queen's door.

He hoped that Tancred was not innocent. It was better to have a culprit, cut and dried, than a Court which simmered with speculation. Rumour, gossip, suspicion and fear. He could sense them now, threatening his Golden Age, his Reign of Piety, his Age of Virtue.

For a third time he knocked and at last the doors were opened by a white-faced maid of honour, still clad in the flimsy costume of a dryad.

"My lord?"

He pushed through. "The Queen? How is the Queen?"

"She weeps, my lord. She loved Mary Perrott."

"Aye." Nonplussed, Montfallcon stalked to the window and stared moodily at the lawns, the fountains and the fanciful shrubs. It was raining forcefully now. Great drops splashed from an uncertain sky through which the sun flashed an occasional ray. Montfallcon scowled and put his back to the window. The room, with its flower scents and its thick curtains, was in half-light, occupied only by the nervous dryad.

"Announce me," he said.

"My lord, I was instructed to leave her in complete peace for an hour." A curtsey.

Montfallcon, his face like furious rock, marched grumbling from the room.

"You'll say I was here, girl."

"Of course, my lord."

She closed the door on the terrifying Chancellor and began to shudder. From through the other door there came the sound of weeping, imploring cries, as Gloriana mourned her protégée, her sweet, happy lover, her child. . . .

For Gloriana recalled the jealousy she had felt of Lady Mary's happiness and, in a brain confused by the day's chivalry and fantasy, had conceived the notion that she had by some charm brought death to the girl, had secretly willed it, had somehow, by frustrating Sir Tancred's enthusiasm for arms, arranged it. Perhaps denied satisfaction for his passions, yearning to use his monstrous blade, he had turned it upon the creature he loved. . . .

Moreover, this miserable logic was sustained by her training. For she knew she represented the whole Realm, that she held responsibility for all that occurred in the Realm and that if this terrible crime had taken place then it was because she had not been assiduous in anticipating it and therefore preventing it. And if such horror could come about in her own palace, how much more horror must exist throughout her Empire, how much unseen injustice, hidden cruelty . . . ?

Is all this Golden Age a myth to hide a darker truth? Merely a cleverer disguise protecting an actuality as bad as my father's dreadful Age of Iron? Worse, for this also has hypocrisy. Montfallcon since I was a child convinced me that the dream, if followed and believed, must soon become the truth. Yet Tancred, most of all, believed that dream, and most of all, has been destroyed by it, might even have used it to justify his deed. I allowed Montfallcon to make me his chief Symbol. I accepted the necessity. And Albion prospered, became more joyous, attracted the envy of all other lands, brought scholars and their wisdom, merchants and their trade.

Or is it mere gilding that soon must crack to reveal the rotten wood beneath? Are we all enchanted by this charming fancy of Montfallcon and his fellow dreamers? My father's eye sustained the Myth of Cynicism, denying piety and virtue. Does my own sustain a Myth of Happiness, denying crime? Is the succession of the seasons of Man no more than a pretty tale, to encourage us, to offer us empty Hope, an attempt to give the lie to a grimmer truth than we'll allow? Do we impose this shape on Chaos, as a child imposes shapes upon a pond's weedy surface and is surprised when he returns to find that weed and water have joined together, mutable and never firm? Or do we frame a turbulent sky with our fingers and believe that, because we have narrowed our vision to that small sphere, we have captured and contained the elements?

Or is it Gloriana who is at fault, unworthy to represent the Age . . . ?

"Oh, Mary! Mary! Mary!"

Instantly, the Countess of Scaith was upon her, bearing down on her with her strong, boyish body, gripping her, kissing her.

"Hush!"

"Oh, Mary!"

"Hush, my dear."

"I was her mother. Sir Thomas Perrott entrusted her to me. I swore she would be protected. I took her virtue, her virginity. I took her innocence. I allowed her this assignation. I encouraged it. I relished it. And I hated it, as well, but could not deny her that affectionate Sir Tancred, for she seemed so happy, and I had taken . . ."

"You took nothing. You gave. You were generous and she loved you for that generosity. Like all of us, she would do anything for you, not because you are the Queen, but because you are Gloriana."

"Tancred shall hang."

"No!"

"Hang!"

"He shall not."

"He should . . ."

"Where's the proof he murdered Mary? None."

"His sword." Gloriana raised red eyes.

"The only weapon of its kind, save those carried by Lord Rhoone and his men. Any wishing to kill her could have used the sword. What did Tancred say?"

"Lady Mary is murdered. Little else."

"Has he admitted guilt?"

"He wept too bitterly."

"Tancred is innocent." Una was adamant. "Rather blame Montfallcon. Tancred has no habit of violence. His lust for it, in your name, is proof of that. His only experience has been at the Tilt, in mock battle. He could not kill anyone. We have both of us always known that. It is why you made him Champion, you'll recall."

Gloriana nodded. "True."

"The murderer's one of Rhoone's guard, with a passion for

Lady Mary. You'll discover he was there. Servants will be questioned. A guard. Certainly."

"But murder should not happen at my Court, Una!"

"Murder has happened. The first in thirteen years. And public. Why, I doubt if there's a Court in all the world could claim such an untroubled span."

"By what effort, by what hypocrisies is this peace maintained?"

"By good will, by Faith, by a belief in justice, Your Majesty." The Countess of Scaith was tired. "Honour's but an invention of Man and by Man's honour is maintained. Do not doubt that Gloriana's Court is Virtuous. . . ."

"I spend too long about my own affairs, my own conceits, my own satisfactions."

"You spend too little, my dear." The Countess of Scaith stroked her friend's sobbing head. It seemed to Una, in her heart, that all this had come about as a result of her irresponsible adventure into the walls. Since that day, when they had both discovered the secret nomads of the depths, Una had had the entrance to her passage bricked in. But still she felt as if, by breaking through, she had released a dark spirit into the brilliance of the palace proper—a spirit which had inhabited one of them (possibly Sir Tancred) and destroyed Lady Mary. Now, even if the spirit had fled, it had left an inheritance. It would be many months before life at the Court would recapture any of its old optimism.

A tap at the door.

The Countess of Scaith left her friend's side and went to speak to the maid of honour.

"Lord Montfallcon was here, my lady, and left a message. Now Doctor Dee awaits outside."

Una left the Queen's room and closed the door. "I will speak to him."

The dryad pulled back the door and in strode Dee, magnificent in mourning black, his white beard emphasising the dark dignity of his robes.

"The Queen rests," said the Countess of Scaith.

"I have encouraging news," Doctor Dee told her. "I am convinced of Sir Tancred's innocence."

"A witness?" Una moved towards the Queen's door, to call the news.

"No."

Una paused.

"Not exactly," continued Dee. "I believe that a visitor of Master Tolcharde's could have committed the crime. He came but recently, accompanying the Thane of Hermiston, who had been on one of his journeys to some astral plane. A ferocious creature this—a barbarian, with sword, axe and mace—daggers—in iron and polished copper, fur and horn—with some outlandish name I forget. Well, in short, he escaped the Thane and we thought him borne back by demons into his own netherworld. Now I believe he is somewhere in the palace."

"But what proof have you, Doctor Dee?"

"I know Sir Tancred for a gentle, chivalrous creature whose love for Lady Mary matched his love for Albion."

"His sword," she reminded the sage. "Her blood on his armour."

"From where he held her against him. I have visited him. Lord Rhoone has him in one of the older apartments—with bars and locks and so forth."

"He is comfortable?"

"His physical needs are provided for. But he screams. He raves. He is possessed."

"Possessed by your demon?" she said.

"Mine? My demon visitors are tame, I assure you, and their work is beneficial."

"I say what others might," she told him.

"Aye. You are a sceptic, my lady, I know."

"Not a sceptic exactly, Doctor Dee. I differ so far as interpretation is concerned. But we discuss Sir Tancred."

"I believe him sane. That is to say, I believe that he was sane until the moment he found her murdered corpse. Now he cannot believe what has happened. His mind seeks to escape the truth.

Alternately, he weeps and then his countenance grows sunny and he seems to speak rationally, save that he refers to Lady Mary and how they are soon to be wed, and asks that she may visit him, and so forth. It is a sad madness he has. Not the madness of guilt, but the madness of grief."

"So this escaped barbarian is the culprit?"

"I can think of no other who would perform such a bestial, such a meaningless deed. For it is not ordinary wickedness that inspired her death."

"I think the same. But as for your barbarian . . ."

"I've set the Thane to finding him. Lord Rhoone's men, too, join in the search, for Rhoone is with me in his feeling for Tancred's innocence."

"I do not think you will find him," said Una, scarcely conscious that she spoke.

"Eh?"

"Yet I hope that you do, Doctor Dee. Has anyone else seen him, this one you suspect?"

"Not in the palace. The Thane, of course, and Master Tolcharde."

"Such a barbarian would be noted."

"Aye—save that we were all in disguise today. We'll find witnesses at least."

"If he exists."

"You doubt . . . ?"

"I doubt nothing save that he's the murderer. I believe that he returned, as you first thought, to his own sphere. My instinct leads me to suspect an enemy within the Court."

"Better to blame an interloper, surely?" Doctor Dee added a particular emphasis to his words.

"So as to calm the Court?"

"Aye."

The Countess of Scaith put a hand upon her hip and nodded slowly.

"And we must save Sir Tancred," added the alchemist. "He is surely innocent."

"Save him by a lie? For expediency?"

"'Tis not a lie, but a speculation."

Una's smile was bleak. "A fine difference, Doctor Dee."

"It ensures that the innocent shall not suffer."

"'Tis bad logic and leads to worse."

Doctor Dee shrugged. "I'm no politician. You could be right. Besides, the barbarian might yet be found."

"Let us hope he is."

"You'll tell the Queen? You'll give her hope?"

"If it pleases you, Doctor Dee."

"You think me a fool, eh?"

"You have my respect, Doctor Dee. More than you shall ever realise, I think."

"What?" Doctor Dee rubbed at his bearded chin. "You're a mystery to me, my lady. It has surprised me you show such suspicion of my enquiries, when you have a brain so quick and flexible."

"Possibly I merely argue with your methods of research, good sage."

"Then we must debate. I am always willing. . . ."

"This is not the time."

"Of course. But you will reassure the Queen. I would not have her grieve more than she should. I know that Lady Mary was close to her. . . ."

"I understand your motives, sir."

"Then my thanks to you, Countess of Scaith."

Doctor Dee entered the passage, looking right and left, as if uncertain of his direction. Then he set off back towards his own apartments, through Hern's Throne Room, in the East Wing. It was true, as the Countess of Scaith had guessed, that he only half-believed the Thane's story of a mysterious barbarian, but he fully believed Sir Tancred innocent and his mission had been to make certain that the Queen knew of this. Now he was reassured and could return to his experiments, wondering if the ancient art of necromancy might be employed to raise Lady Mary from the dead, if only for a moment, and learn her murderer's name from her own lips. However, he did not maintain much faith in such practices. He believed that there were better, alchemical means of producing the effects claimed by the old sorcerers of Hern's time, whom he, Dee, had helped discredit.

Yet, he thought, if the dead could be raised, by whatever means, what knowledge might be gained! All the lost knowledge of the ancients, of those distant pre-Classical ages, the previous Gold and Silver Ages of the world's youth. The secrets of the stars, of transmutation, of navigation . . .

Thus, by hopeful reverie, did Doctor Dee distract his thoughts from gloom, until he came into his chambers, wading through paper, to hesitate at his bedroom.

He had made up his mind to enter when he noticed, with mild surprise, that he had a visitor.

The figure sat at Doctor Dee's desk, inspecting a half-constructed star-glass, trying to fit into it the lens which Doctor Dee had not yet finished grinding to his satisfaction.

Dee frowned. "Sir?"

"Sir," said the visitor, a flat echo. A doppelgänger?

"Do I know you?" Dee enquired. "Are you one of Murdoch's acquaintances?" He felt a thrill as if, at last, he confronted a true demon face to face.

"I know you, sir, and I know your deepest desires."

"Indeed!" Dee was amused.

"Indeed." Another echo.

The figure rose, remaining in shadow as it moved the length of the wall, coming closer to where Dee stood with a palm upon the handle of his bedchamber.

"Shall we enter, Doctor Dee?"

"Why so?" Dee had too often confronted both the peculiarities of Nature and the various manifestations of the Supernatural to feel any real perturbation, but his bedchamber contained the one secret he refused to share.

"Because," said the figure slowly, "I would offer you a bargain. I know what you have in there. I know the problems you have experienced. I can solve them."

Dee hesitated. He heard his heart begin to thump. "You know, you say?"

"And I can give you what you have sought for so long."

"The price?"

A shrug.

Doctor Dee laughed as he turned the handle and flung open the door, to let his guest precede him.

"You've come to purchase my soul, have you?" His eyes flamed.

"No, sir. I've come to sell you one—or, at least, grant you the means of obtaining one."

The door closed on the pair. The papers stirred for a moment, in the draught, and then settled. A black rat, which had hidden itself on Doctor Dee's entering, re-emerged and ran across the room to a bench and began to climb. On the bench was a cage. In the cage sat another rat, a white female, staring with wary fascination at her wild visitor, her whiskers twitching, her heart pulsing.

The black rat reached the bars, sniffing at her as she squatted in the corner of her cage. The black rat squeaked an order. Slowly, compulsively, the white rat began to move towards him until at last they were nose to nose.

From within the bedroom there came a sudden shout and the black rat looked up, ready to run.

"It is not possible!"

"Oh, it is, sir, I assure you."

"In which case, my friend, I would give you anything at all!"

The black rat returned to its nuzzling.

The Eighteenth Chapter

In Which Lord and Lady Rhoone Discuss the Appearance of Mysterious Disturbances in the Order of the Court

"THERE SHOULD," SAID Lord Rhoone, taking the last of the beef from the salver presented by the servant, "have been a trial, my dear."

They broke fast in their own over-furnished apartments, warmed by the early June sunshine. Lady Rhoone, on the other side of the table, put her large red chin upon her hand and laid down a knife, picked up a piece of bread at which she stared rather dully. "Of Tancred?"

"He is innocent, I'll swear."

"He seems happy, in Bran's Tower. He believes himself a Knight of Chivalry, imprisoned by an ogre. He awaits the coming of some warrior-maid, some Clorinda, to rescue him. Innocent or guilty, my dear heart, he is mad and therefore must be held somewhere. The Queen visits him. Others do." She bit at the bread.

"But he should have been proved innocent and a greater effort made to discover the real murderer." Lord Rhoone dabbed at his black beard with a napkin and sniffed. "This way, there still remains suspicion that the murderer's abroad and might kill again. No trial—no ceremony—no resolution. That's what set Sir Thomas to stalking. . . ."

"Lord Montfallcon has made all efforts, Bramandil. None but Tancred was seen in Lady Mary's apartments. For a month Montfallcon searched and investigated. He still pursues his inquisitions, as best he can."

"Aye—and reassures no-one. Look how strangely Doctor Dee acts—can there be something on his conscience? Or Sir Orlando

Hawes, become stern and ferocious. Or Sir Amadis Cornfield, who has conceived a hatred of Lord Gorius Ransley—or Master Florestan Wallis, who makes excuse upon excuse to be free of duties and who was, until recently, the most conscientious of the Queen's servants. All since Lady Mary's death. While Sir Thomas Perrott comes to Court with all his sons, swearing to cut Tancred to pieces and then, after an interview, also claiming Tancred innocent and haunting the palace night and day in his quest for the true murderer." Lord Rhoone lowered his voice. "Then vanishing. Vanishing, my dear, in the night. And none can find him. Who saw him last? It must be the murderer himself! And killed the father as he killed the daughter, but this time hiding the corpse. And his sons maintain the search, then leave, in a pack, claiming the Saracens as culprits and refusing to name their informant."

"Why Arabia?" She chewed.

"In revenge for the murder of one Lord Ibram—you recall?"

"Lady Mary was Ibram's slayer, then?" Lady Rhoone shook. "Oh, my dear heart!"

"The story goes that Ibram loved her and insulted her: that she was avenged, perhaps by that faceless spy of Montfallcon's, and that, in turn, she was slain."

"But where's the spy?"

"Dead. Killed by the Saracens."

"You are sure?"

"It's common knowledge."

"So the Perrott brothers now seek the Moor who did the deed."

"Rumoured to be Lord Shahryar, the ambassador, who has temporarily returned to his homeland."

"The Perrotts pursue him to Arabia?"

"They would not say. But they are one of the greatest of ship-owning families. They've many noble kin. They've a large enough fleet to threaten war and seem serious."

"They would not act against the Queen's interest, surely?" Lady Rhoone discovered that she was still hungry and signed for a servant to return with a tray of fries. She watched as they were piled upon her pewter. "The Perrotts are famous for their loyalty."

"There's a hint they believe themselves betrayed by the Queen."

"And the Queen?"

"She believes she has betrayed them, for the Lady Mary was under her protection. She believes she's betrayed a trust. So when the Perrotts put it to her that she protected the murderer, from political considerations, she swore that she did not, yet in such a tone they believed she lied. For her voice shook, d'you see, my love?"

"They took this for an admission?"

"Aye."

"Ah, the poor Queen. As if her grief were not already overbearing!" Lady Rhoone sadly chewed a fry. "And she with no artifice at all to disguise her true feelings, save her dignity, which is natural. Did not Montfallcon speak to the Perrotts?"

"They mistrust him. They always have, for in Hern's time Montfallcon betrayed their uncle to his death."

"So they have precedents."

"Exactly. Old scores, which their father buried on Gloriana's accession. He was loyal and he was ambitious for his girls. One married well, to Sir Amadis Cornfield, and another fairly well, to young Sir Lepsius Lee (who had been a lover of the Queen's), and all three girls were much in favour at Court. Through this favour Sir Thomas Perrott expanded his estates and his fleets, giving good service to Albion in return, as all would swear. But now the sons call their sisters little better than traitors and, I heard, at least five of their ships are already refitted as war-vessels. Montfallcon, of course, is at his wits' end."

"Great Mithras, Bramandil, my lord! You are suggesting civil war? In Albion? Under the Queen?"

"Not civil war, for none would join the Perrotts. Not yet, anyhow. But a bloody uprising to disturb the Realm and shatter the faith of the common folk. Unless the Perrotts are allowed to attack Arabia—meaning war with one of our own protectorates, and the most powerful. So civil war of sorts abroad, indeed, if the Perrotts are not stopped."

"And Sir Thomasin Ffynne?"

"The Queen has paid what is virtually a ransom for his restoration.

She has agreed to make amends for the shipping he destroyed in the sea-fight. With his return, Her Majesty will receive advice, at least. And he'll not be affected by the madness affecting the rest of the Court since Lady Mary's murder. He'll have intelligence from Arabia, also."

"You think, my love, that Arabia is responsible for the murder?"

"I think it unlikely. Lord Shahryar struck me always as a practical man."

"Then someone works to turn one against the other?" Lady Rhoone frowned, surprised at her own insight. "It can only be that."

"In whose interest is such disruption?" Lord Rhoone moved his bulk and stood, feet spread, stretching in his green-and-red uniform, his brass breastplate seeming to swell as his chest swelled. "The Court depends on stability. This is not Hern's time, when advantage could be gained by murder and treachery. Now advantage is gained by service, charity and loyalty."

"Some foreign plot?"

"We are all too ready," said Lord Rhoone wisely, "to blame some outside source for our dismay. I am ever reluctant to shift the blame onto strangers before I am certain that the malaise is not indigenous."

His wife embraced him, her great bosom engulfing his armour. "You are too just, dear heart. Too cautious. Too kindly for your position."

"I protect the Queen."

"And sturdily."

"To protect her, I must not give rein to the night-horses of the imagination, which would bear my thoughts off, willy-nilly, away from my simple duty. Therefore I refuse speculation. As does Lord Montfallcon, though his task is harder. If the Court suffers a summer madness worse than some it has suffered in the past, then it is my task to counter it with common sense."

She kissed him. "But you would not object if I were to visit our estates, taking the children with me?"

"My own thoughts. Go soon."

Lord Rhoone lifted his massive head to stare pensively at a plate of apples.

The Nineteenth Chapter

In Which Questions of Diplomacy Are Debated and Lord Montfallcon's Mind Grows Darker Still

IGUANAS AND PEACOCKS gave a singular, tropical quality to the Queen's summer lawns as they stalked and prowled the grass, the flower beds and the terraces of her gardens. The strange, leathery smell of the huge iridescent reptiles, brought as a present by Sir Tom Ffynne and kept through most of the year sleeping near the furnaces heating the palace, reached Gloriana's nostrils through her open windows as she studied the plans presented to her by Master Marcilius Gallimari, Master of her Revels.

"It will as usual be a bright and elaborate affair, Your Majesty," he told her eagerly, "with all the trappings of ancestral Chivalry. In the great courtyard, to remind the people of their fortune. With yourself as Queen Urganda, to attend the Tilt . . ."

She sighed. "The plans seem most cleverly conceived, Master Gallimari." She leaned back upon her couch and moved a lassitudinous fan near her face. She was clad all in light-coloured linens, muslins, lace and silk, with a little lace cap upon her glowing hair. "I assure you of my approval."

"I shall ask Master Wheldrake for some verses—since the topic is so close to his heart."

"Verses? Of course. And you should commission a few lines, at least, from Master Wallis, or he will be offended."

"Perhaps a prelude and a song?"

"Excellent."

"Master Tolcharde will create the illusions. And the parts—of knights, gods, goddesses, monsters and so forth?"

"Choose whom you will."

"Some already have chosen their own parts. Your permission is required, Your Majesty." His dark face sought a smile.

"They have it."

Master Gallimari was somewhat frustrated; disheartened by the Queen's evident uninterest in his elaborate entertainment, planned for Accession Day. He had, however, become used to her apparent indifference since the Spring Festivities. He was sure, sometimes, that she blamed him for Lady Mary's death. Hesitating, in the hope of detecting denial or confirmation of his fears, he added: "And the music, Your Majesty?"

"Commission some."

"Composer and consort must be paid."

"We shall pay them."

"And dancers."

"Master Priest can supply dancers, as usual."

"Aye, Your Majesty."

Master Gallimari looked down upon the heavy, tragic face of Albion's Queen. "Your Majesty is not displeased?"

"With the Summer Entertainment? Your inventions, as ever, Master Gallimari, are excellent. There should be jolly sport."

He was certain he detected irony.

"It seems, Your Majesty, that you have lost interest in my work. If there is something lacking . . ."

She smiled and became gracious. "Master Gallimari, your only fault is that you interpret disapproval when all you find in me is sadness." She was brave. "I look to you, Master Gallimari, to improve my humour. Make your best efforts. They shall be appreciated by us."

Relieved, the handsome Neapolitan swept, bent and backwards, from her presence.

The Queen saw Una, Countess of Scaith, in summer silks and swinging farthingale, crossing the lawn in the company of a listing Lady Lyst who widened blue eyes at the heavy reptiles and clutched, with comical gesture, at the Countess's arm. "Dragons, in faith!"

"They guard the Queen," Una was saying lightly, "as the dragons of old guarded Queen Gwynifer."

"She needs 'em." Lady Lyst straightened. "We're all in danger.

Women especially. There's more femicide planned. Wheldrake thinks it, too." She exchanged a glance with a cold-eyed lizard.

"You've heard something?"

"Sensed, that's all."

"Unlike you, Lady Lyst, to trust to a feeling only."

"These are not days for trusting to logic. The greater one's intelligence, the greater the confusion. And my poor brain is ever confused, at the best of times." Lady Lyst smiled self-mockingly, then curtseyed when she saw the Queen emerge into the garden. "Your Majesty."

"Lady Lyst. Una. A lovely day."

"Too hot for me, I fear," said Lady Lyst, adjusting cuffs and collar, straying honey curls. "One thirsts so."

The three moved in the direction of a marble fountain: King Alexander the Great at the Court of Queen Hecate of Iberia, with water-nymphs and dolphins. They lifted their faces to the spray.

"It is our hottest summer." The Queen brushed moisture from stomacher and skirts. "It seems to infect the whole palace, arousing strange passions, unsuspected passions in the most unlikely persons."

"Your Majesty believes it is only the weather creates the mood?" Lady Lyst spoke as one who hoped for hope.

"Weather has a great deal to do with everything." Gloriana turned her eyes towards the blue sky, shading out the sun with a lace-sheathed hand. "That's always been my strong fancy, Lady Lyst. You'll see. As the weather grows milder, so shall our sensibilities find better balance."

Lady Lyst tripped upon a small step and ran forward, with arms flailing, before she righted herself. "I am encouraged, madam." She cast about her, as if for a seat, or perhaps a bottle.

There came a yell from behind a large dodo, a carved bush, and a long-legged creature, apparently armoured in chequered plate, ran into view, across the path, through another hedge and onto a lawn. The Queen and her ladies stopped dead in astonishment, for now came a trio of guards, with ruffs and tabards flapping, caps askew, swords drawn, giving chase to the armoured, flashing figure, while behind these, panting, imploring, in stained smock and velvet cap, Master Tolcharde cried, "Hold! Hold! Do not harm him!"

"Master Tolcharde!" The Queen's voice brought him to a stumbling halt which he turned into a ragged bow, though his eyes still followed the soldiers and their quarry. "Who's that, sir?" The Queen was imperious, by habit and, perhaps, to amuse her two friends. "Whom do they chase, Master Tolcharde?"

He tried to speak. He flapped his hands. He was in agony, a quandary. "Madam. A minor adjustment's all that's necessary. Forgive me."

"Some servant of yours? Some captive of the Thane's?"

"No, Your Majesty. Not quite a servant. Oh, dear!" He was eager to continue the pursuit. He cast anxious eyes after the flashing, chequered figure who now ran round and round a large yew bush, cut to resemble a castle, flattening a bed of pansies, knocking over one of the soldiers.

"I thought at first," said Lady Lyst, "that it was Sir Tancred escaped from the Tower." She regretted her lack of tact and shut her glorious lips.

"Who is it, sir?" asked the Queen.

"A harlekin, madam."

"A comedian? What has he to do with you?"

"He's mine, madam. Made by me, madam. A mechanical creature, madam. I meant to present him to you in a—I'll present him later. Only, I beg you, madam, tell your guards not to harm him. The machinery is delicate."

"And easily displaced?" The Queen was amused.

"At present. That will all be made right. If I may continue, madam."

"Try not to destroy our whole garden, Master Tolcharde."

The inventor bowed rapidly, gratefully, and was on the run again, crying out to the remaining guards, "Hold! You'll harm him further. Let me just reach the lever and he'll stop!"

The three women seated themselves upon a stone bench and laughed with a spontaneity none had enjoyed for many weeks.

Yet it was this laughter which reminded poor Gloriana of her duty once more, for she wished to bring back to her Court that certainty, that happy faith, which now was threatened. Montfallcon, lost in dark suspicion, no longer exerted his will in the cause of tranquillity, though he swore his ambition was unchanged. Lord Ingleborough, steadily growing more sickly, could not support her, and half her Council seemed abstracted, self-involved. Even Doctor Dee's enthusiasm for his investigations had waned, though he spent most of his hours in his lodgings. Seeing herself as Lady Mary's betrayer, she in turn felt betrayed by her Council, though it might be she expected too much of them. She determined that it was to be by her effort alone that optimism and good will should return to the Court. She must fire her men. She must whip them from their bad humours. She must be Albion, and act an imperial part for them. There was none, at present, upon whom she could rely, save Una—and Una was primarily a private friend, with Gloriana's private needs her paramount concern. Gloriana gathered herself from laughter and from the seat and bade farewell to them. "I have convened my Privy Council and it awaits me now," she said.

The Countess of Scaith became serious and began a question, but Gloriana was moving between hissing iguanas and trumpeting peacocks, back to the doors of her apartments.

In the Privy Chamber, their sweating faces dappled with burning colours from the grandiose glass above, their bodies clad in hues to rival that window's glory, magnificent in their summer finery, the Queen's Council assembled somewhat tardily.

On a chair, made with poles into a litter, Lord Ingleborough was carried in by servants. His heart still faltered; there was gout, now, in all his limbs, so that he could barely sign his own name on his documents, and he was in considerable pain, relieved a little by a variety of potions, but none satisfactory. He still wore his full, formal dress, his robes and chain of office, his air of authority, but his intelligent eyes frequently clouded with pain. The gout had spread so suddenly, as if carried on the same air which brought murder to the Court, that Sir Amadis Cornfield, prone sometimes to superstition, considered the thought that Lady Mary had been a sacrifice to a demon, summoned by one of Doctor Dee's profession, and that the demon itself moved unchecked everywhere, bringing madness, sickness, grief. He looked across at Doctor Dee, who seemed older, frailer, almost as weak as Ingleborough, yet oddly animated. Sir Amadis pushed the thought away and dwelt on pleasanter things: his little mistress, who had come to relieve all his burdens, just in time. This moment was soon gone as Sir Amadis recalled Lord Gorius Ransley's ruthless attempts to woo the girl away from him, even hinting, recently, that Sir Amadis's wife would be informed. Lord Gorius, a widower and courted by many unwed ladies, sought, in Sir Amadis's opinion, to seduce his girl from mere spite. In the old days he would have been tempted to settle the matter with a challenge. He regretted the passing of some of Hern's customs. He glared across the table at his would-be rival. Lord Gorius pretended to ignore him.

Elsewhere Master Florestan Wallis sat, composing verses upon his paper, a look of almost ludicrous serenity on his thin scholar's features, while beside him Master Orme hummed a tune and sniffed at a posy, apparently as content, in his way, as his fellow councillor. Master Gallimari was busy with his arrangements. Sir Vivien Rich grumbled a little about the heat and dropped perspiration on table and tools, with many apologies. Masters Palfreyman and Fowler both yawned and chatted over Sir Vivien's head, their subject being the sapping nature of the heat which made them wish to sleep all day.

Lord Montfallcon, resting himself in his chair, his face darkened with care, looked down the long table at the Privy Council and wondered how he had ever come to assemble such a gutless rabble of fops and flapmouths. He determined to begin to replace them all, even Lisuarte Ingleborough, who grew too frail for duty. He recalled how cautiously he had selected these men, for qualities of character and intelligence. Again he began to question his own judgement, but was interrupted by, of all people, Sir Orlando Hawes, panting, in white, securing a button of his doublet, apologising for lateness. His ebony skin seemed to have an unhealthy cast to it and he, too, sweated, stinking strongly of lavender water and a woman's bedchamber, as most of the others stank of roses or poppies. A fine collection of wilting blooms, Montfallcon thought. The first crisis close to home in nearly thirteen years and they broke. And yet, he wondered, could it be merely the murder that had changed them so? It seemed unlikely. He yearned for some of his old, grim colleagues, now dead or exiled or retired, who would have responded to the problem with practical understanding. A servant or two on the rack, a noble or two threatened with accusations of treachery, and the truth would have come shouting forth.

The doors were opened. They rose, even Ingleborough, at the Queen's entrance. In heavy finery she moved slowly to her chair, and as they bowed they were blinded by the bright light from the window behind her. She stood at the table for a moment, contemplating them, thoughtful, then she sat down, allowing them to resume their own chairs.

"Good morning, gentlemen."

Montfallcon was surprised by the animation in her voice. "What business have we?" she asked, when they had responded with their greetings.

Lord Ingleborough, forgetful of protocol, announced: "Tom Ffynne's ransom is accepted. He returns in his own vessel shortly."

"Excellent news. But he must be chastised, my Lord Admiral. All his booty—if he has any—confiscated. And he must make over a sum towards his own ransom."

Lord Ingleborough nodded, agreeing with this justice.

Montfallcon felt his own spirits lift. Lately the Queen had been careless of the Council's business, offering scant guidance to them. Now she was once more valiant. A warmth bloomed within him that had nothing to do with the heat of the sun. His Gloriana was showing her father's strength again. The Council was becoming more animated, looking expectantly down the table to where the Queen sat, upright and smiling.

"Your Majesty," he began, "in the matter of the murder of Lady Mary, I regret . . ."

She waved a royal hand. "That business is best forgot, my lord. Though we feel sympathy for poor, mad Sir Tancred, there seems little doubt he was the murderer, after all."

She brought relief to them. They had, it seemed, waited only for her positive word. Darkness was dismissed from every skull.

"There remains the matter of the Perrott lads," said Lord Montfallcon. "We have news they're arming ships at rapid rate."

"To attack Arabia?"

"It seems so, Your Majesty."

"Then they must be stopped."

"Agreed, Your Majesty. However, it is a delicate problem, for they act surreptitiously."

"Summon them to Court. There'll be no secrets in this State. We have always said so."

"They will not come, Your Majesty." Sir Amadis, as a Perrott relative, spoke with some embarrassment.

Sir Orlando said: "Cannot the guns be spiked, the ships holed?" He looked to Ingleborough.

"Possibly." The old man drew a deep breath. "But this would only delay and worsen the situation."

"Have you the men to do it?" asked Sir Orlando of Montfallcon.

Lord Montfallcon once again regretted Quire's death. If he agreed, he would have to send Tinkler and Hogge and some like them. And they would bungle it. He might even be forced to recruit Webster and his garrulous mock gentlemen.

"You hesitate, my lord." Sir Orlando was again his stoical self.

The Queen looked on, frowning, unhappy.

"I do, Sir Orlando. I am not certain it is the best scheme. It is underhand . . ."

"Then we must be underhand, if the Perrotts are underhand."

Now he realised that Hawes was speaking uncommonly wildly, believing himself to be forceful. Montfallcon became doubtful and looked to the silent Queen. "Your Majesty has never permitted such methods in the past. She has always been most sensible to the fact that the Crown must be seen to be without blemish." Now that she appeared to acquiesce in the kind of scheme with which he was all too familiar, he grew alarmed. All his life he had protected her from knowledge of how he maintained her security, her diplomacy. To hear a scheme discussed in open forum and not immediately dismissed by her was shocking to him. "I think not."

"Otherwise we risk an Arabian war, eh?" said Master Orme.

"Exactly, but —"

"Then let's have one." Master Palfreyman was on his feet. The Secretary for Arms was unusually fierce. "Let's punish 'em. Show 'em their place. They have been allowed to scheme too long—murdering our folk, challenging our power, having the gall to propose marriage to our Queen. Let's raze Baghdad, Your Majesty!"

The Queen was pale, as if by imitating her father's mood she realised for the first time what could be released in her name, but she smiled. "There can be no war," she said. "It has always been our agreed policy, with Sir Orlando, that war wastes lives and money, that it introduces a false sense of unity while it is being fought and creates unexpected dissension when it is over, for once men get the habit of making war they find it hard to lose, and must look for other wars, other enemies."

"So we attack the brave Perrotts, instead. Betray their cause, which is a just one," said sardonic Master Fowler. "I beg your pardon, Your Majesty." He sat down.

"The Perrotts have been summoned and refuse to come," she told them. "Such disobedience angers us, but yet we sympathise. We forgive them their wrath. They have lost first a sister and then a father. But what proof is there that Arabia is at fault?"

"It is well known, Your Majesty," said Sir Amadis. "Some vengeance taken by Lord Shahryar before he returned to Baghdad. You must admit he hurried away soon after."

"Recalled by his Caliph. This rumour sprang from nowhere. Sir Tancred, I insist, was the murderer." She seemed to burn with regal fury. "I'll not permit war. Never that, unless attacked."

"Arabia proves herself aggressive, daily. She'll strike soon enough." This from saturnine Master Palfreyman again.

"If she strikes," said Gloriana, "we'll strike back. We are Albion. It is our duty to resist the old habits of the Age of Iron. Are not all of you here, as every one of our people, across three continents, convinced of that? Do you wish this delicate Golden Age to survive? To become sturdy? To become set, firm-moulded, inviolable? You do, gentlemen, I know. It is the dream we all share. The dream Lord

Montfallcon and Lord Ingleborough dreamed while day by terrible day feet tramped the steps of the scaffold and the headsman's axe was never dry. We show the whole world the road back to true Chivalry. We stand against injustice, immorality, cruelty, tyranny. And this is why we are secure. One base act on Albion's part, and the structure crumbles, the dream is destroyed. I am your Gloriana, your Queen, your conscience and your Faith. I remind you of a Duty which I have not forgotten and which you must not forget."

Montfallcon's face was shining as he listened. He saw the expressions of selfishness, of rage, of disappointment, of cynicism, despair and malice melting from every face. Lord Ingleborough waved gouty fists and called "Hear! Hear!" in counterpoint, looking about him as if to challenge any who declined assent.

And Queen Gloriana laughed and grew to her full height, her stiffened collar a white, glowing aurora behind the blazing auburn of her hair, and the green-blue eyes in her head, the proud unflinching eyes, were the eyes of King Hern, whom some had believed to be the very Prince of Demons, the leader of the Wild Hunt, hiding antlers beneath his tall, iron crown; and the hands on her hips were the strong hands of her warrior forebears, while the smile, following the laughter, was the sweet, wistful smile of her mother, Flana, who, at the age of thirteen, had given her life for Gloriana's. By this means, half-spontaneously, half-deliberately, she reminded her Council of her legend and her power; and of her origins which even they could believe, as she stood thus before them, were at least half-supernatural.

Lord Montfallcon bowed before her. "You do well, madam, to remind us. We shall do our duty, every one of us."

"One petty action," she said, "and we betray all else."

Then, disguising her own exhaustion and her inner fears, she bid them good morrow and left them to continue their debate in terms of honour, virtue and idealism.

Only Lord Ingleborough, drowsy in his chair, looked after her and understood what generosity and what courage she had displayed that day.

The Twentieth Chapter

In Which the Queen Continues Her Search for Consolation and the Countess of Scaith Makes a Dreadful Discovery

AND THAT NIGHT the mood of the Court was lighter than it had been for many weeks. There was a dance, at which the Queen led her courtiers in the Escalad and the Vatori, and the musicians played merrily the best and most complex compositions, and for many hours there was laughter in the corridors and apartments when the official entertainments were completed; then Gloriana, weary and solitary, made her way to her secret halls to find reward for the brilliant part she had performed to cheer the Court and lift the cloud. She sought the clever attentions of her dwarves and children dressed as fanciful creatures of mythology; the caresses of her geishas and their soft, thrilling words; the scented, yielding bodies of her youths; the harsh hands of cruel women who instructed her in every indignity; the brainless bestial men of the jungles; the cold harlots, male and female, in their skins of white silk; the quivering girls who whimpered at her whips. From room to overheated room she went, hopeful that, her duty so splendidly done, she might now find escape from her body's craving: but no escape came. Limp with weariness she returned at last to her own bed. Alone, she closed the heavy curtains and in darkness sorrowed at the injustice of her fate.

Lord Montfallcon, more carefree and easy since Gloriana had risen to her challenges and thus assured him that the Dream would yet be sustained, awoke to hear her distant weeping voice, while beside him his wives stirred, half-fearful but yet asleep. He was astonished that she did not feel as he now felt. His new mood could not dissipate at once. He thought, without much fervour:

Ah, Albion, still unfulfilled, as the fullness of my purpose is unfulfilled; and are the two so closely linked? This collection, these creatures she maintains, are distractions only and bring her more grief, yet her duty to them tells her she must keep them, though they fail her. They go unpunished, these wanton, depraved, distorted monsters, because she is too generous. Instead they are rewarded with every luxury. She would be happier free of them, free of all these private responsibilities—retainers, entertainers, children—but she continues to accumulate them. This is not the quality of conscience I instilled in her from girlhood. It is mere sentimentalism. She is exhausted by all of that. Who benefits? Not Albion. Marriage must surely be the answer—but to whom?

Hern had destroyed so many of his own relatives that there were few in the Realm who could claim large amounts of royal blood. Montfallcon considered the Counts, the Dukes and the Earls of Hibernia, Eire, Valentia or Virginia. Would that Scaith had had a son and not the girl who acted husband for the Queen so well that Gloriana felt no loss. The Grand Caliph was too greedy for power and would not be controlled as consort; besides, there was a strong chance he would not produce an heir, and it was an heir Albion most lacked. Casimir of Poland could not be wed without giving offence to the Caliph. Elsewhere there were princes too old and princes too young, princes mad or princes diseased. The Queen of Corinth had slain all her brothers just the previous month. In Venice, as in Genoa, Athens and Wien, some form of republic existed and royalty was killed or exiled and therefore useless for match-making. The Aethiopes were all crazed. Prince Henri of Paris lay dying even now. No, it must be some noble of Albion, perhaps one who could be elevated first. Her voice came to him again and, as always, he drew his wives to him, to muffle the sounds.

"This blood—all rhythm and fractured melody—and never a resolution!"

The Countess of Scaith heard the desperate words and awoke from a deep and pleasant sleep in which she dreamed she explored a simpler, more innocent world—one of John Dee's other spheres. . . .

And John Dee himself, in his dark bed, also heard the Queen, but answered her lustily as he drove his body into that of the creature beneath him. "Here! Rise! Sing! Crescendo and then climax come!" And his bizarre paramour joined him in delicious consummation as he shouted: "Gloriana!" and flung himself shuddering from her. "Gloriana . . ." He stroked her auburn hair, her strong, lovely features, her shoulders, her breasts, her thighs and her belly. "Oh, Gloriana, you are mine and we are both fulfilled."

And Sir Amadis Cornfield, on his way to the old Throne Room, there to keep his illicit tryst with his own nymph of the night, his darling, laughing beauty, paused at Gloriana's distant, whispering voice in the corridor and frowned.

"I am betrayed by my body's cravings and yet my body refuses respite. . . . Oh, this burden, this burning, shameful burden . . ." The voice faded as Gloriana slept at last.

Sir Amadis padded on, leaving his wife and his own duty behind, his brain pounding with lustful anticipation, for it must surely be tonight she would consent to give him more than her kisses. . . .

In Master Wheldrake's darkened chamber Lady Lyst took a heavy glass goblet of wine in one hand and a thin horsewhip in the other and moved her nightgown a fraction so that her poor, panting, naked poet could press lips to shoe and murmur "Your Majesty" to her, for she must, as always when these moods were on him, be the Queen for him. "Your Majesty's punishment is just, for I am wicked and unworthy. Let your whip inspire me to virtue and drive me closer to the muse so that my verse can once again aspire to the ecstasy it possessed when I first beheld your picture and determined to present myself at your Court, your feet. . . . Your Majesty!"

"Now, Wheldrake?" Lady Lyst lifted the whip. Her voice was slurred.

"Aye. Now! Now!"

The whip fell.

Lady Lyst winced. She had thrashed her own left leg.

* * *

The Countess of Scaith began to return to sleep as the Queen's voice died at last, but she was alerted again by another sound, from overhead, as if a rat negotiated some hollow in her roof. A groan, not Gloriana's distant note, but much closer to hand, caused her to sit up, seeking the dagger with which, by habit, she had slept since Lady Mary's murder. She found it, gripped it, drew back her curtain and found a candle on the little carved table beside the bed. Flint sparked, tinder drew, and the candle was alight, making the room more sinister for the shadows thus created. In heavy linen, the Countess stood upright, dagger poised, candlestick lifted, and looked about her.

The groan came again, from above. She remembered the grille and looked up. Did this one also lead into the walls? Was there movement there? A glitter, as of eyes?

"Who?"

The groan again, distinct but weak.

"What do you want?"

The groan.

She took a chair, thinking to investigate. Then she paused. "Begone!"

A mewling sound.

She placed the chair against the wall, against the tapestry, blue and green, of Tristram and Isolde, the castle and the sea, and stood upon it, daring herself to stare into the grille with the candle. The same glittering, the same faint groan. And now a word: "Help . . ."

"Who are you?"

"Please, I beg . . ."

She thrust the point of the dagger into the side of the lattice panel and prised. It fell away suddenly, as if it had always been imperfectly secured. It fell with a clatter first upon the chair and then to the carpeted floor.

A tiny, piteous sound. She thrust in the candle and her first sight was a small black-and-white cat, its yellow eyes glaring with pain. It sprang towards her, not to attack, but for security, and she almost toppled. It clung to her shoulder and she saw that it was wounded—a terrible gash in its side, its fur all matted with blood.

Carefully, she carried it down and put it on a tallboy where stood a jug of water and a bowl. She had begun to bathe away the blood when she realised that the cat could not have spoken.

She turned and, looking upward, saw a white, stark face staring down at her. The mouth was a crooked gash, bubbling with blood. She could not move. But, as she watched, it thrust more of its body through the gap until it lolled, a stranded frog, still staring at her, still gasping, half-free of the hole, its body hanging down upon her tapestry to reveal the round-pommelled dagger quivering in its back.

"Tallow!" cried the Countess. She recognised the one who had elected himself to guide her and the Queen through the depths.

Then the body fell, arms limp, down to the chair, which skidded across the room, crumpling the carpet, down to the floor to lie upon its back to show how the dagger's point poked through the patched doublet, to admit further blood. Tallow tried to arch himself, to roll, but he was dying too rapidly. She ran to him and helped him sit, causing more blood to gush, like vomit, from his mouth.

"He has killed me. I resisted him."

"Who has killed you, Tallow?"

But Tallow's head had fallen and he no longer breathed. The flow of blood gradually slackened and then stopped, and Una, Countess of Scaith, stood upright, staring down in horror on Jephraim Tallow's corpse, while his wounded cat mewled from the bowl in which she had placed it.

She stroked the cat. She bathed it as best she could. She dragged a sheet from her bed and threw it over Tallow. She seized the lattice panel and pushed the chair to the wall again, to replace the panel, as if she feared more corpses would come squeezing through into her room. She took another sheet and wrapped the cat in it, laying the little beast on her pillow. She dragged on a robe while Elizabeth Moffett knocked at the door. "Madam! My lady?"

"Back to your bed, Elizabeth!" The Countess would not involve that simple girl. "'Tis nothing."

"You are safe, my lady?"

"Safe."

There were political matters in Una's mind. Another death, and this one even more mysterious, for the victim would not be known, and the Court would be aflame, worse than before. Sir Tancred was blamed, imprisoned. The affair was over, and everyone relieved. She drove out a thought that somehow Tallow had been sent to her, as a warning. She could not involve the Queen. She could not remind Gloriana of what lay beyond the walls, not now. And yet she must have help.

The robe buttoned, she left her room and locked it behind her. Elizabeth was no longer in the antechamber. She unbolted the door into the corridor. Elaborate lanterns illuminated the passage. Guards moved through the corridors, but none challenged her as she made her way swiftly to Master Wheldrake's rooms. She tapped on oak. She heard a murmur and a yell from within. She waited.

"Who's there?"

"Scaith."

"Is that you, Una?" Lady Lyst was drunk.

"Admit me."

There was hesitation. Una grew impatient. At length the keys were turned and two dishevelled figures stood there, Wheldrake shamefaced, Lyst tipsy, hiding something behind her back. Both wore nightgowns.

"Wheldrake and I . . ." began Lady Lyst. Whatever she held, it now clattered down behind a table. "We . . ."

Master Wheldrake helped his mistress to a chair and signed for the Countess to seat herself, but Una continued to stand. "There has been a murder," she whispered.

"Another?" Lady Lyst frowned and sipped from a nearby decanter. "Mithras!"

"Here in the palace?" squeaked Wheldrake, becoming serious. "Oh, Countess! Who is it?"

"A stranger. Happily, I suppose. I know him slightly." She noted Lady Lyst's expression. "I did not invite him to the palace. He—crawled here. Evidently murdered in the gardens. At any rate it seemed to me that if the palace is not to be alarmed further, we must hide the corpse."

"You did not—you were not—protecting yourself?" asked Wheldrake.

"If he were dead by my hand, sir, I should have said so." The Countess was sharp.

"I apologise."

"I need help in burying him, however. I thought of the disused gardens. You're familiar with them? Near the foreign embassies."

"Now?" Master Wheldrake looked doubtfully at the hiccupping Lady Lyst.

"It must be. You know what a shadow Lady Mary's death cast. Suspicion, talk of revenge. Let's have no more. If Tallow, the dead man, is buried, he'll not be missed. And there is no way the Court can discover the murderer, I assure you."

"He was some kind of thief, eh?" said Wheldrake. "From one of those taverns . . ."

The Countess knew that Wheldrake was familiar with the riverside taverns. "Aye," she said. "He was that kind. A messenger. He brought me news sometimes. You'll forgive me if I say no more."

"Of course." Wheldrake mistook her for a fellow nightbird and was glad to be discreet. "Come, Lady Lyst, let's to the Countess's apartments."

Valiantly, Lady Lyst staggered upright. "Lead on."

She required aid from them for only a few yards of the corridors and then she was steady again, almost sober, as ever.

They slipped into the Countess's rooms and she showed them the blood-soaked sheet in which Tallow was wrapped. "We must carry him. You and I, Master Wheldrake. Lady Lyst, the lantern."

From her pillow the cat mewed. She looked at it, studying its wound. It was not bad and would heal readily. Its concern seemed entirely for its own fate. It made no attempt to approach the body of its dead master.

"He's light." The small poet took the feet and Una the shoulders. They left her apartment by the outside door, carrying Tallow's body in moonlight, while Lady Lyst led the way to the old gardens where, a few months since, Tallow himself had occupied the balcony high above and seen Oubacha Khan and Lady Yashi Akuya in conference there.

It was now that Una realised she had brought no spade. But Wheldrake indicated the broken rim of a well and poor little Tallow was pitched down into it, while the three of them rested against the stonework, panting and anxious if they had been seen. But no lights glowed from any of the nearby windows and they were able to return, whispering and tripping, as Lady Lyst lost herself twice and led them through shrubberies, until they were once more in the Countess's room.

"I am obliged to you both," said Una. "You understand the necessity?"

"How did he come here?" asked Lady Lyst, sitting on the bed and stroking the cat. "There seems a great deal of blood about. On you. The floor. The bed."

"Murdered bringing a message." Una was happy for them to think she had a city lover. "Some thief sought his purse."

"And found it," said Wheldrake. "For he had none upon him I could feel." He added: "And no weapons, save the dagger in his back. Poor devil." He became thoughtful. "You are sure the murder was not performed in the palace proper? There has been speculation that Lady Mary's murderer still goes free amongst us. Or Sir Thomas Perrott? Was this messenger of yours the murderer? Did Sir Thomas find him?"

"It was to forestall such speculation I asked your help, Master Wheldrake," said the Countess of Scaith.

He smiled. "Forgive me."

Lady Lyst was breathing heavily, as if realisation came that second. "A murder!" Her voice was unusually loud and Una flinched.

"I beg you, Lady Lyst. . . ."

Lady Lyst lowered her face. She seemed to sleep. "She is tired," said Wheldrake.

"You were the only people I felt could be trusted." The Countess gestured. "It was important to me to remove the corpse. I hardly thought. Perhaps I acted hastily . . . ?"

"Wisely," said Wheldrake. "The Court just recovers. This

would make life intolerable for all. As long as you are certain that Lady Mary's murderer was not that fellow's murderer, too."

"I cannot be certain." The Countess of Scaith looked at the small black-and-white cat, which was licking its wound. "But I assure you, Master Wheldrake, I shall attempt to discover the truth and shall act upon it."

"Surely," said Lady Lyst, "Lord Rhoone at least should be informed. Or Montfallcon, eh?"

"Perhaps. I must consider the implications."

"You keep silent to protect the Queen?" Lady Lyst stood up. "Is that it, Una?"

"I suppose that is much of my motive."

"A worthy one," said Wheldrake.

"Aye," said Lady Lyst a little doubtfully.

"You think silence leads to suspicion. That I could make matters worse?" the Countess of Scaith asked her friend.

"I am too drunk to think."

"I respect your logic."

"I have no logic. My logic leaves me daily. It never helped. . . ." Lady Lyst moved away. "Wheldrake."

"Coming." A sympathetic nod to the Countess of Scaith and Wheldrake was skipping backwards, in his mistress's wake.

When they had gone Una found that she was looking again at the grille. It seemed to her that blood still oozed from it and down the wall, as if a hundred corpses lay behind it. Until now she had never considered the possibility that Lady Mary's murderer might be from within the palace depths—perhaps Tallow himself. Yet it was, of course, the most likely explanation. She determined to investigate—perhaps taking Lord Rhoone into her confidence and going with a detachment of sturdy guards. It could even be that war of some sort was being fought in the old tunnels and halls—rival nations squabbling for supremacy of those dark and dreadful subterranean corridors, those rotting rooms, those ruined apartments and abandoned grottoes. The notion began to seem reasonable.

She spent the rest of the night nursing the cat and staring

frequently towards the grille, but no more sounds came from behind it. When it was light she cleaned as much of the blood from the carpet as she could and bundled up the sheets. There was a good deal of blood on the tapestry down which Tallow had slid. She used water to wipe the worst of this away. If Elizabeth Moffett noticed, then Una would have to swear her to silence and make up some story of gentlemen fighting here—the kind of tale Elizabeth would wish to believe.

And then, dressing herself, she once more left the apartment, going now to Lord Rhoone, whom she had decided to recruit.

The doors of the Rhoone apartments were open as she knocked. To her surprise she heard Doctor Dee's flat tones and Lord Rhoone's boom, full of tension.

A maid came. "My lady?" The maid was weeping.

"What is it? I need to see Lord Rhoone."

"Lady Rhoone. And the children!"

The Countess became weak with horror. "What? Dead?"

The maid led her into the dining room. There, laid upon the floor, was stout, red-cheeked Lady Rhoone and the plump girl and boy of thirteen and fourteen years, their joy.

Doctor Dee knelt beside the girl, his ear to her heart, while a distracted, terrified Rhoone hovered. "The kidneys," he said. "It must be the kidneys."

"They are most certainly poisoned," said Dee, nodding to Una as she entered. "And you had none of the kidneys?"

"Not quite. Almost."

"Who?" said Una. She was helpless. Had there been a massacre in the night? Were Tallow and the three Rhoones only a portion of the victims?

"Bad meat," said Doctor Dee. "The stomachs must be cleared."

"They'll live?" begged Rhoone.

"Have your servants bring them to my apartments. No," Doctor Dee became almost shifty, "to Master Tolcharde's. There is a physician I can recruit. Antidotes I can try. Stretchers, now!"

Una was unnoticed as Lord Rhoone and Doctor Dee supervised the servants bearing the woman and the two children from the room. She continued to follow, uncertain why she did so.

She became part of a procession behind the stretchers. They went through the old sections of the palace, through the Throne Room, up the broken staircases, along the galleries, to Master Tolcharde's evil-smelling laboratories. Dee knocked loudly. It was some time before an apprentice answered. Dee turned.

"No-one in here," he said. "No-one but Rhoone. Secrets."

Una paused. John Dee looked at her curiously, then pulled her into the musty chambers before shutting and bolting the door. "Countess? You heard of this? You came quickly."

She shook her head. Rhoone and the stretchers were moving on into the mystery of Master Tolcharde's chambers. Dee made a decision to continue with them, but held Una's arm to keep her back. "You think foul play, do you?"

"What's your analysis, Doctor?"

He sighed. He spoke reluctantly. "Foul play."

The Twenty-First Chapter

In Which Various of
the Queen's Courtiers Are Resurrected
and Another Is Interred

LORD RHOONE CAME, perspiring and in confusion, grinning to the Queen's Withdrawing Room, to sink upon a footstool and with grateful lips kiss the comforting hand of Gloriana.

"Saved," he said. "Some seer, some apothecary of Dee's."

"Not Dee himself, dear Bramandil?" She used his given name to assure him of the depths of her affection just then.

"He could not. As they died, he admitted it. Then Tolcharde brought in this other. After you had gone, Countess. You recall? To tell the Queen."

He addressed Una's weary back. She nodded.

"A sniffing of my dear ones' breath and an antidote was created to revive them. They recover now, in our lodgings."

"The seer?" asked Gloriana. "Who's he?"

"Perhaps a traveller. Dee said he came from another world."

"Ah. A captive of the Thane's." She restrained her scepticism.

"Possibly."

Una moved from where she had been contemplating the Great Yard and the azure lake through the tall, half-opened window. She was very pale and breathing deeply, wearing dark blue with cornflowers stitched on petticoats, pearls and light blue lace. "They'll live?" Her voice was small.

Lord Rhoone rose to take her hands. "Countess. You, too, are unwell, I fear. You must forgive me." He squeezed. "Anxiety turned me blind to all other considerations. . . ."

She smiled, but was close to madness at that moment. "I thought we had a plague of murders. When Doctor Dee was so certain . . ."

"We were all infected by the suddenness of it, and by suspicion based on past events."

"We must forget Mary," said Queen Gloriana importantly.

"We must forget so much nowadays." Una glared about her as if suspecting attack, her hands still in Rhoone's. "Should that be so?"

"Whether it should or should not, we've scarcely choice in the matter." Gloriana rose, informally splendid in mellow bronze and red gold coronet. "There's no more murders. Bad kidneys were the cause of your family's calamity, eh, my lord?"

"This heat, madam, turns all tripes foul, faster than any other meat. We should not have eaten them, save I thought them fresh-cut from a newly slaughtered beast."

"We have already sent word to our Butchery. And to the Larder, also."

"They were not deliberately poisoned, then?" The Countess removed her hands and returned to a pretended contemplation of the brightly painted panels overhead: Cupid and Psyche, Jupiter and Semele, Titania and the Weaver, Leda and the Swan, all at odds in mood and style and no consolation to a chaotic mind.

"The evidence is against it." Lord Rhoone stood between reassuring Queen and despairing Countess, anxious at once to be soothed and to soothe. The solution was natural and cheered him. "I must return to them."

"May we meet this seer and reward him?" The Queen smiled as Rhoone bent his leg, preparatory to leaving.

Lord Rhoone scratched his head. "He's gone—perhaps back to his own sphere. He did not linger for thanks. A good man. A true follower of Asclepius."

The Queen frowned. "Let us hope he comes again. I'll speak to Doctor Dee. Have him invited, Una."

"I'll enquire," promised her Private Secretary, grateful for a duty to perform. "I'll speak to Doctor Dee today, Your Majesty."

Lord Rhoone bowed twice while behind him a footman opened the door, then closed it gently on the two women.

"Lady Castora and her children's escape has excited your blood and put you in poor humour." Gloriana came to her friend. The Queen was evidently also weary.

Too much nobility all round, thought Una, created over-refined sensibilities, pitched like tight-strung instruments and prone to snapping. And yet she could not confide her fears to the Queen, for all that her silence produced unspecific yet significant pauses in the conversation which gave Gloriana doubts and thus increased her own imaginings. So she replied: "It has, madam."

"You'd best return to bed and rest. It's my intention to do the same. My night . . . Well." A stiffening: further recourse to Lethe. Una had no more sympathy. Her fears for the Rhoones had exhausted her for the moment, though she felt guilt from being unable to console the human creature she loved most in the world. It was best for her to leave, for she suspected her mood drained the Queen. "I will, madam. I thank you and pray we'll both be recovered by this afternoon. Then I'll make enquiries of Doctor Dee and seek out this foreign philosopher. I'll bring him to you, if I can. With all speed."

"Mayhap we can encourage him to divine some of our other mysteries." Gloriana spoke seriously. She kissed the Countess. They parted.

Una of Scaith returned to her apartments, noting how merrier was the general mood of the Presence Chambers as she went through, and wishing that she could share in the atmosphere; resisting her impulse to warn them of the danger she guessed threatened the whole Court but which she could not name. She saw the outer palace as the surface of a sunny lovely pool in which bright little goldfish swam, unaware of the lurking predator in unseen weedy deeps.

Now that Lord Rhoone, from mercy, could not be recruited to help flush the monster, she yet feared to seek allies elsewhere; none at this moment could be trusted for silence. And discretion, though her temperament hated it as that which destroyed more than it protected, was of the greatest necessity until Tallow's murderer and, she was certain, Lady Mary's was identified. She must have perfect proof and knowledge of where to strike, or he'd be lost again, in those secret, unwholesome tunnels; escaped for ever. She took the wide curving Queen's Staircase, on which courtiers, including Sir Amadis Cornfield and Master Auberon Orme, passed the time of day, wittily and cheerfully, down to her own lodgings' lower floor, there to dismiss Elizabeth Moffett and her other maids, changing into the costume she had come to associate with her foreboding and her fresh-discovered melancholy: her hose and doublet, her sword and boots. The weapons could be used (she added two daggers to her belt), for she had been trained in arms as a girl in Scaith and more than once, an Amazon in full armour, had entertained the Queen in the Accession Day Tilt. This year she was to play the Peasant Knight in Sir Tancred's stead. She dismissed these expectations, went to her writing desk, considered a note, then left quill on empty paper, and pushed the chair to the place it had occupied when Tallow came through. There were bloodstains to be seen, still, on the tapestry, if the eye sought for them. She pulled away the grille, considered putting it on the bed, then remembered discretion.

From a basket (brought by a maternal Elizabeth Moffet) the little black-and-white cat mewed, as if to warn her. She stroked his head, pondering the problem of leaving an unwanted trail. She took a long cord from one of the bed-curtains and tied it to the grille, looping the other tasselled end about her wrist. Then she returned to the chair, a candle and flint and tinder in her purse, to stand there, to put her hands upon the ledge, to scramble, feet snagging in the tapestry so that, to her dismay, it came partially loose from its moorings. But she was up and would have to risk the tapestry's clue. She squeezed through the hole, the grille bumping and following behind on the cord, to clatter against the gap as she passed down the tunnel. In dust and rubble she wriggled on until the passage widened and she could turn, drawing the cord to close the panel and securing the loose end to a piece of jutting beam which stuck from the stones. Her means of entry disguised and her means of return assured, she continued in darkness for a while, moving by memory along the route that last night brought the dying Tallow to her.

She lit a cautious candle and found herself in the narrow passage, able to stand upright. She wished she had thought to bring a dark lantern, for the candle could betray her. She crept on a short distance, then drew her sword. This action reassured her. The balance of the steel in her hand gave her the illusion of invulnerability, and thus she progressed on lighter feet until she reached the gallery with its little prison chambers off to one side, where the carvings seemed no longer quaint, but menacing. More tunnels, another gallery and then, leading from this landing, a stairway into a wide, dark, deserted hall which might, two or three centuries earlier, have led to an outer door. Mistaking this for the hall to which Tallow had led her and the Queen, she descended the stair to a midway landing, then peered over. The hall was smaller than she had imagined, and unused. Albino rats rose on hindquarters to stare at her with pink, unfrightened eyes.

She began to return up the shivering staircase, to find her bearings. There came some scufflings, which she ignored, ascribing them to the rats. She heard a whisper which could be either human or bestial in origin, but it was of a sort she had detected on previous adventures, so she was not discouraged. However, she made the light of the candle fall on her blade, in case malicious eyes watched and considered attack. She noted another glint at the top of the stair and then she felt her heart's beat increase.

"Eh?"

She raised her flame. A glimpse of silver. Her voice echoed from below, as if changelings mocked her, readying themselves to replace her. Then blackness was utter again.

She paused, realising the foolhardiness of this venture into the walls. She should have slept first. She should have sought advice, if only from Wheldrake and Lady Lyst. They would have accompanied her, too. But she could trust neither to be level-headed: one too imaginative, the other too drunk. This need to know what had killed Tallow could betray her to her own death. Yet there was nothing to fear from the wretches she had seen. What if one had murdered Tallow? What if another, or the same, had killed Lady Mary when detected, as Una thought, in some crime? Her head, like a mine-stream, ran clear and then cloudy again, moment by moment. She began to tremble. She considered her danger: Tallow had not been armed as she was now armed; Lady Mary had not been armed at all. The nomads of the walls would be in awe of a gentleman with a sword. They were not courageous, on evidence, for why else would they be in hiding here?

"What?"

The echoes seemed to increase. More shadows gathered at her back. She was at last upon the boards of the gallery again and moving forward. She felt the presences fall away and she was alone once more, calling herself a fool, panicked by childish fancy.

Then a slender, ragged figure was revealed by her candlelight, shielding eyes, gibbering as it retreated. "No!"

It was gone. A creaking hinge sounded from somewhere.

If this were a fair example of the enemy, she was much encouraged. She moved more swiftly through the passages, ignoring doors on either side of her as she sought the large hall again.

The passage opened out and she saw that she stood in a stairwell. The staircase zigzagged up, storey upon storey, and through the rococo railings faces peered, as prisoners from bars, regarding her with frank but neutral curiosity. The faces were oddly distorted, not by the filigree of the banisters but in keeping with their bodies. She realised that she was observed by a large tribe of dwarves, male and female, children and youths, which she had disturbed in some progress between the floors, for they all bore bundles and packs. She became relaxed and smiled up at them. "Good morrow to you!"

Her voice's echoes were high, now, like tremolo'd viol notes, and were sweet to her ears. Several of the dwarves grinned back at her, revealing their teeth. She saw that the teeth were filed and her own smile faded. She bowed farewell and moved on as quickly as she thought prudent. But she was not to be their prey, for even as she continued her own progress, they continued theirs, up the endless stairway, shuffling and muttering.

It came to Una, as she passed through into another gallery, that the dwarves had something of the characteristics of an evicted people, and she was reminded again of her own image—of a struggle for power, partly territorial, partly philosophical, within the walls. She recalled Tallow's only phrase: *He has killed me. I resisted him.*

This chamber had a painted ceiling: the adventures of Ulysses depicted with such artistry that Una was forced to pause and detect as much of them as dust and candlelight permitted. She was awed. She had never seen painting to match it, yet it had gone out of fashion, evidently, and been forgotten as another part of the palace was added and all this built around, built over, buried by changing tastes and embarrassment with a previous era's art, no matter how consummate or enduring it seemed. Una reflected that very few monarchs possessed the finer sensibilities the world might reasonably expect to find in them. As a race they were vulgar and their ostentation and grandiose pomp, even their simpler pursuits (such as riding to hounds and gaming), were in such perfect accord with the general taste of their subjects that they symbolised and represented the majority far more satisfactorily than any body of elected republicans. She was reluctant to leave these paintings, but she must.

She took a large doorway and crept through a number of apartments—withdrawing rooms, bedchambers and the like—whose rotting silks and linens were evidently still in use. Once she went by a bed and saw that a man and a woman, gaunt and filthy, both wearing plush-padded golden crowns, lay asleep in it. She stepped aside for a procession of musty lords and ladies, whose crumbling trains were supported by the hands of blind children, and she stared, making no attempt to stop them or ask directions from them, until they were gone. They were flesh and blood, as was evident from their smell, but she could not see them as anything but ghosts; as if the original rulers of Albion continued to maintain their Courts, as layer was heaped on layer.

The Countess of Scaith knew that she must, sooner or later, make enquiries of some denizen, or she could be lost in the walls for the rest of her life, sharing the fate of these insane creatures. She found herself upon a back staircase, narrow and winding and somewhat comforting in its scale. She descended, ignoring the doorways she passed on the landings, until she reached the very bottom of the stairs. She moved on, but her foot struck bulky flesh, and she lowered her candle, expecting to find another corpse. Instead the mild, alien eyes of a huge reptile contemplated her, blinking very slowly in the light. A hiss, the opening and shutting of the long red mouth, once, then the thing was on the move, heavy, confident and, Una thought, amiable. She considered following it, as a lost traveller might follow a friendly dog, but it had taken a tunnel too low and too narrow for her to progress in any comfort, and she did not think it wise to risk meeting a herd of the creatures. As she turned away, seeking another door, she saw a girl dressed in the simple, cleanly garments of a country maid, standing close by and staring at her in wonder.

The girl was, in contrast to all others Una had seen here, so ordinary as to seem abnormal. "Sir? Do you come to help me?"

"Help you?" Una hesitated. "You need it?"

"Aye." The girl lowered her eyes. "I hoped . . . But there's none in this frightful place who has the courage. . . ."

"I'll help you if I can." Una stepped up to her, to peer into the features, to find that they were real. "But you must help me, too. How do you come to be here?"

"My father brought me, sir. To escape creditors. He thought we should be safe. He had heard of the entrance from his grandfather." The girl began to weep silently. "Oh, sir, I have been here a year, at least!"

"Where is your father?"

"Dead, sir. Slain by the infamous Lords Evius and Picus D'Amville."

"Hern's henchmen? Alive?"

"Old, sir, but surviving here, by retaining habits learned at Court."

"Montfallcon sent them to Lydia, to fight in the war. They were killed by brigands."

"They returned, in secret, after King Hern's death, and have been here ever since." The maid dropped her voice. "They have men at their command—a few, but bloodthirsty—and rule a great territory."

"This is part of it?"

"No, sir. This was once the kingdom of another disgraced knight, lately slain."

"You know a great deal of what goes on within the walls. If I help you escape, you'll be my informant?"

"Willingly, sir."

"There is a hall somewhere—I think nearby, but I am lost—where families camp. Do you know it?"

"I think so, sir."

"You've heard of Tallow?"

"Aye, sir. He's his own master. He was kind to me."

"Well, Tallow inhabited this hall. Or so I'd guess."

"Then I know it, sir." The maid took Una's hand. "Come. It's safe to go that way."

"I can find our way back from there." Una felt that it might, for the moment, be enough to save this young girl from death and return her safely to the outer palace. There, too, she would have a witness to what might be found within the walls—enough evidence to make Gloriana agree to send in expeditions, to arrest the tyrants, to save the persecuted. But even as she thought this she wondered at the enormity of it. And would Gloriana accept the need? Perhaps, for generations, her family had allowed this microcosm to exist, the denizens of the walls being some sort of sacrifice to the dead ancestors who had built the original houses; courtiers to attend so many royal ghosts.

The young girl led Una swiftly and surely through the twisting corridors, to pause at a door, to bite her lip and look enquiringly up at her benefactress. "Here, sir, I think."

Cautiously, Una pulled back the door. It creaked; there was familiar firelight behind it. She opened it a foot or two and recognised the huge hall. But it had otherwise changed, for in the centre there was now erected a dais, made of slabs of granite and marble which had been hauled from a dozen disparate sources, for some were plain while others bore sections of elaborate bas-reliefs. And mounted on this crazy dais, the components of which formed irregular steps, was a barbaric ivory chair, evidently of East Indies workmanship, intricately carved with scenes of martial glory and amorous conquest. And there was a figure lying back in the chair, its face hidden in a hood, its hands hidden by long black sleeves, its feet hidden by the folds of the skirt. And fitted over the hood was a tall, spiked crown—a crown of steel and diamonds and emeralds; a war-crown, of the sort one of Gloriana's distant ancestors might have taken into battle with him. And, replacing the nomads Una had first seen here, there was now a noisy concourse of ragamuffin gallants and fantasticos, painted whorish women, who, with trays of gold and silver, waited upon this hooded monarch of the dispossessed, who might have been Death himself and who certainly possessed Death's power over the posturing rabble. In their filched finery, their antique, mouldering costumes which looked to have been stolen from corpses, they might have been corpses themselves, raised by the lord in the ivory throne.

Was this sorcery?

The young girl spoke innocently and far too loudly for Una's peace of mind. "Is it the place you sought, sir? Are we safe here?"

"It has changed." Una put herself between the rabble (which had fallen silent and was staring at them both) and the girl.

The hooded creature raised a mysterious arm, apparently beckoning them towards him.

"Whom do I address?" demanded Una, remaining where she was. She was full of fear now.

Then the maid was running forward; running to the throne and through the parting crowd, up the steps, to kneel at the feet of the hooded figure, to huddle there, as if secure. Una pushed against the door through which she had entered. The door would not move.

"I've been tricked. Lured by a witch, eh?" Una spoke with crazy irony. "What are you, all of you?"

Again the apparition in the throne gestured and the mob began to converge upon her. She threatened with her sword. Rusty blades were produced. Diseased hands reached out for her. Faces corrupted with sores and boils leered at her. She feinted again. She cut the back of a wrist so that the owner howled and dropped its flencher. She stabbed. Her blow was blocked by a dozen swords and filthy fingers seized her in every private place of her body. She flailed. She screamed. She tried to break free. Beyond her attackers she saw the hooded figure stroking the head of its Judas goat, the cowering girl who, through eyes half-terrified, half-triumphant, watched as Una was wrapped about with thongs and strips of cloth and borne up on the shoulders of the mob, her sword flung away.

Una, shuddering, babbling demands, was carried closer and closer to the throne to be placed, almost gently, on the lowest step. She glared and fell silent.

The figure stood up, face and limbs still hidden, and looked down on her. It spoke to the young girl. "Excellently done. It is she, sure enough."

Una stared back, finding courage as she controlled her heart's rapid beat. "You were expecting me?"

"We hoped, that's all, my lady. You are the Countess of Scaith, the Queen's closest friend. Dark Una—the deceptive Truth . . ."

"Truth, sir, is a mirror. Peer away." Una disdained to struggle in her filthy bonds. She had become cool.

Her captor seemed amused by her answer. "The best of all of them. Better than Montfallcon, even. An enemy to fear. Well, madam, we've a use for you. Not much, really. You might keep the old man quiet. Do you find madness embarrassing?"

"What?"

His question had been rhetorical. He signalled her dismissal and again she was picked up, carried through the shifting shadows of the hall, along a short passage. A barred door was opened. She smelt ordure, the stink of a human being who had been incarcerated for some time. She heard an animal noise—a shriek, a roar, a rattling of iron. The mob laughed as she was hurled into the room to land on rotting cloth, and one of them cried out with considerable relish:

"Here you are, old man. Here's what you need to calm you down! It's a woman! All to yourself!"

The door was shut, a key turned, and Una, in the darkness, listened to the inhuman noises issuing from the creature which now, through reeking straw, slowly advanced towards her.

The Twenty-Second Chapter

In Which Rivalries and Mysteries Bloom and Spread and Lord Montfallcon Sees the End of All His Victories

"NONETHELESS," LORD MONTFALLCON maintained his stand, "the Accession Day Tilt must take place and thereafter the Queen must make her Annual Progress. Never has it been more necessary. These ceremonies, Sir Amadis, are not empty ritual. Their function is to assure the people of the Queen's majesty, her reality, her charity. Already rumours proliferate in the capital and must be spreading across the nation, across the very world. If the Queen does not appear, then the rumours will fatten like flies on dung and infect the Realm with an hundred moral diseases, weakening us in every quarter. We have dismantled the Rule of Might and replaced it with the Rule of Justice. That Justice is symbolised by the Queen. We maintain our provinces, our world empire, not by soldiers, but by means of a philosophy exemplified in the person of Gloriana. Mithras! Our own faith is implicit in her and how she acts."

Sir Amadis Cornfield felt discomforted by the surroundings of Lord Montfallcon's oppressive rooms which were, as ever, unaired and overheated. He felt that it might be possible to catch a very ordinary disease of the body here. Yet he was reluctant to go without convincing his fellow councillor. "The Queen mourns," he said. "She is enfeebled by so many terrible events. With her greatest friend suspected of murder . . ."

"She's free of an enemy." Montfallcon was glad and grim. "The Countess of Scaith's influence threatened the security of the Court and the Realm. It is evident that she plotted with Sir Tancred to murder Lady Mary, that she killed Sir Thomas Perrott in her own rooms—the blood has been discovered, on floor, bed, tapestry; there is blood everywhere. Doubtless Sir Thomas's body will be found anon."

"This is evil gossip, my lord." Sir Amadis was shocked.

"Then why has the Countess fled the palace?"

"Could she not also be a victim?"

"She is not the kind to be a victim, Sir Amadis."

"I did not know, my lord, that victims were chosen according to their temperaments."

"Your knowledge, sir, is not informed by my experience."

"Nonetheless, the Queen grieves, half-mad with uncertainty."

"Public business will steady her."

"And who's to replace the Countess at the Tilt? First Tancred's gone, now her. It's as if Fate takes any who would be the Queen's Champion."

"Lord Rhoone has agreed to play the Peasant Knight."

"Then let's hope he survives until Accession Day." Sir Amadis looked at the clock, all brass and polished oak, above the fireplace. The hand stood near to the half-hour. He had no time for further pleading. "I've spoken my mind on it."

"So you have, sir."

"It could be put out that the Queen is ill. . . ."

"And make matters worse? I have steered this ship for many years. I know what is good for Albion. I know the tides—the powerful tides of the common will. I know the shallows and the reefs. I know what cargo to carry and when to hold it, when to dispose of it. That is why the Queen relies on my judgement. Why she will do as I suggest. Why she must not be weak or be thought to be weak at this time! At the Tilt every important noble will be watching her, to take news of her mood across the world."

Sir Amadis shrugged and, with the curtest of nods, was off.

He made his way swiftly to the disused suite of rooms behind the old Throne Chamber, where his little mistress—minx, trollop, virgin innocent—had agreed to meet him and, at last, be fully his. Her decision had been taken at the instigation of a gentleman, her guardian, who had pitied Sir Amadis in his discomfort, his distraction and his grief, and informed the girl that her interests would be best served by kindness to a Queen's Councillor.

Sir Amadis felt warm gratitude towards this courteous gentleman who had concerned himself with the relief of the heart's ache, the frail body's pain, and Sir Amadis also felt a pleasant sense of victory over Lord Gorius, his rival, who would now be thwarted.

As he reached the half-deserted East Wing he came suddenly upon Master Florestan Wallis fancifully attired in floral reds and yellows, in deep conversation with someone Sir Amadis took for a kitchen doxy. Master Wallis peered around (a guilty flash) then took a dignified defiant stance, his back to the girl. "Sir Amadis."

"Good morning, Master Wallis." Cornfield was careful to pay the girl no attention, but he was amused, for he had never visualised the Secretary as anything but asexual, a celibate. To see him thus (gaudy, embarrassed) added further to Sir Amadis's cheer, though he felt no malice. Rather he enjoyed something of a sense of conspiracy with his fellow councillor.

He passed on, leaving them murmuring. He dismissed a very small suspicion that crossed his mind, linking kitchens with kidneys.

Lord Montfallcon glowered up from under his heavy brows, and Master Tinkler, scratching a head that was the chosen field of warring tribes of vermin, shifted his feet, cleared his throat, rubbed his nose, before settling.

Lord Montfallcon re-read his list, knowing that the longer he kept Tinkler waiting, the more rapidly Tinkler would answer his questions and therefore have less of a chance to colour his information with pointless interpretation.

"No Quire?" It was his usual opening.

"Dead, sir, for certain." Tinkler was helpless. "And I was not the only one who hunted him. Six months have passed, sir. We must give him up."

"Who else hunted him?"

"Fathers of daughters, and of sons, he'd wronged. Kidnapped or killed. Who knows now?"

"The mood in the town?"

"Quire's forgotten by most."

"Fool. I meant the Queen."

"Loved, as always, my lord. Revered."

"Gossip?"

"Unimportant."

"Aye?" A sceptical twitch of the eyebrows.

"Not —" began Tinkler awkwardly. "Not worthy —"

"What's the gossip, Tinkler?"

"Of several murders, of a return to the days of Hern's mad Court, of a Queen driven insane by her —"

"Unfulfilled lust?"

"You might say. . . ."

"What else?"

"Sir Thomas Perrott imprisoned by you, my lord, and tortured. The Perrotts banished and planning rebellion. And the Queen's favourites ravishing any virtuous girl they can find."

"Worthy of Quire, that gossip." Lord Montfallcon's short laugh was horrible. "The old days, in truth. What's the remedy suggested in the ordinaries?"

"Every man and woman has a different one, sir." Tinkler began to warm to his subject now that he knew what was expected of him.

"But in general."

"There's a common belief Her Majesty should marry, my lord. A strong man, they say. Like yourself."

"They'd have me marry her?"

"No, sir. Well, not many . . ."

"Because I'm not trusted, eh?"

Tinkler blushed. "They think you too grim, sir, and too old."

"So who?"

"A suitor, you mean, my lord?"

"Who does the mob think the Queen should marry?"

"A king, sir."

"Poland?"

"No, sir, for Poland's king is not considered strong enough for a hard-willed woman. As consort, many think that the Saracen monarch, who was much admired during this winter's visit for a handsome, manly, martial king, would be the proper candidate."

"Why? We are not at war."

"The broadsheets. The street songs. I brought you some, my lord. All speak of it. Do they not? Of civil war. Of war with Arabia. Or war against the Tatars."

"Where there's a will to war, a war will always follow," mused Montfallcon. "That intent must be changed."

"I didn't hear you, my lord, I regret . . ."

Montfallcon studied Tinkler. "So the Queen shall marry the Grand Caliph, who will master her, lead Albion to victory . . ."

"Many sympathise with the Perrotts, sir. The murder of Lady Mary sparked their imaginations."

"Such murders always do. And that contained all the proper elements. Innocence destroyed!"

"So they believe the Perrotts will rise, my lord, and that many will join them. They think that the Perrotts will support the Queen and clear the palace of—" Again Tinkler paused.

"Of Hern's old men?"

"Aye, my lord."

"The Queen is virtuous. But not her servants?"

"Aye, my lord."

"She's too weak to rule alone?"

"Pretty much what they do say, my lord."

Montfallcon lowered his head, fingered his lip, nodding slowly. "And they fear that a weak Queen means a weak Albion."

"A strong-willed woman badly advised is closer to the mark." Tinkler moved his dented velvet hat upon his head. "This is not shared opinion. Some disagree."

"But Faith weakens, eh?"

"Not too much. Save for the murders, all would be forgotten in a day. Even the murders will be forgotten in time. If there had been no more—but I heard . . ."

"There have been no more murders."

"The Countess of Scaith fled, I heard, after attempting to poison Lord Rhoone, killing his children."

Lord Montfallcon waved a hand. "Nonsense. She fled for other reasons."

"Some say you had her incarcerated, my lord. In Bran's Tower. With Sir Tancred. Sir Tancred was popular, too."

"And I never was." Lord Montfallcon smiled. "How easy it is to give them heroes and villains. And I was content it should be thus, until that murder. If only I had Quire. What a beautiful ferret. What a golden-tongued spreader of tales. Well, it's up to you, Tinkler. You must tell them how the Queen is strong, that she considers dismissing me, that I am close to the end, that my health fails, as does Lord Ingleborough's. . . ."

Tinkler's eyes were widening. "This cannot be, my lord. . . ."

Montfallcon threw down gold. "Your pay's safe, Master Tinkler. Tell them the Accession Tilt may be witnessed as usual, for a week from walls and roofs, by the commons, that the Queen will appear and that, shortly thereafter, she'll begin her Annual Progress through the Realm. Tell them Sir Thomas Perrott was almost certainly murdered by the Countess of Scaith, who has herself fled Albion—that's the truth—and that when the Perrotts realise this they'll become wholly loyal and obedient again. We'll not say, yet, if the Queen plans marriage, for that's the best counter-rumour we have, and it would be foolish to use it too soon, before suitors were selected. . . ."

"The Queen receives suitors, my lord?"

"Tell them that, if you wish."

"I think it will cheer the commons to know all this," said Tinkler soberly.

"Aye, it might." Lord Montfallcon put a quill to his teeth and picked. "You may go, Tinkler."

The obsequious quasi-Quire padded away. Lord Montfallcon rang his bell and the little page Patch, in green velvet, entered, doffing his cap and bowing low. "My master's without, sir. With Sir Thomasin Ffynne."

"Let them enter."

Patch signed and stepped aside. Lackeys came slowly forward, with the poles of Lord Ingleborough's litter upon their shoulders.

In his chair, dreamy with pain, left hand on weakening heart, Ingleborough swayed as he was lowered. He reached out a knotted fist to Patch who ran forward. There was love—father and son, husband and wife—between the two, and even Montfallcon was touched by the affection they displayed. Ingleborough was so consumed by gout that there was hardly a muscle free of some degree of agony, but his brain remained good, when he did not attempt to drug himself with drink or opiates. Behind him hobbled Sir Thomasin Ffynne, serious of face, in dark velvets and black linen. Patch closed the doors on the departing lackeys and, at a word from Lord Montfallcon, locked them.

Lord Montfallcon sighed. He offered Sir Tom a chair, which Sir Tom took, lifting the weight from his ivory foot. "It's hot." He massaged the joint above the foot. "Like the Indies."

"Would that you'd gone there, Tom," grumbled Ingleborough. "The diplomacy involved in freeing you! The Moors have been tardy as a matter of policy. Neptune knows why! They've ambitions. . . ."

"We can be sure of that," said Lord Montfallcon.

"It all smells of war." Ingleborough winced, for he had clenched his hand too hard. Patch stroked the pulsing knots. "I've never known it more imminent, since Hern's time. What's the answer, Perion?"

"The Queen must marry."

"But she won't."

"She must."

"But she won't." Lord Ingleborough laughed. "Gods! She's worse than Hern, for she can't be deceived and flattered as he was. She knows us too well—we three in particular. She's been privy to our casual talk since she was a child. She knows all our tricks."

"But she also loves us and will follow our advice," said Montfallcon significantly. "Now, Tom, what have you to say concerning Arabia's and Poland's rivalry?"

"Since New Year's this was hatching." Tom Ffynne's ruddy cheeks seemed to shine the brighter as, smiling, he reported his heavy news. "Casimir and Hassan left here deadly rivals, each thinking that with the other dead the Queen would be his. A familiar tale—the woman or the man is never asked, the rivals develop their feud as fully as the lack of facts permits. The fewer facts, the greater the development. The less interested the courted object, the more the rivals are certain she pines for one of them and will be his, if the other's gone."

"We know these failings, Tom." Montfallcon was impatient by nature and, of late, had begun to lose the self-control he had for so long maintained. "But the specific rivalry . . . ?"

"There's to be a duel between Poland and Arabia."

"No!" Montfallcon was amused, disbelieving.

"I have it from the Emir of Babylon, who's close to the Caliph."

"Where do they fight?"

"On a ship. A Turkish ship. In the very middle of the Middle Sea."

"With swords?"

"With all the weapons of Chivalry."

"Horsed? They can't be!"

"So I hear. The ship is large—the whole deck will be given to the tournament. Lance, sword, mace and so on."

"To the death?"

"Or a wounding."

"But death's possible? Is it, Tom?"

"Aye."

"So we'll have the threat of war between Arabia, whom we protect, and Poland, our best friend." Montfallcon was very grey. He fell in his chair. He looked at his two friends. He bit his lip.

"And Tatary will move," said Lord Ingleborough. "They are poised to detect a weakening in the fabric we've woven for thirteen years."

"The Queen should choose one of them. That would stop 'em. But which?" Lord Montfallcon straightened his back. "Poland, whom our people can't respect, or Arabia, who couldn't give us the heir we'll need? Which?"

Tom Ffynne put his finger along his nose. "Arabia. There's plenty who'll sire the heir for him."

Montfallcon continued to brood. "A little more of this talk and there'll be a hundred claimants for kinship with the Queen's nine daughters. You know that, do you, gentlemen? You've considered that?"

"For the crown?"

"It's likely."

"Things aren't so bad," said Tom Ffynne.

"Not quite. But in thirteen years we have created the Golden Age. Such creation takes very little time. But it takes still less for terror to descend, willy-nilly, upon a nation. Gloriana should marry Arabia. Hassan is a citizen of Albion, after all. There are Roman precedents. Greek."

"He'll give us further trouble. For the Saracens wait only for our sanction to make war on Tatary. The Queen knows that. It is one of the reasons she'll not consider marriage to Hassan. She fears that she will put too much power into the hands of another Hern." Lord Ingleborough's voice trembled as pain seized him.

"We shall have to control him," said Montfallcon.

"There'll be Saracens at the Court, seeking to control the Queen—and us," said Tom Ffynne. "I think we'd be poorly off with Hassan as consort."

"It could be made plain he *is* consort, and not king."

"In words?" said Lord Ingleborough. "Certainly, that can be agreed. But in actuality? He has ambitions to use Albion's might against the Tatar Empire. All know that. And if there's a hint of a marriage, we can be certain that the Tatars will attack Arabia, at least, before they are attacked. It's better, Perion, to stand alone, behind the Queen. Or find a husband closer to home and scotch the reason for the fight. Albion's seen worse threats."

"War would destroy all we've achieved," said Lord Montfallcon. He groaned. "How has this happened? In a few months we have become threatened from within as well as from without! I kept everything in perfect balance. How did I lose control?"

"With Lady Mary's murder," said Lord Ingleborough, "and dissension here, amongst us."

"One murder? Impossible!"

"Perhaps Poland learned of your scheme to kidnap him, Perion," said Tom Ffynne. "If so . . ."

"He'd need that verified. And there's none, now, who can be believed. The main kidnapper's dead."

"You had him killed?" Lord Ingleborough struggled in his chair.

"Not I. Arabia."

"Why?"

Montfallcon shrugged. "He overreached himself in a matter of espionage."

"On your behalf?"

"On Albion's."

"Now you have it!" said Lord Ingleborough. There was sweat on him. "It is as I always warned. Use the old methods—and you see the old results emerging."

Montfallcon shook his head. "That's nought to do with Lady Mary's murder and the rest of the business with the Perrotts. For we must not forget them. If they attack Arabia . . ."

"They'll be popular for it," said Tom Ffynne.

"We'll not be able to support them." The Lord High Admiral was wincing as he spoke. "We cannot."

"And if we stop 'em," said Tom Ffynne, "half the nobles in Albion will be against us, as well as the commons. We could have some sort of uprising. Not a large one, possibly. But who knows? One thing leads swiftly to another."

The pain in Ingleborough's face was reflected in Montfallcon's, who again saw his great dream fading, even as they spoke. He stood up. "There must be a way to save all that we have schemed for, all the good we have created!"

"Not by the old methods." Lord Ingleborough drew Patch to him, as if to protect the lad from Montfallcon's rage. "We acquired bad habits in Hern's service, even as we worked against him. You cannot help yourself, Perion. You continue to use the instruments of secrecy and terror—modified, perhaps, but you still use them. You plot along conventional lines. . . ."

"To protect our Queen and Albion!" Montfallcon did not raise his voice, but his tone intensified and was therefore much more fearsome. "To protect the innocence of the girl whose life we three protected for so long from the cruelty and caprice of the father! My whole soul has been invested in this service—as have yours. I refuse to accept your inference, Lisuarte, that my actions have been in any way misguided."

"Or immoral?" Ingleborough spoke quietly, his teeth clenching. The pain continued to increase in him. A hand to the heart again.

"Most morally have I protected Albion and all Albion means to us. The world's not perfect. I have had to use certain tactics . . . but never have they touched the Queen. No stain . . ."

"Spilling blood for Albion is spilling blood in the Queen's name." Ingleborough sighed, lowering his chin upon his chest.

Tom Ffynne was up. "This is no good. If we three quarrel, then all we've achieved is surely lost."

"I have never acted," continued Lord Montfallcon, "unless the Queen (and therefore the Realm) was in some way threatened. Many of the dead were amiable enough, I suppose, but foolish, luring the Queen into like foolishness—indirectly, often. She never knew. We could not have the Realm discredited."

"I fear your next admission," groaned Ingleborough, "that you've had the Countess killed. And those others."

"The Countess's influence upon the Queen was never good. Her advice paid scant respect to Duty. And the Queen is Albion and Albion is Duty."

Tom Ffynne cried: "Friends! No more of this. You drive yourselves to opposing ends of a brittle plank. When it snaps you'll both fall. Let's keep to the middle. Remember. Our business is to maintain the balance. It is what we have always agreed. And you, Lisuarte, are in monstrous bad pain. You must retire. I'll talk to Perion. He claims more than is true, as a man will become drunk on his own poetry and add substance to his stories and thus maintain the song."

Montfallcon sat down behind his desk. Patch ran for the lackeys to bear away his master's chair. Tom Ffynne stood beside the empty fireplace and listened to the ticking, to the grinding levers, of the clock above his head.

When Lord Ingleborough had gone, Sir Thomasin Ffynne

looked down at his remaining friend. "There can be no more killing, Perion. Another death here and our plans are defeated for ever."

"I've killed nobody. Not the ones Ingleborough speaks of, at any rate."

"I said nought of culprits." Tom Ffynne stretched himself. "Besides, in conscience, I can't imitate Lisuarte's tone. I've done my share. And come adrift. This last venture was a stupid trick and I'll not sail out again. I'm shorebound from now on. I merely said we must have no more. We must see to it that there is no more. We clear the air, Perion. We must bring back the light. We must make the Queen happy. For all our sakes. It cannot be done with the old ways of iron."

"What other ways are there?" Montfallcon sulked, but he did not deny, in his stance, the truth of Ffynne's words. "Iron threatens: iron defends."

"Gold defends, too."

"We pay our way clear? That's never worked in all history!"

"Golden ideas." Sir Tom laughed at himself. "Golden dreams. It's what we've lived on, you and I, for many years. Golden faith."

Montfallcon agreed. "The Queen responded. She brought us back our faith for a little while. It seemed that all was well again. Then the Countess of Scaith is proven a murderess and the Queen crumbles. She's been moping ever since. She'll see no-one. Count Korzeniowski wishes an audience on important matters concerning Poland—perhaps he wishes her to stop this duel, for he loves his Casimir. Oubacha Khan talks openly of Tatar armies gathering at Arabia's borders while spreading rumours, got from his crony, Lady Yashi, that Lady Lyst and Master Wheldrake aided in Perrott's murder and threw his body down a disused well, so now Lyst and Wheldrake go fearful for their lives, lest the Perrotts catch the rumour. . . ."

"You believe them innocent?"

"Aye. Those two have no murder in them."

"There's gossip of perversity. . . ."

"Mild. I know his tastes. He would be chastised by the Queen every day, and Lady Lyst's his substitute. And her taste's for nought but wine. The Queen could make such gossip disappear, but she will not. She has not carried her sceptre for more than a week. She has not received ambassadors. She has not entered the Audience Chamber. She refuses to listen to me. And now there comes a deputation of Saracens, some fifty strong, to speak urgently—doubtless on the same matter as Korzeniowski—and she spurns them, virtually insults them, and they wait daily in the Second Presence Chamber—all etched steel and warlike battle-silks (though they bear no weapons) like an army giving siege."

"The Countess of Scaith. If she were found?"

"She's gone for good."

"You're prejudiced against her."

"So I am. But I can read character. She was softening the Queen."

"The Queen believes now that she was a traitress?" Ffynne was perplexed.

"The Queen says nothing to me."

"She thinks you deceive her, Perion, perhaps?"

"Perhaps."

"Does Ingleborough have her ear?"

"He dodders."

"He did not today."

"He has spoken some conventional comfort to her, Tom, but she dismissed him, also. Apparently she half-suspects that the Countess of Scaith was murdered, too. She thinks the blood in the room was her friend's."

"Could it not be?"

"There would have been signs of a struggle."

"And no signs of Perrott's death, then?" Ffynne was sceptical of the theory.

"The whole mystery has been debated." Montfallcon rose slowly. "She had all the time in the calendar to make sure she was not detected in Perrott's death. She would not flee unless she felt suspected. Would she?"

"But was she suspected?"

"By me. I have always been suspicious of her."

"And no news of her in Scaith?"

"None. None. She'll be abroad. She has estates everywhere. Some even say the Emperor of Tatary is her lover."

Tom Ffynne wiped his face with his sleeve. "The Queen needs support, Perion. If she'll not accept it from me, she'll find it elsewhere. Una of Scaith was her closest friend. Perhaps her only friend, in private life."

"The Queen is not a private personage," said Lord Montfallcon. "She'll recall soon enough that Albion's friends are her friends. It's a simple equation."

Sir Thomasin Ffynne pursed his lips. "It could be, my lord, that we have made our equations too simple. Where, by the by, is Doctor Dee? I should have thought he'd be pleased to comfort Her Majesty."

"Obsessed with his experiments. He scarcely emerges from his lodgings, these days."

"It seems we're all divorced from her at once." He limped towards the door. "What explanations are there for that, d'ye think, Perion?"

Montfallcon looked up. "What? You blame me, too?"

Tom Ffynne turned back to study him. "You're quick to suspect accusation. I but asked the question, hoping that your subtler brain might find an answer."

"I'm plagued by many questions." Montfallcon had become ashamed of himself. "Forgive me, Tom."

"Well, think on it. Your mission is, after all, to maintain the unity of the Court and the Realm. And the core of that unity is, as always, Gloriana. Should the core collapse, the whole structure collapses, eh?"

"I have always said so."

"Yet we are not thinking too much of protecting the core. Of healing it, if it is wounded." Tom Ffynne spoke kindly. "We must be gentle. She is still, in one sense at any rate, not a woman. So think of her as a child, Perion."

But Lord Montfallcon drew in a weary breath. "The tenderness is all gone, Tom. Now there is only Duty."

"By such means are marriages turned sour and cynical, I think." Tom Ffynne was leaving. "But, like Lisuarte, I never married, so I'm not the best judge, perhaps."

"I have been married many times," said Montfallcon, his voice deepening with grief.

The Twenty-Third Chapter

In Which the Queen
Attends Her Accession Day Celebrations;
in Which Chivalry Is Affirmed;
in Which She Discovers a New Champion

In burning gold and blazing silver, in shimmering jet and glinting steel, in plate and chain, in surcoats of the finest rippling silk, in bright blues and reds, in greens and yellows, in purples and browns, in a dancing sea of rainbow plumes, with lances bound with samite scarves, with shields fabulously charged, with standards starched and brilliant, their horses clad as gaudily and armoured as fancifully as they, the Queen's Jousters clattered through the wide gates into the Great Square and began their procession around the perimeter. Above them, on walls and roofs, according to ancient privilege, from four sides the commons roared and cheered their favourites. From the old balcony on the East Wing, where her father and grandfather had sat, Queen Gloriana waved to her knights, distributed roses (flung at random) and was saluted, to louder shouts and wilder huzzahs by a crowd delirious from the pageantry and the heat of high summer. Lances were raised and dipped; bucklers were displayed while heralds called the Rolls of Arms. From throughout the Realm the knights had come to compete before the Queen. Here were famous names—Tirante, Duke of Lyonesse, from the Isles of the West; Sir Gandalac of the Vale of Lune in the North Country; Sir Esplandian of Valentia; Sir Hector of the Ranach in Hibernia; Sir Turquine of Lincoln; all with their yeomen, their pages and their gentlemen, their heralds and their squires. And from beyond Albion came Sir Hakan of Tauron, the Huron King, with his armour all decorated with war-feathers and beads; Sir Herlwin of Wicheetaw; King Desrame of

Mauretania; the Emir of Saragossa; Prince Hira of Bom Bai; the Sultan Matroco of Aethiopia; Prince Shan of Cathay; Sir Bulamwe of Benin—many of them familiar to the crowd, for they attended the Tilt every year, competing not only in arms, but in the splendour of their accoutrements, their weapons, their horses and their attendants; who were clad in fantastical costumes as fauns, wild-men, godlings. Some brought beasts, such as unicorns, elephants and camelopards, to draw their marvellous chariots; some rode as if to hounds, with packs of trained hyaenas, or apes; and Sir Miles Cockaigne, whose boast was that he had never won a fight in his whole career, had fiddlers and dancers in his entourage, while his yeomen carried sackbuts instead of arms and he himself, in chequered surcoat and loose, lozenge-linked motley-coloured mail, came as Sir Harlekin the Bold, to bring laughter to both Queen and Crowd.

All sought to please Gloriana, yet the nobles from the castles and the great houses of Albion, who maintained their estates and tenants in her name and the name of Chivalry, who administered her laws, who belonged to that generation which worshipped her and for whom she was a symbol of faithfulness and idealism, they studied her, anxious for affirmation which she must supply, knowing how easily the virtues of Romance can transmogrify and become the vices of Cynicism. Through her, and with her absolute support, Montfallcon had re-fashioned the mood of Albion, through a subtle use of pageantry and myth—telling a golden lie in the strong belief that it stood, in time, to become a silver truth—a lie which almost all were ready to accept, for the same reasons as Montfallcon gave it out. And the Accession celebrations, which would last the full week, were a visible sign of their participation in and commitment to those principles. So they saluted Gloriana, and were merry, fighting in good friendship and according to complicated Chivalric codes, in a display to please the commons, to confirm their loyalty to all that Gloriana meant, to compete not merely in matters of physical grace, but in rituals of honour and humility, to give visible reality to their will towards spirituality, towards the true meaning of Chivalry.

* * *

The Queen, withdrawing into the long gallery, where, as was the royal habit, she might sit and watch the tourney through the glass which protected her from dust and, to a degree, from noise, behaved in manner so easily that some of those who did not know her might have thought her callous, that she forgot lost friends so swiftly. Many foreign ambassadors filled the gallery, as well as favourite maids of honour and companions, their suitors, relatives of Privy Councillors, wives and children of the competitors below, acquaintances of the Queen from the provinces who took this chance to visit her, as well as the best part of the Privy Council itself, which would not today attend the Tilt, but would wait upon her, in the colours of Romance, on the last day, Accession Day, when she must appear as Queen Urganda the Unknown, mysterious and beneficent sorceress of legend, friend of heroes, saviour of the noble and the brave.

Gloriana acted the rôle of Gracious Sovereign with an energy derived from unfamiliar anger at the injustice of her position. Montfallcon had insisted she be there, recalling to her those pledges she had made to him even before she took the throne, reminding her of Albion's heritage, its meaning and its worth. Her conscience had been awakened by him, but not her spirit. She had seen the sense of his insistence, but nonetheless resented it. She had always, in the past twelve years, enjoyed her Accession Day ceremonies, culminating in the Masque in which she played the central rôle, but with Una gone, with Mary gone, with kind, silly Sir Tancred gone, she could only feel their absence more poignantly, and she mourned for them while she smiled and chatted and from time to time lifted a gay hand to the window.

She felt betrayed—by the innocent Una, by the knowing Montfallcon, by Council, companions and friends—for she had no friends now, only subjects, dependents, her servants, her secrets. Such feelings drove her to great displays of wit. She was no longer herself. She played Gloriana's part at full stretch, and few guessed she might soon snap, and of the few who guessed, fewer cared. She was like a splendid flagship, all sails unfurled to catch the wind, all colours flying, brass and woodwork, gilding and paint flashing in the sunlight, cheered on by everyone who watched her glide across the water, and none to know that, below the waterline, she had no rudder and no anchor.

The first tourney commenced, in the special yard erected upon the large artificial island in the middle of the ornamental lake, so that the whole mass of people might have a fair view of the proceedings.

Sir Timon of the Bridge of Graveny, a young knight in blue and white, jousted against the more experienced Sir Peregrine of Kilcolman Castle, in red, gold and black, and Sir Timon was soon unhorsed, whereupon Sir Peregrine dismounted, took two pikes and, helping his antagonist to his feet, handed him one so that they might continue their fight until one fell or five pikes broke. In their heavy, fanciful tilting armour, in closed helms and full plate, the knights moved slowly and deliberately about the field, and, like dancers in an ancient mime, struck at one another with stylised gracefulness. Above them, surrounding them, the crowd was quiet, sweating in the August heat and conscious of the discomfort of the jousters who roasted slowly as they fought.

Lord Oubacha Khan caught Queen Gloriana's eye as she turned from the scene. He smiled and bowed and she cried out: "Good my lord, come and sit with me. It has been a while since we talked."

The tall Tatar, in his golden surcoat and silver mail, the formal costume of a noble of his own land, approached and kissed the Queen's hand. "I was concerned," he said in a low voice, "for the well-being of the Countess of Scaith."

Gloriana drew him down upon the couch. "As are we all, my lord." She spoke lightly.

"I admired the lady very much."

Gloriana did not drop her guard, but she was sure she read sincerity in the oriental's dark eyes. "As did I, Lord Oubacha Khan."

"There is talk that she is dead."

"And talk that she is fled. And talk, indeed, my lord, that she has gone to live with your own master, in Tatary, at your Muscovian capital."

Oubacha Khan smiled very slightly. "Would that she had, Your Majesty."

"You do not seem to think she was a murderess."

"I do not care. If she is alive, I would find her."

Gloriana was surprised by his intensity, but she remained a formal Queen. "That is Lord Rhoone's responsibility, and Lord Montfallcon's."

Oubacha Khan murmured a secret. "My own people also search."

"In Albion?"

"Everywhere, Your Majesty."

"Then you must be sure to tell Lord Rhoone of anything you hear, my lord."

"I shall, of course, Your Majesty. But strangely we have heard nothing. There is no evidence she left the palace at all."

"Ah, indeed?" So painful was the subject that Queen Gloriana turned away, pretending boredom, so that she should hide her true feelings, her interest.

"We continue to search."

"We have heard, my lord, that Tatar merchants do good trade," began Gloriana in a voice slightly higher than was natural, "with the peoples of our East Indian provinces, the mountain states of Pathania and Afghania especially. Do your merchants grow rich?"

He, too, became a public man. He said: "Merchants grow rich or they perish, Your Majesty. Some grow rich, doubtless."

"Trade between nations brings knowledge and knowledge brings wisdom, my lord. Do your merchants become wise, also?" She performed the function Montfallcon expected of her, so that she need not think of Una.

"The Tatar nation is famous for its wisdom, Your Majesty."

"Wisdom teaches that trade builds peace and prosperity, while war brings only poverty and further strife." She pursued this conscientious reasoning, yet seemed to the Khan to be half entranced as her attention went to the window.

"There is a kind of wisdom, Your Majesty," he continued,

virtually as automatic as she, "that is merely caution disguised by sophistry. There is another kind, unadorned, that tells us that too much emphasis on the merchant's needs creates a nation both morally and physically weak, a prey to stronger nations."

"So would many of our Stoics agree, in this land," she said. "But the world should support all manner of philosophies, I think, and it should be the duty of the righteous to protect the weak while encouraging the strong." She hardly knew what she said, for the words were almost rote, diplomatic habit; yet Oubacha Khan, though he responded in similar terms, found them significant.

"For there is considerable strength in apparent weakness," she continued, casting another glance towards the Tilt, where two new knights now fought. "Of course, the Tatar people are famous for their subtlety, and must know that."

Oubacha Khan said: "That belief can become dangerous to the one who holds it. Strength can melt away without his realising."

"Unless he is reminded always of the necessity for maintaining his strength, my lord." She smiled, rising to watch as the knights levelled their lances and, mantling streaming, went upon one another at full gallop. There came a crash, a cheer, as both knights broke their spears but retained their seats, returning to their positions for fresh weapons. "If I, for instance, should grow weak, you, as a friend, would be ready to remind me, I am sure."

"Indeed, Your Majesty." Oubacha Khan had enjoyed the exchange much more than had the Queen. He understood her to mean that Tatary's gathering of arms along Arabia's borders would act as a signal for Albion to grow alert. And he was satisfied, for this was what he expected of diplomacy.

"My Lord of Kansas!" The Queen greeted the bronzed, long face with genuine pleasure. "You have not yet returned to your Virginian estates?"

"Soon, Your Majesty. There is a great deal to keep me here. And I would not miss the Tilt." The soft-spoken noble smiled, bowing to kiss her gloved hand. He was clad in doublet and puffed hose of varying yellows, with a short purple cape upon his shoulder, a broad-brimmed, befeathered hat upon his head, and this he removed as he bent.

She teased him. "You are most gaudily dressed, for a Stoic, my lord."

"I am dressed, today, for a Queen," he said.

"You become a perfect courtier, my lord." As Oubacha Khan politely departed, she patted the couch to bring Lord Kansas down beside her.

He grinned, complying. "In honesty, madam, I feel like a stuffed pumpkin."

She was comically grave. "You look very handsome, my lord. Do you enjoy the Tilt?"

"I do."

"You do not take part?"

"No, madam. I've little experience at formal arms and I haven't the retainers sufficient to support me. Not here."

"You brought a very small household, so I heard."

"It's my habit, madam, for often I travel only in the company of soldiers, as you know."

"You have tilts in Virginia. I have read of them."

"Elaborate ones, Your Majesty."

"But, as a Stoic, you deplore the pomp, eh?"

"I accept its necessity, madam. Here, at any rate. I share with the Countess of Scaith"—it was evident that he regretted his lack of tact, but he continued almost without pause—"a preference for simpler methods of maintaining the State's dignity. But they will come, in time, I think. Old memories must be crushed beneath a weight of gallantry."

"I shared that belief, also," said the Queen. "I envy you your pastoral Virginian life. Is it peaceful, in Kansas, my lord?"

"Too peaceful for a man of my kind, sometimes, madam. You know the Virginian temperament, by and large, I suppose. We enjoy the land. We are secure. At peace with our fellow nations and, now, with Albion."

"The rebellions were small enough."

"And not against the Realm, only its representative." He made it clear he referred to Hern.

"Yes." Gloriana rubbed an eye and dipped her chin into her ruff. "But if there were war? Would the Virginian nobles pledge support to us?"

Lord Kansas was surprised. "War?"

She put fingers upon his forearm. "There are no wars starting today, my lord. Not, at least, that we know of. I merely asked a speculative question."

"Virginia would come to war. Reluctantly. But she would come."

"It is as I thought."

"This Perrott business, madam. Surely it has not reached such proportions—?"

"It has reached nowhere, my lord. Save that the Perrotts are justly angered at the slaying of their sister and the disappearance of their father. But they will cool."

"There are none at the Tilt."

"You have noticed?" She admitted a weary smile. "Aye. They stay away this year. The Perrotts and their kinsmen. Who can blame them? But they will, I assure you, come round."

"I hope so, madam. Sir Amadis. His wife was a Perrott, eh?"

"Recalled to home. Sir Amadis had leave to go with her, but declined. They are separated. It will not last. Sir Lepsius Lee has gone to Kent with his wife, taking his retainers from the Court."

"You are not hurt by such disloyalty, madam?"

"We are the Realm, my lord, and thus have no human feelings." Her expression hooded, she looked again towards the tournament. She kept her hand on his arm. "Your direct farmer's ways are refreshing to us, Lord Kansas, but not always suited to Court life."

He chuckled. "You'll forgive me?"

"You charm us, as always, my lord."

Lord Montfallcon approached with narrowed eyes. "My Lord of Kansas?"

Kansas rose and Kansas bowed. "Your grace."

At that moment Queen Gloriana understood her Lord Chancellor: he saw the Virginian noble as a possible suitor. Did he approve? And did Kansas pay court to her? she wondered. She looked at one and then the other. She waved a fan against her cheek.

"You have grown to love our Court, apparently," said Lord Montfallcon.

"As I love the whole island." Kansas hesitated. He seemed reluctant to speak further, perhaps because he feared Montfallcon's oversensitive interpretation.

The grey lord moved in black robes slowly towards the Queen, almost as if he menaced her, and Lord Kansas began to raise his hand, by impulse, perhaps to stop him. Then he dropped the hand to the pommel of his dress dagger.

"Madam," said Lord Montfallcon, hardly conscious of these gestures, "the ambassador from Cathay would speak with you."

"Let him approach, my lord." Gloriana smiled farewell to Kansas and returned to Duty.

And Duty she did, throughout the week, as the sun grew hotter and hotter, the crowd more boisterous, the Chivalric contests more glamorous, with silk, steel and water, dust and haze combining to create a scene which came, daily, to resemble a dream. She attended banquets and enchanted everyone. She bestowed honours, accepted gifts, gave out praise to all, while the general opinion was that this was the finest of Summer Festivals, that it would never be equalled in perfection and merriment. Not a knight, nor yeoman, nor ambassador, nor lady, nor dignitary, nor merchant, but left the Queen's presence with joyful heart and hopeful step. And if the Queen had come to rely a little more each day upon her paint pots to maintain her bloom, none made adverse comment upon the fact, or even saw, as silent Sir Thomasin Ffynne or aching Ingleborough saw, how pale she became.

And Lord Montfallcon, moving amongst the guests, amplifying and sustaining the Queen's good work, refused to see, or to listen to Tom Ffynne or Lisuarte Ingleborough when they mentioned it to him. He had become almost hearty towards his potential enemies, to his many acquaintances, but grew colder towards his friends.

Meanwhile, Sir Amadis Cornfield attended only those ceremonies at which he must be missed, while speeding often to the old

East Wing; and Doctor Dee, absent-minded but amiable, came forth from his lodgings only rarely, ever careful to lock his door behind him; and Lord Gorius Ransley, at different times, lurked the passages of the old palace; and Master Florestan Wallis came weak and breathing very heavily to his own duties, when beholden. Even loyal Lord Rhoone spent more of his hours in private company with his wife and children than was usual, but this was to be expected.

And when the Queen missed Master Wheldrake or Lady Lyst, she knew what they feared and did not ask for them. Besides, Master Wheldrake was still at work on his last verses for Accession Day. Lord Shahryar returned from Baghdad, bearing the compliments of his master, Hassan, the Grand Caliph, and bringing expensive gifts, but he would say nothing of a rumour concerning a duel forthcoming upon the deck of a ship. And Lord Montfallcon was hard put to smile on the man who had robbed him of his best servant, Quire.

Sir Vivien Rich took part in a tilt and won it, but was much bruised, complaining he would not be able to sit a horse for a month and would therefore miss the early September hunting. Sir Orlando Hawes challenged a cousin, the Nubian knight of great renown, Sir Vulturnus, and, by chance, defeated him, thereafter going about the Court in something of a daze.

There were expeditions to the fields beyond the city and great open-air evening feasts, much drunkenness, so that some of the guests were lost, to be found next day in haylofts, ricks, hedges or ditches, or, upon two or three occasions, the comfortable beds of farmers' widows.

The August air burned, but it also soothed; and if tempers rose they were soon shrivelled by the universal good cheer. Parties of courtiers, out riding early, or at twilight, could look across the beautiful hills and see the corn being gathered, see the richly decorated barges on the long straight canals leading to the river, and the city and the ships loading and unloading the cargoes of a wealthy world; and they could see a peaceful, happy, industrious Albion, and know that the Queen's rule was good. The shades of

Lady Mary and the rest had vanished. News reaching the Perrotts caused a weakening of their general hatred, and some Perrotts counselled their kinsmen to consider making peace with the Queen, who had always been their friend. Poles, Saracens and Tatars mingled with the folk of Albion, proving themselves human, decent men and women, and Mars fell back below the horizon.

Accession Day itself dawned, and in the morning the last four fights were fought, to decide the two Champions who would, that evening, tilt once more before the Queen and the winner receive the garland from the Queen's own hand. Between these two events would come the Masque, attended by the Queen and members of her Court, to personate the characters and speak the lines. There was much happy anticipation of this event, the peak of the celebrations. Praise for Gloriana was on all lips; scandal was banished; the morality, bravery and piety of the Realm was assured, so that Lord Montfallcon's stern features bore an expression that was almost pleasant.

In her apartments, surrounded by companions, by maids and pages, pale Gloriana suffered herself to be painted and disguised in the magnificent, glittering costume of her rôle: damask silk and starched linen, velvet and brocade, stitched with thousands of jewels—sapphires, amethysts, turquoises, rubies, pearls and, predominantly, diamonds. On her stranded head was a tall, pointed crown, with a thin veil of lace, to add mystery to her countenance. Behind her head rose a wired collar, so high as to give an overall stretch of seven feet, so that she would tower over every knight. Corseted, bound, entwined with ribbons, weighted with metal and precious stones, embellished with rouge and kohl, she stared at her reflection in the mirror and silently yearned for Una, who would laugh with her, make a joke of what she did, yet never seem cynical, always be sympathetic to both her private feelings and the demands of her public duties. Her bright, lonely grieving eyes stared from within the paint and gradually grew hard.

She was ready.

Led by attendants, she entered Master Tolcharde's carriage, which would bear her to the island, where Master Wheldrake already proclaimed the story of the Masque.

"Now that great sorceress, URGANDA, did she come,
As ever from her Land Unknown,
In sea-borne chariot, a fiery sphere,
To our Firm Isle, where every year
Twelve paladins of bold renown
Assembled them a fight to make
And fame to take as Champion."

Master Wheldrake's voice lacked its usual steadiness as he piped his lines to a respectful crowd. He wore a simple toga, a laurel crown and sandals, and was perhaps the most comfortably clad of all the people there, whether they watched from the gallery, the surrounding pavilions or the roofs and walls of the palace itself. He read from a scroll, and, as he read, the participants began to ride over the little bridge from courtyard to island—each knight in a predominant colour, each bearing a large shield charged with the device of the character he represented.

"These famous knights each bore great arms:
The first he was the Knight of Silver Charm,
The second the Knight of the Flaming Brand,
The third was called the Jewelled Hand,
The fourth was named the Unthron'd King,
The fifth the Knight of the Broken Spear,
The sixth, of youngest year, was Golden Ring."

As Wheldrake spoke, the named knight raised his lance—Sir Amadis Cornfield in silver mail; Lord Vortigern of Glastonbury, in scarlet armour, his shield charged with the flaming sword; Sir Orlando Hawes, in greens and red, with the jewelled gauntlet upon his right hand and the same motif on his buckler and surcoat; Sir Felixmarte of Hyrcania, whose arms were a divided crown, and whose armour was of brass; Master Auberon Orme, in blue edged with silver, with the broken lance as his badge; and Master Perigot Fowler, in golden armour, with the ring as his charge. Facing these six, on the other side of the island (now fringed with small imitation trees, over which the horsemen loomed), were the remaining six knights, and it was to these that Master Wheldrake now pointed.

"The seventh brave knight was Raven Head;
The eighth was the Son Consider'd Dead,
And nine the Knight of the Moon was he,
While ten was call'd Prometheus Set Free,
The eleventh was he of the Misty Foss
And the twelfth, whose eyes had lost their sight,
Was the noble knight of the bright Black Cross."

Here was Master Isador Palfreyman, with his black armour and his raven crest; Master Marcilius Gallimari, in unmarked armour; Sir Sylvanus Spence, brother of young Sir Peregrine, with his pale yellow armour and his arms displaying a radiant moon; Lord Gorius Ransley, in fiery scarlet, with appropriate symbols; Sir Cirus of Malta in pale grey; Sir Vivien Rich was last, in pure white armour bearing black crosses, his helm already closed to signify his blindness.

Master Wheldrake withdrew across the bridge as a trumpet was blown—a signal for the knights to charge, couple by couple, with specially weakened lances which broke at once. Then all dismounted and began to fight, with monstrous clashing broadswords, on foot.

For a while this mock battle continued to be waged, with several of the contestants showing every sign of fatigue, until suddenly, from a silken pavilion close to the West Wing, there appeared a vast bronze sphere, rolling on mighty wheels of brass, decorated with raised motifs of myriad description, rumbling and groaning and pulled and pushed by dwarves dressed in grotesque dolphin costumes so that they seemed to slither along the ground. From the sides of the sphere, in cunning sockets, fireworks fizzed and screamed as the elaborate contraption was trundled towards the bridge, while Master Wheldrake, his voice almost a gull's shriek above the noise, continued to recite:

"So for almost seven days they were engag'd,
Weapon for weapon, gauge for flaunted gauge,
Each hero of equal skill and might
Fought all from morning until night
Until upon the seventh day there came,
To cause these lords their noble sport to still,
A noise so shrill: A carriage built of flame!"

Across the shivering bridge rolled the sphere, the dolphin dwarves dragging it to the far side of the island and then jumping into the lake to swim for their lives to the shore, while the knights, in pretence of great awe, fell upon their knees, raised their hands, dropped their weapons and stared at the carriage, which was now silent. Master Florestan Wallis clambered to his feet, forced open a reluctant helm, waved his arms and cried to the crowd:

"What magical terror can this be
Come to fright my fellow knights and me!"

(his own lines—he disdained to be supplied by Wheldrake), while Sir Amadis Cornfield, as the Knight of the Silver Charm, sang out:

"This is Leviathan of which our legends speak,
And 'pon our Firm Isle shall great destruction wreak!"

(and Wheldrake sneered from the other side of the bridge and shrugged in an effort to show the uncaring crowd that he was not the author of this poor stuff). But one must indulge a minister of the Crown, he thought, even though that minister be feeble-minded, sexless, full of much learning and no knowledge, bombastic, possessed of an ear which could not tell a nightingale's song from a lapdog's fart . . .

Wheldrake watched through weary eyes as the two sides of the carriage fell apart to reveal an enormous green serpent, all of papier mâché, with glittering scales, rolling eyes, lolling tongue and clashing teeth, one of Master Tolcharde's best creations. That the crowd found this by far the grandest entertainment so far was obvious from its noise. A score or so of maidens, in flimsy linen, came past Wheldrake now. The garlanded nymphs were dancers supplied by Master Josias Priest, who simpered nearby, urging the girls on. They were all young, their figures as yet not quite fully defined, boyish, attractively hermaphrodite, led by one of the most beautiful creatures Wheldrake had ever seen (*Mithras! What an exquisite, youthful tyrant she would make!*). Now behind them came a faun, with huge, wicked, lustful eyes, capering and blowing upon a reed pipe, while from another pavilion, hidden from the crowd, music began to play, to represent the faun's ethereal voice.

The green serpent moved free of the sphere, towards the knights, who lined themselves before it, raising their weapons, preparing for the fray.

Then, a further transformation, as the serpent seemed to shrivel and collapse, to become a lovely barge bearing a beautiful giantess seated upon a coral throne. Six and a half feet tall, magnificent, auburn-haired, radiating virtue, a pointed silver crown upon her veiled head, flaming with jewels enough to blind those who beheld her, she raised a pearly wand and smiled upon the dazzled heroes, while her maidens danced about them, covering them with flowers, and the fauns leapt and twisted, seeming to fill the air with his silvery music as the maidens sweetly sang:

> *"With golden flutes and harps we hail our Queen,*
> *The wonderful URGANDA, the Wise Unseen,*
> *Now doth she beg ye gentle knights your war to cease*
> *And, laying down your arms, to swear enduring peace.*

For there's no greater sorceress in all our wide Globe's span,
Than this grand Monarch, whom all Heroes woo,
Whose voice and heart are ever true, this Queen of Fairy Land!"

And Wheldrake glared at Florestan Wallis who, with more flourishes and crow-caws, called out:

"My peers! This is the noblest Sovereign
To whom we all swear fealty and love.
By fighting thus we shame her name!
Farewell war-eagle—Welcome dove!"

Then music and maidens continued with the song:

"As Man's ignorance a hideous form can oft create,
And sick imaginings small lies inflate,
Thus too can truth and beauty wear a fierce disguise
So that her enemies shall all be hard appris'd
That though the kindlier virtues are encouraged,
As in that distant noble land of Albion,
URGANDA's wrath can burn full strong, and fill the hearts of evil men with dread!"

Master Florestan Wallis's eyes were upon the faun, who seemed to fascinate him, so that there was a pause before he recalled his next contortion:

"But madam, how shall we choose our Champion,
To rule above the others and make all One,
To order spirit as Time doth order Space,
If not by test of martial arms and grace?"

Wheldrake leaned heavily on the bridge and glanced towards the pavilion from which, very soon, Lord Bramandil Rhoone must ride, in his rôle.

The Queen spoke (Wallis's lines, for diplomacy's sake):

"Noble-blooded paladins, there's one I'll give to you
Who is my chosen Champion, his peers are few,
Yet from no landed castle does this hero come,
Though noble is his soul and of vices he has none.
For years his only weapon was a shepherd's hook,
The sky his roof, the fluttering fire his book.
His name ye will not find in Herald's Rolls,
But carved upon a beam of some poor peasant's fold,
The lowly pasture was this brave knight's domain
And yet I'll warrant that ye all do know his name
This goodly Peasant Knight, so free of sin —
My great lords—bow the knee to PALMERIN!"

They were bending already, but Wheldrake, looking towards Lord Rhoone's pavilion, was astonished to see a small, unmounted figure leaving it. The figure was clad in faded black, with a wide-brimmed black hat, a couple of black crow's feathers stuck into a worn band, black ringlets falling to the shoulders, black brows shadowing glinting eyes, pale features, long nose, a lantern jaw, thin sensual lips; a cloak clasped about the neck with twisting silver, boots of black, broken leather, hands hidden, head down, walking boldly for the bridge, crossing it as Wheldrake stared (recognising the figure from somewhere but not recalling where), and moving between the ranks of kneeling knights as the leading maiden and the faun ran forward to put garlands about his neck: presenting himself as Palmerin, the Peasant Knight, appraising the gathered courtiers on both banks and in galleries, seeking friends and enemies in one long look before the head bowed as it reached the carriage and the leg was made:

"My Queen."

From behind her veil Gloriana's expression was one of astonishment, quickly hidden, for the stranger was speaking Lord Rhoone's lines—the lines that the Countess of Scaith would have spoken were she here—and Gloriana guessed that Rhoone was sick and had sent some servant as a substitute. She refused to consider the crazily flickering thought—that another Champion was dead before he could perform his rôle today.

"My lady, though I be of lowly station,
Most loyally I've served your name and nation."

The dark, cold, sardonic eyes were looking through her veil as if they peered through flesh and into her soul. She was fixed by the gaze. And there was humour in his eyes, too, which attracted her. It was as if she had been sent another Una.

And through the rest of the Masque, Queen Gloriana found herself forgetting fear, forgetting duty, forgetting grief, fascinated by those wonderful, intelligent, unkind eyes.

Of the courtiers who stood as knights of this and that, somewhat bewildered by the newcomer, so confident in his lines, so familiar in his attitude, there were some who knew him and smiled as men might smile who recognise a friend turned up in paradoxical circumstances. Sir Amadis Cornfield recognised him as the gentleman who had been gracious enough to secure him the favours of Alys Finch, the girl who led the dance today; Master Florestan Wallis recognised him as the protector of his paramour, the lovely "Philomena," who played the faun in Josias Priest's troop; Lord Gorius Ransley also recognised him as the friendly intermediary between himself and Alys Finch, who promised consolation soon; Lord Rhoone, peering cheerfully from his tent and a willing party to the joke, knew him for the apothecary who had supplied the antidote and saved the lives of his wife and children; while Doctor John Dee, staggering forward in conical cap and swirling blue robes, to play his personation of Merlin, Urganda's consort, paused upon the bridge, recognising this "Sir Palmerin" as the benefactor, the seer that had supplied him with his whole desire.

But standing in the gallery, face gaunt with rage and consternation, Lord Montfallcon recognised his ear, his mouth, his sword, his instrument, and knew how thoroughly and with what audacious cunning he had been deceived and manipulated by Captain Quire, who was even now offering his arm to Queen Gloriana, speaking verse neither by Wheldrake nor by Wallis, and leading her, compliant, against the progress of the Masque, towards the bridge.

"So shall they come together, side by side,
And simple shepherd take the mighty for his bride."

The crowd was delighted by the sentiments and the outcome. Noble and commoner wed was ever a favourite theme, and reinforced the Masque's intent, to show how, in all ways, Albion was a unity. The Queen had not been meant to leave her throne, but here was Quire leading her around the square, waving his hat, while she, elated by surprise, waved her wand, to the mob's huge delight, to the applause of her nobles. The maidens and the faun continued to dance before them, while the twelve paladins, horsed once again, rode behind, and a bemused Merlin, having been usurped his handful of couplets, hobbled in their wake, shaking his head.

That this display, though vulgar, served perfectly his needs, Montfallcon admitted to himself, even as he trembled in his anger. Quire had always boasted of his understanding of the mob and now he proved it.

But to see that creature, that symbol of every ignoble deed, every perverse trick, every lie and deceit, used secretly by him to maintain the Realm, arm in arm with the innocent girl whom Montfallcon had protected through the years from any hint of infamy or guilt, whom he had protected against cynicism, against the understanding that some iron had been mixed in with the gold, perforce, to give it the strength it needed—to see that appalling pairing of vice and virtue—brought the blood thundering into his skull and made him want to scream from the window, there and then, for the Guard to drag Quire to the island, to bring out block and axe, to behead the upstart on the spot where, from this same window, Hern had watched a thousand far more innocent heads fall in a single day, when the lake had turned dark red with his victims' lifeblood, including that of five members of Montfallcon's immediate family, whom Montfallcon had let perish without a defending word, so that Gloriana might live to gain the throne.

But, being reminded of those deaths, Montfallcon was also

reminded of his self-control. He drew deep breaths, he tried to smile. All around him the nobles of Albion, of Arabia, of Tatary, of Poland, of the world, were clapping as Captain Quire led the Queen for a second turn about the courtyard.

And, from without, the cheering, stamping, whistling, cap-waving crowd threatened to shake the whole palace to the ground.

Montfallcon moved slowly along the gallery, looking down at the scene, then he opened a door into a tunnel and, within a short while, stood alone in the silence and the darkness of Hern's Throne Room, listening to the beating of his own heart, the hissing of his own breath.

"Oh, what a destroyer Romance can be."

It was as if he confided his thoughts to Hern's ghost, for he was almost friendly in his tone. It had been Montfallcon who had killed the king, whispering him into the final madness, encouraging him to put the noose about his throat, to jump from the battlement above, to hang against the wall, with dead, bulging eyes staring into the same courtyard where Quire defied both convention and retribution and brought the Summer Pageant to a joyous peak.

The Twenty-Fourth Chapter

In Which Lord Montfallcon Considers Means to Rectify His Cause

"AN EARLDOM FOR a Perrott, then a Perrott for the Queen." Lord Montfallcon's lip quivered as he saw how simply all could be saved. "Though she'll have to be rid of certain encumbrances. The seraglio, the children . . ." He was back in the old Throne Room, after two days in which he had kept to his bed, cooling his head and scheming. "As for Quire, I cannot do what has to be done. It must be for Ingleborough to speak to her, to tell her enough, to warn her. . . ." He rubbed an itching nose. He blinked about him in the dusty light from above.

Clack-slap, clack-slap from amongst the looming simian statuary. Tom Ffynne entered. "Why here, Perion?"

"I feel that it is safer."

"Than your own study?"

"I feel that, aye."

Ffynne shrugged. "This recalls unwanted memories."

From the tunnels beyond the old Throne Room there came the noise of several crazed clocks, and through the doors came lackeys with Lord Ingleborough upon their sticks, the sticks supporting a chair. Ingleborough's white, knotted face swung overhead, tight with pain. Patch, in blue and silver, ran beside the litter.

Lord Montfallcon moved his hand and pointed at a place, at the flagstones; the litter was lowered, the lackeys waved away. The three men sat there in the beam of dirty sunlight—Montfallcon with folded robes upon the throne's first step, Tom Ffynne, his leg stretched out beside him, upon the stone block, Ingleborough in his chair. Patch, discreet boy, paced his way around the vaulted perimeter.

"So this Shepherd Knight, this son of Tatyrus, shares the

Queen's bed already!" Tom Ffynne was admiring. "That can't be what's worrying you so much, Perion, can it? He's not the first commoner. . . ."

"He might be the first murderer, however." Montfallcon shuddered as he calmed his hard-breathing body.

"You suspect him?" Ingleborough's voice was a whisper. "Of what?"

"I know him. I know what he is. I know Quire."

"So long as he pleases the Queen," continued Tom Ffynne, even as he was struck by the passion in Montfallcon's words, "what does it matter if he's of lowly birth?" He stopped, giving sudden close attention to his friend. "Eh?"

"He pleases her. Oh, aye. It is his trade. Deception and flattery." Montfallcon had heard some of what Quire had whispered to the Queen that first night, heard her responses, and had been helpless as Quire had charmed her, reassured her, played father, brother, husband, all at once; trading on her weariness, her sense of loss, her self-pity, to make her love him. Quire had been so gentle. His caresses (Montfallcon had heard her say this) were like moth's wings. And instead of leading her to crisis, Quire had calmed her towards reconciliation, as no lover had done before, bringing her peace and a protective arm. Montfallcon had gone mad that night. Now one of his wives lay upon her own bed, close to death, as a result of his rage.

Into the silence his words had made, Montfallcon added:

"I am convinced that this is Lady Mary's murderer. Probably Sir Thomas Perrott's, too."

"But it's his first appearance at the palace."

"He has been in the walls, creating the scene he required before he decided upon his entrance. He is a great actor."

"The walls are death. There are creatures there. I've heard!" Tom Ffynne looked at the solid granite of the inner stones. "Half-human vermin, impossible to root out, for they hide in lost crypts, far below the surface."

"All expeditions have been unsuccessful." Lord Ingleborough spoke very slowly, his voice hardly more than a murmur amplified in the pointed ceilings of the chamber. "But we have never been seriously threatened by them, any more than we are threatened by rats. A little poison answers."

"Well," said Montfallcon, "that is where I believe he has been hiding. He knows the walls as only a few from the outside can. He might have entered them at any time."

"Do you invent hypothesis, Perion?" Tom Ffynne would know.

"Not a bit. Quire was my agent. He turned against me."

"You outlawed him?"

"He outlawed himself. He has ambitions on the throne, I'd swear. He's gone mad for power. I once thought he might."

"He'd be our king, then? Other commoners have raised themselves thus, in Albion."

"The line's remained pure for the past fifteen hundred years," whispered Lord Ingleborough. "Direct from Oberon and Titania of legend. And they, in turn, were descended from fabled Brutus who overthrew Gogmagog. She is of the blood of Elficleos."

"Are we not all, by this time?" Tom Ffynne smiled.

"It isn't the blood I seek to protect," Montfallcon told them impatiently, "it's the flesh, the soul, the very life of our Gloriana. If Quire were nought but a tavern ruffler and could protect Albion by marrying the Queen I'd make him a noble, prove him highborn, if necessary, or change the Law. But Quire's birth is not the question. I fear Quire's intentions. Quire killed the Saracen. He kidnapped Poland's king. Oh, and he has done much, much more. He began the events which have led us to our present pass."

"And you have not told the Queen?" Ingleborough frowned. "Why not?" He turned his aching neck to watch his page, pacing the flagstones in the distance. The sound of Patch's footfalls was like slow dripping water.

"Quire knows why. It's his gamble."

"Because to reveal his character you must reveal your own secrets, is that it?" Tom Ffynne pursed his lips.

Montfallcon admitted it.

Lord Ingleborough sighed. It was as if a far-off storm was heard amongst the buttresses of the roof. "Shall timocracy threaten us so early? Shall we fall through all the stages in a single reign—next to oligarchy, then to democracy, and finally return to tyranny? You must, indeed, reveal your secrets."

"And do more harm?" Montfallcon was contemptuous of the entire argument. "No, Lisuarte, you shall talk to her. Tell her you have heard that this Quire is a thief, killer, spy. Tell her, if you like, that he is probably the murderer of all her friends—including the Countess of Scaith."

"I'd lie." Ingleborough swayed in his chair. "What do you mean?"

"You would not lie!" Montfallcon stood up, clambering towards the madman's throne, his robes swaying. "You would repeat what you had heard."

"But you killed her. Did you not tell me? You?"

"I did not."

"I am confused." Lisuarte Ingleborough moistened his mouth. "You wish me to play false witness against a man of whom I had no knowledge until two days past? This is mindless plotting, Perion. I said I'd not be involved in your schemes!"

"It is critical." Dust danced as Montfallcon turned at the top of the dais and slumped into the asymmetrical chair. "She'll believe you. She mistrusts me, at present. Quire has helped her to that conclusion. She'll think me merely jealous."

"Give her the facts, then," said Ffynne with common sense.

"The facts will corrupt her." He sulked.

"You say that Quire does that already—and threatens to bring her to the final corruption." Sir Thomasin scratched his ear. "What do you think you'll lose, Perion?"

"Albion. This nobility we have made."

"You do not respect her." Lord Ingleborough looked hard at his friend. "You think the knowledge will break her."

"Such knowledge as that would make her find fault with everything. She would sneer at virtue, lose belief in sincerity. And become Hern reborn, to rule with cynic tyranny." Montfallcon's fist struck the arm of the throne. "Would you bring all this back? Have you the courage to risk it, my lord? Would that result be to your conscience's liking, my lord? Would you congratulate yourself if you were the one to release Hern's spirit howling upon the world again?"

"She resists that spirit as firmly as any of us," said Tom Ffynne. "I'm with Lisuarte in this. You should respect her. Give her the knowledge."

"And be misbelieved? Thus bring her suspicion without proof? How can I prove all I say without revealing every underhand thing I have done in her name? I beg you tell her, Lisuarte. You know she'll listen."

The pain-haunted eyes were lowered. "If you think so, Perion. But you swear you had nought to do with the murders in the palace?"

"I swear it."

"And you promise me you'll contemplate no killing? That Quire will be justly dealt with—exiled, say?"

Montfallcon knew there could be no more corpses. Another hint of murder and the Court would return to a mood worse than that existing before the Summer Tilt. "I swear that, also. Quire shall not die at my hand, nor by my instigation. But banished he must be."

"Then I shall speak to her tomorrow." Ingleborough raised a twisted hand to his face. "I am easier, in the morning."

"You'll serve Albion—and the Queen," Montfallcon promised.

"I hope so." He winced. His heart. "Patch! Fetch the men, lad, for the chair."

The little page had gone, perhaps already anticipating his master's wishes.

The three men waited together in silence, for there was nothing more to say. It seemed each one was sceptical of the others, at that moment, and must test his thoughts alone.

Eventually, Tom Ffynne grew impatient, and went to seek page and lackeys for himself. He discovered the lackeys and ordered them to work, but Patch was not to be found and Ingleborough, almost fainting in his agony, scarcely noticed his little catamite's absence as he was returned to his lodgings.

The Twenty-Fifth Chapter

In Which Lord Ingleborough
Receives a Visitation, a Warning
and a Release

Lord Ingleborough lay with his hand clutched about the arm of his chair, with his head upon the rest behind him, square before the open door of his lodgings which opened onto a small, homely courtyard that, in turn, opened onto the great square beyond. In Ingleborough's courtyard grew marigolds and roses, while a small fountain played from the centre of a pool. It was a warm evening and he was watching insects form patterns with the water's spray. His footmen waited on him, with brandy wine to hand, while from time to time he would ask after the missing Patch, affectionately believing the lad to have strayed off, indulging, as he sometimes did, in games with his fellows.

The gate of the courtyard opened with a creak, to make him focus his eyes, in the hope of seeing Patch. But the approaching figure was somewhat taller (though by no means a tall man) and wore faded black. It was Captain Quire, the Queen's new favourite, the man whom tomorrow Ingleborough had promised to accuse. Ingleborough thought it possible that Montfallcon, in his fury, had apprised Quire of this intent and that Quire now came to placate him, or to parley. The old man straightened in his chair.

Captain Quire had already doffed his headgear, to display the mass of thick black hair framing his face. His sombrero was beneath his cloak, in hidden right hand, while his hidden left was upon the hidden pommel of the sword which the Queen, in her infatuation—naming him her Champion—had allowed him to retain.

"My Lord High Admiral." The man's voice was level and even gentle in its tones. He bowed civilly. "You enjoy these evenings, my lord?"

"The warmth loosens my bones a little, Captain Quire." Ingleborough, always the most sentimental of the three survivors, found himself unable to adopt any kind of haughtiness to the stranger, particularly since he had also taken a large amount of brandy and so further mellowed a mellow nature. "They are seizing up, you know, day by day. Petrifying, my physician says." He twisted his lips—a smile. "Soon I shall be all stone, and the agony, at least, shall be gone. I'll stand over there," a nod into the courtyard, "and save a mason the trouble of carving my memorial."

Captain Quire allowed amusement to show.

"Some wine, Captain?" Ingleborough made a painful movement.

"Thank you, sir, but I will not."

"You do not have the look of a drinker. Are you one of those who believes all wine an evil?"

"Merely a time-waster, my lord. A clouder. Nations have been made great or brought to disaster by the stuff. I acknowledge its power. And power is not necessarily evil."

"I've heard you've a taste for power."

"You've heard of me, my lord. I'm flattered. From whom?"

"Lord Montfallcon, who is my old friend. He tells me you were in his employ."

"He was my patron for a while, aye." Quire leaned against the doorframe so that he was half in shadow, half in light, sideways to the Lord High Admiral.

"I formed the impression from him that you were a rough sort of fellow." Lord Ingleborough was studying him. "And something of a villain."

"I do have that reputation in certain quarters, my lord. As has Lord Montfallcon. And Sir Thomasin Ffynne. All have had to be harsh, on occasions, for expediency's sake."

"And I?"

Quire seemed almost surprised. "You, my lord? You have led an exemplary life, all things considered. Oddly, you are not thought secretly wicked."

"Oho, Captain. You came to flatter me, after all!"

"No, my lord. Besides, Lord Montfallcon and Sir Thomasin are in the main admired for their cunning. I was not praising you."

"But I am more pious, eh?"

"Innocent of blood, at least." Quire continued to speak softly and casually, as if he passed a little time with a sick friend whom he regularly visited. "And it must have been a rare soul could remain innocent through King Hern's reign."

"I have never been called innocent before. Why, I'm a known sodomist. All these footmen of mine—these young men—have been my lovers." Ingleborough shifted in his chair. He turned to look at his grinning servants. He was piqued. "Innocent!" Yet Quire had managed to please him. "Ho, ho!" He winced as the pain ran through him. "Hypocrates, Hypocrates! I do so need thy aid! More wine, Crozier." The footman filled a pewter cup with brandy from a jug and put the cup to Ingleborough's lips. "I thank you."

He looked sharply up at Quire. "I've played my share in building the new Albion, you know. I've gone against my chosen beliefs once or twice, for the Queen's sake—to protect the Realm. And I'll protect the Realm against any enemy."

"As would we all, I think. I have served the Queen's interests consistently."

"Have you, truly?"

Captain Quire put a finger to a lifted lip. "Well, sir, shall we say that I have taken actions which others have told me were in the Queen's interest?"

"You have no opinion? Is that what you are saying? Or are you sceptical?"

"I have no opinion."

"Then you are amoral."

"I think, my lord, that that is probably what I am." Quire smiled delightedly as if Ingleborough had all of a sudden enlightened him. "Amoral. As any artist must be, in many respects—save, of course, in the defence of his art."

"You are an artist, sir?" Ingleborough gestured rapidly for more wine to be poured into him. "In paint? In stone? Or are you a playwright? A poet? A writer of prose?"

"Closer to the last, I would say."

"You are modest. You must tell me more of your art," Ingleborough had taken a strong liking to Quire, though his opinion of the man would not alter his pledge to Montfallcon.

"I think not, my lord."

"You must. You have my attention, Captain Quire. Why hide a talent? Tell me what you do. Music? Mime? Or are you, in your private rooms, a dancer?"

Quire laughed. "No, sir. But I'll give you an example of my art if it's to you alone."

"Excellent. I'll dismiss the servants." He moved his head slightly and was interpreted. The footmen left their master and Quire together.

"Lord Montfallcon has told you that I aided him in his policies," said Quire, as if he had overheard that morning's conversation. "He has mentioned a Saracen, the King of Poland. I laboured mightily in his cause, my lord. I travelled the whole globe. I have been to the famous land of Panama, where the Queen's ex-Secretary now rules as king. I put him there, on Albion's behalf. And since then savage, bloody, unthinking customs have given way to civilised justice. I have always despised savages, my lord, as I despise all who are ignorant and put precedent before interpretation. Such habits give birth to hypocrisy."

"Not knowingly, Captain Quire."

"Of course not, sir. But enlightenment is better."

"Much better, Captain." Lord Ingleborough humoured his visitor. "God-worship is a great destroyer of Man's dignity, for instance."

"Quite so. Well, I'll not list all my achievements, but they have spanned the world."

"But you mentioned your art. A demonstration."

"That is my art."

"Espionage?"

"If you like. Part of it. Politics in general."

"And you do have a moral purpose. Albeit a general one—of enlightenment."

Quire listened keenly. He considered Lord Ingleborough's statement. "Possibly I have. Aye. A very general one."

"Continue."

Quire's stance grew more relaxed. "My art encompasses many talents. I work directly upon the stuff of the world, whereas other artists seek only to influence it, or represent it."

"A difficult art. There must be dangers in it, not found by other artists."

"Of course. My life and liberty are constantly at risk." Quire became serious. "Constantly, my lord. When, tomorrow morning, you visit the Queen, on Lord Montfallcon's behalf, you will be putting my plans and possibly my liberty in danger."

Lord Ingleborough smiled, almost forgetting his pain. "So Montfallcon has told you. And you are here to plead."

"No, my lord."

"Then to charm me into giving up my word."

"I meant, my lord, that Lord Montfallcon has told me nothing directly and that I am not here to plead. I overheard your conversation. I saw you gathering and followed. I am, as Lord Montfallcon guessed, familiar with the palace's secret parts."

"You were eavesdropping, eh? Well, I've done the same, in the old days. Did you kill the Countess of Scaith?"

"No."

"I thought not."

"You believe Lord Montfallcon slew her?" Quire's tone was neutral.

"Well, he was never her friend."

"The rumour says she's fled the land."

"There's no evidence. More evidence to say she's dead. But we are off the original subject, Captain Quire." Lord Ingleborough's strength was leaving him again. The twilight grew steadily deeper. "Well, I had best tell you what I intend to do. It is my duty to honour my word to Montfallcon and inform the Queen of her danger from you. You have confessed to me that you are a killer, a spy, and worse. I admire your honesty as I admire all honesty—honest cruelty, honest greed, honest crime. I prefer it, as many of us, to the hypocritical kind. And I'll tell that to the Queen."

"She knows what I am already," said Quire in a small, furious voice.

"You have told her everything?"

"She recognises me for the artist that I am. She is deceived because she would rather be deceived by me than by you, or Lord Montfallcon or the Grand Caliph of Arabia."

"I understand you. But I must list your crimes—as Montfallcon sees them—in the morning. I do not think you mean personal harm to the Queen. Not now. But I think you could, in time, do great harm to the Realm, and corrupt the Queen. You are much cleverer, you see, than Lord Montfallcon gave me to understand."

Captain Quire bowed acknowledgement. "If you had been my patron, this position would not have come about between us."

"What are your plans, Captain Quire? What do you seek to achieve here?"

"To amplify and define my senses," said Captain Quire. "I answer the same to all such questions."

"But you must have plans. Are you loyal to Albion?"

"Anyone can claim that. What is loyalty? A belief that what one does for another is the best thing one can do? Well, I do not interpret. I have been told that what I do is best for Albion."

"So you do serve a master. Who?"

"I have a patron, my lord."

Ingleborough gasped as pain came hard into him again. Quire stepped to the brandy and poured, putting the cup to the writhing lips.

"Thank you, Captain Quire. Who is this patron?"

"It is not my habit to disclose such names."

"You spoke freely of Montfallcon."

"Never when in his service, my lord."

"This patron's task for you?"

"The same, he tells me, as Lord Montfallcon's. To save Albion."

"But he is at odds with Montfallcon?"

"In some respects."

"Perrott? Is Perrott alive and employing you?"

Quire shook his head. It was growing cool. He stirred. "So you will speak with the Queen?"

"Aye, Captain."

Captain Quire folded back his cloak and displayed a scabbarded dagger.

Lord Ingleborough looked at him through the gloom and shrugged. "Murder me? With so many witnesses?"

"Of course not. I am not sufficiently well-established at Court."

"Yet your gesture was calculated."

"I promised an example of my art."

"So you did."

Quire looked into the darkness of the courtyard. "Well, I have caught your catamite."

"You have Patch!" Lord Ingleborough raised both swollen hands to his face. "Ah!"

"I secured him as soon as I knew your intention. I have been playing with him this afternoon." The dagger was touched. "He's mine. Yours again, if you swear silence regarding me."

"No." Ingleborough was shaking, his voice all but inaudible. "Oh, I will not."

"He'll be safe. If you tell he'll be killed."

"No."

"You admitted you had no evidence against me. The Queen will want some. She will be anxious to retain the friend she has in me. You can imagine that, my lord."

"Of course. But I must do my duty—all the more so now. I must warn the Queen."

"Then Patch will begin to die."

"Spare him." The voice was a far-away wind. "I beg you. You'll serve no purpose in harming Patch. I love him."

Captain Quire drew out the slender dagger in his gloved fist. "Already my little pudding prick has pricked poor Patch's little pudding. Heated and inserted—so . . . Why, he'll die the old, famous buggers' death."

Lord Ingleborough groaned.

"Promise silence, my lord—from Patch as well as yourself, of course—and your page shall be restored."

"No."

"You cling to a word reluctantly given—and slay, in terror and in pain, your darling."

Lord Ingleborough was weeping. The side of his mouth twisted.

Quire straightened up. "Shall I go to fetch him, my lord?"

"Just bring him back, Quire." His speech slurred.

"And—?"

"Bring him back, I beg you."

"You'll be silent?"

"No."

"Then I must keep my word, too. Whatever befalls, I'll bring you a memento. An eye? Or a tender, tiny testicle?"

"Please spare him."

"No."

"I love him."

"That's the point of my capturing him."

Ingleborough began to tremble. His mouth opened and shut rapidly. His eyes glared and his colour became quite ruddy, then turned blue.

With some delight Captain Quire recognised the symptoms. "Easy, my lord. Your heart is failing." He took the brandy from the table and held it a little way from the hand that reached for it. "Frequently it is the heart which fails first, when folk are afflicted as you. An uncle of mine . . . No, no—wine can only do harm. Shall you die and not save Patch? Patch must perish, without you to force silence. Tell me, my lord."

Ingleborough whimpered from the back of his throat. His mouth went wide, wide, as if a rope strangled him. His tongue came forth. The eyes popped.

Quire called out with great concern in his voice:

"Footmen! Quickly! Your master's ill!"

The young servants were slow in arriving, for they had been playing cards, several rooms distant.

They found Quire trying to put brandy into their master's mouth. It was Crozier who removed the jug from Quire's hand, saying sadly: "It is too late, sir. He is dead. I think he died happily. You cheered him mightily, sir. But perhaps the stimulation was too much."

"I fear that you are right," agreed Quire.

The Twenty-Sixth Chapter

In Which the Queen
Receives Several Courtiers and Reaches
a Decision

HER COSTUME, WORN in answer to the day's great heat as well as to advertise her mood, was of oriental influence—glowing silks and cotton veils, many strands of pearls and ornaments of baroque Saracen gold. Quire remained, in black, at her side, upon a couch placed next to her chair by the open window of her Withdrawing Room. She had retired here, disdaining the Audience Chamber: it reminded her too much of the petitioners still occupying the Presence Chambers to which, in hope, they had come after Accession Day. She was languorous: an Egyptian Empress. And her manner was satirical, as if she mocked her own appearance, yet she was gentle, smiling on everyone; a little sad, still, at the loss of Ingleborough. "Yet it was inevitable and I am glad he did not die alone," she had said to her lover that morning, after he had soothed her to her current, and novel, tranquillity; then she had discovered and satisfied his desire. She lived to please him. She had never known one who accepted love so gracefully. His hard, handsome little body inspired her to creative achievement as a fine musical instrument might inspire a composer. A touch would reveal to her such fresh, sweet notes which could content her wonderfully; now she could with ease utterly forget her own flesh, for he made no effort to arouse her, and she was so grateful; it proved his understanding and his love.

Her ladies, dressed to match her, sharing her mood, had become almost the giggling waiting women of some Indian harem, and found Quire very curious. He received a great deal of their attention. As John Dee, in robes of white and gold, joined them, the ladies fell back into an antechamber. The doctor was pale and discomforted, but his nod to Quire was not merely friendly and he bowed very low before the Queen with much more of a courtier's flourish than had once been usual in him. "Your Majesty. I have obeyed my Lord Montfallcon, as you desired me to do. And there were physicians attending, also, for he is, as you know, suspicious of me. The corpse was opened and its contents sniffed. Save for brandy it was clean. No food had been consumed at all in the past twenty-four hours. Not a hint of poison, in colour, smell or condition."

She moved a fan as if to wave away the image he conjured. "Thank you, Doctor Dee."

"In my opinion, madam, Lord Montfallcon has become plot-hungry. He craves traitors the way a dog craves rats; he lives only to hunt them."

"My Lord Montfallcon protects the Realm. He performs his duty, Doctor Dee, as he sees it." The Queen made only languid defence.

John Dee clawed his snowy beard and snorted. "The wheels of Montfallcon's mind spin like those of a clock without a pendulum."

"Lord Ingleborough was his oldest friend. He grieves. And, grieving, he seeks a villain to personify the fate which befalls us all." The Queen became more sympathetic. "His attention therefore comes upon the most suspicious, in his eyes—the stranger to the Court. The newcomer. Captain Quire."

"He wished to find Ingleborough poisoned, and now he is dismayed." Dee looked fondly at Quire. "He is jealous of you, Captain, and would believe you guilty of every crime in the land."

Quire shrugged and moved his mouth in a wistful smile. "He thinks he knows me. He told me so."

"He could not," said Dee gravely, "know you, sir, for it is only a few months since you came to our sphere, in Master Tolcharde's chariot."

Quire stretched himself along the couch. "So you insist, Doctor Dee." For Dee, in this matter, he feigned amnesia. Yet it suited him, as it suited the Queen, that he should possess no past in Albion.

The rose-carved doors of the Withdrawing Room were opened and a footman stood there. "Your Majesty. Sir Thomasin Ffynne awaits your pleasure."

"He is expected." Gloriana closed her fan and extended her hand as Tom Ffynne hobbled in to kiss it. A grunt at Dee, a smile at Quire, and he lowered himself, in answer to the Queen's sign, to a white silk chair. "Good morrow, Your Majesty. Gentlemen, Perion Montfallcon's finished his gruesome work, then?"

"I have just come from there." Doctor Dee shared a look. "Aye."

"And no poison?"

"None."

Tom Ffynne was satisfied. "His little page ran off, you know. Patch? Ran off, doubtless, when he heard the news, or saw his master dead. He can't be found."

"He'll reappear in time, I'm sure," said Captain Quire.

"It would be grief. Patch was very fond of Lisuarte. But the poor fellow was in too much pain. That body was best dead. Though he lives in here." Ffynne tapped his forehead. "The finest of all of us. The noblest of Hern's old men. What's to become of his estates, there being no direct heir?"

"A nephew in the Dale Country," Gloriana told him, "who has for many years acted as his steward."

"A true nephew or . . . ?"

"There are papers sufficient to prove blood ties." Queen Gloriana smiled. "In such matters, so long as there are no contesters, birth can be adjusted according to certain diplomatic requirements. His nephew is the new lord."

"And where's Perion now?" Tom Ffynne asked Doctor Dee.

Meanwhile Gloriana and Captain Quire exchanged glances, exclusive and knowing, not hearing what he said.

"Returned, I suppose, to his offices." Dee shifted his gold cap upon his white head. "I am not in Montfallcon's confidence, Sir Thomasin."

"Aye. He's a difficult old fellow now. I remember when he was younger, and his family alive, he was somewhat softer in his emotions. But gradually, in the cause of Albion, his spirit has grown as inflexible as poor Lisuarte's limbs—and, I'd suspect, gives him as much pain. You must not think too badly of him, Doctor Dee."

"I do not, Sir Thomasin. It is Lord Montfallcon thinks ill of me. He sees me as a sorcerer who puts a glamour on the Queen."

"There, there," Sir Tom smiled. "You are not the adventurer you once were, in his eyes. There are greater threats now. Captain Quire, for instance." The shrewd eyes looked across at Quire.

Quire laughed carelessly. "What does he say of me, Sir Thomasin?"

"Oh, many things. You are the cause of all strife in Albion."

"So I have been learning. Is he exact?"

Sir Thomasin grinned. He knew that Quire must be aware of Montfallcon's confidence in him. He knew that Quire dared him to reveal what even Montfallcon dared not reveal to the Queen. He shook his head and was admiring. "He says he marks you for a murderer, a spy, an abductor, a rapist, a thief. The list is almost endless."

The Queen laughed. "How can he have so much intelligence of you, Quire? Are you a lover who has rejected him? Now, now—we must dismiss this topic. My Lord Montfallcon is the loyalest noble in the Realm and serves us well. I'll not have him mocked."

"I do not think we mock him, madam," said Sir Thomasin. "He is my friend. We discuss him because we fear for his sanity. He should be sent to one of his houses—somewhere in the country—to rest."

"He would deem himself exiled."

"I know. You must concede to him as much as is tolerable to you, Your Majesty." Tom Ffynne was serious. "I would not have him follow Lisuarte at once."

"There's little danger of that, surely?" Captain Quire spoke diffidently, as one not well informed of matters on which others discourse.

"He weakens himself with these wild-goose chases."

Ffynne scratched at his weather-stained forehead. "And summer's ever the season for strange fancies. The sun draws forth hidden humours as it draws forth sweat."

"You think the autumn will find him cooler?" the Queen asked.

"If he's handled kindly."

"I have conceded to him a great deal in my life, Sir Tom."

"Indeed, madam. In turn, he's devoted his entire soul to your well-being."

"For the sake of the Realm."

"And from affection, Your Majesty."

"Yet he calls any other who befriends me 'traitor.' The Countess of Scaith. Doctor Dee. Captain Quire. He is jealous of them all. Lady Mary Perrott was not held by him in any high esteem. Should I fear for the lives of every person I love, Sir Tom?"

Ffynne was horrified. "You do not think, madam, that he would take such guilt upon himself. To play executioner . . ."

"He seems content to place the guilt on me," murmured Gloriana. "Guilt inherited is one thing. I have borne it through my childhood, through my reign. I am resentful of new guilts, sir. Your friend, our Chancellor, accuses me by accusing my friends. Is this the loyalty you would have me show to him?"

"He has many burdens, madam, he cannot share. He lightens your load in a number of ways."

"What? Tell me how."

Tom Ffynne became confused. "I do not know, Your Majesty. I refer to the business of statecraft in general."

"He has statecraft at the root of his nature. He enjoys his schemes."

The Admiral could not deny this. One glance at Quire, nearly beseeching him to speak, and Quire was rising, to walk around the couch and peer through the window into the floral extravagance, the thousand eyes of the peacocks' rustling displays, the green blandness of lawns on which heavy iguanas lazed. Quire pretended the stranger's embarrassment. Tom Ffynne knew a flash of resentment, then was reconciled: Why should Quire involve himself? He was already much victimised by Montfallcon who, in Ffynne's opinion, was angry at the loss of a servant now threatening to become his effective master.

Doctor Dee was conscious that his own remark might be taken for hypocrisy, but he made it, for practicality's sake. "A sedative. If Lord Montfallcon were to sleep . . . I have a philtre I can prepare."

"Lord Montfallcon accept a draught from your hands, my innocent sage?" Queen Gloriana laughed and showed him a mild eye. "Oh, I think not!"

"Lord Montfallcon . . ." began Quire before the door opened and the footman spoke.

"Lord Montfallcon, Your Majesty."

Gloriana was reluctant. She looked imploringly to Tom Ffynne who was helpless. She was conquered by her old loyalty, her good heart, by convention. "Admit him."

Lord Montfallcon, in his dignified black, with his gold chain, his iron head of a paler cast than usual, strode into the room and stood before them, like Death himself come calling. He stared suspiciously from face to face, then bowed before the Queen, still keeping his distance.

"Ingleborough's demise, it seems, was natural," he said.

"Aye, my lord." The Queen inclined her head towards John Dee. "So we have heard."

"In these days it is wise to be sure." Tom Ffynne rallied a little weakly to his friend.

"In these days, very true." Montfallcon stared hard at Quire, to the Queen's resentment. She rose up.

"My lord?" she said impatiently. "My lord?"

"I intrude upon some private conference." Montfallcon made no attempt to advance into the room. He saw no allies, save Ffynne, and Ffynne was apparently an uncertain one. "But my business is urgent, Your Majesty."

"Then do, my good lord, tell us what it is." She looked at Quire as she spoke. The captain looked back.

"It concerns your public duties, Your Majesty. I must make arrangements. Since the Countess of Scaith no longer acts as your Secretary, I must suppose I fill the rôle. Unless your—unless this Captain Quire . . ."

"Captain Quire has no official function, my lord."

"Then? Your Majesty?"

"What are the duties, in specific, Lord Montfallcon?"

"There are many who would speak with you. Ambassadors

and so forth. In these days, when war is threatened, it would be wise to insist, in your person, upon our power."

"Let them know some mystery, my lord. It could be argued it makes us more powerful, if we are not seen."

"There is also the Progress, Your Majesty. Through the Realm your most loyal nobles await your coming. They must be informed when they may expect you. They prepare entertainments, as is usual, from South to North, West to East, in all the great houses of the Realm. With the Perrotts presently mollified a degree or two, it is of importance that you spend time with these families, who will support you, should the Perrotts begin again to speak of secret enterprises and look for allies amongst fellow nobles."

The Queen had hardly been listening. Her voice was casual when she replied, "We have decided against a Progress this year, my lord. We feel that the Summer Tilt was sufficient to advertise our friends of our favour and health and our enemies of our strength and support."

"It was a gain, madam, certainly. But it must be ratified. The Progress will be crucial, this year of all years. The Court can go about the land, reinforcing the buttresses of the Realm's structure."

"They need no reinforcing, surely?" Captain Quire seemed to regret his outburst. "I only meant to say that Albion has never seemed stronger."

Montfallcon glared at him. "A structure's as strong as its proprietor's vigilance. Lice and vermin and rot can occupy its walls, destroying its beams and its foundations, so that it seems by its outer signs the best-made house in all the world—until one day it falls, all of a sudden."

"I have heard of merchants who fear so much for the safety of their buildings that they will saw through perfectly healthy beams in a search for worms, dig up the best-laid foundations in a quest for suspected pests, and thus bring their houses down upon their own heads." Captain Quire fell silent at the Queen's warning glance. "But I know nothing of such matters, my lord. Forgive me for speaking on them."

"You seem thoroughly conversant, 'Sir Palmerin,'" Lord Montfallcon let weary contempt infect his tone, "in all matters concerning the control of vermin. Have you perhaps suffered the attentions of some terrier in your own time? Or been a terrier yourself?"

"You become obscure, my lord," answered Quire mildly, but he was able to show to the Queen that his feelings had been hurt and she became engaged.

"My Lord Montfallcon. You overreach!"

"For what, madam?" Bleakly.

"Show courtesy to our guest! What harm has he done to you that you should display such disaffection?"

"Harm?" Montfallcon frowned. He opened his mouth. He said lamely: "He—I know his like."

"What like is that, my lord?" Quire seemed to tremble with self-control as he spoke.

"Enough!" The Queen was fierce. "You are distraught, my lord, for reasons that we all do know. If you would rest, and return this afternoon, we should be pleased to speak more on the matter. Explain our reasons fully, if you so desire."

"Excuse yourself from Duty, madam? Is that what you mean? You must make your Progress!"

"Perion!" cried Tom Ffynne, springing up and limping forward. "Wait a few hours . . ."

"You must make your Progress, madam!" He used his quiet, furious voice. "The Realm depends upon it."

"The Realm is secure."

"The Realm has never been more threatened."

"How so?"

"Believe me that it is so, madam."

"Show me proof, Lord Montfallcon."

"The proof will manifest itself soon enough."

"Very well, my lord, then we shall wait to see it."

Montfallcon's pallor gave way to purple. "Oh, madam . . ." His breathing became huge. "You are listening to bad advice."

"I listen to my own conscience, my lord. For this once."

"It is Hern's philosophy I hear!" He held his ground, by the door. "Familiar speeches to me, madam."

He had angered her again. "You may go, my lord."

His grey finger pointed at Quire. "This maggot, madam, will infect you with the Sophist's plague and make you cruel and hated, turning all to darkness."

"My lord! I am the Queen!"

Tom Ffynne was lurching to take Montfallcon's arm. "Perion. What you say is almost treachery—and would have been judged so under Hern. Come."

Montfallcon remained. "You are with them, now, Tom. You serve them. Already you've expressed your liking for Quire. Well, Lisuarte had a similar liking and he died. A taste for Quire is a taste for hemlock."

"You're weary, Perion. Let us go to your lodgings and continue our discussion there."

Ffynne's hand was shaken free. "I am alone now. Alone I protect Albion. And protect her I shall, against any threat, from any quarter. For too long has secret voluptuousness been tolerated at Court. Selfish lust weakens all. We shall have Hern back, mark my words."

"That is nonsense, my lord." The Queen was once more placatory.

"Then marry, madam. Marry and have done with it all! The temptations with which you beguile your private hours, they now become your whole world. Find a husband—of noble birth—and marry him. Thus shall war be averted thoroughly. Marry strength, to take the burden of your private grief, to share the weight of the Realm's responsibilities. Don't demean yourself with these wicked, little, common, clownish knaves who'll only do you harm, who understand nothing of Chivalry!"

"Arabia would have me marry the Grand Caliph. You'd like him for a master, eh, my lord? And he'll help me share my private grief, eh, my lord?"

"A few more months and the nobles and the people shall welcome the Arabian fleet as our saviour. Cannot you see into what dangers we slip if you do not make your Progress, letting suitors court you as you go? I had the plans all arranged, the most likely bachelors listed—and if you were to favour a Perrott, so much the better. If you do not make your Progress, and possibly make peace with the Perrotts by visiting them or a nearby house, they'll be arming for private war again."

"All these plans, my lord, and no consultation!" She shrugged. "Be off with you, sir, and make further plans, since that is your will. But do not, I beg thee, ask for my affirmation and involvement."

Montfallcon scarcely heard her as he stood breathing deeply and glowering at the man who had robbed him of his power. Quire moved to the Queen's side, as a guard might, out of concern.

Montfallcon whispered: "He is capable of any crime. He is more terrible than Hern, for he is not mad or vain, as Hern was."

"Sir Thomasin—please escort the Lord Chancellor back to his apartments and make him to rest. Return, my lord, when you are in more civil humour. Doctor Dee, if you can help, please do so, though I fear . . ."

Montfallcon looked from Dee to Ffynne as they stood on either side of him. "Am I arrested?"

"Of course not, Perion," said Ffynne, "but you are distressed. The Queen's concern is for your health. Doctor Dee could attend you, if you so wished, giving you some drug to help this mood pass."

"What? Am I to be poisoned by the magus?"

With these predictable words, he was led away.

Gloriana embraced her Quire. "Oh, my love, that you should suffer so much insult!"

Quire was brave. "I do not blame him, madam." He stroked her face as she stretched beside him on the couch. "He is, as you say, distracted by his friend's death."

"Tell me that I shall not have to make the Progress. It would mean parting from you for so long. And I do not think it will do any good to our cause."

"You must not exhaust yourself, madam, by a journey of that length. Albion needs you at the Court. Who knows what evil would develop here? Already so much, as I understand it, is unexplained. It could be that the Countess of Scaith is still alive. . . ."

"Oh, Quire my dear, if it were only so. What two good friends I should have then." And she hugged him tightly, burying her head on his shoulder as he seemed to reel, with frowning, puzzled eyes, beneath the force of her love.

The Twenty-Seventh Chapter

In Which Old Acquaintances
Are Resumed and Old Issues Are Debated

LORD SHAHRYAR OF Baghdad drew off his pointed helm, causing its silver curtain to clash as he placed it beside his curved sword on the table in the tavern's private room. It was almost dawn and he had been waiting for Quire for three hours; it would be their third meeting since their original bargain had been struck. Near the shuttered window the gagtoothed Tinkler, who now sported threadbare brocade and a crumpled ruff, drained the last of the bottle he had brought for them both but which the Saracen had disdained. "He'll be here soon, my lord."

"You know? It was I sent you the message of where to be."

"I know my old master, the Captain."

"It's your new master who concerns me." Lord Shahryar seemed nervous. "What shall you report, eh?"

"Lord Montfallcon gave me to understand that I carried on Captain Quire's work. And so I served him. Now that Captain Quire is back, well, I serve the same master as he serves." Tinkler, however, was uncomfortable. "I shan't betray you, sir—it would mean betraying the Captain." He scratched at his itching head.

In came Quire, hastily, a little short of breath. "There are disadvantages in being so close to the monarch." He slammed the door shut, pushing back his cloak. As well as his usual black he now wore a wide red sash, knotted on the right. It was as if the lower part of his body was stained with blood, so unlikely was the sight. He placed his sombrero near the Saracen's helm. "You prepare for war already, my lord?"

"This is court dress. I have been waiting a week in the Presence Chamber for audience with the Queen. Together with a large deputation from the Caliph, who is growing doubtful, Quire, about the success of our scheme."

"He should not be. Everything progresses." A wink at Tinkler. "You're looking quite a gallant, Tink. Montfallcon's gold?"

"He paid me your wages in full."

"He's generous. You should continue to serve him."

"Not now you're returned, Captain." Tinkler became relaxed.

Quire seated himself opposite Lord Shahryar and put folded arms upon the table. "Forgive me if I seem weary. My duties exhaust me."

Tinkler laughed coarsely. Lord Shahryar feigned suitable disgust and said: "I need more specific news. Matters seemed to move well, but now I suspect your plans stick. The death of the girl created all that you told me would be created. On Accession Day your plan could not have been better realised. But now there is silence from you and, save for Ingleborough's death, which was to be expected and which achieved nothing (the page, by the way, is embarked for Arabia, a present for the Caliph), it is almost as if you had given up on us."

"I have a handful of Privy Councillors with me. Upstanding gentlemen become besotted fops, who support every decision I encourage the Queen to make." Quire lifted his lip. "Montfallcon is all but exiled, he is so disgraced, and the Queen will no longer listen to him for she is convinced he is mad with jealousy. The Court divides into two main camps—those who share Montfallcon's opinions and those who share the Queen's—and further divisions are to be expected. The Progress is halted and so the Realm will not be reassured. The Perrotts continue with their fleet and shall soon sail against Arabia—giving you just cause for war, but also allowing you to hold off and make kindly terms (though you may have to defeat the Perrotts first, as well as those who choose to sail with them). There are enough, and more coming to the Perrott side, particularly nobles who feel slighted by the Queen's refusal of their invitations. And there are details of other schemes I bring to fruition. And you are unhappy, my lord? If that is so"—a theatrical reaching for the hat—"then I can always find a fresh patron, and change these advantages about . . ."

"You owe me your life, Captain Quire. And you swore you would serve my interests."

Quire fell back against the chair's rest. "But if I'm not serving them well enough, my lord, I see no reason why you should continue to employ me. Can any one man do what I have done? As Montfallcon almost single-handedly built up the Golden Age, so am I destroying it. As, in all reason, it deserves to be destroyed; Myth is but another word for Ignorance."

"How long, then? Before everything is ready?"

"Another month. By October the nobles will be glad of a marriage between Gloriana and Hassan, if it soothes their fears."

"And what can I be doing for you, Captain?" eagerly said Tinkler, drunk on the talk he had overheard. "I could kill Montfallcon for you."

"And throw suspicion immediately onto me? No—he destroys himself. I want you to continue working for him, Tink."

"What? I can't!"

"It's best. You'll bring me information I can use."

"You don't want me to come back with you, Captain, into the old partnership?"

"No. Serve Montfallcon in every way he tells you—only report to me when it is possible."

Tinkler shrugged. "If you say so, Captain Quire."

"Your position is perfect for us."

"Very well, Captain." He seemed to be sulking.

Lord Shahryar picked up his helmet. "Then what shall I tell my Caliph?"

"That the Queen's bewitched by me, that she will do anything I say, that when the time comes I shall give her decisions which shall put her firmly into the marriage bed with him, though I know not what good it will do either. . . ."

"Captain Quire!" Shahryar snatched up the curved sword. "You'll make no offensive jests concerning my master!"

"I'll make what jests I care to make," said Quire coldly. "For my secrets are recorded, as always. And if I die, your plans are given away. If that were to happen, the Realm would unite at once. It would undo all our work. Thus, too, Lord Montfallcon fears to betray me. For years he has sustained the myth through lies and espionage, murder, torture and destruction of contrary opinion. If evidence should emerge—as I might allow it to do, at the right moment—that Gloriana's golden reign is based as firmly on blood as was her father's, then you'll have a thousand nobles turning on her, snatching down the figurehead in the vulgar belief that they destroy the ship."

"Quire—do you plan to trade these secrets for a crown?" Lord Shahryar slipped the scabbard into his belt. "Is that it? You deceive every one of us?"

"To become a king is to become a cripple, my lord—with all movement, all power, restricted. Even Hern was borne down by it. Why, at the beginning of his reign he had, like his daughter, many fine ideals. But as the weight crushed him, he gradually gave way to self-pity. He's called a cynic for that. But a true cynic is one who controls the weak as well as the weakness in himself. Hern was controlled by both."

"And you are not?"

"No, my lord. An artist demands freedom in which to accomplish his work. No king is ever free."

"I hope you are not deceiving me in this." The Saracen tucked his robe around him and pulled his hood over his helm. "I hope, also, your tardiness is not a result of any sympathy you feel for your new mistress. She'll be happier when our Caliph marries her."

"And it's all the more important that she does soon," said Quire with a grin. "for you have not told me every factor, have you, my lord? You deceive me a little and fear I do the same."

"Deceive you? How?"

"The duel between Poland and Arabia was fought—on the ship. Count Korzeniowski told Lord Rhoone, who told me, as being closest now to the Queen, in case I thought she should know."

"What of it?"

"Poland is badly wounded and returned home. His parliament placed him under arrest and a new king was elected."

"I've heard the same."

"And the new king, who was the warlike Prince Pyat of Ukrainia (known for his inclinations and supported by parliament), wants vengeance upon Arabia."

"It was a fair tourney and my master won."

"I believe you. Pyat, however, fears that if Arabia goes unpunished it will make her too much of a threat. There is some fear she'll unite with Tatary."

"Impossible."

"But you cannot reassure Poland sufficiently—for you have such large battle fleets in preparation. You stand to be attacked from two sides."

"Then Albion would come to our assistance, under the treaty."

"Aye—which would give Albion much trouble, but it would not show your Caliph as the Pure Knight, the Saviour of the Empire. Indeed, the rôles would be reversed. The duel was foolish."

"There was a question of honour."

"There is no such thing. There is pride."

"Self-respect, Captain Quire. But if you do not recognise that quality . . ."

"I have a great deal of it. It is not the same as pride. And pride could throw my plans and yours into a whirlpool, losing us everything. That is why you must have me bring all to a head quickly."

"If you like." Lord Shahryar made to shrug.

"And I suspect, my lord, that your head's at stake, also, is it not?"

The Saracen's black eyes grew hot. "And yours, Captain Quire, at very least!"

In a swirl of dark cloth he was gone out of the tavern room, leaving Quire and Tinkler staring at one another as old friends do who have become awkward and whose interests are no longer identical. Tinkler was untalkative. Then he said: "Is it true, Captain, that you'd bring Albion down?"

"You cannot bring a nation down so easily, Tink. I'll merely change the structure a little. Gloriana and the Caliph as joint rulers over a great Empire. An Empire which will make enemies, of course, and require to expand itself—into Poland, Tatary, the world."

"So the future shall have much to do with war."

"I should think so, Tink."

"And what shall we do then, Captain?"

Quire drew his sombrero down over his eyes and smoothed back the crow's feathers on the crown. "We shall thrive, Tink, in such a world."

Tinkler, given this vision, could only look upon it with a shifting eye. He cleared his throat. "It would be a simpler place, in some ways."

"It is the business of war to simplify, Tink. Most men prefer it, when it comes, because their lives are far too complicated. Peace throws men into a kind of confusion few of them have the strength to bear for long—responsibilities blossom. Most of the world is made up of weaklings, Tink—and in war they flourish. Oh, how the weak love to fight!"

He was on his way, blowing a kiss to his bemused and frightened friend.

The Twenty-Eighth Chapter

In Which the Queen's Favourites Disport Themselves and Wherein Lord Montfallcon Warns of the Catastrophe Which Follows upon Impiety

FROM A HIDDEN fountain, water squirted suddenly out of a bed of white horehounds so that Lady Lyst, already unsteady, fell over with an astonished cry, dropping her brimmer, her legs sprawling in the folds of her Indian gown while the Queen, her attendants and her courtiers laughed heartily in the intense late August sunshine falling now upon the gardens of Gloriana's private apartments. Flowers of all sorts, arranged by colour to contrast, bloomed in geometrical squares, circles, crescents and half-moons divided by the narrow gravel paths and the moist lawns, the yew hedges, the ornamental shrubs of these symmetrical and comforting examples of a tamed nature. Ernest Wheldrake, pocketing a small book, helped his mistress to her feet. He, too, was dressed for the current summer fashion, with a great deal of black and gold in the Moorish style, so that he was inclined to resemble a small cockerel who had somehow borrowed an eagle's plumage. His turban slipped over his twitching face as he struggled with Lady Lyst and eventually, after much slipping about, restored her to an upright stance. She swayed. "Death! I'm soaked, inside and out!"

Again there was laughter.

As usual, Captain Quire did not sport the fashion, but remained in pauper's black, his sombrero shading his face (a crow to Wheldrake's fancier fowl), but he smiled with the Queen. Of the rest, Sir Thomasin Ffynne could not bring himself to personation and he wore mourning purple (for Lisuarte) with an earring as a concession to gallantry. Sir Amadis Cornfield was opulent, half-naked in the gold and feathers of some Inca king, and Lord Gorius vied with him, as another East Indian potentate, embellished with beads and coral bangles. They paid their usual attentions to little Alys Finch, who danced for them now, in a sarong, through the rainbow fountains which damped her gown, outlined her boyish figure, heated up their ardour. "Ah!"

Phil Starling, the dancer, wore some gold things and a breechclout, along with the usual paint, and lay upon a lawn at the feet of his half-swooning Wallis, an unlikely mandarin. Master Auberon Orme, a Tatar fantastico, ran from the entrance of the nearby maze pursued by two of the Queen's ladies who were clad as Burmese courtesans, and almost tripped over young Phil, who pouted, looking beyond him at Marcilius Gallimari, resembling a slender Turk, his arm around two little blackamoors whose modesty was protected by nothing more than aprons of pale gold chain at back and front. All were besotted by the euphoria, the erotic air which of late had filled the Queen's personal court.

The Queen embraced and kissed Lady Lyst. "Rest here." They lounged together on a marble bench, laughing up at Quire and Wheldrake. "When shall this summer end!" It was rhetoric; few there expected or would welcome a hint of autumn. "We were discussing some official employment for Captain Quire. Now that Lord Rhoone's to the country with his family, we require a temporary Master of the Queen's Pensioners. What do you say to such an appointment, Captain?"

Quire shook his head. "I have not the conscience of good, bluff Lord Rhoone." He pretended to frown and consider alternatives. He had been much relieved at Lord Rhoone's removal from the Court (by Quire's own suggestion). He remained nervous of all those he had encountered before assuming his present rôle. Rhoone, in his gratitude for the apparent saving of his family's lives, had never suspected Quire to be the same hooded villain he had once led to Lord Montfallcon's presence; at Montfallcon's constant urging, however, two could be added to two at any time and Rhoone become a potential enemy instead of a useful friend. The first victim of this enterprise had been Sir Christopher (who had been poisoned because he might have remembered Quire's face as well as his name), but now there was none close to the throne, save Montfallcon, whom he daily discredited, with any knowledge of his intimate past. He considered, for a moment, hinting at Lord Ingleborough's position, but this was already Sir Thomasin's. He looked towards Ffynne, arm in arm with a maid of honour, who had come up to them as they talked. "The Queen believes I should seek honest employment, Sir Tom."

The old sailor was shrewd behind his twinkle. "What's your vocation, Captain, I wonder?"

Hilarity. The Queen and Lady Lyst fell into one another's arms again. Quire pretended embarrassment while he and Ffynne exchanged their private irony in a swift glance. "Not much, I fear. A small talent for acting, I suppose." He referred, they thought, to his performance at the Tilt.

Sir Thomasin said: "My friend Montfallcon considers you a spy. Sir Christopher Martin is not yet permanently replaced."

"Oh, Sir Tom!" cried the Queen. "Captain Quire would be nothing so base as a thief-taker!"

"Secretary, then?" Lady Lyst blinked, hearing her own slurred voice with some shock. She relapsed.

Gloriana became sad, then stifled the emotion. Quire was quick to understand and changed his tone at once. "My vocation is to serve the Queen in any way she will. I'll let her decide my fate."

She took his hand and sat him down between herself and Lady Lyst. "It will take much consideration. I shall question you, Captain, as to your proficiencies."

Sir Orlando Hawes appeared upon the terrace above. He wore conventional shades of dark colours, purple and black, for he joined in the mourning, as did most of the court, of Lord Ingleborough, whose funeral had earlier taken place. With his black skin, he was almost a shadow, but Quire noticed the eyes linger on little Alys as she danced and ogled her lovers. Quire was greatly satisfied with her work. She had become his stalking bitch, and he had developed in her a lust for treachery as another might develop a lust for gold or pleasure.

Sir Orlando hesitated, seemingly saddened by the sight of this private masquerade, perhaps embarrassed by its echoing of the costumes of his own ancestors. Then, slowly, he took the steps into the garden, removing his black feathered hat as he bowed. "Your Majesty. Lord Ingleborough is entombed."

The Queen resisted guilt as, the minute before, she had resisted sadness. "Did the funeral go well, Sir Orlando?"

"It was attended by a great many, Your Majesty, for Lord Ingleborough was loved by the people."

"As we loved him," she said firmly. "The people were apprised of our inability to attend?"

"Through ill-health, aye." He straightened his back and stared about him.

"I have seen too much of misery these past months," she told him. "I'll remember Ingleborough alive."

Sir Orlando looked towards Sir Thomasin. "We missed you at the feast, sir."

"I saw Lisuarte buried. It was enough. I was never one for public ceremonies, as you know."

Sir Orlando disapproved. His opinion of Sir Thomasin had ever been low. He did not acknowledge Captain Quire at all.

"Lord Montfallcon spoke in the Queen's name, Your Majesty," he continued. "As her representative."

"So Sir Thomasin has already informed me."

"He is with me. And Lord Kansas. He sent me ahead to request . . ."

"Perhaps he would prefer an interview this evening?" she suggested.

"He is wearied by the day's events. It would be best, Your Majesty, if you saw him now." Sir Orlando gestured back at the terrace. "He is on the other side of the gate."

The Queen looked enquiringly at Quire, who shrugged acquiescence. It would not do to show malice toward Montfallcon. Not yet.

"We shall receive the gentlemen," said Gloriana.

Another bow and Sir Orlando had returned to the gate to bring back Lord Montfallcon and Lord Kansas who were also in the uniform of mourning.

Quire saw the Queen become guiltily aware of her own unsober costume. He squeezed her hand and whispered: "They'll drag you down if they can. Remember my words—trust no-one who would make you feel guilt."

She rose, as if he controlled her, and went smiling to greet the three nobles. "My lords. I thank you for coming here so soon. The funeral went off, I'm informed, with proper dignity."

"Aye, madam." Montfallcon bowed slowly. Kansas followed his example. The Virginian was troubled and sympathetic, whereas Montfallcon was merely accusatory. Quire knew a moment's anxiety when he contemplated Kansas. "You'll forgive us for intruding upon your"—Montfallcon cast a mighty glare over the garden and its occupants—"games."

"Of course we do, my lord. In such melancholy times we must divert ourselves. It does no good to brood on death. We must be optimists, eh?"

These were unfamiliar words from her, and Montfallcon looked to Quire as the suspected author.

"Will you not join us, my lord?" asked Quire with mock humility. Then, as though he checked his malice, "But I forget myself. Lord Ingleborough was your dearest friend."

"Aye." Montfallcon looked through Tom Ffynne. "I have none left now. I must be self-reliant."

"You are the strong central pillar of the Realm," flattered Gloriana, linking her arm through his. He started, as if he would pull free, but courtesy forbade it, as did habit.

He let her lead him towards the maze. "There was a reason for my visit, madam."

Lord Kansas, Captain Quire and Sir Orlando Hawes stalked in the wake of this pair, three black and ill-matched birds of passage.

"And what's that, my lord?"

"Business of State, madam. A meeting of the Privy Council must shortly be convened. We have news. Your guidance is required."

"Then I shall call the Council together for the morning." She was anxious to show that she did not reject all Duty.

"Later today would be better, madam."

"We entertain our friends presently."

They went into the maze. Montfallcon's head disappeared entirely, but Gloriana's could be seen, together with her silk-clad shoulders, over the top of the hedges. Then Quire went in, then Kansas, and finally Hawes.

From where she sat, Lady Lyst began to giggle. She saw the Queen's auburn, ruby-studded hair. She saw the crown of Sir Orlando's tall hat, the top of Lord Kansas's head, with its cap and feathers. Wheldrake came to sit beside her, wanting to know why she laughed. She pointed. The two visible faces, at different points in the maze, were very grave. The bobbing feathers looked like carrion birds, scuttling along the tops of the hedges. Even Wheldrake, who was at his composition, allowed himself a smile or two.

"Why have they gone into the maze?" he asked.

Lady Lyst was unable to answer.

When Doctor Dee came up, having changed from black to robes of lightish purple, the Thane of Hermiston, in the dark mourning set of his clan, beside him, he could not see the joke at all.

"Where is Captain Quire?" asked the Thane, placing his large hand upon his red beard. "And what's all this idolatry? Is there no piety left at Court at all? Why is everyone so naked? And with Ingleborough scarcely put to rest?"

Master Wheldrake said: "It is the Queen's pleasure. She is bored with Death's company."

"Captain Quire," said Lady Lyst with significant hilarity, "is in there!"

The Thane and Dee looked towards the maze. "Everyone is drunk, I think," softly said the Thane, by way of interpretation and possible excuse. "Though I would not expect it of our visiting sage." He spoke of Quire, whom he regarded as his greatest prize.

Phil Starling screamed. They all gave him their attention.

Master Wallis had borne him to the ground and was wrestling with him in a peculiar way. It was not possible to tell if this were true violence or play. The Thane took a step towards them, then halted as the couple began to roll over and over on the grass.

"How swiftly manners change," murmured the Thane, who was just back from an adventure. "The Queen permits all of this?"

"She encourages us," said Lady Lyst, very suddenly serious. She pulled herself up. "It has happened since the Countess of Scaith disappeared. We all grieve for her."

"Where's she gone to?" the Thane would know.

"Perhaps to one of your other spheres," Wheldrake suggested, "for she's nowhere to be found. Oubacha Khan has been searching for her. He thinks she's still somewhere in the palace."

"How?"

"In the walls," said Lady Lyst. "But where?"

"Montfallcon thinks she murdered Perrott," Doctor Dee told the Thane.

"Not Perrott," said Lady Lyst.

"Not anyone," pointedly remarked her lover.

"Not anyone." Lady Lyst rubbed at her weary eyes. "We're suspected of Perrott, Wheldrake and I." She sighed.

"Montfallcon seems to think Quire came from the walls." Doctor Dee was dry. "He'll not believe the truth, that's why. But Montfallcon and Kansas discussed the matter at the feast today. They were for going in, not to seek the Countess, but to find proof of Quire's origins."

The Thane chuckled. "They'll have to look further afield for those."

"Captain Quire has powers that are not of our world," Doctor Dee murmured. "He is a brilliant alchemist."

"He has said nothing to us." Lady Lyst became interested, for her own tastes were shared between the wine bottle and natural philosophy.

"He is a greatly modest man," said the Thane approvingly. "He will give the Queen good advice."

"Yet some blame him for all this idleness," Wheldrake told him.

"It cannot be so." Hermiston was firm.

"Or if it is so," added Doctor Dee, noting that the Queen and

Montfallcon, still arm in arm, were emerging from the maze again, "it is for sane reason and the Queen's well-being."

Montfallcon seemed a little mollified. Wheldrake saw Tom Ffynne turn the corner of a hedge, note his old friend, and turn back again, taking a maid or two with him.

Kansas, Hawes and Quire were still within the maze.

"Then we shall see you this evening, madam?" Montfallcon said.

"This evening," she promised. She asked of Wheldrake: "Where is Captain Quire?"

"Yonder, madam." Wheldrake showed her. "He followed you in."

She seemed agitated to be parted from him so long. "Will someone fetch him here?"

The Thane began his stride towards the tall hedges. As he reached the entrance he stopped with a hint of a yell as Phil Starling flew out, still giggling, pursued by Master Wallis. There was sweat on Master Wallis's pale skin. Some of Phil's kohl had smeared, giving him the rakish appearance of a dissolute foxhound. The Thane made another effort to enter and did so. They saw the feather of his bonnet for a moment.

Panting, Phil and Wallis came on. Montfallcon grew angry. "Master Wallis!"

Florestan Wallis came to a halt, one hand on the boy's soft arm. He cleared his throat. "Aye, my lord?" Phil continued to grin.

"There is a meeting of the Council called."

"I shall be there, my lord." Wallis dropped his hand. Phil stared through bold, luscious eyes at Lord Montfallcon, smiling at him as a harlot might smile on a potential client. This was too much for Gloriana. Once again regal, she dismissed them both with a wave.

"The impiety spreads," said Montfallcon in his cobra's hiss. "One understands the Queen's desire to maintain her whores. She feels responsibility towards them. Let us hope that one day soon the responsibility will be removed"—he broke deliberately from this to his next phrase—"but when the denizens of the seraglio are brought out into the open, to be displayed for all to see, one wonders if, after all, the Queen is wise to continue with her old customs. What was reasonable and private divertissement now becomes public, senseless and all-consuming rapture! Shall we soon see in Albion some pasha's opulent and decadent court? Is this to become Hern's Albion, where no maid nor youth was ever safe from infamy?"

"We shall meet again, my lord, when the Council meets," said Gloriana distantly. "Where is Captain Quire? Is he lost?"

No-one answered. Lord Montfallcon could not leave, or did not desire to leave, without his friends, and they were in the maze with Quire. The Queen caught sight of Sir Amadis, looking a little sorry for himself, coming along the broad walk, and she seized on him. "Sir Amadis!" He looked up, doing his best to soften brooding features. Alys Finch had slighted him for the third or fourth time that day and had linked hands with Lord Gorius, even as she had flirted at two of the Queen's maids. He had turned his back on them, though he knew he would return to her if she called. He was helpless. He was that treacherous nymph's absolute slave. "Sir Amadis!"

He joined the Queen's party. "Your Majesty?"

"We wondered if you had news of your wife's kinsmen. Any letter from there?"

The Queen was singularly cruel, he thought, to remind him of his inconstancy, just as he brooded so satisfyingly upon fickle Alys's. "No letter, madam."

Under Montfallcon's dreadful gaze he toyed with an oriental bangle.

"Her brothers will not let her communicate with anyone at Court," he continued, anxious to be released from this double ordeal.

"And you've no urge to join them, sir?" Montfallcon knew nothing of Sir Amadis's infatuation, so his question, in that respect, was innocent.

"I serve the Queen, my lord."

Lord Montfallcon grunted. "As we all do, Sir Amadis. There is a meeting of the Privy Council. All other business set aside until our debate's over."

"What's the cause, my lord?" Sir Amadis became almost sober.

Lord Montfallcon would not discuss such matters before those who were not of the Council. He looked around him, back and front, side to side, to show his fellow councillor how Sir Amadis momentarily forgot himself. He made some sounds in his throat.

Sir Amadis noted Quire striding from the maze to save him. "Here's Captain Quire . . ."

The Queen brightened.

Montfallcon, seeing how swiftly her colour altered, likened this blush to the unnatural shade of those poppies fed by alchemists with blood and rare earth to give forth an intoxicating and intense perfume for a few hours before withering. "Be wary, madam," he murmured before he remembered to check himself.

She ignored him.

Montfallcon looked for Kansas and Hawes, but they were not yet free of the maze. Tonight, he thought, he and Kansas would go into the walls, as they had agreed, and there discover the evidence he must have before Quire could be convicted and disgraced. In the meantime he had sent for Tinkler. He would use Quire's former servant against the plotter.

Captain Quire came up and stood close by the Queen.

Montfallcon turned to Doctor Dee. "Are all our members now aware of when we hold the meeting?"

"I think so, my lord," said Dee, a little taken aback by Montfallcon's civility. Montfallcon, these days, found new virtue in old enemies.

The Queen cried: "Ladies. To my chambers. I must change."

With Quire still beside her she was strolling for her terrace, the maids gathering to attend her. Lifting their backs, the various courtiers looked one to the other, perhaps wondering at how much a number of them had altered in the past few weeks. The orientals confronted the sober mourners almost as two alien armies might draw up their ranks before a battle.

Sir Amadis, hearing a familiar cry from the maze, made his excuses and, with Indian gold rattling upon his flesh, went running as a dog on the scent.

* * *

Within her bedchamber the Queen dismissed her ladies, setting them to seek more formal robes than those she wore, leaving her alone with Quire. She stretched her huge frame upon the sheets and let her head fall into his lap. He stroked her with familiar tenderness. She sighed. "Oh, Quire. Montfallcon's determined to destroy our idyll. He refuses to believe that I shall return to full Duty in time."

"What's so urgent," casually asked Quire, "that he needs to call a sudden meeting?"

"He's afraid of war."

"With Arabia?"

"With everyone. He fears that the Empire must dissolve if present events continue in their courses. The Tatars are ready to make use of any opportunity. There have been disputes for some while concerning Cathay's borders. There have been reports that the Afghanians seek an alliance with the Tatars, with whom they believe they have more in common. The Perrotts, in order to take their vengeance on Arabia for the killing of their father, are now likely to spark off a dozen different wars. We've Poland to consider, and the war they plan. The Tatars will overrun Arabian borders, given the chance, for they know Arabia would attack them. So Montfallcon sees the Perrotts as central to the scheme and would make me marry one of them."

"Perhaps you should," said Quire.

She became alarmed. "We would be separated!"

"But our happiness cannot be considered here."

"It would be stupid to sacrifice my person. You have told me that yourself. Quire—you said that I should not give my soul or my body to the Realm, merely my presence and my brain!" She craned to look, as a small, frightened child might look, into his saturnine face.

He reassured her. "Aye. I think Montfallcon's mistaken, anyway. Who's to say the Perrotts in their angry mood would agree to any match? They want vengeance. Besides, I doubt if a marriage could stop war now. Unless it be marriage to Hassan himself."

"I could not marry Hassan."

"Marriage to him would at least leave us free to be lovers," said Quire with a quiet smile. "He would be glad to encourage us, if we were discreet."

She put a hand to his lips. He kissed the fingers. She stroked his heavy jaw. "No cynicism. Besides, Hassan would demand too much. There are many nobles, I know, who favour the match, for he's seen as strong and manly. My master."

Quire nodded. "If you were ever to make a sacrifice—and I say that you should not, as you know—then you should consider marriage to Hassan. It would be the only sane decision."

She drew him down to her. "Stop. I'll have too much of this talk later. I love you, Quire."

His voice contained a note he had never heard in it before as he steadied himself against her passion and said to her: "I love you, too."

She was Gloriana Regina now, in all her conventional magnificence, the orb in one hand, the sceptre in the other, two gauzy collars behind her back, like fairy wings, a massive starched ruff, stomacher and farthingale, varicoloured brocade and embroidered silks, huge pearls covering her person like tears, diamonds encrusting sleeves and breast. He removed the sombrero and kissed her hand. She was returned from the Council. He took the sceptre and the orb from her and handed them to a footman to replace in their cabinet. He brought her a glass of wine, which she sipped, smiling down on this courteous dwarf.

"You are pale," he said. He went behind her to loosen her stomacher, barely able to reach over the frame of the farthingale. He fumbled with the laces and she laughed, calling in her ladies.

"There was more to the meeting than I had anticipated," she said to him.

He sat down in a chair as she was stripped. The ladies smiled at him a great deal. He was a success, for he made the Queen so womanly, which was all they desired for her.

"War's with us?" he suggested.

"Not yet. Montfallcon spoke much of you."

"He continues to accuse me?"

"He believes he'll find evidence. Did you know that these apartments are built upon far older structures? Of course, I told you of my adventure with Una. The one which has given me so many nightmares. Which you, my dear, have banished with so many of my other fears."

"Aye. She blocked the entrance."

"Well, Montfallcon thinks there are other doors—in the old wing—near my father's Throne Room. I told you of what happened to me. . . ."

He raised a hand to stop this drift. "What of these entrances?"

"He says that you were living there for many months before you first appeared at the Tilt. He says that you were the killer of all those who have died or disappeared. He has fallen in with Lord Kansas—who is a good man and a brave one—and together they mount an expedition to hunt out witnesses who'll testify against you."

Quire smiled. "Were these murders, then, committed before an audience of rats?"

"It distressed me, Quire, my love. I do not want the walls disturbed. I . . ." She hesitated. She was in her shift now and was kicking free her shoes. "They are the past."

"You think they'll find your father still alive?" He let her come to him, in soft white, to sit at his feet while he stroked her neck and shoulders, waving the women from the room. The door was closed. He mocked her, but was kind.

"His spirit," she said. "There are demons there."

"Demons, eh?"

"I told you. Such wretches. I felt sorry for them, but I could not bear to consider them. They are my father's victims. Living in dungeons. Living like vermin."

"Then forbid Montfallcon to enter."

"I tried, but I could give him no reason. I know, too, that it is my own weakness which says to forget the walls and what's within them. Therefore I cannot indulge myself. . . . Oh, Quire!"

"I have told you—it is not indulgence to admit weakness. And, once admitted, weaknesses must sometimes be indulged. That is rational, my dearest heart. You must protect yourself or you cannot protect the Realm."

"You have said so many times, aye. Yet I gave him permission. He dared me to refuse. To show that I had faith in you, I had to let him mount the expedition."

"How many?"

"Montfallcon, Kansas and a few men-at-arms—members of the City Guard. And I think they have a guide. I am not sure. Montfallcon was somewhat mysterious."

"A denizen of the walls?"

"We met one, Una and I. Perhaps it is the same."

She could not see Quire's face, so he permitted himself a little wistful smile. "Well," he said, "do you think they'll come back with a hundred people who saw me try to poison the Rhoones?"

"You saved the Rhoones. It is well known." She stroked his leg. "Do not fear, my love. They shall not be allowed to accuse you further. Even now Montfallcon makes statements my father would have called unquestionable treachery. But he will calm, as he forgets his grief. And so will the others who spoke against you."

"I have other enemies?" He was ostentatiously merry. "I'm flattered."

"And many friends. Doctor Dee respects you and speaks for you at the Council. Sir Thomasin Ffynne, who serves there now, thinks you a rogue but a good-hearted one"—she smiled—"as do I. And Sir Amadis will hear no harm of you. Or Lord Gorius—and it's well known how much those two dislike one another these days. And Master Wallis. And several more are, at very least, rational concerning you. Of the Council, only Hawes is firmly with Montfallcon, while Sir Vivien tends to that position. They share certain qualities of temperament."

"I am surprised by the attention," mused Quire.

"Why so? They are jealous. They see a commoner usurping power that they feel only the nobility should own."

"Power? What power have I?"

"They think you rule me—and therefore could come to rule the Realm. It has happened with the mistresses of kings, they argue."

"Who argues?"

"Well, Sir Orlando, mainly. But he'll be persuaded of your reasonable nature in time."

"Perhaps they are right," said Quire, as if he struggled with a conscience. "Do I help you in your decisions? Subtly, I mean? When I argue for your good health, your sanity, your privacy, am I not arguing against the security of the Realm?"

She refused to hear him. "Quire! I shall not let you be troubled. If it continues, Montfallcon shall be dismissed. I'll make you a baron, stage by stage, and put you in his place."

"Arioch forbid!" He was deliberately old-fashioned, using phrases subtly reminiscent of her father in his kindlier moods, for he knew that this reinforced her wish to please him. "Such responsibility isn't for Quire!"

"It's not in your nature to want high office, that I do know. I have told Montfallcon again and again."

"He disbelieves you."

"He becomes surly. He cannot say it is not so."

Quire continued to stroke her, but he had let himself grow quiet. She looked up at him. She was anxious. "You are hurt by these accusations. I should not have mentioned them."

He sighed. He let his hand fall onto the arm of his chair. She got to her feet. "Oh, I am cruel! In that Montfallcon is right—he often warned me of it when I was a child. I have much of my father in me. I should control it more!"

"No, no," said Quire and shook his head. "But I admit I am disturbed by this. In innocence I sought to please you at the Tilt. I suppose that it was a silly scheme. While I guested with Master Tolcharde and he showed me the device, the chariot he'd made for you, I conceived the escapade in a spirit of Romance. Then this began to happen: Love. Now I find there is also a great deal of hate. I am," he said, turning his head away, "not used to being so hated."

"My love will vanquish all that hate," she promised. "My love is strong. Never has anyone loved as I love you, my darling Quire!" She drew him in. "This will all pass soon," she promised.

He stood away from her, kissing her hands. "I'll walk a little," he said. "In the grounds."

Diffidently, she asked: "Shall I walk with you? I'd enjoy the cool air."

He shook his head. "Let me gather myself. I'll return to you soon and, you shall see, I'll be amusing. Happy once more. And that happiness I'll share with you."

She was reluctant to set him free, but she knew she must resist all jealousy or it would threaten her marvellous temper. She became grave. "Very well. But do come back to me soon."

A smile of acquiescence, a kiss of encouragement, and Quire opened the doors, moving between her cheerful ladies, down the stairs, past silent, darkened rooms, out of the windows, into the garden. He remained on the terrace, looking this way and that, then swiftly stepped through moonlight, crossing the lawns and entering the maze, where he had earlier arranged his usual appointment with his most important pawns, his two personally trained and by now proficient traitors.

The Twenty-Ninth Chapter

In Which Lord Montfallcon's Expedition Returns from the Walls with News of Further Death and Presents Captain Quire with a Small Astonishment

"We have still to hear from Lord Montfallcon." The Queen spoke with casual amusement as she sat with sampler and needle on the couch beside Quire, who had borrowed some Greek book from Doctor Dee and was reading it. The mood of the Withdrawing Room this morning was relaxed. A few ladies attended the Queen, Tom Ffynne had been and gone, to say that Lord Montfallcon and Lord Kansas had entered the walls the previous night, taking torches and swordsmen, finding an opening in a gallery above the old Throne Chamber.

"You would think a search would not take so many hours," agreed Quire from the other side of his book.

"You do not know those tunnels. There are many. They are intricate."

"Aha," said Quire vaguely, as if he did not properly listen to her. Then he said: "Should I, perhaps, go with some of your pensioners to look for him?"

"Oh, no! Why seek the one who would accuse you? He spends longer than he needs because he won't admit there's no evidence there against you."

"Nonetheless," said Quire, closing his book, "it might be practical to take a few guards to the Throne Room, at least, and to wait for them."

"You are too charitable." Gloriana concentrated upon a difficult stitch. "Why should you be concerned for them?"

"Perhaps I wish my own ordeal ended?" he suggested.

"Forgive me." She set aside her sewing. "Now I understand.

Very well, you can take some pensioners, if you desire, but do not enter the walls, I beg you."

"You humour me." He rose and kissed her. "Thanks." Entering her Audience Chamber, that great, brilliant, empty room, Quire glanced around at it for a moment before calling over one of the guards. "Bring six men and come with me on the Queen's business."

They had been told by her to obey him. The guard ran off to gather his fellows.

Quire strained his luck, he knew, by allowing himself this luxury, but he felt that if Montfallcon did recover some little piece of evidence, it would be best if the Queen were not present when it was shown to him.

Soon Quire was surrounded by Hern's gloomy vault, staring up into the pointed ceilings and recalling, with a certain pleasure, the deeds he had performed here. It was from here that he had sent Alys and Phil about their initial seductions; where Cornfield, Ransley and Wallis had come to pursue their passions. He had overheard conversations. He had kidnapped little Patch. And now he returned commanding the Queen's own guard, looking for the gallery he had used more than once himself, which Tallow had shown him: the entrance to the walls. Quire regretted Tallow's death, though it had been convenient and, rather more, he regretted the man's escape, his crawling away for aid.

He smiled to himself, wondering how Montfallcon fared against the vagabond army; the rabble Quire had turned from individual scavengers into a pack which ruled the tunnels, terrorising all other occupants. It had terrified Tallow. It had run him down and killed him because he would not join it. Quire sighed. That had been the simplest part of his plan. He was nostalgic for those easy early days.

At length there came a noise from above, a torch's flickering, and he was instinctively drawn into shadow to watch as Montfallcon, cursing, burst through. Then came two of the city guards. Montfallcon leaned against the gallery rail, not seeing anyone below. Both guards were slightly wounded. There had been a confrontation and a chase.

"Where's Kansas, my lord?" asked Quire softly from where he stood, knowing his voice would grow in the vastness of the hall.

Montfallcon turned, still leaning, and looked down at him. "Villain! Kansas is dead and half a dozen soldiers with him. There's a mob in there. Your mob, eh?"

"You continue to credit me with far too much power," said Quire. "What will you do? Send in a rival mob?"

"Possibly." Supported by the guards, Montfallcon moved along the gallery and began to descend unseen stairs, until he stood staring with cold hatred upon his catlike enemy. "You taught them to think, eh, Quire? Those rats."

"Your reasoning's too subtle for me to follow. Will the Queen allow more activities in the wall? She would rather —"

"Do not speak so familiarly for the Queen, rogue! Not to me! You have corrupted her. That horrible seraglio . . ."

"It was always there, my lord. I did not invent it. Why, she's hardly used it since I've known her."

"It is the symbol of her private indulgence, of what she has become. It is that part of Hern she allows to flourish —"

"It is possibly where she escapes from Hern —"

"—and you! Oh, you, Quire, are Hern personified. I know his logic. I had full experience of it, eh? And now we hear it made more subtle in his daughter's soft mouth. You are Evil's tool, Quire!"

"I assure you, my lord, I've no symbolic value—I work for myself alone."

Montfallcon spat at him. "You'll perish! I'll see to it. All the corruption shall perish! Kansas wished to marry the Queen. Did you know that? He was courting her and would have won her, but you appeared! I wanted a Perrott for a consort, but, by Xiombarg, I'd have settled for him. And now he's dead. Killed by you!"

"By me?" Quire showed comical astonishment. "It was the two of you went willingly into the walls, ignoring the Queen's desire, all common sense, all warnings. How can I have killed him?"

Then Quire frowned as he realised that the face of the guard on Montfallcon's right was familiar. He hesitated. He recalled the face; it was the face of the survivor who had witnessed Quire's killing of Ibram the Saracen last New Year's Eve. The man was too astonished, too shocked to speak, for he was still reeling from the encounter in the walls, but it was plain that he also recognised Quire.

Quire turned away. "I'll report this to the Queen, shall I? You'll be wanting to send another expedition in, will you, my lord? And another?"

"We'll find a means of controlling them," Montfallcon promised, "and of bringing you to justice, Captain Quire."

Quire knew that the guard would soon be speaking to Montfallcon and that justice might be closer than the grey lord realised. He instructed a palace pensioner to take the bad news to the Queen. "Tell her Kansas is killed in a fight there. Tell her it would be best if the walls were sealed, in case this rabble of Lord Montfallcon's breaks through."

Quire himself remained where he was, with his back to Montfallcon and the others. He bit a knuckle.

Behind him, Montfallcon lifted his sword, then lowered it again. He had sworn to have no more public bloodshed, and he knew that if he killed Quire outright the Queen would hang him for certain. He was prepared to give his own life for Albion, but could not die until he was sure that the Realm's course was assured.

Without a further word to them, Quire was rapidly on his way, sending his guards back to their quarters, as he took the stairs that would lead him, eventually, to Doctor Dee's apartments. He must demand a further favour of the doctor. He must demand poison. And then Alys Finch must lure the guard and make him drink the poison. It could be easily done, that part, Quire was sure, for Alys had murdered Sir Christopher with no trouble at all. Dee was the only problem, but there was one threat to Dee which would work, as it had worked before, though Quire regretted it must now be openly made. Previously he had arranged his arguments so well that it had always seemed he must disappoint the magus through no fault of his own. Possibly it could still be done, but he had little time for his usual clever rhetoric. He must get the poison and give it to Alys, returning to the Queen before he was missed. There was no way in which he could permit that particular witness to live: he was able to identify Quire as a murderer, and now that Sir Christopher was dead, there would be nothing Montfallcon need consider dangerous. Quire could be accused, simply, and tried, simply, for a simple crime. Anything Quire might say would be interpreted as an attempt of his to escape sentence.

Quire realised that there were extra subtleties to his position, and that it was possible Montfallcon would not use the guard against him, but he was too close to fulfilment to take the risk. And the death of an ordinary guard would not be remarked. The body could, indeed, be hidden for ever, if necessary.

He reached Doctor Dee's door and knocked upon it. There came cautious sounds from within. A grille was moved. Dee's somewhat bloodshot eyes looked out and became less wary as he recognised his benefactor.

"Come in, sir! I was just preparing her. I fear, however, that I must increase the strength of the philtre. She becomes a little difficult to control. Look!" He chuckled, pulling down his shift. "She has scratched my neck. Perhaps you can help me, Captain Quire, as you have helped me before?"

Quire showed concern. "Of course, Doctor."

"She is the most marvellous creation. I have never known a simulacrum so fine. But I have told you this many times. Our own science has no means to produce such a perfect, near-human creature. Well, you are aware how I failed. How Master Tolcharde failed. You understand that I do not complain to you of any minor malfunction, but . . ."

"I understand. She becomes fierce."

Doctor Dee nodded and sighed. "She is not tame, sir. No longer. And she is very strong."

"I'll do what I can. In the meantime, use caution."

"Oh, she is so lovely. Irresistible. If she were to kill me, sir, I should die very happily."

"I came on another matter, Doctor Dee. I need help. There is trouble in the walls. A madman leads a pack of ruffians. The madman must be killed."

"Killed? Zeus! Who is he? Are we in danger?"

"There's a chance of defeating him. But I need more of that poison you loaned me once before. The kind that is so hard to detect."

Dee nodded. "Aye. I have some still. But why should it be necessary to slay a madman with poison of that sort? Any simple poison would do, if he must be poisoned. I should have thought it best if he were put to the sword, Captain Quire. You can use your sword, sir, I am sure."

"I must have the poison swiftly."

Dee was reluctant, alarmed by Quire's manner. "I think . . ." Then he checked himself. He became afraid. "You will help me with her?"

"As soon as my business is completed."

"You swear it, Captain?" He was pathetic.

"I have been good to you, Doctor, and asked few favours."

"You are a very clever philosopher, sir, that I do know." Doubtfully: "So I suppose your business cannot be evil." Thus Dee convinced himself as he moved towards his cabinet. He handed Quire a phial. "You'll return soon?"

"As I promised. And remember—be cautious, Doctor." Quire skipped from the room, his spirits beginning to rise. Then he was off to find his stalking bitch, his little Alys Finch.

The Thirtieth Chapter

In Which the Queen and Captain Quire Go Hunting

THE SUMMER LEFT its stamp most solidly upon the autumn so that October in this thirteenth year of Gloriana was the warmest any had known. No breezes came to blow away the threat of war, and neither was Gloriana's ardour for her little lover cooled. The Court's euphoria increased, if anything, in private—while angry ambassadors prowled the corridors and Presence Chambers and grew impatient, as their masters grew impatient, for intelligence, becoming more and more dependent upon rumour, gossip and fabulation (which had increased a hundred-fold since Quire's appearance at the palace); the ambassadors, in the main, wanted reassurance from the Queen so they could inform their homelands of the practicality of peace, but, unable to provide news, they were helpless to counter the heady talk of fleets and armies, cannon and cavalry, the authority of precise-sounding terms which disguised the ugly and ludicrous facts of the chaos they pretended to describe. Maps were got out and paper fleets were launched with all the usual silly ritual and sane men looked desperately to Gloriana, hoping for the regal, maternal command to put the toys away before the squabbling became earnest.

Albion's nobles mingled with the ambassadors, growing uncertain and quarrelsome as they waited for instruction, dismayed and disheartened by the Queen's new mood, for she gave audience so rarely and with such misinterest that she made worse what her silence had begun. The Empire, founded on a grand myth, must have the myth sustained if it were not to disintegrate. There were many in the palace who saw the disintegration already beginning and spoke of Hern's bad blood showing at last, and they whispered stories of the Queen's monstrous appetites, of the legendary seraglio where every night scenes were enacted to make those of Hern's time seem like good-hearted, innocent frolics. Yet only Montfallcon and a few of his party saw Quire as the instigator of all this. He represented himself, when he appeared, as one who sought to remind the Queen of Duty and who failed. He was, he told them, as dismayed as they were, for they must know how much infected he was by the Romantic spirit of Albion—after all, it was how he had come to meet the Queen. So they thought him a kindly dupe of the Queen's, a sop to her tormented conscience, and said that it might be well for them all if, as Montfallcon raved, Quire did control her—that he would make the better monarch.

The walls had been closed up again, on the Queen's orders, and she considered plans to destroy those interiors or, at least, to bury them more solidly. She blamed Montfallcon for the death of Lord Kansas, of whom she had been very fond, and she blamed him for the other deaths; for the death of the city guard who had somehow died of minor wounds a day after the expedition had returned. Montfallcon was disgraced. She did not see him at all. He received communications from her through intermediaries—through Sir Orlando Hawes and Sir Vivien Rich, who were not so outspoken against Quire and who, it seemed, gradually grew to accept Tom Ffynne's opinion of her lover: "Lucky, rather than cunning, though he thinks himself a complete rogue." All could see that Quire loved the Queen, as if he had never loved anyone before.

Meanwhile Oubacha Khan advised his lord that Tatar might soon reclaim lands regarded as rightfully their own; Lord Shahryar sent optimistic reports to Arabia; Count Korzeniowski begged his new king to hold his forces, without success; and the Perrotts, in Kent, gained allies almost by the hour. Quire was proud of his achievement. There remained but one main move to make. "She was infatuated," he told the Saracen ambassador, "and now the infatuation slowly deepens into love. Then I'll withdraw and down she'll tumble—into your master's arms."

The Queen, when she asked advice from any but Quire, sought

portents from a Dee who steadily became stranger, but who supported Quire's opinion with increasing certainty. Sir Tancred flung himself from the battlements of Bran's Tower, and it seemed that Chivalry died with him in Albion that morning, and from its corpse grew the richer, darker, morbid blossoms of inward-looking erotomania which, as it often will, adopted the trappings of Romance. Alys Finch, who had given herself twice each to Sir Amadis Cornfield and Lord Gorius Ransley and had then, at the right moment, resumed a kind of modesty, had them, as she put it, panting for her like dogs no longer content with bones but drooling for the richer meat. Both had reached the stage of being willing to promise her anything in order to have her again, while berating her, accusing her, hating her for what she did to them. Phil Starling shared this lust for treachery, the consolation of the unimaginative, and slipped free of Master Wallis whenever he could, into the beds of a dozen minor courtiers, or into the Queen's own seraglio where he discovered himself a treasure-house of pleasures. Lord Rhoone returned from the country to find the Court so altered he was entirely baffled. He did not see the Queen, but he spoke to Tom Ffynne of his bewilderment. "Is this Quire to be king? What becomes of Albion?" Tom Ffynne held the opinion that Quire would make an excellent candidate for consort—a realist was Quire, with a bit of experience of the world—and not of the generation, as Montfallcon was, which feared a return to Hern's ways so thoroughly that it was actually likely to bring about the terror by brooding on it too much. Oubacha Khan found the small black-and-white cat, now completely healed, and made enquiries of Elizabeth Moffett. He discovered an unexpected ally in Sir Orlando Hawes. Alys Finch was put by Quire to stalking Hawes. She won her way to his bed but, she told Quire, had to give him rather more than she had given the others. It would be worth the expenditure, Quire was certain. Oubacha Khan visited the members of his retinue, warriors all, who lodged outside the palace gates. Quire heard of this with some amusement. Tinkler reported that Montfallcon had sent him into the walls to try to parley with the rabble there

(Montfallcon did not know that Tinkler had captained it when it had killed Kansas and the others, for Quire had put him in charge, then). Quire instructed Tinkler to continue to obey Montfallcon, to serve him to the letter until such time he countermanded his command. Montfallcon spoke secretly with Count Korzeniowski, telling him of Quire's part (but not his own) in the abduction of the king. He hoped that Korzeniowski would then tell the Queen. Instead Korzeniowski withdrew himself from the Court and sailed for Poland, to advise swift war. Montfallcon grew madder. Quire grew stronger. The Queen continued to be in love.

Ernest Wheldrake received a knighthood; the only honour in the whole season.

"In autumn, when the wind and sea
Rejoice to live and laugh to be,
And scarce the blast that curbs the tree
And bids before it quail and flee
    The fiery foliage, where its brand
Is radiant as the seal of spring,
Sounds less delight, and waves a wing
Less lustrous, life's loud thanksgiving
    Puts life in sea and land,"

quoted the poet, perched upon a monstrous stallion in the stable-yard of the palace, and clad all in tawny colours, his red hair blazing, his stiff arms waving as he found his stirrups and caused Lady Lyst, leaning a little in her saddle, to sigh.

"Splendid, Sir Ernest!" cried the Queen, who had not understood a word. She was in doublet and hose astride her chestnut beast. She wore forest green save for white ruff and cuffs, with a little hunting sword at her belt and a pointed cap upon her own red curls. Captain Quire, in black, climbed into the saddle of his black mare and grinned at them all as they prepared for the hunt, which would be led by Sir Vivien Rich, plump and happy, glad that he had, in his own mind, lured the Queen and her favourites to healthier pursuits. "Hurrah!"

To horns, the hounds came forth eagerly, a brown and white sea, swirling and savage around the legs of the horses. Sir Orlando Hawes, close by his friend Sir Vivien, wore russet and gold, while Alys Finch rode, ladylike, upon a little gelding, in velvet skirts of soft red. Sir Amadis Cornfield was mounted and close to her, looking from Quire to the girl, anxious for an answer that could not be supplied. And Lord Gorius rode up on the other side. Both rivals wore shades of green.

Sir Thomasin Ffynne, riding in on his own horse, saluted the Queen.

"Where's Lord Rhoone?" She had been expecting him.

"Gone back to the country, after all," he told her.

She shrugged and handed down her stirrup cup to a groom. The hounds were on the move and the huntsmen trotted through the gates, towards the open country where a little mist could be seen on the fields. "He's best away from the Court, I think."

"Aye." Sir Thomasin's horse began to buck as the hounds went by. He was not a hunter. "And I saw Lord Montfallcon this morning."

"He never sleeps at all." She was careless. "Was he wandering the corridors looking for spies again?"

"He says the Perrotts have half the houses in Albion in sympathy with them."

She spurred at flanks. "Let 'em have the whole damned Realm!"

They were away.

Soon the Queen was a good distance ahead of Quire. With flapping cloak and bending brim, he sought to catch her. Through mellow fields and over hedges moist with dew, sniffing the first scent of autumn now that they were in open country, and relishing it, Quire knew October was to be his month, his greatest success, and he could let his elation show as, chasing behind her, he entered the red trees and green shrubs of the forest, galloping on springy moss, trampling the autumn flowers as, ahead, the hounds bayed the imminence of game. "Would you not be free for ever, madam—a forest spirit?" he called. "Robin Hood and Maid Marian?" And he sang a traditional snatch:

"Bold Robin came down to the water's side
For his lady fair was there,
'Oh, Marian, I would make of ye my bride
Out of love for your red-gold hair.'"

This pleased her but she did not draw rein. Again she raced ahead of him and again he must use every effort to keep her in sight, ducking beneath the branches, causing leaves of yellow and brown to shower.

Through the forest the hunt pounded, with yells and halloos, and while Quire gave chase to the Queen, Sir Amadis and Lord Gorius gave chase to Alys and Sir Orlando, who rode very close, while Lady Lyst kept on her Wheldrake's track as he giggled and shrieked every time the branches lashed his face and body so that he barely kept his saddle at all. And only Sir Thomasin and Sir Vivien, it seemed, attended to the hunt itself.

Out of the forest and into soft sunlight, a broad, hilly clearing, of dark moss and blue autumn crocuses, labouring for the crest, then seeing, over the tops of the flowing beeches, the hounds in full cry after a fox that clove through dense bracken as a salmon through water. Gloriana rested her horse for a moment, allowing Quire to catch her. She was flushed. "Oh, Quire! We shall hunt every day!"

"Every day, my glory."

The chestnut was set off again, springing forward and down the hill, while Quire, becoming aware of certain aches and pains, followed.

The beeches went past and his ears were full of their hiss, the thudding of the hoofs, the gasp of his own breath. He was not her match, but he refused to lose her. The horns sounded some distance off. They broke out of the beeches and into the golden bracken. Quire caught a rich taste of earth and was astonished by the pleasure it gave him. He shut his mouth tight, lest he receive the shock again. Fences were leapt, and gates, and streams, and the hunt was spread out now, following the hounds who had their quarry for certain.

"Halloo!"

Quire moved his head and looked over his shoulder. Sir Amadis and Lord Gorius were well behind and had almost lost the hunt. To his right were Alys and Sir Orlando; ahead of him, also on the right, were Sir Vivien and Tom Ffynne; while immediately ahead was Gloriana, shouting for him to keep up. Hounds and huntsmen streamed away before them, down the golden hill towards the broad waters of the Thames.

"There!" cried Sir Vivien. "There! He's sighted!" He turned to call to the Queen, swayed strangely in his saddle, grabbed at his horse's mane, then fell awkwardly, saddle and all, from the racing beast.

The Queen was past him before she could draw rein, but Quire had pulled his black mare short and had jumped down to kneel beside the groaning knight. "My back. Damn! I think it's broken, Quire."

"Bruised, that's all," said Quire. "What happened?"

"Groom betrayed me. Girth slipped. Off I came. Should have seen to it myself. Those palace grooms are useless for anything but the harnessing of coach-horses. Ah!" He was in great pain.

The Queen and Tom Ffynne were galloping back. In the distance, below, the hounds' baying grew louder and fiercer. Sir Orlando Hawes, with Alys Finch beside him, looked darkly down at Quire. "What? Another accident? Are you injured badly, Sir Vivien?"

"Back's broke. I'm alive." He sweated in pain. "Better fetch some grooms and a gate, eh?" He looked up at his friend. "How does the hunt go, Sir Orlando?"

Hawes looked coolly down the hill. "Oh, I think they'll soon have caught the little fox."

The Thirty-First Chapter

In Which Master Tolcharde Presents His Greatest Achievement and in Which Matters Between Rivals and Lovers Come to a Head

THE PUBLIC ROOMS almost entirely abandoned, the Queen entertained her guests in the caverns, the heavy-scented interconnected rooms of her seraglio, where celebrants were waited on by boys and girls with oiled, naked bodies, and all manner of strange people—dwarves, giants, hermaphrodites. Where last year the theme of her Autumn Masque had been the Feast of Bacchus, this year was a more directly Bacchanalian affair, looked upon by a sleepy Queen and a sardonic Quire from their common couch on a dais above the main floor where, as if they revelled in some northern Byzantium, guests lay upon cushions and grew lazy with food and lust and wine.

Hidden musicians played languid music to which some of Master Priest's dancers, led by Alys Finch and Phil Starling, capered rather slowly. It was as if the world wound down, in luxury and impious carelessness. A few lamps and torches gave the scene light, but darkness was sought by all, and the colours of their costumes, as well as the furnishings, were all deep.

Sir Ernest Wheldrake, stripped to the waist and revealing a criss-crossed back, lifted a wine-cup to Lady Lyst's near-senseless lips. With his other hand he held his book, from which he read:

"Red was the fruit of the vine
As if it bled,
Ruby red, the grape sublime
And magical its power
So that it said 'Stop' to Time,

As hour by mooning hour
And head to swooning head
We shared that bower,
That bower sublime,
Thee and thine, me and mine,
And pined for the love of the dead."

Frowning, Lady Lyst opened her eyes, the wine dribbling down her chin, and stared with some curiosity at the small bunch of lilies in her right hand. She closed her eyes again and began to breathe more deeply.

Sir Ernest was about to read again when the twin giants, black and white, pushed open the asymmetrical doors of the room to allow Doctor Dee, in his gown of magical symbols, his scrolls, to hurry in, with Master Tolcharde, in his best, behind him, and the Thane of Hermiston, in clan plaids, coming last.

"Why," said Phil Starling from the floor, putting an arrogant hand upon an unremarkable hip, "here's Master Tolcharde all puffed and stuffed and ruffed and covered over in jewels." There was some laughter, but not from Quire or the Queen.

Doctor Dee frowned at Phil in distaste, Master Wallis pulled at the boy, who tugged away, grinning, moving from place to place, greeting his several friends, while Wallis opened mouth and eyes to implore him, then turned.

The Thane of Hermiston stood as if he had received the Gorgon's glare. "Arioch! What's all here?" His great beard bristled. "I've seen no worse in all my travels between the worlds."

This made the Queen smile. She raised fingers. "Come to us, my dearest Thane. Have you news of your adventures? Have you more captives to bring us, as you brought us Captain Quire?"

The Thane blushed, then glared at Quire. "Captain, this woman has corrupted ye!"

The Queen was amused again. "On the contrary, sir!"

"What is this place?"

"It is a place of pleasure," she said.

"Madam . . ." Doctor Dee's face was drawn. He had a long,

partially healing scar down the side of his face. He had tried to hide it with his white hair. "We brought the Thane to you because he wishes to tell you something. . . ."

"Is it amusing, dear Thane? Remember, you attend the Autumn Feast."

"Amusing? No, it is not, madam. I have seen the Margrave of Simla. Tatars line the Empire's borders and ready themselves to attack us. They have news that war shall begin in the middle of this month. There is a traitor here, who informs them."

"Who is the traitor, sir?" Easily.

"The Margrave does not know."

The Queen looked down to Sir Orlando Hawes, who sat a little uncomfortably on his cushions. "You see a great deal of the Tatar ambassador, Sir Orlando. Has he said much to you?"

Sir Orlando shrugged. "Nothing definite, madam. I think the Tatars want war, as everyone else seems to want it. But you are unwilling to hear such talk, I know."

"It is not very specific, sir."

"Oubacha Khan has hinted that Tatary means to attack parts of India and Cathay as soon as war begins between the other nations. They think it will be easy work then, for, as he put it, the whole globe will be on fire." Sir Orlando spoke with careless voice, as one who no longer has hope of convincing another of his opinion.

"But no certain news?"

"No, madam. When the Perrotts go against Arabia, it will doubtless be the sign."

"Have some Perrotts brought to Court," she said.

He looked hopefully at her. "Tomorrow, madam?"

"Next week," she said.

"Aye, madam."

Quire whispered: "Perhaps you should act a little more swiftly in this. A threat, say, to the Perrotts, that they stand to be executed as traitors."

"There is no execution in Albion."

"Just the threat."

"Aye. Sir Orlando!" She called again. "Have the Perrotts informed that they commit acts of treachery against the Realm. Remind them of the old penalty."

Sir Amadis Cornfield looked up from where he sulked. He rubbed at his forehead as if to clear his mind.

"Is that all ye'll do with my news, madam?" asked the Thane.

"What else can we do, sir?"

"Investigate. The Realm slips closer to Chaos by the day!"

She took a large cup of wine down into her, as if to answer him. "I'll have no unnecessary bloodshed, sir, as well you know."

"Ye've kept the world from large wars for thirteen years," he said. "Now ye set the match to the cannon which will signal the hugest war of all. I have seen such worldwide wars in my journeys. I have seen whole continents wasted—burned to nothing. Is this to be Albion's fate?"

"Of course not, sir."

The Thane scowled. "I'll be away, to seek a saner place than this." He looked to Quire. "She seduces ye, sage, with all her wiles and obfuscations."

Quire was silent.

The Thane looked to Dee and Tolcharde, even to Quire, as if he expected them to accompany him, but they remained. He strode from the seraglio, an angry skirl of tartan. "The woman should be married! It should all be dismantled! Bah!"

Master Tolcharde was tactful, waiting for his friend to leave; then he stepped forward, awkward in his finery. "Madam, I have been promising you this spectacle for some months." Diffidently. "It is ready at last. If the consort will play the music I have prepared for them, your dancers shall appear."

"We are eager, Master Tolcharde." She spoke gratefully at his bald and sweating head.

A wave to the musicians' gallery and brisk, brilliant music began to play, in considerable contrast to that which had begun the evening. The Queen took another glass of wine. Quire leaned back in the couch, absently stroking her arm.

Master Tolcharde clapped his hands. From the far end of the long room figures began to appear. They were dancers clad in glittering costumes, so light-footed and elegant as to make Master Priest's troupe seem crippled. They danced closer and closer, pirouetting, leaping, touching hands, and, as they neared the cleared arena, it seemed they bore frozen masks upon their faces—metallic masks, with eyes that were blank and mouths which showed no expression. There was Harlekin, in chequered costume, and several different clowns—a Zany, a Pierro—Columbina, Isabella—the Doctor and old Pantalon. There was Scaramouche, with swagger and sword, a red-faced musketeer. And they danced in a line before the Queen; then, with a single movement, they bowed and curtseyed as the music momentarily stopped. Every part of the costumes was of metal. The hands and feet were metal, glaring with colour. The faces were metal.

"Behold," said Master Tolcharde with pride, "my Mechanical Harlekinade!"

"They are not human, Master Tolcharde?" The Queen gasped. "Not a scrap? They are so beautiful!"

"Metal through and through, madam. There have never been finer creatures made."

(Doctor Dee enjoyed a look with Captain Quire.)

They began to dance again; acting out an entire play: of love thwarted, of love gained, of love attacked and love revenged. And though their hard metal faces showed no expression, their mechanical bodies movingly expressed the tale. Gloriana settled closer to Quire and Quire to Gloriana. The play continued. Harlekin thought himself deceived by Columbina, for Isabella was jealous and wanted Harlekin for herself, so made it appear that Columbina made love to Scaramouche. In turn, out of spite, Harlekin gave himself to Isabella, only to discover the truth too late and, as he rushed to tell Columbina, he was killed by her vengeful knife. Upon learning the truth, she herself took poison. The last movement of the dance was a slow, funeral step, echoing the earlier dance of Master Priest's ensemble.

Most of the audience was considerably moved, particularly Masters Cornfield, Ransley and Wallis, all of whom felt themselves betrayed in love. Alys Finch wept a great deal, too, and was comforted by Sir Orlando. Quire did not care for the mime, but since the Queen found it satisfying, he clapped enthusiastically. The mechanical creatures danced away.

"You must present them again, sir," the Queen told Master Tolcharde. "Many times. Do they perform other tales?"

Master Tolcharde was apologetic. "Not yet, madam. Just that one. But they can be adjusted. For comedy as well as tragedy. If you will allow me, I'll bring them to your next entertainment."

"Again and again, Master Tolcharde. We thank you."

Tolcharde had never been more pleased. Beaming, he followed in the wake of his Harlekinade.

Quire thought he had seen the dead dancing. He got up. He required, he said, to relieve himself.

As he went by, Sir Amadis plucked at his cloak. "Captain Quire?" The tone was pleading. From a distance, on golden cushions, suffering the attentions of two geishas, Ransley glowered.

"Aye, Sir Amadis? What can I do for you?"

"Your ward—your charge—your dell—the girl."

"Alys is not my responsibility, sir. Not any longer. Once I protected her virginity, but now there is nothing to protect." Quire was firm. He was moral.

"But you spoke for me once."

"I should not have done so."

"Will you speak for me again, Captain?"

"I cannot, Sir Amadis. You must speak for yourself."

Ransley had risen and was stumbling over to them. "Be wary, Amadis, of any plotting you do. I can hear. I can hear."

Quire pulled himself away from them. "I cannot. You must decide this for yourselves, gentlemen. I am not a god."

"You have a god's power, Quire," Lord Gorius said. "In some respects, at least. Zeus! How you've seduced us all!"

Quire paused, his back to them. "How's that, my lord?"

"Look at us. Drunk, besotted with lust, like some tyrannical Roman court of old. And all your doing, Quire."

"Indeed." Quire swung about. "Then I must be a god, as you say, my lord."

"When the inquest's done on the death of Albion's honour, at the end of the world—not far off, I'd say—the verdict'll be murder. And the murderer, sir, shall be named Quire."

Quire scratched the back of his head. "The corruption lies in the fact that a myth was used to manufacture an imitation of reality. Could Albion fall so swiftly if the foundations were secure?"

"You don't deny . . . ?"

"I deny everything, my lord."

"What of Alys Finch?" Lord Gorius became weak. "Won't you intercede? Or select one of us?"

"I am not a god," said Quire. "I am not even a king. I am Quire. You must settle your problem for yourselves." He continued on his way, leaving Ransley and Cornfield in conference, mouths to ears.

Sir Orlando Hawes was talking politics to Alys Finch, who had the flatterer's trick of rephrasing the words of her companion and handing them back as her own opinion. "I blame Montfallcon. He clung so desperately to his belief. He felt the only way to hold the Empire together was by making Gloriana seem a goddess and, to ensure she believed the tale herself, keeping her in innocence of all he did to preserve the legend. He clung on to the point of madness. As it happens, I believe he is a victim of Quire's as much as he believed others were Quire's victims. I gather evidence, even now, but not so publicly as Montfallcon."

"You think Captain Quire a villain then, with his eye upon the throne?"

"I have no great dislike for Quire. He would make an excellent king. If his motives were not at odds with mine I'd tolerate him. But Albion's fabric rots before our eyes. The glamorous tapestry Montfallcon wove cannot be allowed to drop all at once and reveal the reality beneath—neither nobles nor commons could accept it. The curtain must be raised inch by inch, over a period of years."

"There are holes in the tapestry already. That is why so many nobles side with the Perrotts. They see corruption beneath the brocade—or think they do."

"There's no real corruption here. Just a bereaved woman's euphoria, which will pass. But Quire has let the extremes of it be seen. Some view the entirety—a little entertainment like this one—and think it must represent a greater, unseen horror. Romance inspires the imagination and makes imagination grow—but if that imagination's misapplied, searching for ugliness rather than for beauty, then a terrible force is unleashed."

"You share Captain Quire's dislike of Romance."

"I share that. But I do not share his hatreds, Alys. And worst, most destructive of all, is his hatred of himself. It is what binds him so, though neither will admit it, to the Queen."

"You think he loves the Queen truly?"

"If it is possible for Quire to love anything."

"You were speaking of Oubacha Khan and the expedition you plan with him—following Montfallcon's tracks into the walls."

"Aye. The cat, Oubacha Khan thinks, might lead us to the Countess of Scaith. It's a faint hope—but we go secretly, with fifty Tatars, fully armed. They'll easily defeat the rabble, I'm certain. They are the greatest fighters in the world. Oubacha Khan, you see, loves the Countess. He thinks her the victim of a plot—either Montfallcon's or Quire's—and would find her, even if it means finding her corpse."

"You dredged the well, you two?"

"Aye, and discovered only a vagabond, probably some denizen of the walls."

"When do you leave?"

"Very soon."

"You'll tell Montfallcon?"

"No. He's bound to betray us—inadvertently. He is no longer in control of any of his senses. He has not been for some time, or he would long since have detected Quire's work, since the murder of Lady Mary. He now speaks of destruction as the only answer to our ills."

Alys Finch saw her master, Quire, returning, and she frowned to herself.

Quire was stopped by a weeping Wallis. "Quire—Captain—the boy betrays me," Wallis whispered. "Speak to him. I am dying with the pain he causes me."

Quire smiled down at poor Wallis and patted him on the head. "Of course, I shall." He looked about for Phil. Starling was enjoying the attentions of half a dozen ladies and seraglio gallants, but he saw Quire at once and he laughed, mocking them both. Quire sighed. "He lacks grace, that youth. He always did."

"You must make him behave." Wallis was tense.

Quire's gesture was not encouraging. "How?"

"He is your responsibility."

Quire smiled slowly. "As the Queen discards them, I accumulate them." He would be happier when his work was finished.

"He kills me," said Wallis simply.

"Find another," said Quire. "There are so many here. They'd be flattered by attention from one of your station."

"I love him."

"Ah," said Quire. He was looking over to where Sir Amadis and Lord Gorius were rising, ready to leave. He put a hand to his lips. Then he saw the Queen. She was very drunk, beckoning to him. "I must go. Duty, Master Wallis."

Abandoning the wretched Secretary, he moved between the cushions, ascending the dais at Gloriana's summons.

"Let us retire," she said. She could scarcely speak for drunkenness.

Quire saw that Sir Ernest had fallen over the sleeping body of Lady Lyst and now slept also. Half the guests were in a like state. The denizens of the seraglio crept quietly back to their various quarters. Quire let Gloriana put a hand on his shoulder and steady herself. She towered over him. He summoned more of his strength than he would normally reveal and began to help her down the steps.

"My children," she said.

Quire was puzzled.

"I promised to see the girls." She pointed towards the end of the hall. "They are through there. In the adjoining apartments. Not in contact, of course, with . . ."

"I know," he said. "But it will have to be tomorrow. You spend the day with them tomorrow."

She remembered, or was prepared to think that she did. She let him lead her past the twin guards, along the passage, through one set of rooms, until finally they reached her ordinary bedchamber. With a jingle of jewels, she fell upon the bed and immediately was snoring.

Quire had helped her to this state and was satisfied she would sleep for several hours. Employing a tenderness which had become a habit with him, he dragged off most of her trinkets and what clothes would come away easily, pulled a coverlet over her and left the room. A finger to his lips and servants were aware of the Queen's condition. He went to the main door into the corridor and was about to open it when he heard voices murmuring on the other side. A phrase: "Are we to be ruled by a whore and a cut-purse?" He gave himself a crack to see through. "It must be destroyed. It is Albion's shame. There is a way."

The Thane of Hermiston and Lord Montfallcon were speaking softly as they walked together along the passage. Quire had not expected this combination. They were unlikely companions. He did not think there was much to fear from them, however. Doubtless their respective delusions brought them together. He closed the crack and when they were gone he was off along a familiar route to the East Wing where he would later keep an appointment. He went early because it was always his habit to be on the scene much sooner than he was expected. By this means he had, in other days, kept himself alive.

He reached the gallery overlooking the garden where, that spring, Gloriana had played her rôle as May Queen. He walked swiftly. Moonlight passed through all the many windows so that it was almost as bright within the gallery as it was in the garden below. Casually, Quire looked out as he moved. Then he paused and found himself a shadow into which he could withdraw. He could hear peculiar sounds coming from the garden, a creaking and a rustling, a clattering, as if someone tried to chop branches from the trees. He let his eyes grow used to the darkness and began to notice that the growth which surrounded the entire garden, providing food and shelter for the deer, seemed to be swaying. He realised that someone was on the Tree Walk. He had used it himself, once or twice, and knew that it was firm. At last he heard sharp, almost regular sounds—*snick-snick, snick-snick*—and saw two figures come into view. They were fighting with swords as the Tree Walk swayed and groaned. They staggered this way and that, falling against the rope rails, sometimes making the walk swing at right angles, clinging on as they continued to duel.

Quire watched for some time, conscious that now he might be keeping his visitor waiting, but he must see the outcome, even though he had guessed who the duellists were. After all, he had almost encouraged the fight.

Snick-snick, snick-snick. It was as if some mad gardener had chosen this hour to trim the trees. The creaking grew more animated. The rustling increased. The duellists shuffled and danced along the Tree Walk, sometimes in sight, sometimes not.

Then there was a silence, a lack of movement. Quire saw a figure standing, leaning hard against the rope, then the walk tipped and he went down.

Quire ran for the steps which would take him into the garden.

When he reached the body, the victor was standing there. Sir Amadis was breathing deeply as he sheathed his sword. "I think I killed him," he said, "before he fell. I hope. Poor Gorius."

"This is stupidity," said Quire.

"You saw it? How many other witnesses?"

"Who knows?" Quire believed there was only himself. "You'll be imprisoned for this. Exiled."

"I wanted Alys. As did he."

"She'll have no part of you now."

"I know."

"You must return to your wife," said Quire on impulse. He became thoughtful. "Aye—to Kent. The Perrotts will protect you."

"What shall I tell them?"

"That you are a victim. That you quarrelled over their position—that Ransley called the Perrotts traitors and wanted them hanged. He tried to murder you. Something of the sort. They'll receive you in Kent, as you know."

"Aye. My wife wanted me with her. I could not. My loyalty. My lust."

"If you're still loyal to the Queen, then save her a scandal." Quire was delighted. This would confirm the Perrotts in their hatred. It would ensure that their fleet sailed. "Go you now. You can be in Kent by morning. A horse is all you need."

Sir Amadis looked doubtfully at Quire. "You are eager to be rid of me, Captain."

"You know I've always sought your friendship. Now I seek to save you from retribution, that's all."

"Kent's the answer, right enough." Sir Amadis was already parting from Quire. "I'll do my best to make them see sense and save Albion from war. If I can do that . . ."

"You will be more powerful than Quire," said Quire under his breath as he waved.

He walked without haste back to the gallery, congratulating himself that he was free of two encumbrances and that his luck stayed with him.

He met Lord Shahryar in what had been a laundry. Once servants had laboured here for Hern. The sweat and the steam had gone up, the water down, running over the flagstones, going the gods knew where. The rounded ceilings were still caked with soap which had risen with the steam and the whole place stank of lye. Quire leaned against a wooden tub and smiled at Lord Shahryar, who did not find this a fit meeting-place.

"Another few days, that's all," said Quire very quietly, "and the Perrotts sail."

"Our fleet's already on the move, but will harbour in Iberia. Until we need to come to Albion's rescue." Lord Shahryar's tone was depressed. "Is it really happening, Quire?"

"Aye," said Quire. "Really." It seemed he shared the Saracen's mood.

"We'll restore the glory." Shahryar was eager. "It is in reality scarcely harmed at all. The people will respond well to handsome Hassan."

"Aye. You'll have an even better lie, within a year, than Montfallcon could conceive."

Shahryar noticed Quire's own bitterness. "You wouldn't thwart us, would you?"

"Now? How could I? It is all too far gone."

"What will you do?"

"Find another patron, I suppose." He did not like the drift of the conversation.

Shahryar laughed. "So. You've come to love her. It's the classic tale."

"I'm fond of the poor creature, now that she is on the verge of defeat. I am always fond of my victims, sir."

"No! It's more than that. You hesitate." Shahryar took a step or two nearer. "I wonder if you would betray us if you could. There are means. Sir Thomasin Ffynne is ready at Portsmouth with a great fleet, to forestall the Perrotts. Yet if it were turned on us . . ."

"Fear not, my lord. I've kept my word. I am renowned for it."

"And renowned for hiding the truth by means of a well-chosen platitude." Lord Shahryar shrugged. "Well, I must trust you. But I have often wondered why you went so readily from Montfallcon's service and into mine. . . ."

"That day? It was fated. I had lost my temper with Lord Montfallcon. I was piqued. If you had captured me on another day, this whole story would have been a different one. I'd have thwarted all your plans, in Montfallcon's name. But, perhaps in haste I gave my word—and I kept it. . . ."

"You have a regretful tone, Captain Quire."

Quire had finished with him. Before Shahryar realised it he had begun his journey back to Gloriana's room, for she would be waking soon.

But she was already awake when he arrived. She was pale and her mind was clogged. Sir Orlando Hawes stood by the bed. He nodded to Quire as Quire appeared.

"What's this? Is the Queen ill?" Quire went to her. He was surprised when she waved him away, intent on the note she read and re-read.

"What is it?" Quire asked Hawes. "War declared?" He hated this ignorance. He lived for knowledge. "What's in the note?"

Gloriana showed it to him. It was from Wallis.

"We found him. In one of those little rooms off the main seraglio," said Sir Orlando. He was sad, but he was triumphant, too. "He used a leaf from Sir Ernest's book, and the poet's pen and inkhorn. He had stabbed himself with a dagger. Through the heart. Neatly, with proper calculation."

"Oh, Quire!" Gloriana accused him.

The note was addressed to him.

To Captain Quire. Sir, Being in doubt as to your advice, I have decided to do away with doubt and pain for ever and take this step. You did me a service and caused me great misery thereby, but the fault lies with me. I believe I have repaid any debt I have to you, and thus may take my leave with clear conscience. I have betrayed the Queen's faith and cannot thank you for your help in this. But I am avenged—betrayed by you and by your creature as I know you have betrayed so many—to their deaths. I remain, I suppose until life vanishes entirely, your servant. Florestan Wallis, Secretary for the High Tongue of Albion. By this deed, once more a loyal friend of the Queen.

"You are lost, Quire," said Sir Orlando. "This poor fellow has accused you and died to prove his case."

Gloriana began to weep.

The Thirty-Second Chapter

In Which
Captain Quire's Plans Are Further
Inconvenienced

"IT PROVES NOTHING," said Quire. "He was mad with guilt and despair. I know young Phil. He's one of Priest's dancers and has been under Wallis's protection. He was playing flirt to all. Wallis asked me to help him and I did what I could. Thus he considered me to be in his debt. It's the import of the entire letter. That and his belief he shunned duty to pursue lust."

They sat side by side upon the bed while she read the letter over. She ignored him. "Sir Orlando was right. This proves infamy of some description."

"Only in Wallis's eyes."

"He recorded all the business of the Realm. He could have been the spy for Tatary and you his agent. Or the reverse. I recall everything Montfallcon hinted at . . ."

"There's scarcely a lackey in the Court could not gain that information," he said. "I've spoken to no Tatars, that I swear. How can you believe this?" He was aggrieved—accused, inadvertently, by a man he had not killed, of something he had not done.

"Oh, Quire, I have been betrayed by so many in my life and have always kept my faith." She looked hopelessly at him. "I believed in Chivalry and in Albion, in my service and duty to the Realm. You teach me self-love and say that is for the sake of the Realm. I think, however, that you are trying to betray me again, in a new way. You force me to betray myself. Is there anything crueller?"

"This will not do. You are tired. And you are still drunk."

"I am not."

He became sullen. "You debate non-existent problems. I love

you. Not four hours since, you agreed that our love was enough to sustain all else."

"I have turned my back on Albion. I have become cynical. And so many have died."

"They died before," he said. "Only you did not know—save for a few. How many were murdered far more horribly than Lady Mary?"

"What do you say?" She turned, frowning. "What do you know?"

He grew cautious. "What I have heard. Ask Montfallcon." He risked his own security. If Montfallcon guessed that he had revealed those secrets, his safety was all gone.

"In my father's time, you mean?"

He retreated. "Aye."

It was as if she strapped armour about her, moment by moment. He sought a chink with: "I love you."

She shook her head and let the letter fall. "You think you do. And I you, little Quire. But this —" She rose to pace the dark chamber. "The Court crumbles. The dead increase. I believed that I acted to save us from further death. Yet here's poor Wallis gone. And in our own secret quarters that represented our retreat from death, from the past. It is too much, Quire."

"You seem to blame me."

"Wallis did."

"Aye. His brain was disordered. Many would make a scapegoat of me."

"The Phoenician scapegoat bore the whole tribe's sins and was killed to free them. I do not want you killed, my love. I do not want a Realm which requires a scapegoat."

"I assure you, I agree."

"I must look to the safety of Albion's spirit. I must stop these wars. I must reunite the nobles."

"It is too late." He saw his power weakening. Again he shifted his ground. "So, I'm to go away? You have no more use for Quire's comforting."

"I need it more than ever," she said. "Yet it diverts me too greatly."

"You trust me so little that one vague letter can turn you against me?"

"I do not know. There is much I have refused to consider. I know you, Quire, because I love you. Yet I have no words for that knowledge. I am confused."

"Come to bed. Let me banish confusion."

"No. I would debate this with myself."

He realised that the morning would bring news of Lord Gorius's death and Sir Amadis's flight. He had perhaps overreached himself, for he had also been accused of injuring Sir Vivien. He lay on their bed, brooding. He must consider urgent plans. He must win her back to him for the few days needed until his great plan was brought to full bloom. He must appeal to her in some way. He must pretend to agree. So he waited in silence for a while in the hope that she would feel the need to fill it. He knew her nature.

And at last she said, sadly:

"I am unworthy of my people. I have no intelligence. I have made a monstrous mad thing of my wisest councillor."

He continued in his silence.

"I have betrayed my duty. I have allowed my friends to perish, to suffer, while those who are not my friends prosper. I am infamous and my subjects turn against me, for I betray their faith by losing my own. In my pain and my fear I sought help from Eros—but Eros rewards only those who bring him virtue and good will. I have been foolish."

He climbed from the bed with a great display of impatience. "This is mere self-pity."

"What?"

"You continue to blame yourself for the crimes and weaknesses of others. You'll never test your own strength if you follow this course. You were Montfallcon's foil—now you claim me as your influence. You must consider your own decisions and make 'em. So I'll leave, as you desire."

She halted. "Forgive me. I am distressed."

"You fear to take any form of retribution on your enemies in case it should reveal your father's cruelty in you. You are not cruel—but there must be firmer justice. You have been only the reflection of your nation's needs. Now you must impose your will and show that you are strong. It is the way to end all this madness."

She drew massive, beautiful brows together. "You stand to suffer most from any retribution," she reminded him.

"Do I? Put me to trial, then. By whatever jury you select. Or try me yourself."

He drove her back to tears; he exploited her general guilt; he offered her escape through hysteria. She did not take it. Instead she found dignity. She rose, huge and sympathetic, and took him, to his astonishment, to her breast. "Oh, Quire, Quire."

"You must rest. For a day or so." His voice was muffled. "Then make your decisions."

"Do not advise me, my dear. Do not try any further to reduce my aspirations. You taught me not to mind my affliction. But it was that very affliction which represented my love of Albion. I shall risk the pain, in order to serve the Realm again."

"This is weighty. . . ."

"I shall decide, in the course of the coming week, on what I must do."

He felt thwarted, even though he saw success.

He gave himself up to her awesome kindness.

Next morning there came the news of Ransley and word that Sir Vivien was dead of his fall. The Queen, in her puzzling and novel mood, took both deaths with a kind of tolerant dismay and had Tom Ffynne sent for. She intended to discuss the problem of Cornfield's disappearance from the palace, though it was by now well known he had ridden south-east on the Dover road and almost certainly went to his kinsmen.

Quire was not ignored by Gloriana, but he was not consulted any longer by her. She continued to show towards him the affectionate detachment of a mother for a charming but demanding child. And she allowed him to go with her when she robed herself in her encrusted gown, her crown, and took her orb and sceptre, to return to the Audience Chamber she had all but abandoned. As she moved through the Presence Chambers she greeted astonished petitioners who had long since given up any real belief they might be granted an interview. She was distant; she was friendly. Her humanity was all but gone and she was little else but habit, a monarch. Quire followed, nodding and bowing to those he knew, showing a confidence which, for once, was not much with him, attempting to give the impression that he had at last persuaded the Queen to do her duty.

She was enthroned and Quire took the chair at the foot of the dais; the Countess of Scaith's chair. Lord Montfallcon was summoned but did not immediately appear.

Lord Shahryar was the first foreign ambassador to be received. He looked hard at Quire, not daring to ask, even with his eyes. He was tall and self-contained, in his silks, and his steel, and his gold. "Gracious Majesty. My master Hassan, Grand Caliph of Arabia, sends his greetings and asks me to express his deepest affection for your self. An affection, he asks me to tell you, that goes deeper than mere admiration for the world's most beautiful, most loved, most honourable sovereign, ruler of the world's mightiest and noblest Empire. He awaits the moment when you will send him a sign that you share this affection, so that he might fly to your side, to help you in this troubled hour of history."

"Troubled hour, my lord?" She seemed amused. "What troubled hour is that?"

"Well, Your Majesty, there are rumours. Certain of your subjects—unruly and unwise—disobey your wishes. . . ."

"A minor domestic matter, my lord."

"Of course, Your Majesty." He said no more. He did not look at Quire at all. Quire knew, however, that Shahryar might believe himself betrayed and, in turn (for he had nothing to lose), might betray Quire.

The doors of the Audience Chamber groaned open on unoiled hinges. Montfallcon entered. He wore his black robes of office, his gold chain. His grey face was drawn and there were blotches of red, like a drunkard's blush, on his cheekbones, showing that he had slept hardly at all for many nights. His eyes shifted in his head as he noted the Queen, then Quire, then Shahryar. He had one hand wrapped in the heavy folds of his cloak as if he clutched his own costume to steady himself, and when he spoke, his voice was rapid, ragged. "Your Majesty sent for me?"

"We hope we do not inconvenience you, dear Lord Montfallcon."

His glance was suspicious. "What are we doing here?"

"We are giving audience, my lord. We are debating important matters of State."

Montfallcon pointed. "Then why is he here? That spy. Sir Orlando told me of the note."

"The note said nothing." The Queen's tone continued to be light. "There was no evidence against Captain Quire."

"There is evidence everywhere," said Montfallcon. "In your own actions." He looked hard at Lord Shahryar, who pretended embarrassment. He fell silent.

Lord Shahryar was eager to remain but could not, by custom, do so. He bowed and withdrew, leaving the three of them in the vastness of the room filled with warm, autumn light, making the tapestries, panels and wall hangings seem richer than ever.

"We sought your advice, my lord," said the Queen softly.

"I have given it. I have told you what to do. Abandon Quire. Abandon your secrets. Abandon wanton epicureanism!"

"My charges? My children?"

"Abandon all of that."

"And will you abandon your own secrets, my lord?" she asked.

"What?" A glare at Quire. Quire was able to shake his head to let Montfallcon know that he had said nothing.

"We have heard you have been into the walls again. We forbade you, or any other, the walls. We ordered the entrances closed up."

"There are many entrances, as I am discovering. Possibly hundreds."

"Is that so, Captain Quire?" she asked.

"I do not know, madam," he answered innocently.

She laughed. "Oh, come now, Captain. You are a villain from the walls. Admit it. All the evidence shows it now. I do not accuse you. Perhaps with Lord Montfallcon's help you could rid us of the creatures who so distress us and who are almost certainly causing this plague of deaths. It is the most obvious explanation. And therefore I would suggest to you that the Realm be apprised of our decision. We must tell everyone that we have discovered murderers and criminals hiding at the very roots of the State—that all our recent troubles were caused by them; that they murdered Lady Mary and others, seduced some of our councillors (now dead or fled), tried to poison the Queen herself. And we shall assure everyone that, with this discovery, we shall send expeditions into the walls to destroy every creature found there."

Quire smiled. She had found perhaps the only means of uniting the nobles swiftly in a common aim. It was a clever notion and he admired her for it, even though it threatened his own plans.

"The walls?" Montfallcon rubbed at his eyelids, mumbling to himself. "No—there is something to be done—there can be no-one sent to the walls. Not yet."

"What do you say, my lord? I do not hear you."

Quire had heard and was on his feet. "It is a splendid plan. Shall we join forces then, Lord Montfallcon?"

Montfallcon was contemptuous. "The wall rabble is not the cause of our dissolution. Base appetites are the cause. Bad blood. There is a canker here and it must be burned away. All evil must be swept from the palace. All!"

Quire pursed his lips. "We could begin with the walls, however, my lord." He pretended to humour Montfallcon. "First the corruption within, then the corruption without, eh?"

Montfallcon would not listen to him. "They must die," he told the Queen. He trembled as he moved further into the Throne Room. "There can be no ambiguity. Not now. Show Albion that you are pure, by destroying all that is impure within the palace!"

"But, good Lord Montfallcon," she said, "that is what we suggest."

"Then let me send men to do it."

"It is our will." She frowned, looking to Quire for aid, but he could not help. He shrugged.

"Good." Montfallcon turned to leave.

"My lord," she said, "there are other matters. The Perrotts. Know you when they plan to sail for Arabia?"

"Three days." He was gone.

"Ah." She turned to Quire. "Word must be sent to Tom Ffynne at Portsmouth with the fleet. But what shall he do? Attack the Perrotts or join them? If he joins them we'll be at war with half the world—or more than half. If he attacks, we'll have civil war. And Arabia's movements are strange. There's news of a great fleet, but no news of what it intends. Does Lord Shahryar threaten us—war or marriage?"

"Possibly," agreed Quire. "If we were to avoid war . . ."

"Oho!" She looked down at him from her throne. "Give myself to Hassan? Would you agree to that, Quire?"

He dropped his gaze.

"You may go," she said.

"Eh?"

"It is bad diplomacy to have you here." She was demonstrating her power over him. "It incensed Montfallcon. It might incense others. Tell me, do you think the expedition into the walls will save us?"

"Several might. Led by a variety of your nobles, given important tasks." He was sullen.

"Then you find my statecraft good."

"I have never doubted it." He did not want to leave. On the other hand he needed to see Alys, and Phil, to contact Tinkler, if he could. They must all be warned and set to work. He made a show of dignity. He stood up, bowing. "When does Your Majesty desire me to return?"

"We'll keep you from the public eye today, I think. We'll meet tonight. In my bedchamber?"

Quire was dry. "I'm to be the secret lover, then, am I? Because I seem a villain."

She shook her head. "Because you are a villain, clever little Quire. It is your nature. I understand that now."

"You punish me?"

"Why so? I love you still."

Baffled, Quire made his way from the official rooms, back to the private apartments, doing his best to order his thoughts and scarcely able to understand how, since Wallis's suicide, their rôles had reversed in this subtle way. He would, in the past, never have allowed himself to be placed in such a position as this. He must immediately consider ways of re-establishing his authority. He went first to the seraglio and found Phil, taking him away and punishing him for his foolishness. Then he told Phil to find Alys Finch at once and send her to meet him in the maze. Then he gave a messenger a note to take to the town in the hope that Tinkler would be found. He was frustrated, needing to take action, but not possessing sufficient information, as yet. He went to see Doctor Dee, who received him reluctantly, staunching a wound in his arm. "She grows fiercer. The philtres no longer function. You must make me a new one soon." Doctor Dee was too weak to visit the Audience Chamber and be Quire's ear.

Quire considered entering the walls and going through familiar routes, where he would be able to overhear almost everything, but there was too much danger of meeting either the Tatars or Montfallcon. He did not wish to betray himself by admitting a connection with the rabble which would soon be blamed for so many crimes. So he fumed.

He went to the maze and Alys Finch did not come to him. Was she, too, in the walls? With Oubacha Khan and Sir Orlando Hawes? Misleading them, as he had told her to do? Was half the Court in that province he had only lately claimed as his own? Tinkler was not found. There was no-one else to work for him. He had lost three useful councillors in a single night and suddenly had no allies on whom he could call. Dee was useless. The Queen, having cleansed herself of all sentiment, would be of no help at present. He brooded on this problem, which was central to his cause. How could he again tap the huge well of feeling that lay within the woman?

He spent the day waiting. He had never known a more terrifying one. He was impotent. And when, at last, she joined him in the bed, she talked of all her efforts to unite the Realm, to pacify the world, and wondered why he had no praise for her. She told him that Montfallcon had gone, probably into the walls, and that she feared the old lord, suddenly. She told him of her efforts to send messages to the Perrotts, begging them not to sail. She told him of a brief meeting with Oubacha Khan and Sir Orlando Hawes, and he became more interested. But the pair, it seemed, had said nothing of their plans to the Queen. She made love to him and he was passive, barely able to respond at all. She gave him up and readied herself for sleep. He wondered if he should go again to the maze and hope that Alys was there. He watched her, stroked her absently, as she began to breathe more deeply.

He was unable to interpret his own state of mind; for this unexpected mood of hers had thrown him entirely off balance. He realised, with some astonishment, that he feared the mood, that he would do anything, pay almost any price, to lift it. And yet he had weathered worse humours in his time; why should he be so discomfited now?

It dawned on him, then, that he cared for her good opinion of him—or that, at any rate, he desired her to exhibit some kind of opinion. The desire was new. He sat up in bed and was considering waking her when, from several rooms distant, there came a shriek.

Gloriana was awake. "Eh?"

Quire began to scramble from the bed, pushing back the curtains. His long shift tangled his feet. He found his sword and went to the door to listen: a babble of women's voices, coming closer. "Some maid," he said. "A fit."

He opened the door. There was light in the rooms beyond—lamps, candles, torches. Shadows moving; women everywhere, like hens about a fox. A giant stumbled through a door. He staggered between the ranks of night-clad ladies; he was almost naked and blood pumped out of him from three or four wounds, falling on the writhing body of the little girl he held in his arms. It was the albino twin, the guard from the seraglio, and he was dying. Quire ran towards him. The girl was one of Gloriana's children, perhaps the youngest. Gloriana took the child from the giant and said: "Do they fight? In there?"

Quire darted past the guard even as the man fell to his knees, then sprawled as the last of his blood burst from him. The little figure in his encumbering shift, the long Iberian sword in his right hand, ran into the semi-private rooms. He pulled back draperies, sought for the door to the seraglio and found it partly opened, broken by the giant's weight, and he was squeezing past, running up the steps, hearing the screams ahead; through the dark gem-studded caverns he ran, with the deep carpets hampering his naked feet, to reach the door where the two guards had stood. The black twin was not at his post. Quire pushed through and was in the main seraglio, looking down at the giant's corpse. "Arioch!"

Lurking bloodletters swarmed through the low-ceilinged vaults, slaying any that showed life. Even as Quire watched, the shrieks became fewer and fewer.

It was the rabble from the walls. They were slaughtering the entire seraglio. Already most of the poor, soft creatures were dead. A few ran here and there or hid themselves, whimpering; all the dwarves and geishas, the cripples and youths Gloriana had protected here in this menagerie of sensuality. A bewildered, lumbering ape-man crashed against a jewelled fountain and fell into the bowl, two long pikes sticking from his hairy back. A little boy ran past Quire, waving the stump of a severed arm. Elsewhere was butchery even more obscene: a hellish shambles.

The rabble had come through two or three of the secret entrances Quire thought only he had known about. He looked down the long central walk to the apartments where the children had been kept. There were corpses here, too, small and large: the girls and their guardians. Eight of the Queen's nine children. Quire had known battlefields, ship-fights, massacres a-plenty, but never one as appalling. He was overawed by the scene. He moved through the knee-deep fresh-killed bodies, trying to speak.

Phil Starling came running towards him, all his bangles jingling on his oiled and painted body. "Oh, save me, master! Save me, Captain! I did not mean to let them in. I sought Alys!"

Quire made a movement to draw back, then realised Gloriana was behind him. He shrugged and went forward. "Phil—go through—quickly."

But a scrawny swordsman had pounced, cutting Phil from the

back of his neck to the base of his spine, opening him up as an expert fishmonger might open a sole. Phil fell forward, cloven, and was dead.

Phil's killer stood over the body. He was panting, intoxicated by the terror of his own actions, searching for further eyes that might accuse him. He wore a fur cap, askew on his head, to match a twisted, gagtoothed face. His silk coat was all blood, as were his breeches. Quire recognised him and cried:

"Tink!"

Tinkler blinked, motioned with his sword, looked hard through the semi-darkness. "Captain?"

Quire gathered himself. "Is it you leads this rabble?"

"In your name, Captain," said Tinkler from force of habit. "In your name." He began to gasp, as a man will who is plunged suddenly into cold water.

"Mine?" Quire moved his mouth in a horrible grin. "Mine, Tink?" Slowly he approached his servant. His voice was flat. "You brought them here and did this in *my* name?"

"Montfallcon gave me my instructions. He knew you had left me in charge of the mob—or guessed it. I don't know. But you said to obey him. I could not find you, Captain. It was too dangerous to look for you. And then Montfallcon said that the Queen had ordered us to do it. That you agreed. It seemed he spoke the truth." He looked past Quire to Gloriana. "He said that you desired the seraglio destroyed, Your Majesty. Did I do wrong?"

"Wrong?" Gloriana shared Quire's hideous mirth. "Montfallcon . . ? Ah, vengeful, sullen Achilles!"

"Your Majesty?" Tinkler began to bow, as one who has accomplished a difficult task.

Then, with a cry both agonised and vengeful, Quire drew back his arm and drove his sword deep into his servant's heart.

"Villain!" He sobbed. "Literal-minded sloplicker!" He withdrew the sword and aimed for another thrust.

The Queen was shouting at him. "No more! Call them off if you can. But no more death!"

Quire became calm as he lowered his sword above Tinkler's

twitching body. He cleared his throat and spoke loud and clear. "That's enough, lads." He knew he betrayed himself, gave her firm evidence of his connection with the rabble. "Come to me! This is your Captain. This is Quire."

Slowly, in twos and threes, the weary ruffians presented themselves before him, almost eager, upon command, to pile their glistening swords at his feet.

He turned, saying to Gloriana: "I did not do this. Montfallcon ordered it."

"I know," she said, and went to find the palace soldiers.

As the rabble was led off, she and Quire squatted amongst the dead children, looking for life. There was none. He had expected arrest, with his men, but she had given no order of that sort, showed hardly any emotion at all as she looked into the faces of the girls she had borne. "This is what he meant, Montfallcon, when he asked me to give him permission to destroy 'all that was impure.' And it was why he would allow no inspection of the walls. He used your mob against me. Against both of us, in a sense." She sighed. "He asked my permission and I agreed. Do you recall me agreeing, Quire?"

He would not reply to her.

"It was my first true attempt at independent statecraft. I thought myself in command at last. Do you remember, Quire? I sent you away after that display."

He nodded.

"I gave him permission to kill my children. My first decision."

"You did not." He reached out for her. Then his hand dropped. It was useless. He began to consider his own escape, certain that she must soon turn on him, realise the guilt he shared—for the mob and its commander had been his invention.

"Has Montfallcon been found?" she asked.

He shook his head. "Fled into the walls, it seems. Or perhaps somewhere in the East Wing."

"Poor Montfallcon. I drove him to this."

Quire saw two of the Queen's older companions coming for their mistress. He stood up. He fingered his jaw. He wondered which route to take. He could go out to the town and hope for a ship—or go back into the walls, at least for a while: perhaps to search for Montfallcon and slay him. The Queen must soon grow vengeful. She was weeping now. She would want her scapegoat soon. The ladies who came to her were thrust back. She turned her dreadful face up to look into his. "Quire?"

He awaited the condemnation.

"Aye."

"You must replace Montfallcon truly now. You must be my adviser. My Chancellor. I cannot make another decision. I will not."

Quire opened his mouth, then he shut it again. He bit his lower lip. He was entirely surprised. He said: "I am honoured, madam." He had dreamed of this but never expected it, least of all now. At once the whole of Albion was his.

He helped her to her feet. She said, leaning on him: "Can you stop the war, Quire? Is there any way?"

He hesitated.

"Quire?"

He controlled himself and said: "There may be one way. I have already spoken of it. It would involve a great sacrifice on both our parts."

"I'll make the sacrifice," she said. "I must make it."

"Later," he said.

He was mystified by this success. He felt defeated. In the morning Lord Shahryar could be informed. The Grand Caliph would come sailing up the Thames, to rescue Gloriana and Albion; to crush the Perrotts. And his only emotion was one of disappointment, even fear, and again he could not explain the source of this unusual emotion. As he got her back to the bedchamber he said in a low, puzzled voice: "Why should you trust me now? I have been proven a liar and a traitor."

And she replied, very coldly: "I trust you for Montfallcon's work. Who else is there?"

Which caused Captain Quire to shiver and go, at length, to find another place to sleep.

The next morning she held formal Court for the second time. More ambassadors were interviewed, more intelligence gathered, while Quire stood, in his faded black, beside the throne, in conference whenever they were alone. Slowly, but with little relish for what he did, he manipulated her towards a decision, though he did not mention outright the solution he had already hinted at. Doctor Dee was called for, but sent word that he was ill and could not come just then. And neither Oubacha Khan nor Sir Orlando Hawes could be found.

"Well," she said, when everyone had been seen; when Master Palfreyman had counselled fierce and absolute war against all enemies at once; when nobles had begged her to send word to the Perrotts that their father's killers had been found; when all voices and all opinions had been heard; "what must I do, Chancellor Quire?"

He hesitated, though not for drama's sake. He found that he had difficulty in speaking for other, more mysterious, reasons. At length: "There is only one decision which will save the world and Albion from war." His voice was thick. He licked his long lips.

"Quickly," she said.

He looked into her eyes. She stared above his head. "I'll not be tormented. I can tell your advice is already formed, Chancellor."

"You must marry Hassan al-Giafar."

"It will be popular with the nobles."

"And the commons."

Her huge face grew momentarily sad. Another, smaller face looked out of it, for a second, at Quire, and it was pleading with him. He turned away. Then she was stern. "Lord Shahryar must be sent for."

"I shall summon him myself," said Quire. He began to feel relief, at least for the moment, that it was all done. He was free of obligation to Shahryar. He had done all that he had promised he would do. And he felt only weariness, inexplicable misery. Very heavily he began to walk towards the doors of the Audience Chamber.

Even as he signed for the footmen to open them he knew there was some kind of disturbance on the other side of the doors. He paused, listening. Then he smiled. Gradually he became possessed of a peculiar sense of elation. He recognised at least one of the voices. They were demanding to be admitted.

"Why do you hesitate?" she called across the empty room.

He walked backwards in the direction of the throne.

She cried to him: "Quire! What is it?"

He began to laugh. "You're free of me, I think." Calmly he stared into her astonished eyes. Why was he glad of this? "And there's no excuse for war. I should have killed the old man. But my reasoning's too devious. I saved him up. I am again betrayed by my own brain's convolutions!"

"No riddles!" she commanded. "Who is out there?"

The doors were pushed open from the other side, slowly. They revealed a group: Oubacha Khan, in Tatar war armour, handing his sheathed scimitar to one of the Queen's Gentlemen Pensioners; Sir Orlando Hawes, dusty and grim, in breastplate and helm; Alys Finch, holding a small black-and-white cat, grinning her triumph at Quire; the Countess of Scaith, in male attire, filthy and haggard; and Sir Thomas Perrott, ragged, unkempt, dirty, red-eyed, in a sacking smock.

"Una!"

They all looked at Quire, none at the Queen, though she cried her friend's name.

Quire smiled back at the girl who had rescued these prisoners, both of whom she had originally betrayed to him. "Your lust for treachery is even better developed than I thought, young Alys. So does the pupil seek to excel the teacher."

"One hunts the largest game, Captain." Alys Finch laughed cheerfully into his face. Neither showed malice.

Behind him the Queen was rising. "Una!"

Quire was almost merry. "Albion is saved! Albion is saved! And

Arabia's vile plans are all confused!" He continued to dance backwards, seeking escape.

They moved into the Audience Chamber, to threaten him.

"Una!"

The Countess of Scaith hesitated, then curtseyed to the Queen. "Your Majesty. Alys Finch is here to testify against her master. . . ."

"You'll believe the word of this minx, will you?" cried Quire satirically, throwing back his cloak to free his sword. He still wore the red sash, his concession to passion. "What proof have either of you?" The sword flew out. "Have you ever seen me?"

He knew that they had not. He had been careful to remain hooded. But he knew, just the same, that he was doomed.

"Sir Thomas!" The Queen was jubilant, recognising the elder Perrott at last. She turned to Sir Orlando. "A messenger, immediately, to Kent. And another to Portsmouth."

"It is done, Your Majesty," said Hawes. He moved towards Quire, who was at the door which would lead him to his offices, Montfallcon's rooms. "We're saved from war. But now we must save ourselves from Quire. Once and for all."

"Hurrah!" yelled Quire, drawing his sombrero from his belt, shaking out the feathers and donning the hat. "Virtue triumphs and poor Quire is denounced, disgraced, dismissed."

The kiss he blew to baffled Gloriana seemed sincere. He went behind the drapery. The door slammed. Sir Orlando Hawes and Oubacha Khan ran to it, calling for more assistance. Quire had locked it.

When they entered the apartments at last, there was nothing to be seen but a small fire burning in a grate, some dust moving in the autumn light, as if Quire, like a malicious ghost, had been exorcised entirely.

The Thirty-Third Chapter

In Which Queen Gloriana
and Una, Countess of Scaith
Review the Past

"I FEEL NO guilt," said Gloriana bleakly, "and think that I should not. But then feeling—strong feeling—has gone from me. The seraglio was becoming a museum of failed hopes. My children . . ." She sighed. "I was never fully conscious, Una."

The Countess of Scaith, in voluminous travelling costume, took her friend's hand. They were alone in the Withdrawing Room. Gloriana wore dark colours to match the shades of late autumn. Light rain fell outside.

Gloriana responded to her friend. "But you are recovered, eh, Una?"

"In truth," she said, "I share something of your dilemma, for I know that I should have felt more terror. But there was something comforting about my incarceration. It removed all responsibility from me. And Sir Thomas Perrott, once he understood that I was a friend, proved a kindly companion. We talked a great deal. We were buried so deeply and escape was so impossible that we were able to choose a variety of topics. It was, in many respects, a holiday. For one of a fatalistic disposition, at any rate."

"But you'll not stay at Court?"

"I may return. But not immediately. I need the air of Scaith."

"And you take Oubacha Khan with you?"

"As my guest." Una smiled. "He's celibate, he tells me. A vow."

"Aha. A vow." She became distant.

"You still pine for Quire?"

"He is a traitor."

"Perrott does not think so. Perrott maintains his belief that he was Lord Montfallcon's victim."

Gloriana shrugged. "Well, they are both gone, now."

"I bear him no grudge," said Una. "Because you love him so, Gloriana."

"I love nothing."

"You love Albion."

"I love myself. They are the same." Her tone was not bitter. It was worse: it was hopeless.

Una hesitated. "I'll stay. If you think —"

Gloriana shook her great head. "Go to Scaith with your Tatar." She moved, like a funeral barge, to stand before the window, blotting the light from the room. "You risked your life for the Realm. I'll not have you risking your soul for its symbol."

"Oh, Gloriana!"

The friends embraced. Una was weeping, but there were no tears in the Queen's cool eyes.

The Thirty-Fourth Chapter

In Which the Past Is Invoked Once More and Old Enemies Resolve Their Struggles

ALBION, WITH WAR banished and the Arabian fleet dispersed even before Tom Ffynne and the Perrotts could meet with it, knew optimism again as Chivalry was at last restored. The Queen made plans for a Progress, regretting only that the Countess of Scaith could not accompany her. Sir Orlando Hawes proposed marriage to Alys Finch and was accepted. He had found the innocent in her, now that Quire's influence was gone. Sir Amadis Cornfield and his wife were invited to the palace and came, to receive token recrimination, though the Queen's main purpose was to offer this new, sober Sir Amadis the position of Chancellor, which carried with it an earldom. Sir Amadis begged leave to return to Kent. He said he had lost his taste for statecraft. And Gloriana was alone, as she had never been alone before, and every night she pined for her villainous lover, and her voice was heard through the emptied tunnels and vaults of the hidden palace, the deserted seraglio, as she wept; though she never mentioned his name, even there, in the darkness of her curtained bed. The autumn grew gradually cooler, but the year was still unnaturally warm. Tatary drew back from foreign borders. King Casimir was re-elected Poland's king. The Lady Yashi Akuya, having lost hope of Oubacha Khan, returned to Nipponia. Hassan al-Giafar was accepted as bridegroom by the Princess Sophie, sister of Rudolph of Bohemia, and Lord Shahryar was recalled to Arabia for execution, seeming distressed when he was reprieved. The last leaves began to fall from the trees and lie in drifts on the paths. Sir Orlando Hawes was made Chancellor, head of the Privy Council, and Admiral Ffynne became, with him, the Queen's chief adviser. Master Gallimari and Master Tolcharde arranged a further popular display, in the great courtyard, of the mechanical Harlekinade, attended by Queen, nobles and commons. Sir Ernest Wheldrake proposed marriage, in maudlin verse, to Lady Lyst, who drunkenly and cheerfully accepted him. The Thane of Hermiston, who had unwittingly encouraged Montfallcon's final vengeance, disappeared in Master Tolcharde's roaring globe and never returned to Albion. Dr. Dee remained in his apartments, refusing visits even from the Queen herself. His experiments, he said, were of major importance and should not be witnessed by the uninformed. He was humoured, though he was by now considered entirely mad. There was speculation about the fate of Montfallcon, whom most thought a suicide, and of Quire, who had evidently fled through the Spiders' Door and returned to the underworld before escaping abroad. The Queen would not speak of either. The Countess of Scaith, as she had promised, said nothing of Quire and refused to accuse him. Sir Thomas Perrott maintained the firm belief that Montfallcon was the villain who had imprisoned him. Sir Orlando Hawes kept silent on the matter for two reasons—his natural tact and his need to protect his bride's reputation. Josias Priest emigrated to Mauretania.

The Court resumed its old merriment, and Gloriana presided over it with grace and dignity, though her laughter was never anything but polite and her smiles, when they came at all, never more than wistful. She was as loved as she had always been loved, but it seemed that the passion, which had led her to aspire to fulfilment, was now gone from her. She had become a goddess, almost a living statue, a steady, gentle symbol of the Realm. She took to walking at night in her gardens, unattended, and would spend much of her time in her maze, walking round and round until it became absolutely familiar. Yet still she inhabited it. Sometimes servants, looking from their windows, could see in the moonlight her bodiless head and shoulders drifting as if by levitation over the tops of the yew hedges.

Time went by for Gloriana, hour by slow and lonely hour, and she took no lovers. Her private time was spent with Sir Ernest and

Lady Wheldrake and with her surviving child, Duessa, whose son, many years hence, would come to inherit the Realm. She counselled Duessa towards a moderation she had never herself experienced, to balance Romantic faith against realistic understanding.

One night, as she undressed for bed, a palace servant came to her door with a message. She read the wavering words. It was from Dr. Dee. He wished to see her alone, he said, because he was dying and there was that on his conscience he would communicate. She frowned, wondering whether to go at least part of the way with attendants, but then decided she wasted time, if indeed he was dying. So she drew a huge and heavy brocade gown over her shift, put bare feet into slippers, and went to the East Wing, towards Dr. Dee's apartments, taking with her a candle. The way to Dr. Dee's lay through the chilly old Throne Room, still known as Hern's Chamber, which she had always refused to enter. She began to shudder, hating the place and its memories. She had not been here since her father's death. In common with most of her generation she disliked the pointed or "Saracen" style of architecture, found it barbaric and inhuman. It was almost as if she entered the walls again, and only her regard for her old friend led her on. Save for a single shaft of moonlight, which struck the block and the surrounding mosaics of the floor to form a pool, the chamber was in darkness, dominated by the huge anthropoidal statues, the irregular, vaulted ceilings. She paused. There was nothing to fear now that the rabble had been transported to the new oriental lands of the Empire, save imprecise memories. Yet, as she crossed near the brooding throne dais, she thought she heard a noise from near it and raised her candle to let yellow light fall upon the steps.

She had seen too much blood since the spring, particularly in the seraglio that dreadful night. She recognised the ragged, ruined face of the magus, the toothless mouth opening and closing, the eyes screwed tight shut as the light struck them. There was blood on his beard, blood on the torn nightshirt he wore, blood on hands and legs.

"Dee." She climbed the dais and rested the candle down on a step so that she could take his head in her lap. "What is this? Some seizure?" But now she could see the little wounds all over him. He had been bitten as if by a whole tribe of rats. "Can you stand?" He must have been experimenting with animals, she decided. The animals had escaped and attacked him in the night.

He whispered. "I was coming to you. She is no longer in my control. With Quire gone . . . I feared that she would kill you, too."

"What is it has done this? I must warn the palace."

"You. She is you . . ."

Gloriana tested his weight to see if she could carry him. He was a heavy old man. Now he raved and would not be lifted. She smiled as she tried to get him to his feet. "Me? There is only one me, Dr. Dee. Come."

He was sitting up, an arm about her shoulder. He opened his eyes and she saw in his expression the look of a lover who was intimately familiar with her expressions. She became afraid. He said: "She was you. But she went mad. She was so docile at first. Quire made her for me. Flesh. She was just like flesh. He was a genius. I tried the same experiment—in metal—but failed, as Master Tolcharde failed. Then Quire vanished. I could no longer pay him, I suppose, with potions, with poisons. . . ."

"Quire made what?"

"He made her. The simulacrum. I was ashamed. I wanted to confess. But I was drawn in too deeply. She consoled me so well for so long, Your Majesty. I could not have you, but she was almost you."

"Almost?" She remembered his passion. "Oh, dear Dr. Dee, what have you done and how has Quire ruined you?"

"She was mad. Attacked me. I stunned her. The philtres Quire gave me for her ran out and I was afraid to experiment, though I tried. She was already unstable. Now she wishes to murder me. For using her, she says. Yet she was made for that use. It was as if she woke up—became truly alive. . . ."

"Where is she?" Gloriana did not attempt to follow his ravings.

"She followed me down. She is over there." He made a movement with his head. She lifted the candle, saw a dark shadow on stone behind the anthropoidal statues. He began to shiver.

"Come," she said. "Rise."

"I cannot. You had best go now, Your Majesty. I have given you my confession. Think not too ill of me. My mind was good and, until the end, always at your service, as you know. The poisons. I regret the poisons. I allowed Quire to convince me."

There came a great noise, as if something heavy and metallic were dragging itself across the mosaic flagging, but the shadow remained where it was.

Gloriana could see nothing of the source until, of a sudden, into the shaft of moonlight which fell upon the familiar stone block, came an old man clad in iron, in antique armour, an enormous black sword, made for two hands, upon his shoulder. His red eyes were hot with the habit of rage. His grey face and beard were thin and his cheeks were hollow. It was Montfallcon, wearing the war-suit of his youth.

"He invented for me the most perfect simulacrum," continued Dee, scarcely aware of the newcomer. "A soulless creature. I could worship it, however—have my way with it—and no guilt. Or hardly any . . ."

"Simulacrum!" Montfallcon's frigid, heavy voice was loud in the hall as he turned to observe the shadow, which now, at the sound, began to stir. "You old fool! 'Tis a real woman."

Dee began to breathe rapidly and shallowly. "No, no, Montfallcon. There could not be a twin. There was never any story of a twin or I should have heard it. And all witnessed the birth, did they not? Ah," he smiled, "perhaps—from another world, as I once dreamed? Is that where Quire obtained her?"

"There is only this world." Montfallcon clanked a few steps more, to lean himself against the block. "Dolt! It is the mother!"

"Flana?" Dee's voice grew faint. "Flana died in childbirth."

"She did not. I witnessed her rape and I witnessed the result of that rape nine months later. She was thirteen when she bore the Queen. We were all made to watch—both events. Hern was proud of himself. After all, it was the only time, up to then, he had been able to penetrate a woman. For some reason Flana, who was my daughter, was able to attract him. Flana?"

The shadow groaned.

Gloriana got to her feet. She did not wish to hear this tale. And she was terrified of all of them now. Montfallcon spoke wearily. "It was on this stone he raped my daughter, and on this stone he raped my granddaughter. Twice in his life was he capable of committing the act. I watched both. The blood was always bad, on all sides. I know that now. I sought to burn the knowledge from me. I willed Gloriana to her position. But the blood was bad. Now it is all over. And I am destroyed, hated by all now, because I loved Albion. History will remember your most loyal servant, Your Majesty, as a villain."

The shadow began to rise, muttering to itself. Gloriana was frozen. Her mouth went dry and her eyes refused to close.

Montfallcon gestured to the mad woman. "Come, Flana. Come to your father and your daughter."

Flana moved with peculiar grace into the light. She looked youthful, as mad people sometimes do, though her face was ravaged and her hair, auburn like her daughter's, was dyed in places.

"Here she is," said Lord Montfallcon. "She ran into the walls after you were born, Gloriana, and was there until Quire snared her, drugged her, gave her to Dee in exchange for his secrets and his philtres. I would have known, but I refused to have the walls investigated for the same reasons as you. I hid the fact of Flana from myself. She loved you. Perhaps she still does. Do you love your little girl, Flana?"

"No," said the mad woman in a thick, terrible voice. "She has been bad. She banished her only true suitor."

"She saw Hern rape you. She watched from her hiding place within the walls," said Montfallcon. "He waited until you were exactly the same age, and raped you on your birthday. Do you remember, Gloriana?"

"While the Court looked on. That leering Court." She said: "I remember. Mother . . ."

The mad woman ran towards Montfallcon, who took her by the arm. He said: "Kneel."

She was passive with him. She looked into her father's eyes. Into her hero's eyes. She smiled and knelt.

Her head was resting on the block and Montfallcon's sword was lifting before Gloriana could cry out. "No!"

The broadsword fell. The auburn head burst free of the shoulders. Dee whimpered and then he, too, died.

"Your own flesh," said Gloriana. "Why?" She left Dee and began to crawl up the steps, one by one, away from the corpses.

"Corrupt flesh," Montfallcon equably explained, putting the sword on his shoulder again and looking down at his victim. "She should have died when the rest of the girls died. But she agreed to Hern's proposal. To save her life. I could not stop her then. When you were born, I hoped that you would come to redeem all that had taken place here. But you followed her to corruption, soon enough. My wife and the boys went next. I would not let him have the boys, you see, or my wife. He had a poor imagination, your father, like most monsters. What it was, to be in the power of an all but mindless beast! Yet I waited. I made my plans, developed my ambition. I wanted you to be the golden creature who would give point to all my suffering. You and Albion. And for almost thirteen years it seemed my work, my sacrifices, proved worthwhile and that together we achieved the Age of Virtue. Then you, too, gave yourself to a monster. And now I shall kill you and be done with it."

She had expected this. She could make no appeal to him. She began to scramble up the steps, one by one, faster and faster, as he came after her, in creaking iron, his eyes fixed upon her throat. She reached the throne, was seated in it before she knew it. He paused. "It can begin again soon," he said. "With the bad blood extinguished once and for all."

She began to fear for her surviving child.

"Come," he said, and gestured towards the block. "You shall die where you were born. You should never have existed. You are a nightmare."

She made a gasping sound, pleading not so much for her own life, but for his soul, for the life of the great-granddaughter he did not, at this moment, know had been saved from his revenging mob.

"Sin upon sin," he said. "I should have stopped it then. It went on for too long and Albion was almost brought to ruin by it. Come."

"No."

He reached out his grey, gauntleted hand and he took her almost gently by the wrist. "Come."

Her great strength was all gone. She became reconciled. She rose slowly and was obedient. At her feet the candle began to gutter.

She reached the circle of moonlight. With his hand still on her, Montfallcon pushed her mother's headless body away from the block. Gloriana, swooning, fell to her knees. Fell into blood.

From the gallery a cool, amused voice called out to her. "Aha, Glory. I see you've found your old friend."

Montfallcon growled and forced her head towards the granite.

"Here I am," said Quire. He spoke conversationally, as if to Gloriana. "He's been searching for me for weeks. 'Tis a game we've been playing, Mont and me, in the walls."

"Ah!" She broke free and began to crawl back towards the dais.

Montfallcon stumbled over the corpse of his daughter, regained his footing and slowly began to raise his broadsword as he pursued her.

Then Quire was flitting down the steps, his own rapier in his little hand, his black cloak flying, his sombrero thrown clear, his thick hair bouncing around his long face, darting towards Montfallcon as a terrier at a bear, until he stood grinning between them. "Here I am, Mont."

The broadsword swept down, whistling, to crash with all its weight on Quire's guard. Montfallcon voiced frightful glee as Quire went down. Quire steadied himself with his free hand and tried to reach for the dagger in the scabbard on his hip, but it had slipped too far around his waist. He ducked, instead, and came up behind the turning Montfallcon, who sideswept with a blow that would have cut Quire in two at the thigh. But Quire had danced back, aiming his riposte at Montfallcon's cheek, just below the eye, but was knocked back with an iron arm. The broadsword rose again.

Gloriana cried to them: "No!" She could tolerate no more killing. She would rather die herself.

Quire was smiling as his thin blade struck into Montfallcon's right eye and pierced the head.

The crash of the grey lord's falling echoed and echoed in Gloriana's brain. She covered her ears. She closed her eyes. She was weeping.

Through the darkness Quire approached her and again she began to climb backwards towards the throne, as afraid of him as she had been afraid of her grandfather.

Quire paused. "I have saved you, Glory."

"It does not matter," she said.

"What? No gratitude left? No love?"

"Nothing," she said. "You taught me well. You taught me to love only myself."

He was pleased with his victory over Montfallcon. He advanced with his old swagger. "But I am a hero today, not a villain. Surely I have reprieved myself a little? A kiss, at least, Glory. For your Quire, who loves you dearly and always shall."

"You are a liar! You cannot love. You are a creature made up entirely of hate. You can imitate any emotion. You can feel very few."

He considered this. "True enough," he agreed. "Once." He came on again. "But I love you." He sheathed his sword. "I'll go. Only thank me first."

"How long were you there? How long were you watching? Did you let the drama run its course to maximum effect until you acted? Could you not have saved that poor creature's life—my mother, whom you used so badly?"

"Dee found her pleasant and, while her mind was soothed by what I gave her, she was pleased by Dee. They were happy for several months. Happier than they had ever been before. And she killed Dr. Dee, do not forget."

"You could have saved her."

He shrugged. "Why?"

"You are still the old cruel Quire, then."

"I am still a practical fellow, I know that. It is others who put these definitions on me. My name is Captain Arturus Quire. I am a scholar and a soldier of good family."

"And the mightiest, most evil rogue in Albion." She mocked

him. "You'll have no kiss from me, Quire. You are a deserter! You fled. You removed your support."

"What? With all those witnesses accusing me? I was tactful, certainly." Quire took another pace forward.

She smiled. "None accuse you now. There's the real irony. Your victims forgive you or refuse to believe you the cause of their distress!" She retreated.

He stopped. He put his hands on his hips. "I see no point in playing hero. I was always told that when one saved a fair lady from death one received a favour." His tone became serious. "I want you, Glory."

"You cannot have me, Captain Quire. I am Albion's Queen. I am not mortal. Besides, you taught me how to hate. I was innocent of that emotion before."

He began to lose his temper. "I have waited for you. I have been patient. I taught you strength. And I learned love from you. Name your terms. I'll accept 'em. I love you, Glory."

"Patience has no reward save itself," she said, still full of fear. "I used to give myself to anyone whose loins ached a little, because I knew what it was to ache. I ached so, Quire. Then you soothed it away and I lost myself. Now I ache again, but I have no sympathy for you or anyone at all. I would rather ache than satisfy another's lust, because always, when that lust is satisfied, I remain—aching still."

"Romance is ever attended by Guilt," he said casually. He drew his sword again. He motioned. "Come to me, Glory." He glared.

"You threaten me now. With the very death from which you saved me, and so proudly, too. Very well, Captain Quire. I'll return to the block for you." She began to descend.

He snarled and he took her with both his hands, abandoning his blade. "Gloriana!"

"Captain Quire." She was stone in his grip.

He dropped his hands.

She walked past him, through the cold, haunted corridors, and into the gardens. They smelled of warm autumn, still.

She crossed the gardens and went through her private gate.

She passed her maze, her silent fountains, her dying flowers. She entered her own bedroom.

He had not followed.

Recalling her anxiety, she thought, for her daughter, she entered her old secret lodgings and faced the door to the seraglio.

She passed, on yielding carpet, through into the soothing dark. None lived here now. She recalled that her daughter had been sent to Sussex. She made to return, but paused. Suddenly a thousand bloody images came to her. "Oh!"

In the absolute darkness of the seraglio she fell upon her cushions and began to weep. "Quire!"

Quire spoke from somewhere. "Glory."

A delusion. She looked up. Beyond the archway into the next vault there was a candle burning. It moved towards her, revealing Quire's tortured face, floating.

She stood up, stone again.

He sighed and put the candle into a bracket on one of the buttresses. "I love you. I shall have you. It's my right, Glory."

"You have none. You are a murderer, a spy, a deceiver."

"You hate me?"

"I know you. You are selfish. You have no heart."

"Enough," he said. "It was no wish of mine. I betray all my own faith. But you taught me to believe in love, to accept it. Won't you accept mine? And love yourself, too."

"I love Albion. Nothing but Albion. And Gloriana is Albion."

"Is Gloriana never mere Self?"

For the brevity of an insect's memory this notion gave her pause, placing thought where only blazing impulse ruled. Then she shook her fiery head and blood spoke: "We are the same. Gloriana and Albion are One. That is our destiny, Captain Quire."

"It is your doom, madam." A beast moved beneath his skin and then was immediately harnessed. His voice bore all the innuendo and amusement which had charmed her and sought to charm her still. "Shall I, then, rape Albion?" He drew his sword and as if in play placed the point to her throat. In her turn, she pressed towards it, challenging him to kill her; and her smile bore all the deadly power, all the reasoning sincerity he had seen on no other face but his own.

"Albion is not commanded by brute force, Captain Quire." She stroked her neck like a cat's against his rapier, her playfulness in imitation of his own, her voice a soft purr, its note as accurate as a Ludgate chorister's. "Albion is not raped."

The beast took control of his eyes. He reached and twisted a fold of her gown in his fingers, his shaking fingers, and he tore it away from her. The beast took control of his breath, his noises. She did not move as he tore with both his hands at her shift and tore and tore at every scrap of cloth until she was naked. And still she did not move, but now stared with contemptuous dismay into his face. She was a vibrant lioness to his thwarted lion. He dropped his sword. He seized her breasts and her buttocks, her womb, her mouth. She would not move, save to sway a little when he threatened to make her fall. He reached, half-clambering up her thigh, towards her head.

He pulled her down to the cushions. He spread her legs. He ripped away his breeches to reveal what she had seen so many times before.

It was then that a sudden determination came upon her. She refused to weep for the love he meant to destroy; she refused to plead with him not to reduce himself and her to this. She became filled by an overwhelming sense of outrage—a resolve that this should *not* happen to her, that he, in turn, should *not* commit the act he intended, should not destroy the one thing, other than himself, he had ever valued.

She felt as if she were awakening at last from a trance only a shade less deep than her mother's, and one which had like origin; a trance half Terror, half Divine Power. A burden of unseemly responsibility.

Now she understood the only way in which she might stop Quire's terrible deed from taking place. She could not let that deed occur, be it in the name of Albion, in the name of Peace, or Revenge—or any name that disguised or brought spurious Chivalry and false Romance to the brutal actuality of his intended crime.

Now, by the medium of her furious certainty, all her emotions were brought in check. She studied his well-muscled arse as it arched to plunge. Over his shoulder she saw the knife, sheathed at his belt, its hilt easily found. She took the silk-bound bone in her hand and pulled the weapon from its scabbard as he grunted and cursed and kissed and prepared for his important heave.

She raised the dagger, looking beyond him into the candlelight and a sudden image of blood-washed stone, sharp and hard, as it appeared so frequently in her dreams. The image brought burning tears, yet served only to strengthen her resolve.

She could have struck him easily, slain him almost before he knew the truth. But there was no hesitation in her actions. She had set her course and would not falter. For the first time in her life she acted with a sureness born not of physical terror but of psychic dread. Her anger grew as she thought of Montfallcon, training her like a bird, to know the fear of failing in her duties so that he might then place the burden of her blood upon her and then, again, teach her the ways not of losing that burden but of bearing it. And thus had Hern's daughter been made Albion and tranquillity enforced upon the Realm.

"No!" she cried. "No! You shall not rape *me*!" And with easy strength she placed the knife directly between his legs, startled to sense a power so awful that it thrilled every nerve in her body. Her queenly conscience was shed not through the familiar submissions with which she had earlier sought to grant herself release, but through this manlier understanding of habitual threat, of naked power, unchecked by courtesy or chivalry. Her threat carried with it an unwavering intention of pursuit to the bitter end. It was a threat as chilling and deliberate as any Quire had ever employed against his victims. Perhaps for the first time in his life Captain Quire knew hindrance, knew dread, knew fearful respect as she smiled, in mirror of his old habitual triumph, and she let the razoring steel rest upon his retreating manhood.

Me.

That single word, that brief syllable, had released her, had returned to her the ownership of her spirit and her flesh. She possessed her senses, her blood, her sex. She possessed them for no-one else. She had responsibility to no-one else. She knew an exhilaration which yet did not confuse her threat to the baffled captain who in her face perceived something which distracted him from his own imminent unsexing and brought a different, disbelieving smile. "Glory?"

She was no longer Albion. No longer justice, mercy and wisdom, no longer the personification of righteousness, the hope and ideal of her people. She was Glory. She was Self. She was fighting not for principle but in her own interest, for everything she had ever honoured. Now she understood her commonality as well as her singularity, of what she shared with all women, of what she shared with men and of what was unique in her. At that moment she ceased to be the embodiment of anything but her own desperate, uncorrupted soul.

He stumbled back, tangled in his dark velvet clothing. The beast cowered for an instant in his eyes before fleeing entirely exorcised, and leaving him looking at her with the awe some ancient hermit might have lavished upon the face of a deity revealed, for the first time, in all its mighty omnipotence. He could not speak.

"You shall do nothing to *me*, Captain Quire, that I do not command."

Whereupon, weeping, he fell to his knees upon the flags, no longer able to raise his head to look at her, as if he felt unworthy. He had been able to plot the dragging down of this Queen, this nation, but could not even begin to conceive the humbling of this woman. He bowed before the only authority he had ever recognised. He bowed before this supreme manifestation of the Self.

And then, as he knelt before her, Gloriana gasped, her newly discovered sensibilities overwhelming her, even as she stood, knife in hand, like some Tragic revenger, and she began to tremble, thinking that the whole palace quaked, that the roof must fall. And she cried out, yet still he dared not look at her. And she cried out again and her voice was so powerful it seemed to increase the space constricting it: some Cosmos-striding goddess displaying her triumphant pleasure.

Gloriana shook again, mightily. She had never known more than a hint of this ecstasy. It was as if she received recompense for every disappointment she had ever known. She lifted her head to let forth another, wilder, celebratory shout which pierced the walls and rang through the entire palace, disturbing the dust of centuries, and echoed through every inch of Albion. Now Gloriana knew that one thing for which she had always ached and which had always been denied her. She had claimed back her own soul, her own urgent humanity.

She did not celebrate Albion. She celebrated nothing but herself. It was she who had resisted and defeated the power of the beast, not her nation, not her duty. Her blood was furious with caressing heat. She seemed to become a furnace illuminating the whole chamber and the palace beyond and the fires that she generated poured through corridors and crannies cleansing away for ever the bloodstains and old bones, the old hypocrisies and lies.

And still she quaked, groaning and roaring, like some ethereal sphere in the first moments of its creation. She extinguished Guilt, banished Horror. She raised her hands, dangerous with iron, and screamed her triumph for the third time, oblivious of Quire sobbing at her feet and drowning in a remorse harder to bear for its complete unfamiliarity.

Her skin looked to her like mercurial gold, as if she had passed into Dee's great crucible to be forged into this ideal not of the State but of a natural woman, unfettered by the demands of an alien philosophy, a free agent.

"I need only be Queen if I choose," she said. She paused to stare down at him through heated yet tranquil eyes. "Or if they choose." She smiled. "Oh, little Quire." She was forgiving. Her wonderful body still moved by a profound sensuality, she reached towards him and kissed his forehead.

At that burning touch he raised his eyes and in them was the expression she had known she would find. "I'm sorry, Glory."

In her eyes now he saw tenderness and the promise of reconciliation. His features were quite innocent. He jumped up, quick and free as a child, somehow redeemed by her refusal to let him destroy their love. Her action had given meaning again to the emotions and the words he had all his life plundered and devalued. She had demonstrated her active refusal of his terms, put deed to word, and restored him afresh, just as she restored herself.

Still Gloriana trembled with the pleasure of her renaissance. And she roared again. And now it seemed a sudden dawn had risen upon the whole Realm; through this fundamental humanity she knew she could drive away the darkness and deception of the past and ensure that it should never return.

Tugging absently at his breeches, Quire believed that her extraordinary courage, her resistance to his cowardly crime, that all-hating abuse of power, had freed her of her unjust burden—but also had lifted every sin from his own soul. By some noble alchemy she had, by re-creating herself, also re-created him.

Again her huge, perfect body shook. Again her great voice roared its triumphant pleasure.

Quire knew a baffling sensation which he guessed was happiness. And he, laughing loudly into the dying echo of her shout, watched while she brought the dagger down with such mighty force upon the stone that the steel shattered into fragments which fell like silvery rain upon the dirty granite of that awful chamber. "Ha, Gloriana!" And he bowed.

Then she allowed herself, with such sublime relief, to weep.

"Oh, Quire. Now we are both fulfilled."

The Thirty-Fifth Chapter

In Which Albion Shall Begin a New Age
That Shall Be Truly One of Golden Moderation with
Romance and Reason in Balance at Last

As the warmth of Autumn shall give way at last to the cool of Winter, so shall the Moon of Romance be married to the Sun of Reason and Gloriana, Queen of Albion, be wed to her Prince Arthur of Valentia, causing much celebration throughout the Empire, for it shall be revealed, by way of Sir Thomasin Ffynne, the Queen's High Admiral, that Captain Arturus Quire was, in fact, his ward—the last surviving nephew of Lord Montfallcon, whose family was slain by King Hern. The tale of Captain Quire's commoner's upbringing and how he came to Court, taking part in a pageant and winning the attention, and later the love, of the Queen, shall be on all lips, as shall its sequel, of how Quire's enemies grew jealous of him, how poor Lord Montfallcon, not realising Quire's true birth, schemed against him and others, including Sir Thomas Perrott, then killed himself when he realised the truth, that he had sought to destroy his own nephew. It shall be told how Quire almost single-handedly saved the Realm and brought reconciliation to the Queen, to the rival factions, to Albion and to the world itself.

Chivalry shall flourish again, but it shall be of a more practical order under Prince Arthur's influence, for he will reduce a little of the romance (feeling his own tale, perhaps, to contain enough of that) and increase the realism, so that honour shall be seen to be at once a stranger and more ordinary thing than many previously knew.

They shall be married in November, in time to begin a Progress throughout the Realm, to span the Yuletide season. And, while they are gone, the walls of the great palace shall be revealed, with all their antique rooms, and light brought to every corner, and the vagabonds still dwelling there shall be made comfortable in hostelries especially prepared for them, and large parts of the once hidden palace shall be opened to the citizens of London, for their recreation.

Prince Arthur and Queen Gloriana shall begin their Progress by taking the State Barge, the old Golden Barge of the Queen's ancestors, down the river towards the sea, there to guest with Sir Amadis Cornfield and his Perrott kinsmen, whose lands abound the great estuary. They shall sail from the dock at Charing Cross, on their high, golden galley, between embankments lined with bare elm trees. Through the rich, dead leaves hiding the hoofs of their brown and black horses, knights shall ride on both sides, escorting the barge. The knights shall wear armour of dark gold and silver, their surcoats shall be russet, and their upright lances shall bear all the great Chivalric arms of Albion. And the Queen shall look down the river, beyond London's walls, to where the hills are, dark green and yellow, and she will turn to her consort, who shall wear black velvet and an awkward crown of near-black rubies and gold, and she will hug him and say to him: "Oh, my love! What a sober little king you have become!"

And behind them will be the palace, with its glinting domes and roofs rising and falling like a glamorous tide; its towers and minarets lifting like the masts and hulks of sinking ships.

Afterword
to the 2004, 2016 Edition
Haunted Palaces and Poisoned Chalices
The World of Gloriana

FOR ALL ITS gratifying press and receipt of several awards, this novel got off to a bit of a rocky start in 1978 when it was published in England. The *Times Literary Supplement* hated it at some length, and this seemed to prime a few famous faces who went on TV to say how much they loathed it, too. Germaine Greer, curling her lip as only she can curl it, and Yehudi Menuhin, shuddering with distaste as only he could shudder, thought it was positively disgusting, while admitting they hadn't actually read it. I began to think I had a stinker on my hands until things picked up a bit and some of the more positive reviews came in. Angela Carter, Carolyn Slaughter and D.M. Thomas were very kind about it, and Peter Ackroyd not only praised it in print but praised it again on both TV and radio. It went on to become a bestseller in the UK and Poland, went into a lot of foreign editions, and I'm pleased to say has never been out of print in English since. In fact it is currently in two different editions in England, since it was included, much to my gratification, in the excellent Fantasy Masterworks series. I mention all this with due humility, I hope, since the book was conceived in relation to two books I greatly admired, both of which are inarguably masterpieces that set a benchmark when they were published, roughly four centuries apart. The first is Spenser's *The Faerie Queene* and the second is Peake's *Titus Groan*.

Needless to say I never had the pleasure of meeting Spenser, but I knew Peake well and he was very kind to me when I first met him as a boy in the 1950s. Subsequently we became friends, and when he developed his terrible illness, I made it my business to do everything I could to keep his name and his work alive, for he had temporarily slipped out of fashion. I am particularly proud of the fact that, with Oliver Caldecott, who died some years ago, I was instrumental in publishing the Titus sequence as a Penguin Modern Classic and assuring it, finally, of a large audience. Peake was an authentic genius, who could draw and paint as well as he could write books and poetry. I was very lucky to have known him and his family. His wife Maeve Gilmore was an outstanding artist in her own right, as is his son Fabian and, at the time of writing, I am preparing a personal memoir with contributions from his children Sebastian, Fabian and Clare about the love Mervyn and Maeve shared for each other and how it was put to the test during his final years. He established a standard both as a man and as an artist, which served me as a model throughout my adult life. It was Peake who made me realise it was possible to confront real human issues through the medium of fantasy, and while much of my early fantasy was characteristically heroic adventure fiction, I wanted to write at least one book that would say thank you to him.

In an early series of articles I had written for the British magazine *Science Fantasy*, called "Aspects of Fantasy," I had dealt with the idea of what Harry Levin calls "the haunted palace of the mind" and was of a generation that recognised not only Kafka's surreal fables as having psychological and philosophical meaning, but which analysed most fantastic art in terms of its relation to the unconscious and how it reflected its society. Like Peake, I had grown up on *The Pilgrim's Progress*, Bunyan's great moral allegory, and innocently thought that all books were supposed to have at least two levels of meaning. I read the Gormenghast stories in this light, though Peake himself denied any secondary intention, just as I read Lovecraft and other fantasts, who also denied any deliberate allegorical intent. In "Aspects of Fantasy," parts of which much later formed the basis of my long essay *Wizardry and Wild Romance*,

I pointed out how Gormenghast could represent a human skull and the warrens and catacombs within stand for the inner workings of the psyche.

Similarly, I read Spenser as the allegory he had intended, understanding it to be about chivalric Christian virtue embodied, as he saw it, in the person of Gloriana, the Faerie Queene, Elizabeth the First of England. Denizens of her fairy court were, in many cases, figures recognisable to his contemporary audience and Spenser was praising Elizabeth for what he had decided were her ideal virtues and therefore the virtues of his England. That this was a political document, intended like the various "Arthurian" Round Tables and other chivalric reproductions created by the Elizabethans at this, the birth of the British Empire as we came to know it, has rarely been disputed. If Ariosto's *Orlando Furioso* is the more complete and possibly better model, I had no particular argument with him. But, being the staunch anti-imperialist that I am, I did have an argument with Spenser, much as I loved his work.

I had read both Spenser and Ariosto originally in editions aimed at young readers. Then I had of course accepted unquestioningly the notions of chivalry they offered (I'm still a bit of a sucker for accounts of noble self-sacrifice). No doubt I absorbed, as every English schoolchild does, Marlowe's and Shakespeare's arguments concerning the divinity of kings. As I got older I never lost my enthusiasm for them, but the world became more complex and I did learn to question some of their assumptions. I began to realise that the idealism they offered was a little at odds with my experience, for I was growing up at a time when the whole basis of British imperialism was in question. Victorian pomp and circumstance was giving way to the rationality of people like Aldous Huxley and George Orwell, who understood how easily our idealism could be harnessed in the service of powerful special interests.

During my first fifteen or twenty years I witnessed the winding down of the British Empire as more and more territories claimed their independence. My contemporaries saw our troops engaged in "policing" duties in countries where they were not welcome and in most cases never had been. The Empire was all over and we learned how unpopular we had made ourselves during all those years in which we had been told how grateful "lesser breeds without the law" were for the benign protection of the Union flag. Increasingly the media began to tell by what mixture of illusion and force that impression had been maintained.

When I began to write my own fiction it would half consciously be about ancient empires (like Elric's Melniboné) which had reached the end of their power; about the pomp and ceremony that maintained them in their power and glory; about the lies and violence that had discouraged dissent. My stories of Lieutenant Bastable and the giant airships of the Pax Britannica, of Jerry Cornelius and the cynical arguments of discredited authority, of the cruel empire of Granbretan, were all variations on similar themes, just as *Gloriana* told the story of a woman who personified the State in public but was full of pain, frustration and confusion in private.

By chivalry the State's maintain'd, I had Montfallcon sing in the uncompleted musical version of *Gloriana* I wrote with Peter Pavli,* deliberately keeping the title of the Britten opera but putting a very different twist on the material. *The Statesman's but a conjuror who magicks wonders for the Crown, to bow and to grin, to balance and spin*, I continued, perhaps making one of the earliest references to political spin doctors, anticipating the illusionist skills of modern media and its efforts to employ our sentiments in its interest, justifying that interest, perhaps rightly, as our own. In a populist, apparently transparent democracy government has to go to greater and greater contortions to persuade us of the virtuous intentions of its realpolitik. In *Gloriana* I asked if the means ever justified the end or whether a glamorous construct ultimately destroyed that which it sought to defend, however successful it at first seemed.

Gloriana is not a moral tale in the narrower sense; in fact it offers an argument against the noble Spenserian ideal, against the

---

* Several early recordings now appear on *The Entropy Tango & Gloriana Demo Sessions* CD, Noh Poetry Records, 2008.

notions of renaissance chivalry that are still offered on occasions by our great public figures. Few intelligent people these days are taken in by the rhetoric of noble imperial crusades or even of heroic self-sacrifice of the kind Alexander Korda or John Ford turned into movies during the 1930s. The realists in our seats of government have all read their John le Carré novels or watched *The West Wing*. We understand enlightened self-interest, even if we don't always understand some of the wars in which we involve ourselves. We even know something about zealotry and fanaticism and what they claim to defend. So *Gloriana* was not in that sense meant to be revelatory. It does deal to some degree with self-deception while it accepts the need for a balance between high morality and low realism.

Gloriana herself was based on an ex-lover of mine, a woman of aristocratic inherited power and liberal conscience, while Quire had something of Marlowe in him, and several other characters were based on a variety of friends, enemies and acquaintances. After Bunyan, Peake had been my chief inspiration to write adult fantasy, and I wanted to pay him homage, to say thanks for everything he meant to me. He had inspired many of my heroic fantasies, as well as my early allegorical novel *The Golden Barge*, but I did not feel I had done him justice.

Gloriana was intended to be my last fantasy. I was planning what was to become *Byzantium Endures* and the volumes that followed it, dealing with the world that had permitted the Nazi Holocaust. Also in the works was *The Brothel in Rosenstrasse*, about sexual obsession and the language that led us into war and its uncontrollable consequences, the understanding that control of the rhetoric is not control of the world, and *Mother London*, another homage, this time to the city of my birth. The fantasy I would write would increasingly become a kind of moral fable, with books like *The War Hound and the World's Pain* or *The War Amongst the Angels*. In a sense *Gloriana* marked a watershed and remains something of a swan song, an affectionate farewell to the gorgeous and exotic, to Fancy of Coleridge's classic definition, if not imagination. Almost everything I wrote afterwards put Fancy in service of the Imagination. If *Breakfast in the Ruins* had been a deliberate attempt to confront whatever unconscious ghosts and demons drove me, so *Gloriana* was a way of saying goodbye to most of them.

Albion, with her Platonic temples and barmy alchemists like John Dee, is not an "alternate England" in any generic sense but a fabulous construct, a version of what the best of a nation might look like if written from a seventeenth-century perspective. I was not trying to imitate the language and thought of the Elizabethan age but was drawing on the attitudes and styles of late-Carolingian England. In this the likes of Defoe and Marvell were great influences. My parodies of Spenser (especially "The Mutability Cantos") and court poetry of the sixteenth century were done from that perspective, when practical, commercial interests had come to dominate the thinking of incipient imperialists.

The book appeared, as I've said, to mixed reviews, some understanding, some not, but nobody, not even Germaine Greer (more vane than pulse) objected to a certain rape scene that makes a difference to events in the book. It was not in fact until a few years after it was published that I began to hear from women who objected to its unstated message. My dear friend and supporter Andrea Dworkin told me that she loved the book but was troubled by that scene. Accordingly, when I got the chance to rewrite it I did so. I would also reiterate here that nothing justifies rape! And since another of my characters was once invoked by a young man to commit such a crime, I have since done everything I can to make sure I do not, however inadvertently, compound the error. I am one of those who believes that writing is action and that we carry varying degrees of responsibility for our actions, dealing with their consequences as seriously as we are able. That scene, however, was the only one I altered, contrary to what some critics believe, and the rest of the book remained as originally written. Meanwhile, I reiterate that no rape is justified, but I do suggest that good can come out of evil, just as evil can come out of good.

Lastly I would like to take the opportunity to acknowledge the help, inspiration and support of some of those I associate with this book including Peter Ackroyd, Edward Blishen, Andrea Dworkin, Angela Carter, John Clute, Giles Gordon, Mike Harrison, Emma Tennant and Angus Wilson. The book's argument, as I have said, is with Spenser and it remains, with great love and admiration, dedicated to the memory of Mervyn Peake.

—Michael Moorcock
Texas, December 2003

Appendix A

Lyrics for a Proposed Musical Version of *Gloriana*

By Michael Moorcock and Peter Pavli

JOHN DEE'S SONG
(Words: Moorcock, Music: Pavli)

In my skull's a multiplicity of spheres
An infinity of Albions,
And in one Dee is King
And she the Sage
(Would she then lust for me
And I refuse to hear her beating blood?)
World upon world
A sea of globes
And only rarely do two meet
Thus I discourse; I bow
(Ah! These pantaloons! A eunuch of me'll make trow!)
"Oh venerable *Dee*—respected *sir;*
So noble *and* refined . . ."
(She cannot guess what thoughts do burn
In my tormented mind. . . .)

And now a word on Nature
Next on God and Good
On Love and Death —
On Art—and High Arithmetik
(How to restrain this leaping prick?)
"Madam, I take my leave, if you'll permit!"
Another bow—oh, my blade! I weep!

As through the door I lurch,
Groaning for surcease . . .
(Girl speaks): *"Good* morrow, *Doctor Dee!"*
(Dee): *"Aside, fair maid, aside!"*
(Girl): *"Advice, good sage, I pray . . ."*
(Dee, aside): (*She'll quench me, temp'ry bride.*)
"Come quickly, maid, to my bedside
And I will fill thee full *of my philosophy. . . ."*

And I will fill thee full
And I will fill thee full
I'll fill thee full
Of my philosophy. . . .

Montfallcon's Song
(Words: Moorcock, Music: Pavli)

I hear you weeping in the night
Oh, my Queen.
If you were only woman and not Albion
These sweet wives I'd leave.
I recall your yearning flesh
Your high despairing breath
Your innocence, your lust
My pleasure in your pain
I breathe your name . . .

I hold their hair to my ears, oh madam,
So that I no longer hear, to sleep . . .

Quire's Song
(Words: Moorcock, Music: Pavli)

Having been commissioned to pull down such goodly prey,
This Empire in the person of its Queen,

My life is much enliven'd and I bless the day
That I receiv'd the chance to vent my spleen
On all that I despise
I hate her eyes,
I hate her face,
I hate her mane
But most of all I hate her grace,
Her innocent nobility.

For I am Quire the shadow,
Quire the thief
Of virtue and ideals.

A clever little Quire am I
Realistic, brave and free
The task I've taken 'fore I die
To disperse this silly gaiety,
To crush the myth of happiness,
Display it for a shell,
A bauble bright before
—before a baby's clutching paw—
To lure it into
Hell . . .

Dangle the bauble and the folk will dance
Promise the false gem and watch them smile,
Tell them that happiness is theirs for the taking,
And see how many friends we're making!

For I'm a clever little Quire
To flags and bunting I'll set fire.
At slogans I will sneer.
The only truth is fear.

The only truth
Is fear.

(Rough recordings made June/July 1977)

Appendix B

Gloriana Review

"Kaleidoscope," 2 May, 1978

KALEIDOSCOPE: BACK NOW—or is it forward?—in time, to the mythical Empire of Queen Gloriana of Albion, supreme ruler of Europe, America and most of Asia:

> Queen Gloriana, only child of King Hern VI (despot and degenerate, traitor to the State, betrayer of his trust, whose hand caused a hundred thousand heads to fall, unmanly self-murderer), of the old blood of Elficleos and of Brutus, who overthrew Gogmagog, is forever aware of [the] love her subjects have for her and she returns their love; yet that love, both given and received, is a burden upon her—a burden so great that she can scarcely admit its presence—a burden, it might be thought, that is the chief cause of her enormous private distress.

K.: Her distress is due to the fact that Gloriana is not a virgin queen, unlike her namesake; far from it. Room upon room of her vast palace is given over to male and female concubines. None, though, can satisfy her. For the Empire of Albion, orgasm has become a matter of State, and the great Golden Age of chivalry, peace and enlightenment that Gloriana's rule has brought is as much of an illusion as her own royal serenity. Those illusions are fostered and maintained, by fair means or foul, generally the latter, by her Chancellor, Lord Montfallcon, the centre of a web of spies, traitors, murderers. Chief among these instruments is the ruthless, amoral Captain Quire, an artist of villainy:

> "I am a sympathetic friend—but only to the weak. I will not tolerate the mad or the strong—those I'll fight or avoid. My good deeds, Lord Montfallcon, are, like all my deeds, self-interested. Your work and mine is greatly aided by my reputation for generosity. We employ a great army of loyal innocents, of faithful feeble-minded men and women, of dull, good-hearted, honest folk—for they are the people never reckoned with by one's enemies. They are always ignored, always condescended to. Therefore they are the most grateful for my good deeds and will bring me all kinds of information, not from greed but from simple loyalty. I am their hero. They worship Captain Quire. They'll forgive him any crime ('he has his reasons') and protect him, as best they can, from any consequences. They are the backbone of every scheme."

K.: A conjunction, then, between this king of passionless vice and the Queen of remote, illusory virtue; that's the meat of Michael Moorcock's plot. In a note on the book's half-title, he insists that, despite the name of Gloriana, the ruffs and doublets worn by his characters, the presence of historical figures of the sixteenth century like Doctor Dee, it's *"neither an 'Elizabethan Fantasia' nor an historical novel."* So, in some perplexity, I turned to Peter Ackroyd, literary editor of *The Spectator*. If neither of these things, what precisely is it?

Peter Ackroyd: Well, I think it's a kind of fable. There are some very good modern novelists who have eschewed realism as a form, and they turn to fable as a way of exploring and inventing new worlds. I think it's very important in the present context that this should be happening, because it means we avoid the limited purities of realism, and it allows writers to become inventive and expansive and imaginative. In this case, for example, Michael Moorcock uses images piling on top of each other; he coins exuberant neologisms. All the way through the book there's this constant strain of almost manic inventiveness which is very important. It means that, once you break the dams of realism, you allow other forms to enter which have been not acknowledged recently. You include, for example, fantasy, you include allegory, you include fable and you also include magic of a certain kind.

K.: Now is it any more than an extraordinarily various and inventive fable? He admits some indebtedness to Spenser's *Faerie Queene*, and *The Faerie Queene* as we all know is an allegory; a political allegory. Do you read this book as a political allegory?

A.: Well, it depends what you mean by political. It seems to me that the strain in the book which is in a sense undisclosed—it's sort of camouflaged—is a sort of magical strain, and if you think of magic as a different way of discussing Man's relationship with himself, and with the environment, I would say that was political. What Moorcock does is he pierces through the veils of ordinary realism, in novelistic terms, and he discloses to us the magical underpinnings of reality; and once we see them we're surprised with a shock of recognition, that this is the way that the world actually can be.

K.: But he surely wants us to go with him a little further than that. His thirty-fifth and last chapter is titled "*In Which Albion Shall Begin a New Age That Shall be Truly One of Golden Moderation with Romance and Reason in Balance at Last*," and I thought, dear me, what an old-fashioned message!

A.: Well, it's old-fashioned, that, I think, because in a sense it's metaphorical. It's not meant to be taken literally. For example, Gloriana's rôle, as the Queen who can't reach orgasm, is, I think—this is probably slightly overplaying it—but it's a sense in which Gloriana's Realm is a metaphor for the conscious mind. She sublimates her wretchedness, she avoids and pretends to ignore the labyrinths and corridors underneath her palace, and it seems to me that that, in a sense, is a statement about the conscious mind laying on top of the unconscious mind.

Quire's rôle is rather more difficult to explain. He is a sort of literary figure. He is a literary stereotype, and yet he constantly comments upon literary modes he's working in. He says at one point, "Myth is but another word for Ignorance." What Moorcock does best, if we're talking about its encroachments upon reality itself—upon the way we understand the world—is he takes certain elements which we normally don't acknowledge in the real world, and he magnifies them. For example, he talks about science in terms of the Lords of Entropy; he talks about London as a city in which temples of contemplation reside. It's like a sort of hallucinogenic trip through the real world, and in that sense it not only sharpens our picture of reality, it enlarges it.

On one level, it is that kind of fantasy. One another level, it's a London which has been transformed. The characters of Gloriana, and Gloriana's henchmen and servants, strike me as being quite explicit parallels with the court of Elizabeth I. The corruption, the tournaments, the jousts, the extraordinary festivals on the frozen Thames, strike me as being a very vivid evocation of sixteenth-century England. Yet, on another level, it's a London transformed; it's a London which could have been, if we had retained those virtues which Moorcock sees in Elizabethan England. It's a world, for example, bound by feudal times, and not by commercial ones.

K.: You seem to be describing what is, in your view, an important book.

A.: Yes, I'd say, despite what other critics have written recently, it's one of the most important books I've read—not to be too portentous about it—in the sense that he is trying to achieve things which no-one has bothered to achieve before; and he is trying very hard, and in part very successfully, to break beyond the barriers of ordinary realism with which we've become familiar.

K.: Well, *there*'s a recommendation! Fervent praise from Peter Ackroyd for *Gloriana; or The Unfulfill'd Queen*, by Michael Moorcock.